TEMPTATION AND TORMENT

Katy was half sitting, half kneeling on the bed. In the flickering candlelight, she presented a lovely picture. Her long hair hung loose on her shoulders, barely covering the creamy breasts that were revealed by the flimsy gown she wore. Desire burned so strongly in Kit that he couldn't trust himself to speak. Fighting the fire that threatened to consume him, he took the ruby pendant from her trembling fingers and placed it about her throat. With the greatest difficulty, he kept himself from kissing the soft flesh of her neck.

The ruby glowed against the satiny smoothness of her skin. Innocently, she gazed up at him, tears brimming in her eyes. He would need to put distance between them or it would be harder and harder to resist this overwhelming temptation.

"It's perfect on you, Katy, as I knew it would be." His voice was level, betraying nothing of his inner struggle. "Perhaps when you wear it, you'll think of me."

Fingering the jewel, she watched him go. How could he be so thoughtful and considerate one minute, and then without warning, so cold and distant? Blowing out the candle, she wondered for the hundredth time if she would ever succeed in making her husband love her.

Lovestorm

Barbara
Benedict

LEISURE BOOKS ❧ NEW YORK CITY

A LEISURE BOOK

Published by

Dorchester Publishing Co., Inc.
6 East 39th Street
New York City

Printed in the United States of America

PART
ONE

Chapter 1

"You can't be serious!"

If he had heard her, he gave no evidence of the fact. He sat at the huge oak desk that failed to dwarf him, glancing over his accounts. As if he could balance them; prices being what they were with this damnable war going on.

Exasperated, she tried again. "You can't do this to me. I won't allow it."

This time, he did look up. Former Admiral James Wilton Farley, Lord Whitney, was unaccustomed to having his orders questioned. "My dear child, the matter is settled. There is nothing you, nor I for that matter, can do about it."

Returning to his papers, he considered the conversation at an end. He would have been surprised to find his granddaughter still in the room. Watching him, Katherine found her temper rising. All too often in the past five years, she had come into this very room with words of protest on her lips and just as often, those words had never been uttered. Not this time. There was too much at stake.

Deciding to be firm was one thing, but making him

listen to her was quite another. Katherine studied him as he concentrated on his accounts. Why, he's getting old, she discovered. There was gray in the dark hair in generous proportions. Lines of worry cut into the once handsome features, distorting them. The thought of his advancing age should have touched her, but try as she might, she could feel no affection for this man. Pity, maybe, when he looked haggard, as now, but never affection. That had been destroyed years ago when a more trusting Katherine had stepped off the boat from Ireland, terrified and sick with grief. She had run to his arms for comfort and found none. Farley had extricated himself from the bewildered child and had maintained the distance between them in the intervening years. Katherine learned quickly, though painfully at first, that affection was neither required nor welcomed from her.

As her eyes wandered nervously around the room, she caught sight of the portraits over the fireplace. One was a likeness of a much younger Farley and next to it, one of his only son. They shared certain characteristics: the firm chin, the patrician nose, the hard mouth; all features set in that arrogant pose she had come to dislike. But the eyes of the younger man were a softer gray and she liked to imagine she saw humor in them. There must have been some sense of humor or her mother never would have married him. Impulsive she might have been, but Maureen Farley would have no use for a man that couldn't laugh at himself. It was a trait Katherine had inherited and it made her life with the admiral an ordeal. Farley had a tendency to take life, and himself, far too seriously.

She gazed at her father's likeness with pride. Twenty years ago, Richard Farley had defied his father, taking his beautiful young bride to Ireland, without a single thought to what he was leaving behind. Katherine prayed for some of his courage now for she would need it to face this bitter, old man.

"Grandfather, you might as well put your books away. I simply won't leave the room until we discuss this."

Farley, startled by the sound of her voice, looked up. "It was my impression that we had terminated the discussion."

"No, grandfather. *You* terminated it. You haven't heard a word I've said. I refuse to marry this man."

He summoned all the dignity of his exalted position for his look of scorn. "Don't work yourself into a state. This is not a matter for discussion. The subject is closed. Now if you don't mind, I have work to do." He spoke slowly and deliberately, as if addressing a child or an idiot.

Feeling like both, she stuck out her chin. "How can you be so unfeeling? To do such a thing to your own flesh and blood!"

He shuddered. But if she had hoped to provoke an argument, she had not allowed for his obvious contempt. "Melodrama does not suit you, my dear. To hear you speak, one would think I was selling you into slavery."

"And what is it then? Am I not being sold to the highest bidder?"

"To the only bidder."

She ignored that. "It's not as if I was to be given a choice."

Farley snorted. "Your father had a choice and look what a disaster that was."

"How dare you say that!" He was getting to her but

she couldn't stop. "Mother was good and kind and she was the best wife possible. They loved each other very much."

"Ha! Where did that love get him? He died a pauper."

"But that was your fault. You disowned him."

He was struggling with temper now. "Among her other faults, your mother showed a deplorable lack of breeding, as is painfully evident in her raising of you. A young lady never raises her voice in that disgusting manner, especially to her elders."

By this time, Katherine was more than tired of hearing what a young lady should and should not do. "But then, I'm not a young lady, am I? Young ladies are cherished and spoiled by their families, not thrown into the hands of a complete stranger."

"For heaven's sake, stop screeching. Have no fear. By the time you marry the fellow, he won't be a stranger. I've made arrangements for Warwick to spend some time with us before the wedding."

"You've made these arrangements without consulting me?"

"Consulting you? Whatever for?"

She couldn't believe him. "It's my life, after all."

"As your guardian, I am the one to make the decisions regarding your future. With my experience I am far better able to determine what is best for you."

"You old hypocrite! As if you ever cared what was best for me! All you care about is getting me out of your house and away from your sight as soon as possible. You'd have thrown me out long ago if you weren't concerned with what people would say. The Honorable James Wilton Farley. Hah!"

"That is enough!" His skin had taken on a purplish hue.

"No, it is *not* enough. I think I deserve to know why you are doing this to me."

As he looked her in the eye, the fragile pretense of civility was gone. In his eyes was hatred, sheer hatred. Katherine shrank back from the force of it. "If you want the truth, I can't stand the sight of you. Once you're out of this house, I can sleep again. Now I am sure you will agree that we have nothing further to say to each other and I find I can work better with you out of the room. Good day."

Suddenly, it was as if she had never existed. Stunned, Katherine backed out of his study. How had it happened? Only a few minutes ago, she had been armed with resolution, determined not to let him win this time, and yet here she was retreating, reduced somehow by his total lack of concern, feeling small and lost and lonely.

Perhaps this marriage wasn't such a bad idea, after all. The romantic Irish side of her still rebelled, but the more practical British side urged her to consider it as a means of escape. True, she had planned a different sort of life for herself but realistically, what were her chances of ever achieving it with Farley to make her decisions for her? She could at least see what the man looked like. Who could tell? There just might be a chance for a happy ending, yet.

Chapter 2

Julian Warwick III presented himself at Whitney Hall late the following afternoon. Preparations had continued throughout the night and by the time he arrived, Whitney Hall was ready for him. Except for Katherine. Blissfully unaware of his imminent arrival, she had chosen to spend the day in her favorite activity—riding Midnight over the sizable estate. As so often in the past, she felt the need to work out her frustrations with the mare. For what had seemed a sensible alternative last night took on the aspect of a nightmare in the light of day. What kind of man could this Julian Warwick be if he was willing to marry her without so much as a peek at what he was getting? He must be a toad. With barely a nudge, Midnight, who always seemed to sense her moods, galloped off with the wind.

Farley was relieved to see her go. Aside from the discomfort he always felt in her presence, he decided quite wisely that it would be best for all concerned if the young man were to meet them one at a time. Ushering his guest into his study, Farley recognized the wisdom of his decision. He had a moment's misgiving about what he might have done to his granddaughter, but it was gone before it could manifest itself. The admiral was never one to regret his actions.

"Mr. Warwick, I trust your journey was a pleasant one?" Farley sat at his desk, leaving the young man to fend for himself.

"Far be it for me to complain, sir, but I sincerely hope that I need never make that trip again. Do you know the deplorable condition of that road? Why, there's dust all over my clothes."

Farley watched him brush the articles in question. Were they clothes? Men of fashion were notorious for being flamboyant but this man had gone too far. Looking like a rainbow, it was obvious that he had gone to great lengths and great expense to impress his intended and her guardian. The latter was not impressed. With an air of restrained annoyance, he gestured for his guest to take a chair. "Mr. Warwick, please be seated. My granddaughter is occupied elsewhere at the moment so if you will indulge me, there are a few things I would like to discuss with you."

Warwick dropped casually into a chair opposite Farley. His long, lean body lounged in the cushions as if it belonged there and he was absentmindedly picking imaginary hairs off his trousers. After an extended silence, he looked up at the admiral and surprised Farley with the hard glint in his stare. A brilliant blue, his eyes shone now like mirrors. Clearing his throat, Farley began again. "Those who know me well are aware that I don't mince my words. I'll be blunt. Before my granddaughter returns, I would like to settle the terms of the marriage contract."

A slow smile spread across Warwick's painted face. "Your Lordship, you are a man after my own heart. I, too, am anxious to have everything settled. But pray, where is your granddaughter?"

"Katherine is riding. There will be sufficient time for pleasantries later. Now, I would prefer to discuss business."

"But of course. I'm listening."

Farley rummaged through the papers on his desk. "Here is a copy of the marriage contract. I took the liberty of having my attorney draft it to facilitate matters." He reached over the desk and handed it to Warwick. "Of primary concern, I would think, is the dowry. When I spoke with your agent in London, I was led to believe that you had need of a sizable one."

Warwick had the audacity to grin. As he read, Farley studied him. A fop, perhaps, but there was intelligence in those cold blue eyes, and a ruthlessness to match his own.

His reading completed, Warwick looked over to the older man, his glance both assessing and questioning. "Very interesting, Your Lordship. You've been quite generous but I can't help but be suspicious. Is there something you're not saying?"

"I beg your pardon?"

"Put yourself in my position. I arrive and immediately am rushed into your study, presented with a marriage contract already drafted with neither my knowledge nor consent, and for some reason unknown to me, my intended is kept from sight. Admittedly, your terms are better than I had hoped, but I wonder. How old is your granddaughter?"

"Katherine is eighteen, but I fail to see why it is important."

"Forgive me, but I fear there must be something hideously wrong with the girl if you are trying to get me

14

to sign the contract before seeing her."

Farley chuckled. "I'm gratified to learn that you are so cautious. Have no fear. I've no intention of rushing you into this. I merely wanted your opinion, not your signature. Katherine will be present at dinner and you may take your time about signing."

"But I am still confused. Why are you so willing, nay, almost anxious, to part with such a great deal of money if there is nothing wrong?"

Farley appraised him. Without hesitation, he chose the direct approach. "Remember, Warwick, that what I am about to tell you must be kept in the strictest confidence. Have I your word?"

Warwick's face was unreadable. "Can you trust the word of a colonial?"

"Don't play games with me, boy. A man in my position is capable of knowing what goes on in this kingdom, even in the colonies." He noticed the barely perceptible flicker of fear and pressed his advantage. "I know of your family and background. Whatever your other faults, I am aware that the word of a Warwick is the word of a gentleman."

"I am honored, Your Lordship. My word, then, is yours."

Ignoring the light tone, Farley leaned toward Warwick across the desk. "Above the fireplace you will see a likeness of my son, done when Richard was first commissioned in the army. He refused to use my influence; wouldn't follow in my footsteps in the navy. Before long, he distinguished himself and made me proud. Until he met her!" He spat out the words.

"She was the daughter of a mere soldier. Irish. Can you imagine? Farley blood mixing with that scum? I warned him not to marry her but he was young and so

15

certain he knew his own mind. Despite my warning, he had to have her. She bewitched him.''

He left the desk to pace across the room. "I am not a hard man, but my family name and honor are my life. I have spent all my many years upholding that honor. I went after them, following them to the cheap tavern where they stayed. I swallowed my pride; I tried to show my son what he was throwing away. I made it easy for him to leave her there, to return home where he belonged. Do you know what they did? They laughed at me. To this day, I can still hear that woman laughing and I can remember the desire to strangle her. Katherine has that laugh.''

He moved to the fire, as if to draw warmth from it. "Three years later, my son and only heir was killed in a barroom brawl. His brilliant career was ended in a low Irish pub, defending his wife's reputation. Ironic, isn't it? His family name meant nothing to him but he died upholding the honor of that slut. I learned soon after that she was with child. I tried to get the name of the father, but she refused to speak to me. Shortly afterward, Katherine was born. She's her mother, all over again. I've tried to be fair, but if there's even an ounce of Farley blood in the girl, I've yet to discover it.''

"Aha!" Warwick was grinning again. "So the girl's illegitimate. That's why you're so anxious to be rid of her.''

Unable to control his passion, Farley lashed out. "I can't endure the sight of her. Every time I see her face, hear her laugh, I see the waste, the absolute squandering of my son's life. Had Katherine been born male, perhaps I wouldn't feel so bitterly toward her, but as it stands now, Whitney Hall will go to a distant relative. Therefore, as stated in the contract, the first le-

16

gitimate male offspring of your union will be recognized as my heir. I doubt it is necessary to point out that as his guardian, you will be in control of a great deal of money."

"This is very interesting, sir, and I can quite understand your feelings. But if I may be so bold as to ask, what does Miss Farley think of all this?"

"Katherine? What does it matter what she thinks?"

"Surely she will be required to sign the contract also."

"I am still her guardian. I am responsible for her actions; not she. When the time comes, she will be informed as to what is expected of her."

"The time has come, Grandfather."

Both men turned quickly, as if a bit guilty to be found discussing her. Warwick straightened in his chair. So this was the girl. Katherine stood in the doorway, framed by the firelight, every bit as arrogant as any Farley. There were two attractive spots of color on her cheeks, but whether they were caused by her anger or the mere exertion of her ride, it was difficult to determine. She stood composed, still in her riding clothes, demanding an answer.

The older man recovered first. Typically, he was infuriated. How dare she burst in here and berate him like a small boy. If he was to be honest, he would have seen his son in the girl now, but all he could see was a Katherine-Maureen who dared to defy him. While he could admit a grudging admiration for her spirit, he could not tolerate defiance. Especially not now. "Katherine, this is Mr. Julian Warwick, from the colonies. Mr. Warwick will be spending the next few weeks with us. Please excuse my granddaughter, Warwick. She is usually not in the habit of interrupt-

17

ing me in private conversations, not does she usually present herself to guests looking as if she had just cleaned the stables."

Under his withering glare, Katherine's attention was diverted to her appearance. With dismay, she cursed her temper. Her only thought, when she learned that the bridegroom had arrived without one word of it to her, had been to confront her grandfather. Mortified, she noticed that Warwick was watching her carefully. She said in a small voice, "I'm sorry; I didn't think."

Farley ignored her. "However, as she is only just out of the schoolroom and as yet unsure of proper behavior, I trust you will be lenient with her. Katherine, you may leave us now to dress for dinner."

This time her cheeks were aflame with humiliation. Schoolroom indeed! How could he speak to her like this in front of the man she was supposed to marry? What would he think?

Actually, if she had been less upset, she would have detected the amusement in Warwick's eyes. He had been pleasantly surprised by the girl. She had a nice face, further enhanced by the anger she was struggling so valiantly to control. He felt a lot happier about the whole business. Feeling generous, he tried to make it easier for her. "Miss Farley, whatever the circumstances, I am delighted to make your acquaintance."

Katherine drew her heated gaze from her grandfather to take her first good look at their guest. Good lord, she thought; he's prettier than I am. But before she could engage in any conversation with him, Farley was back in control.

"Warwick and I will meet you at dinner, Katherine."

His words were polite enough, but through years of experience, she could hear the crack of the whip. There was no hope for it; if she was to leave with an ounce of dignity, it was time for an exit. Pulling herself to her full five feet, four inches, she adopted Farley's tone.

"Gentlemen. I am sorry to have caused any inconvenience. When I came down the hallway, the door was open and as I was being discussed, I assumed my presence might be required. I see now that it was not. Pray, do go on with your discussion. You and I, Mr. Warwick, will have a proper conversation at dinner."

By chance, she looked up into those startling blue eyes. Unaccustomed as she was to male company, she was flustered by his obvious interest. Struggling to maintain her composure, she bid him good day and in what she hoped was a leisurely pace, fled the room.

Upstairs, she sat in front of her mirror to brush her hair. Combing the long brown curls always relaxed her and many was the time she had run to this room for that very purpose after a confrontation with his lordship. Only Farley wasn't the only problem this time; it was the man she was supposed to marry. Let's face facts, she thought; he is not Prince Charming. She was still young enough to feel the need for romance, to be swept off her feet, to be cherished by a strong but gentle man. Her only experience with men was in novels, where the hero was masculine in the extreme, managing always to overcome every obstacle in the path of true love. Hugging herself, she could feel his strong arms around her now. He would come in the night, lifting her off the ground in a warm embrace, silencing Farley with a wave of his strong hand. Then they would be off; she on her black mare and he, being the hero, on a pure white stallion.

19

But try as she might, it was impossible to picture Julian Warwick in the role. Swept off her feet, indeed. Those well-groomed hands had never come near a broom. He was just the sort of suitor she should have suspected her grandfather would produce. Oh, she wanted much more from life. Instead of escape, it was quite likely she could only look forward to a continuation of the past five years. He even had Farley's arrogance. Why, he hadn't even stood when she entered the room. Sitting back in his chair, he had watched her make a fool of herself, enjoying every minute. How amusing it must have been for him.

She winced as she yanked her hair furiously. This would not do. She would soon be bald if she let the two of them annoy her like this. No, she would patiently watch and wait. It was only fair. Neither of them could possibly have been at their best under the circumstances of their first meeting. Perhaps once she learned more about this man, she might discover they shared certain interests. She was inclined to doubt it, but she had to give it a try. Prince Charmng wasn't likely to ride up to her door. And annoying though he might be, Katherine sensed there was something about this Julian Warwick; something that hid below the surface. There had been a glimpse of it when she had stared into his laughing blue eyes.

She became aware of the face staring back at her from the mirror. It was so serious. She had to laugh at herself. When she did, the face lit up. That's better, she thought. No sense getting into a stew about it; not yet, at any rate. It was time to dress for dinner. Her long dark hair already shone with reddish highlights from the brushing, but she pinched her cheeks and bit her full red lips to emphasize their color as well. Long

20

ago, Maureen Farley had warned her daughter that she would never be the type of beauty that fashion favored, but her strength would lie in the fact that she was different. Hoping she was right, Katherine chose a gown of deep burgundy, hoping to make the most of what she did have. She was pleased with the results. No, she would never blend in with the girls of today's society, but she could make her own impression. And that was exactly what she planned to do tonight.

Head held high, she made what she considered her grand entrance into the drawing room, confident in the knowledge that she looked her best. Unfortunately, the reason for her appearance had failed to make an appearance himself. There was only Farley to impress with her entrance and needless to say, he was not. In fact, he never bothered to look up as she swept into the room. Feeling a bit let down, she crossed the room, carefully placing herself in a becoming pose by the fire. The casual pose, however, was spoiled by her fidgeting. By now she should have been accustomed to Farley's moods, but tonight she was far too nervous and she found herself wishing he would say anything to fill the void. Irritatingly he sat there; his face turned away and his thoughts entirely in a different world. If he continued in this vein, it would be a horrible evening. This was her first formal dinner and her already slim hopes for adventure and romance were rapidly dwindling.

Those hopes plunged further when her suitor finally made his appearance. And what an appearance it was. His body was covered in a brilliance of color. Between the rich fabric, the glittering jewels, and the shimmering crystal-blue wig, it was difficult to determine where the finery ended and the man underneath began. It was an assault on the senses. In her surprise, Katherine abandoned her pose and together with Farley, who had by now snapped out of his trance, she greeted their guest. As Warwick bent over to kiss her fingertips, Katherine waited, expecting momentarily to hear the fatal rip in those elegant trousers. Then, as he straightened, she saw the rouge. What a strange man.

Katherine watched him greet her grandfather. Never a one for physical contact, Farley actually shuddered at the thought of touching this dandy. The extended hand was ignored and it dropped to Warwick's side. She noticed it was clenched. How interesting. It wasn't nearly as soft when gathered together in a fist. Perhaps there was hope for defiance, after all.

But it was unlikely to occur this evening; at least as long as he continued to fawn all over the admiral, despite the man's obvious revulsion. It was disgusting.

Dinner was announced and Warwick offered his arm to her. Surprisingly, the flesh underneath all that ridiculous clothing was firm. Katherine wished for more candles, something Farley always scrimped on, so she could study her guest's face, to gain a clue to his character. In a rare moment of patience, she told herself there would be plenty of time for that. A lifetime, most likely.

As her sinking disposition forewarned, dinner was an ordeal. Since Farley controlled the conversation, she was unable to make good her earlier boast. Talk centered around the colonies and the "damned" war. Though she was willing to acknowledge her ignorance on the matter, she resented that they seemed to feel no need to include her in their talk. Granted, she was hardly an authority on the subject, but that did little to quiet her growing impatience with their high-handed manner of dismissing the entire affair as ridiculous. Engaging in a minor rebellion of her own, she felt her sympathies to be more with the riffraff than with these two overbearing men. At least the rebels fought valiantly for what they believed to be right, where as her dinner companions were warm and snug and miles away from any danger. Listening until she heard the American mention that he believed the incident would soon blow over, Katherine discovered that her patience, never very strong, was at an end. "But I do believe, Mr. Warwick, that this incident of yours has been blowing over for nearly five years now."

He seemed to choke of his food. Delicately, he lifted his napkin to wipe the corners of his mouth. "Excuse me, Miss Farley. You are quite right, of course. What a nuisance it's been, too. Do you realize I was forced to come all the way to London just to find a proper tailor?" He turned those magnificent eyes on her. "But that proved so fortunate. How else would I have ever had the opportunity to make your acquaintance?"

She blushed, half in embarrassment, half in anger. "How gallant of you to say so. But surely, wasn't it difficult to enter this country when your own is at war with us?"

Farley was clearly irritated. "Please spare us your ignorance. Until you are familiar with the situation, kindly refrain from questioning those who are."

Warwick's soft voice cut in. "I'm sorry if I misled you, Miss Farley. Though it is true that my country swarms with traitors, members of my family remain loyal subjects to the crown. The Warwick name is held in high esteem here in England. Certainly you couldn't have thought otherwise."

It was increasingly difficult to determine which of them was more annoying. Though conceit was better than condescension, she supposed, it was not at all the way she wanted him to be.

"Unfortunately, Warwick, my granddaughter was born in Ireland and she's chosen to consider it her home. Rest assured, there's more reason to question her loyalty than yours."

"That's not fair!" This would not do at all. As usual, she was letting him goad her into an argument and he would soon have her making a fool of herself. Taking a deep breath, she addressed Warwick. "My grandfather doesn't understand. I admire your loyalty, especially since I imagine it must make life difficult for you and your family."

"No one would dare cause any unpleasantness for Julian Warwick."

She swallowed the urge to shake him out of his complacency. "How comfortable for you. But why then did you decide to settle here in England?"

Warwick raised an eyebrow and in confusion looked to Farley. The old man was smirking. "I warned you not to speak in ignorance, my dear. Warwick has no intention of settling here. In fact, he plans to return to America as soon as his visit is at an end."

Warwick had the good grace to look uncomfortable. Katherine was stunned. This had never entered into her thinking. What had she done to make Farley smile at the thought of her going off with a complete stranger to a land torn in half by war? Not that she would mind leaving him now, but she had invested a good many years of her young life in England, at Whitney Hall. Leaving home, albeit a loveless one,

24

was something she had hoped not to suffer through again. And there was always the hope that someday she could return to Clonmara. America was another continent! If she went there, she would never see her beloved home again. Thinking in those terms, she felt the knot in her stomach return, just like in those feverish weeks following her mother's death. Oh Mother, she thought, how could you leave me to this man? Life in England, with Clonmara close by, might have been tolerable with Warwick, but she would dwindle into insanity in America.

The knot grew tighter, making it hard to breathe. She caught sight of Farley, grinning, gloating. So the sadistic fiend was enjoying this. Her temper flashed. Even if she was powerless to prevent his heartless manipulation of her life, there was no reason for him to see that it bothered her. "America?" she questioned Warwick. "Do you know, I have always had a secret admiration for your country. Imagine! Holding the might of England at bay for five years."

Warwick studied her. "Your sentiments are unusual for a young lady in your position."

Katherine gave him look for look. "Not at all. It's that very position that makes me want to applaud the Americans."

Farley went purple. "That will be enough! I will not have treason spoken in my home. Leave the room, immediately."

"But Lord Whitney, surely this isn't necessary. Miss Farley was only teasing me."

Ignoring him, Farley pointed an accusing finger at Katherine. "Go to your room. While you are there, you will consider the gratitude you owe this country before you start applauding her enemies in front of guests. If I ever hear such talk from you again, I will have you thrown from the house."

Was she never to learn that it didn't pay to cross swords with him? How many humiliating defeats would it take to convince her? Assuming a dignity she didn't feel, she placed her napkin on her seat and marched to the door.

Halfway across the room, Farley's booming voice rang out. "First, you will apologize."

Almost losing her balance, she stopped in her tracks. What arrogance! Deliberately, she turned to face the two of them, struggling to conceal the storm that was brewing inside of her. Warwick was inspecting his fingernails, apparently ill at ease. Katherine hoped he would find dirt in them but she knew better. With a short, exaggerated curtsy, she made her apology.

Warwick pulled himself slowly to his feet. "And I'm sorry, Miss Farley, to be deprived of your presence this evening. I was looking forward to having our proper conversation."

As he bent over her fingertips, he glanced up at her. Why, he was grinning. He was far from embarrassed; he was amused. The twinkle in his eyes would have infuriated Farley, had he seen, but Warwick was careful to prevent that. Before he released her hand, Katherine could have sworn he winked at her.

Upstairs, alone, she considered that wink. Was he laughing at her? Oh, how plaguing to be a woman! If she were a man, she would be with them now, able to study Warwick at her leisure. But then, if she were a man, she would be the heir and there would be no reason to know what went on behind those eyes of his. Oddly, she realized that she did want to know. One moment he infuriated her, and then he'd smile and she'd feel curiously warm all over. He intrigued her in a peculiar way. There was that air of mystery; if only she could discover what he was really like.

The thoughts whirled round and round in her head, but when she finally fell asleep that night, she was no closer to making a decision about this man she was supposed to marry.

Chapter 3

When the first rays of the sun slipped through the curtains and touched her face, Katherine popped out of bed. It was going to be a glorious day. Suppressing the urge to run to the stable and jump on Midnight, she contented herself with the view from her window. As she watched the warm sunlight transform the quiet countryside, she sighed. Only on her horse could she recapture the freedom, that whole way of life that had been hers at Clonmara; feeling again the wind in her hair, the very taste of life itself, able to be the master of her world, in unity with the sun and earth. She could be complete, alive with the knowledge that she was no more, yet no less important than any other creature. She could be herself, and there was comfort in knowing that it was good and right to be she.

But as life would have it, reality tended to force itself upon her here in the house. She felt caged. Pacing about the room, she tried to work off the extra energy. Legs racing and heart pounding, she wondered how she was going to cope with this new situation. If only there was someone to whom she could turn. If her mother was still alive, she could have gone to her, crawled into the big, warm bed and had a good cry. Maureen would have encouraged her to cry and, once the storm of tears was over, would have had comforting, if not always practical advice for her. There would have been warmth and love, but instead there was a cold void so deep that Katherine wondered if it ever would be filled. Ah Mother, she thought, I miss you so! She longed for the tender, sweet voice that sang those haunting lullabies.

And Nanny, who had always forgiven her, no matter what naughty prank she played. She had been torn from the aging woman when Farley's agents had come to bring her to England. She thought of the pain in Nanny's eyes and she prayed that life was going well for her. She needed to believe that.

What I really need, she thought, is a good laugh. It was impossible to remember the last time she had laughed with the kind of laughter she had shared with Maureen. There had been times when they had laughed so hard that they would clutch their sides while the tears streamed down their cheeks. Smiling, she thought back to the night when she had stolen down to the kitchen to sneak a bite of Nanny's special baking, only to discover her mother there before her. The scent of the freshly baked cake had kept them both awake. But before either could manage a bite, Nanny was stomping down the hall to investigate the noise. Running blindly to find a place to hide, they knocked each other down. Nanny had found them on the floor, laughing so hard that their insides hurt. Poor Nanny hadn't undertsood what was so funny, but she had been generous with her cake.

Ah, but that was long ago and Farley had taught her it was best not to dwell in the past. The knot grew taut in her stomach. That was bad; she thought she had outgrown it. The caged-in feeling was on her again. Frantically, she fluttered around the room. I've got to get away, she pleaded with herself. After all, who would I hurt if I was to slip out now for a ride? No one is awake and I will return before they are.

Once she had made her decision, she was anxious to be off. Quickly she threw on her riding habit, scarcely bothering to be decent. With the same urgency, she flew down the stairs and ran outside to the stables. Just as she was about to fling open the doors, she heard a noise behind her. Spinning around, she saw Julian Warwick leaning against the end of the building, watching her.

"Good morning, Miss Farley. You seem to be in a hurry."

Drat! Now she would have to stay and make idle chat with the man. She cast a longing glance at the door and, with a sigh, gave up all hopes of riding this morning. Whatever his opinion of her, Farley would have to admit that she knew her duties as hostess. Recovering from both surprise and disappointment, she tried to make polite conversation. "Good morning, Mr. Warwick. I see you don't keep fashionable hours." She even managed a smile.

"Where I come from it's important to be up with the sun. On a day like today it would be a sin to stay in bed."

Pleased by his words, she beamed up at him. He seemed so different this morning, more approachable. "I know. Only I hadn't expected to see anyone else up this early."

"I'm sorry. I bet you were about to sneak off."

She blushed. "I guess Grandfather is right. I have

deplorable manners. But you see, my mother and I always rode in the morning and it's a habit I find hard to break."

"Quite understandable. Please, don't let me stop you."

"You mean you don't mind?"

"Of course not."

"Won't you join me? I'm sure we could find a horse for you."

A look of horror replaced the casual smile. "Good heavens, no! I quite dislike the odious beasts. The inside of a carriage is as close as I care to get to them. But please, do go yourself."

"Oh, I couldn't."

"Nonsense. If I don't mind, your grandfather can hardly object. It would absolutely ruin my day if I were to go about with the guilty knowledge that I had deprived you of your daily pleasure. Besides, if you don't tell him, how will he know? It can be our secret." Like a conspirator, he grinned at her.

She loved him in that moment. "If you're certain . . ."

"Go ahead. Please. I have some private affairs to attend to, so most likely I will spend the day in my room anyway. So please, do enjoy yourself and don't worry about me."

Taking her hand, he lightly brushed her fingers with his lips. For a minute or two, with her head cocked to one side, Katherine watched him walk away. What a perplexing man. Shaking herself, she realized she couldn't afford to waste time thinking about him now. With a sense of release, she went inside, heading straight for Midnight. She had her saddled and ready to ride when she caught sight of a beautiful white stallion, foaming with sweat, in a stall by the door. She reached out to touch him but withdrew her hand at his look.

"Begging your pardon, ma'am, but I wouldn't be taking chances with that animal if I was you. He's not used to strangers and it's hard to predict how he'll act."

The speaker was barely two inches taller than Katherine, but there was an air of strength that more than made up for his lack of stature. He stood, hat in hand, but the twinkle in his warm brown eyes belied any suggestion of supplication. Automatically, Katherine jumped back. He smiled, lighting up the unshaven face. Without reasoning why, Katherine knew she was going to like this man. "Oh, excuse me. I'm sorry, I just didn't think. He's such a beautiful animal. Is he yours?"

The man shuffled his feet. "He belongs to my master. Mr. Warwick."

"Mr. Warwick? But he just told me he hates horses."

He wouldn't meet her eyes. "Aye, that he does, miss. Poor Mr. Julian doesn't seem to be able to get them to do what he wants. But he sure does like them to decorate his stable."

"Just for decoration?"

"No, uh, that is, he likes them for his carriage, too."

Katherine studied the stallion. "He's using this magnificent animal for his carriage?"

He winked, knowingly. "Your Irish blood shows in you, miss. You and I know what a waste it is, but Mr. Julian, he doesn't. But maybe that's better for the horse?"

"This horse is sweating. He's been running, and

32

running hard."

"Well, now, that's my job. A fine beast like this one isn't happy pulling a carriage, so every morning I take him out for his exercise. Then everyone is happy."

"I imagine we'll bump into each other often. I like to exericse Midnight in the morning, also."

Now it was his turn to admire her mare. "You have a fine horse there, Miss Farley."

"I'm afraid she's not my horse; she belongs to my grandfather. He's a lot like your Mr. Warwick. He prefers his horses to be looked at, so I take it upon myself to exercise her. If you're ever too busy, perhaps I could help you by exercising the stallion, too."

He looked uncomfortable. "We'll have to see. As I said, he doesn't make friends easily."

"I'm sorry, I didn't mean to be forward. I guess I'd best be off on my ride before it's too late. My grandfather has a rule about punctuality. If you don't mind, I'd rather no one knew I was here. I'm not sure Grandfather would approve. I've enjoyed talking with you, Mr. . . . uh . . ."

"Sam, just plain old Sam. That's what everyone calls me. And it's our secret, lass."

Odd, that was what Warwick had said. Smiling at him, she led Midnight into the bright sunshine. Without another thought for the strange two men, she was off into the fields. Soon the wind was whipping her hair and she was riding as if the devil himself was at her heels. Unknown to her, a wistful Julian was watching her disappear from sight. Sam was at his side.

"That sure was a close one."

"Yes, Sam, but I trust you handled it well."

"She noticed the stallion. I had to tell her I rode him."

33

"Good. I'd hate to explain where I was last night."

"I know, but I hate to lie to her. She seems like a nice girl. Do we have to do this?"

"Believe me, if there was any other way . . ."

"She wants to ride the stallion."

"Let her; she has a good seat. I doubt I'll be needing him for a while, anyway. Right now, I want to take advantage of her absence to catch up on some sleep. Take care, Sam."

The older man watched him walk away. Poor boy, it seemed he was always tired. With a shake of his head, he returned to the stable.

When Katherine rode back to the stable, only the regular groom was present. That was a disappointment; she had worked up the courage to question this Sam person about his master. Sighing, she handed Midnight to the waiting groom. Any other day, she would have taken care of the mare, but today it was important to get back to the house. Midnight expressed her disapproval of the situation with a snort. Exasperated, Katherine felt compelled to explain. The groom, long accustomed to the relationship between this girl and her horse, didn't interfere.

But Katherine was far later than she had anticipated in reaching the house. Forced to dress in haste, she rushed to the dining room to meet Farley for breakfast. She slid into her chair, prepared for the ensuing lecture. All he said was, "Hmmmph, young people. No respect for the right way of doing things. Where's Warwick?"

The butler intervened. "Mr. Warwick begs you to excuse him, sir, but he's not feeling well this morning and will not be down for breakfast."

Katherine wondered briefly whether it was illness

34

or private business that kept him in his room, but she was far too grateful at being spared her lecture to question his story. All she had to endure this morning was Farley's grumbling about the war. If the Admiralty would listen to him, they'd send every damn ship they had over there and blow all the colonies off the face of the earth. Then they'd be done with this nonsense.

After a time, she managed to escape the dining room. With her guest in his room for the day, there was little for her to do. The urge to be outside was strong, so she donned old clothes and a pair of work gloves and moved out to the garden. Tending the flowers and vegetables had been one of her responsibilities at Clonmara. She had enjoyed it and she made it her business to do so here at Whitney Hall, whenever possible. Though Farley would have considered it below her station, it was honest work and it occupied her time. It was unlikely that he'd ever know; what she did on her own time was of no interest to him.

She spent the entire day in the garden. Farley was only too happy to assume that Katherine was entertaining their guest, freeing him of the obligation. As each had the day to himself, when they met for the first time in the drawing room, they were each in a good mood. Dinner was a relaxed meal with even Katherine included in the conversation. Julian responded eagerly to her attempts to have him talk about his home. America could hardly be as wonderful as he described, but she couldn't deny his enthusiasm. He actually loves it, she thought, and she warmed up to him. Feeling as she did about Clonmara, it was easy to understand his affection. Imagine owning your own home and never having to fear that someone would take it away.

Julian was attentive, making her uncomfortable. His gallantry confused her; she was unaware of how to respond. She should flirt back, but it didn't come easily. After all, it wasn't easy to find flattering things to say. Could she trust herself to comment on his clothes? His cologne? Yet, he was being awfully nice. When he suggested an evening stroll through the garden, she agreed. Farley smiled in a rare show of approval, but she knew he was thinking that now he could retire. He was so obvious.

Outside they walked leisurely in the moonlight. The promising day had become a beautiful night. It was the first time Katherine had taken this walk with a man beside her, but surprisingly, she wasn't at all nervous. The companionable silence relaxed her. In fact, she was startled when Warwick broke into her thoughts.

"And what can you be thinking about that keeps you so quiet?"

"I didn't mean to be rude. It's just that on a night like this, I miss Clonmara."

"Clonmara? I take it that was your home in Ireland?"

"Yes, it was. I was so happy there. My mother would have said that tonight was a night for the fairies. I'd be bundled up and I could stay up as long as I wanted. Nanny would be furious, but once Mother made up her mind, no one could stop her. We would walk, like this, and she would point out the stars. She knew so much about everything. Before I was ten, I could identify almost every star in the sky and I could tell you which animal made which sound."

"How unusual."

"Oh yes, she was quite unusual. I think that's why my grandfather disliked her so. But I've never met anyone who was so alive, so exciting. She made everything an adventure. It was awful when she died."

"You don't have to talk about it if you'd rather not."

"Oh no, it's all right now. When I first came here, it was so different. You've met Grandfather; you must know what I mean. He's tried hard to wipe out my mother's influence. In a way, I guess he has, but on nights like tonight, I still get the urge to run down this hill and dance in the moonlight. Do I shock you?"

She looked up in his face. It was in shadow, but she could sense he was smiling. "I think we all get that kind of urge sometimes, even your grandfather. But some of us feel we have to deny it."

"I know. Young ladies are not supposed to do that sort of thing."

"Not at all." There was a wicked gleam in his eye. "Come, I'll race you."

Suddenly he was pulling her hand and she was flying along behind him, laughing. Unfortunately, his legs were longer than hers; she got tangled in her skirts and fell headlong into the grass. Unable to recover himself, Warwick stumbled and fell on top of her.

He looked down, concerned. With one glance at her face, however, they were both laughing. "Feel better?"

"Oh yes. Much. It was wonderful. But what will my grandfather say when I return with all these grass stains?"

"Hang your grandfather. Let's just forget the man for a minute, can't we?"

Katherine was surprised by the vehemence in his

37

voice and it must have shown in her face. "Miss Farley—oh, this is absurd." Warwick sat up, clearly annoyed. "I can't go on calling you that. Katherine? No, it doesn't suit you. Kate? No, Katy. Yes, that's more the thing. Can I call you Katy?"

"No one has called me that in years. It was Mother's pet name for me."

"Then if you'd rather I didn't . . ."

She reached for his sleeve. "No, please do. I like it."

He smiled again, touching her with its warmth. The smile faded and she could feel her heart rise into her throat, suddenly all too conscious of his nearness.

"Katy, then. I want to ask you something. Does it really matter to you what your grandfather thinks?"

"I hope you won't be shocked, but no, it doesn't. I've tried to be a dutiful granddaughter, doing what he expects from me, but it is never enough. There's little love lost between us, I'm afraid."

"Then why do you stay? Why do you let him bully you?"

"What choice do I have? I have no family, and under the law, he makes all decisions for me until I come of age. I've dreamed of that day for so long, but realistically, I can't see what difference it will make. Women aren't always equipped to take care of themselves."

He studied her face. "I believe you could take care of yourself."

"Thank you. I take that as a compliment. But I have no skills and I have a face that no one takes seriously. So, with no way to earn a living, I'm afraid I'm dependant on the good will of my grandfather."

"Would you leave if a way presented itself?"

"Once I thought I would do anything to get away. I guess I'm growing up. I'd have to think carefully and

38

it would depend on the opportunity."

"And if it was marriage?"

They were reaching dangerous ground. Feeling the tension in the air, she chose her words with care. "I don't know. After the way it was with my parents, I'm not sure I'd be happy in a marriage that wasn't based on love and trust."

She had been staring at her hands, but with a sudden need to make him understand, she looked up into his eyes. Something in their depths touched her, causing her heart to pump madly. It was hard to find the right words, but it didn't seem to matter. All that mattered in that moment was that he was so close and he was going to kiss her. He leaned closer until his breath was warm on her cheeks.

A frog croaked in the distance and the spell was broken. Julian looked away, coughed, and then rose to his feet, leaving her to wonder if she had imagined the whole thing. He dusted his trousers and extended a hand to her. "Goodness, I've lost track of time. I think I'd better get you back to the house."

What had happened? All too suddenly he was once again the obnoxious young man her grandfather was forcing her to marry. When she thought that seconds ago she had almost let him kiss her, had actually encouraged him to do so, she blazed with humiliation. Well, if he chose to pretend that the moment had never existed, it was fine with her. What had come over her? Farley would say that it was the wanton in her, inherited from her mother. Good lord, she mustn't ever give him that ammunition. Rather than face him, she bid Julian good night at the foot of the stairs, begging him to offer her apologies to Farley. Up in her room, she ripped off the soiled gown and summoned a maid to soak it immediately.

Downstairs, Julian found Farley in his study, hard at work on a bottle of brandy. Rising to meet his guest, Farley tottered a bit. "Ah, Warwick. Care to join me with a brandy? I hope you and Katherine enjoyed your stroll?"

"Yes, thank you. She asked to be excused. It's been a long day."

"I should say so. Well, now that you've had a look at her, are you ready to sign the contract?"

Unnoticed by his host, Warwick's hands tightened on the stem of his glass. He coughed lightly. "Your granddaughter is charming, but I must admit that I didn't expect her to be so, er, so forceful. She strikes me as being a very formidable young lady."

"That's the Irish in her. You just have to be firm. Let her know from the beginning that you are in charge."

"I might say I hadn't looked forward to such a struggle. Katherine's a lovely girl, but I did have a more pliable nature in mind."

Farley wanted to strangle the girl. What could she have done to frighten this young fool away? No, he was not going to slip out of this so easily. "I will be frank with you, Warwick. I am well aware of your financial status. I know that you have gambled away a major portion of your family's fortune and that you need Katherine's dowry to recoup your losses."

Warwick looked crestfallen. "I am mortified; I had no idea that you knew."

Farley tasted victory. "I had warned you that I knew all I needed to know about you."

"But I can assure you, sir, that the money will be used wisely. I have plans for renovating . . ."

"What you do with the dowry is no concern of mine. Just take the money, and Katherine, and be gone!"

The cold words seemed to hang between them. The silence was lessened only by an occasional pop from the logs on the fire.

Draining his glass, Warwick edged his voice with a duplicate chill. "You fail to take into account that I am not exactly desperate. After all, there are many unmarried and wealthy young girls all over London."

"And what are you suggesting?" Farley's glare was now directed at his guest.

"Surely you can understand my position. I have a family name to protect. To keep up my home and that name, I need money. A great deal of money. Admittedly, your terms are generous, but in view of the risk I will be taking with your granddaughter, I'm afraid they don't quite fill my needs."

"Go on."

"I need hardly point out, sir, that there is not exactly a string of admirers at your door."

"I think you drive a hard bargain."

"Only out of necessity, my lord. Come now, if you were in my position, wouldn't you do the same?"

Reluctantly, Farley had to admit he was right. It galled him to think of parting with any more money, but there seemed to be no way out. "How much did you have in mind?"

"I've thought this over carefully and I think I might be able to settle for double the original sum."

Farley gasped. Double the sum? Never! He'd throw the American scoundrel out in the cold. Of all the outrageous . . .

"Of course, with a dowry that size, I would be able to sign the contract immediately, enabling me to leave with Katherine for America. Unfortunately, this would mean that you would never see either of us again." He raised an eyebrow, questioning.

Farley could recognize blackmail, but the thought of being rid of Katherine was too tempting. It might have been a mistake to let Warwick see his desperation; he had obviously underestimated the man. He had made an error, and like a man, he would pay for it.

He slammed his glass on the desk, brandy spilling over its sides. "Very well, Warwick; you win. I will have the papers drawn and ready for you to sign tomorrow. Plan on making your arrangements immediately. I trust we have nothing further to say to each other tonight? Good. If you'll excuse me, I think I'll retire for the evening."

Shuffling to the door, Farley betrayed both his age and the amount of brandy he had consumed. He stiffened, almost managing dignity, at the sound of Warwick's voice.

"Have a good night's sleep, my lord. Rest assured that I will take good care of your granddaughter."

Exasperated, Farley left him. Stretching long legs before the fire, Warwick chuckled to himself. "Very good care, indeed."

Then, helping himself to another glass of his host's very fine brandy, he chuckled again.

Chapter 4

Once again, Katy was up with the sun. Unlike yesterday, however, there was no indecision. No sooner had she opened her eyes than she was up and dressing. Somehow, she had to clear these cobwebs from her brain. The need to be on Midnight was pressing on her. Life at Whitney Hall had been depressing, and all too often boring, but how simple it had been compared to the last few days. How could she ever make up her mind about Julian Warwick when he was a different person every time she saw him? Oh drat, she didn't want to think about him this morning. If she did, she would have to consider her extraordinary behavior last night. She'd go to Midnight; she'd help sort this mess.

In the stable, the day had yet to begin and Katy was grateful. She was in no mood to chat. As it was, the stallion's eyes followed her every movement. In them, Kate read not quite hostility, but certainly suspicion. Anxious to win his trust, she approached slowly with a lump of sugar in her extended hand. He whinnied softly but allowed her to stroke his mane, while his eyes were riveted to the sugar. Amused, Katy presented it to him. With the air that it was he that was doing the favor, he took it. Katy grinned, satisfied with her first attempt.

When she reached Midnight, she noticed suspicion in the mare's eyes. Oh no, she's jealous, Katy realized. Though she took the sugar, as if it was her due, she still seemed to expect special treatment. "Try to understand, love. He's our guest and it's our duty to make him feel at home. Don't you remember how it felt when no one came to see you? Tell me you do understand."

Obviously the horse was not in an understanding frame of mind. The strain of the past few days showed on her, too, and she seemed to have a foreboding of what the future would bring. Resorting to the one thing that never failed to soothe her, Katy settled herself in the stall, brushing the jet black coat. She began to sing. Choosing carefully, she sang the haunting lullabies that had calmed her in her childhood. Though she couldn't claim the deep, rich voice of her mother, her horse understood these songs and many a restless night had ended in peaceful sleep to the sound of the girl's high, clear voice.

"It does a body's heart good to hear the old songs again."

Katy jumped. Looking up, she saw Sam, hat in hand, watching her. How long had he been there? Did he realize that she was baring her soul in those songs?

"I'm sorry if I startled you, miss, but it's been a long while since I've heard those songs and it's brought back many a memory." Pulling out a handkerchief, he wiped at his eyes. "You've the voice of an angel, as fine as me own mother's, God rest her soul, and I want to thank you for bringing it all back."

44

To cover her embarrassment, she spoke too sharply. "I'm not accustomed to an audience."

"Then I'm sorry for disturbing you. But you've no reason to be ashamed of giving an old man a moment of pleasure. Good day to you, miss."

As he started for the door, Katy regretted her thoughtless outburst. He had been nice; she felt like a beast, using him to vent her anger. "Sam, please don't go. If my singing has brought you pleasure, than I'm actually glad. That's what singing is for, isn't it? It's just that I'm not accustomed to having anyone listening to me."

"You never sing for your grandfather?"

"Grandfather? Good heavens, no!"

Sam approached the stall. There was a toughness about him that would have frightened her if not for the gentleness in that rough, weather-beaten face. For a moment, Katy let herself wonder what it might have been like to have him for a grandfather. She knew instinctively that with a man like this, she would never have to face her uncertain future alone.

"That's his loss, I'd say. You could make quite a career for yourself on the stage, if you cared for that sort of life."

She stopped brushing, uncertain whether he was teasing. "You can laugh, if you want, but don't think I haven't considered it. Living here requires some acting talent in itself, and I must admit, it makes me long to do something wicked. But it's not what I want for myself. I want a home, a family, something to build on. You know, all the things everyone wants."

"Life has a way of ignoring what we want sometimes." He took the brush and surprisingly, Midnight allowed him to comb her.

45

"Oh, I know that. But I also know myself. I hate living a lie. I act and live the way Grandfather wishes, but I hate it. I want the chance to be myself, to do and say the things I think are right. And I want a husband that loves me for what I am, and children, and, oh Sam, don't look at me like that."

"Lass, you're so young."

"I can't help that. I'm just telling you what I want."

"I wanted those things, too. Once."

She was struck by his wistful expression. "What happened?"

"Maybe I wanted too much. I had a wife and a little girl. Aye, she was a pretty one, my little Kathleen, with her hair as red as the sunset. She was the very picture of her mother."

"But it sounds wonderful."

"Aye, that it was, until the sassenach came. They said they was owed taxes. Where was a man the like of me to get extra money? At a time when there was no money to be had anywhere? I lost my farm. There was no choice but to go to America."

"America? All that way?"

"There was nothing for us back home. America was a land with a future, it was said; the only chance for a new life. Poor Annie, she was so excited about starting that new life. She never got the chance. Two weeks out of port, both she and my precious Kathleen were sick. Being stuck in that filthy, stinking hole, without fresh air and food, it would have been a miracle if they survived. The good Lord was sparing his miracles that year. I watched them get worse and worse until they died in my arms. Annie, she never gave up hoping, right up until the last. Even then, she made me promise to go on without her. How could I tell her that our baby was dead, too; that there was no reason for me to go on?''

"Oh, Sam, I'm so sorry."

"Don't you go wasting your pity on Sam Culligan." His gruff voice tried to deny the emotion that was shining in his eyes. "It's not a story I go telling often, and never for pity. It must be those songs of yours, stirring up old memories. I've made my life, the best I could, and I'm proud of it. But I want you to see that life doesn't always do what we expect from it.''

"Are you warning me about something?''

"Warning you? No, lass, but I do want you to think carefully before you get railroaded into something.''

"What are you trying to say? Is there something I should know about Mr. Warwick?''

He was all innocence. "Mr. Warwick? What has he to do with anything?''

"Come now, Sam. You know well enough what brings your master to Whitney Hall.''

"And it's not my place to be gossiping about my employer, especially if I want to keep my job.''

She followed him over to the stallion's stall. "Just tell me what he's like. You see him every day; you must know what sort of person he is.''

Sam had said enough. "If you don't stop pestering me with your questions, I'll never get my work done. Be off with you, girl.''

"That's not fair, Sam Culligan. You give these cryptic messages and then quit without telling me what you mean. If you don't tell me what to expect, who will? How can I ever make up my mind about him if I don't even know him?''

There was a sternness about him, now. "You listen

47

to me, lass, and you listen well. He's a good man and I'd trust him with my life. But that's my life; not yours. Nobody but yourself can make your decision. Just keep your eyes and your ears open and learn what you can. When the time comes, you, and only you, can tell whether you want to marry him or not."

"I know you're right." Katy sighed as she helped him saddle the horse. "I guess I wanted someone to talk to, to ask for advice. There's been no one to share my troubles with ever since my mother died." She couldn't help it; her voice cracked.

Compassion on his face, Sam put a large blistered hand on her shoulder. "Tell me now, is it that bad?"

Katy shrugged. "Not so much any more, I guess. It was horrid here, with my grandfather, especially after Clonmara, but I had promised Mother I would give it a try. When Midnight came, it was easier. At least I could talk to her, even if she couldn't answer. Now my grandfather says it's time for a new life, in a new country. Part of me wants to take a chance and part of me is scared. I don't know what to do."

"And what would your mother tell you to do?"

She grinned in a sheepish way. "She'd tell me to keep my eyes open and learn what I can."

"See now, that's what you've got to do. Don't let anyone go bullying you into something you don't want to do, that's all. And if ever you need someone to tell your troubles to, you come right here to Sam Culligan, you hear?"

"Sam, you're an angel." She stood on her toes to kiss his cheek. His rough beard tickled and she was blushing at her own impulsiveness.

Sam was a bit embarrassed, but he was pleased. "Well now, lass, you be careful who you go kissing. I doubt His Lordship would approve of your kissing the likes of me."

"Don't you go teasing me, Sam Culligan. I'll kiss whoever I please and the devil take my grandfather!"

Reminded suddenly of the gentleman, Katy realized with regret that she would have to cancel her ride to go in to change for breakfast. "I guess I'd better be getting back to the house or His Lordship will feel it's his duty to read me a lecture on the virtue of punctuality, and quite frankly, I don't feel up to it this morning."

Sam chuckled. "You hurry along and get your breakfast. Don't worry about your mare. I'll see she gets her exercise after I tend to this monster." He hoisted himself onto the stallion. "Now get out of here and let me get my work done."

"Thank you for everything, Sam."

"Never mind all that. You get up to the house."

They went in different directions; she, to the dubious pleasure of breakfast with the two gentlemen and he, to the freedom of the open fields. How she envied him. But there was no help for it. There was little time before breakfast and she had to dress. She resented being a young lady; it meant that she was constantly changing her clothes. At Clonmara, one dress could last all day and often, to Nanny's absolute horror, she wore trousers. Here at Whitney Hall, it was unheard of to wear the same clothes to every meal and it was forbidden to appear at the table in her riding habit. It was annoying. Perhaps if she had a more varied wardrobe it wouldn't seem quite so inconvenient. Farley might be generous about her dowry, but when it came to her allowance, he was a miser. Not only were her dresses few in number, but they were worn and out

49

of fashion, as well. Some she had sewn herself and some were altered gowns of her mother's. Looking through her wardrobe, she chose a bright yellow dress that was much too young for her, not caring today what impression she made. Let them underestimate her. Both men were determined to consider her a child, anyway. She would remain alert and learn what she could of this Julian Warwick.

She arrived in the dining room before either of the men. Warwick sauntered in while she was buttering a roll. "What a charming picture you make, Miss Farley. Why, you look like the sun itself."

For some reason, his gallantry annoyed her more than ever. After last night, it seemed so contrived. If she had to endure a lifetime of this, she'd go mad. "I thought you were going to call me Katy?"

Unabashed, he grinned at her. Rudeness didn't bother him in the least. "Quite right, my dear. But then, of course, you must call me Julian."

"I doubt my grandfather would approve."

"And where is that formidable gentleman this morning?"

"I have no idea. Didn't you meet him upstairs?"

He looked at her in mock horror. "God forbid! Much more pleasant to start my day in your presence." He slid into a chair. "Perhaps he's reluctant to see me this morning. He and I had words last evening."

Though she was dying to know what those words were, Katy refused to ask him, knowing full well that was what he wanted. There was an uncomfortable silence before he tried again. "It was a business discussion, actually, and I take great pleasure in admitting to you that I bested him at his own game."

You would, she thought. And why are you telling me

all this? Rather than give the conceited bore the satisfaction of seeing her curiosity, she busied herself in
buttering another roll.

"I doubt you are interested in business, as a general
rule, but I thought you might be interested in this.
You see, it concerns you. You and your dowry. I managed to have it doubled."

"You what? How?"

"So you are interested?"

She could have bit her tongue. Damn him and his
silly grin. "You're so sure of yourself, aren't you?"

All of a sudden, he was serious. Leaning closer to
her, he spoke in a whisper. "No, Katy, you misunder-
stand me completely. I am not gloating. I just want
you to know that I think your guardian holds you far
too cheaply. He will pay for his treatment of you, and
in a way that hurts him most; through his purse."

She could only stare at him. This new role confused
her; she still thought of him as Farley's ally. A thousand questions were on her lips, but Farley chose that
moment to enter the room. With a scowl, he seated
himself and opened his newspaper, ignoring them
both. So he *was* angry with Warwick. What had happened last night?

Katy engaged in trivial conversation with Julian
but her mind was on other matters. What had he
meant? If only there had been time to ask him, to really talk. They had been close before Farley joined
them. She watched Julian as he talked. There was
something pleasant about his voice. It wasn't nearly
as soft as she had once thought. In fact, it had an air of
command, the voice of someone over in America.
Whatever had possessed him to cross the ocean to
find a bride? He was quite handsome, in a theatrical

51

fashion. Despite the hideous clothing and his affected manner, she felt drawn to him. Enough of that kind of talk, she warned herself; this was hardly the time to wonder what it would be like to be kissed by this man.

He was talking about the war, his war. Except for biased comments from Farley, Katy knew so little about it. No one seemed much concerned with it here in England. But it was real to Julian, who lived in the midst of it and if she was to marry him, it would be real to her. She would need to know more. "But I don't understand, Julian. Why hasn't this rabble, as you call them, given up yet? After all, we've the finest navy in the world, and our army is second to none. It should be evident to even the most optimistic that it is hopeless. Still, they keep fighting and we never seem to win a decisive victory. Why is that?"

"A very intelligent question and one, I might add, that has baffled military minds more experienced with these affairs than ours. It is difficult to say exactly. Surely part of the reason is that these people have a cause in which they believe strongly."

"But they must know they will lose eventually."

"It's not quite that simple, I'm afraid. We were beaten badly at Saratoga and then again when the French beat us to the negotiation tables."

"I don't understand."

"The Treaty of Vergennes, promising a French alliance, was signed only weeks before Parliament passed a bill that would have given in to their demands. With new allies, the traitors grew cocky and now we find we have to fight the French. And maybe the Spanish."

"But the French are busy with their own affairs. They can't be depended on."

"We know that, but try telling it to those warmongers. Even those who agree with you will tell you it doesn't matter."

"It doesn't make sense to trust the French."

"There's more to it than trust. Remember, France is England's enemy; not America's. And America is a vast expanse of several colonies with differing nationalities. To conquer it all would take thousands of troops; to keep it would take more. After our long wars with France, we no longer have the resources. The colonists are banking on this. We've been forced to concentrate on the ports, to bankrupt them before they bankrupt us."

"This is a war of economics, then?"

"In part, but then, aren't all wars? But in one way, this is a new kind of war. In Europe, the army trains and outfits itself, and then goes on the march. The peasant knows enough to stay in hiding until the soldiers have gone. In the wilderness of America, they seem to know nothing about the etiquette of war. When a British command marches through a town, everyone, sometimes even women and children, pick up whatever arms are at their disposal to protect the land they say is theirs by right. But rather than stand and fight, they hide behind bushes, picking off our soldiers, one by one. Naturally, our army prefers to stay by the coast where the fleet can keep them supplied and protected. Therefore, there are no decisive victories."

Farley put down his paper. "They've all gone soft. Why don't they just send in a command to mop up the countryside, killing anyone who tries to interfere?"

"Surely you don't mean civilians, Grandfather?"

"And why not? If they're stupid enough to get in the way, then they need to be taught a lesson."

"I'm afraid many of our military minds think like your granddaughter, sir. It's not easy to consider killing fellow Englishmen."

"Nonsense! Not if they take a shot at you first."

"It's not a simple matter to determine who is doing the shooting. Under British law, a man is innocent until proven guilty. They have the advantage. To them, it is a life and death struggle against an intolerable tyrant. I'm afraid it's somewhat less vital to the average soldier."

"Bah! The whole system has gone soft. By God, it's treason and in my day we would have hung the whole lot of them. A pox on your damned war; I'm sick of it. I don't want to hear it discussed at my table again." Picking up his papers, he went back to it.

Katy felt disappointment. Julian had talked to her as if he knew she had a mind and was willing to use it, and she had enjoyed the novel experience. She had asked for his opinion and he had impressed her with his knowledge and insight. Coyly, she risked a glance at him. Of course he was grinning. He made a face at Farley and Katy had to stop herself from laughing.

It was good that she had the control because in that instant, Farley dropped his paper. "Didn't you have something more important to discuss with my granddaughter, Warwick?"

Katy was mortified. Did he have to be so obvious?

Julian attempted to smoothe it over. "How perceptive of you, sir. As a matter of fact, I was just about to ask Miss Farley to join me in a stroll through your garden. With your permission, of course."

"In the garden? What's wrong with right here?"

"On such a lovely day? It would be a crime to spend it indoors."

"Nonsense. It's too cold to be out there."

"Do you think so? Perhaps we should discuss this with Katherine. After all, it's her opinion that matters most, don't you think? What do you say, my dear, is it the garden or the dining room?" Though he addressed Katy, his cold blue eyes were assessing Farley.

Katy looked from one scowling face to the other, knowing that there was more to this than the location of their discussion. It was a battle of wills, with her in the middle. At the time, it didn't occur to her that she could refuse them both. She agreed to go out, and by siding with Julian, she made a commitment that would make life with Farley more intolerable than ever.

Shivering with the magnitude of her decision, she ran upstairs to fetch a wrap. Apprehensively, she crept past Farley's study, relieved to find him preoccupied with other matters. Somewhat less than enthusiastically, she sought Julian.

He was standing with his back to her, deep in thought, when she found him. For the first time, Katy realized that it was a broad back and for some reason, this delighted her. If only he didn't wear that awful wig. She suddenly wanted to know the true color of his hair. As he turned to face her, his eyes took on the glare of the sun, making it impossible for her to see into them. All at once, the need to do so was vital, as if he would be vulnerable now, and she would be able to read in those eyes all she would ever need to know. She hurried, but by the time she reached his side, his eyes were as fathomless as ever. Acutely aware of disappointment, she let him take her limp hand. She heard her voice, as if from a long way off, ask more curtly than she had intended. "So, Mr. Warwick, what is it you wish to discuss?"

His voice was gentle and pleading, more gentle than she deserved. "What is it, Katy? Have I said or done anything to offend you?"

Must he watch her so carefully? If he was the one who was supposed to be doing the proposing, why was she so nervous? "No, of course not. I'm just not myself this morning. It's not every day that a man comes all the way from America for the seemingly express purpose of offering for my hand. I must admit the entire affair has me somewhat confused."

"Hmmmm. I was afraid of that. You don't trust me very much, do you?"

Was he pleading with her? "I don't know you well enough to know if I trust you or not. I'm not consciously trying to make this hard for you; I don't mean to blame you. I know none of this is your fault."

"Do you suppose there is somewhere we can sit? I'm certain I could do a better job of it if we were seated."

"There's a bench by the fountain. Will that do?"

"I would be obliged if you would take me there."

Katy led him to the bench, wishing it was miles away. Now that the moment had come, she realized that she still hadn't made a decision. What was she going to say to this strange man that one minute repelled, and in the next, attracted her so?

They arrived at the fountain that had never had water in it for as long as Katy could remember and still she had no idea what she would say. The bench she had promised was covered with dust. What a scene for a proposal, she thought. Julian whipped out a heavily scented handkerchief and busied himself with clearing away the dust. With amusement, she watched him put the filthy article back into the pocket of that immaculate jacket. He was a constant paradox—would she ever know him?

Gesturing for him to sit, Julian joined her on the bench. "I'll be direct. You are evidently aware of why I am here. Your grandfather has arranged our marriage. I need the money he's promised for your dowry, and I need it badly."

"I think I deserve to know why."

"That's the problem. Though I agree with you, I can't tell you. Not yet. I realize this isn't much of a bargain for you. I have precious little to offer but my name. Unlike your grandfather, though, I'm not going to coerce you into this. The choice is yours." He dropped to one knee, silk trousers forgotten. "I'm asking you to be my wife. If you say no, I will leave here today and you need never see me again."

"And what about the money you need so badly?"

"Ah, you've hit my sore spot." He was up and pacing. "I wonder how it would have been if we had met under normal circumstances, if there had been an opportunity for me to court you in the manner that you deserve?"

He stopped moving. "But that's useless speculation. We must face facts. I can't promise you the love and romance you want, but I can offer escape. Under my protection, you need never be subjected to your grandfather's domination again. I honestly believe we can make a good marriage of it, Katy. Trust me, won't you? Trust me, and if you do, I promise that I'll never willingly let you down."

He turned to her then, looking for an answer. Though the doubts still whirled around and around in her brain, Katy was lost in the incredible blue of his eyes, drawn to him as never before. Everything seemed so clear and so simple that she was saying yes before she was aware of it.

In a blur, she felt his cool lips on her forehead. It was a brotherly peck but her skin was tingling in a peculiar way. Then he was pulling out a ring, placing it on her finger, and assuring her that everything would work out splendidly. Still in a daze, she allowed him to lead her to her room.

There, without those eyes compelling her, the doubts returned. Alone in her room, she was left with the uncomfortable feeling that perhaps she had been tricked into this marriage after all.

Chapter 5

After hours of contemplation, Katy emerged from her room with the firm resolution that the next time she saw Julian Warwick, she would keep her wits about her and not allow his physical presence to interfere with her thinking capacities. This, however, proved difficult. When she joined Farley for dinner, she was informed that Julian had gone to London to notify his family of the upcoming nuptials. Promising to return within five days, he had packed his things, left with his horse and groom, and gone off to make his personal arrangements.

Katy was expected to busy herself with her own arrangements. She was horrified to learn that the wedding, no mean affair, was to occur at the end of the week. A bewildered Katy was taken in hand by Farley's sister-in-law and a wedding gown was hastily sewn. Trunk upon trunk was dragged from the attics and items Katy forgot she owned were stuffed into them. Despite Aunt Judith's obvious distaste, Katy saved one trunk for mementos from Clonmara, determined that if she was going to the ends of the earth, part of her past was going with her. If Julian didn't like it, it was too bad.

It was an up and down time for her. One minute she was excited about the prospect of a new life, and in the next she was frightened. Trust coupled with doubt, joy with depression. She longed for Julian to appear at the door to tell her that everything would work itself out. She wanted his arms around her, but at that point she would grow annoyed with herself. After all, he was only after the Farley money. Hadn't he all but admitted it to her? So why did she trust him? Just because he asked her to? There was no getting around it; for some reason, she did. For better or for worse, she was going to marry him Saturday and go off with him to a new world with no more than a promise, a few glib words spoken to a gullible girl.

So it went until Friday afternoon. Warwick was long since due and Katy felt the stirrings of apprehension. Where was he? Had he run off? Everyone would laugh at her, but worse, Farley would blame her, making life miserable. No, Julian wasn't that cruel. And there was the dowry. But what if there was some pretty-faced girl in London with a dowry larger than hers? No. He had asked her to trust him and trust him she would. He'd show.

Katy took the rest of the afternoon for riding with Midnight. Luckily, Aunt Judith went home to prepare for tomorrow's festivities, so she was free to escape. By the time she returned from the somewhat wild ride, she was in better spirits. Of course Julian would arrive in time. There was just some unexpected business to detain him, but he'd be here by tomorrow.

In a buoyant state of mind, she joined Farley for dinner. The foundation of her confidence, unfortunately, was not sound enough to withstand his tauntings. Farley was on the verge of panic, and that, coupled with an afternoon with his brandy bottle, put him in a foul mood. "And where is Warwick this evening? Am I mistaken, or wasn't he supposed to marry you in the morning?"

"Grandfather, please."

"Grandfather, please," he mimicked. "You don't seem to be bothered that the bridegroom is conspicuously absent."

"You forget that this whole idea was yours, not mine."

"Be that as it may, the rest of the world doesn't know that. All everyone else will think is that you were jilted."

"So?"

He looked at her carefully. "So? The man is about to make fools of us all and you can say 'so'? You make me sick. Where's your pride, girl?"

Already, she was on the defensive. "I have as much pride as you or anyone else. Only I don't see the reason to be so upset. If Julian isn't here yet, it simply means his business in London took longer than expected. If it is at all possible, he will be here tomorrow."

"I can't imagine what makes you so sure of yourself."

Katy wished she was as confident as she sounded. Dueling with him again, she knew she had to be careful not to lose her footing and thereby give him an advantage over her. "He gave his word."

He snorted. "Huh! The word of a rogue and a scoundrel. Is that what you put your trust in?"

Ignoring him, she continued. "His business is more complicated than he expected, that's all."

Farley was laughing, a dry, mirthless sound that made her cringe. "His business? Oh my dear, that is funny. Do you have any idea where I found your prospective mate? Dead drunk in a cheap saloon, after he had already gambled away a great deal of money. His business, indeed. Do you actually have enough confidence in your charms to believe you could lure him from the pleasures of London?"

"Don't forget, he needs the dowry."

"You're such a silly girl. I pity you, married to a scoundrel like Warwick. My dear, the contract has been signed and he took off with it. There's nothing to bring him back; he already has the money."

"You mean you let him run off with it?"

"Don't you dare criticize me! Don't forget, he gave his word."

Too late, she realized she had let him see her doubt. "He'll be back. He wants to marry me."

"He wants to marry me." His high, mocking voice was unbearable. "You're more of a fool than I thought. He has no need of you. Nor of any other woman, either."

"Grandfather!"

"Don't act so shocked. Think about it. The way he dresses, that perfume. I doubt the fool has ever even kissed you, though God knows I gave him opportunity enough."

Katy's thoughts ran back to the night when he had come so close to kissing her. Was it true? What had she gotten herself into? Correction. What had this leering old man gotten her into? She hated him, even if he was her grandfather. And Julian. Struggling to keep the tightness out of her voice, she made an attempt at dignity. "It looks as if you'll have to admit

62

you made a mistake, Grandfather. I suppose you'll have to try again."

He was livid. "Try again? If you think that I'll part with another cent for you . . ."

"I've never asked anything from you. This whole affair was your idea."

He ignored her. "No, I won't tolerate this. Who does he think he is, toying with me in this manner? Oh no, I won't let him get away with this."

"And what exactly can you do to stop him? He has the money."

Slyly, he began to smile. "How true. But he doesn't have his beloved bride, does he? We'll have to do something about that."

"What are you talking about?"

"There is an appropriate saying. 'If the mountain cannot come to Mohammed, then Mohammed must go to the mountain', or something like that. Never could understand those heathens, anyway."

"You're not making sense."

"Oh no? It's quite simple, actually. When the guests arrive in the morning, I will have to inform them, regretfully, that my granddaughter and her anxious suitor have eloped and are most likely on their way to America by now."

"Am I expected to hide in the attic for the rest of my life?"

'No, indeed. You will go to the mountain. You will be on your way to London, to meet your precious colonial."

"I don't understand."

"Don't you? And I thought you were more quick-witted than that. I'll spell it out for you. It simply means that my responsibility for you is at an end.

You're Warwick's problem now."

"But I have no idea where to find him."

"Come now, my dear; be resourceful. I can direct you to the gaming houses. Eventually you'll encounter him in one."

"And what if he is already on his way home to America?"

"Then you must follow and present yourself to his family."

"I'd rather die first."

"That is a possibility, of course."

"Why, you cold, arrogant . . "

"Don't you dare speak to me in that manner!"

"How can you?" She was dangerously close to tears. "How can you just discard me, as if I was one of your servants?"

"I've fed and clothed you for five years. You have no further claims on me."

"Claim? But I'm your own flesh and blood."

"No, you are not!" Pounding a fist on the table, he stood towering over her. "I've allowed you to use my name for the sake of family honor, but I can do so no longer. Richard was not your father; no one but your mother knew actually who was and I sometimes doubt that even she was certain."

"No." Her voice was so small that she doubted he heard her.

"My son died defending that slut's name."

"That's not true! He died on a battlefield, a hero. My mother told me so, long ago."

"She could hardly have told you the truth. No, my son died in a dirty tavern, in a sordid duel with your mother's lover. Or at least one of them."

"No!" But he was no longer aware of her; he was

lost in his own hell.

"He had so much here, but he left it for her. Why?"

"He loved my mother."

"Love? Bah!" He spat on the floor. "That's what I think of love. What did it get him? A bullet in the back!"

"I don't believe you!"

"I have no reason to lie. Haven't you ever wondered why I can't stand the sight of you? Why I'm so anxious to be rid of you? It's because you're just like her. If I allowed you to stay, you'd soon prove yourself to be as much of a slut as she was. It's in your eyes. I've seen how you look at Warwick. You make me sick."

It was some time before she was able to breathe. The strength of his hateful assault had taken her by surprise. Rising from the table in a daze, she stumbled out of the dining room and into the hallway. As if it was planned, Julian stood there waiting and she went unthinkingly into his arms. There was comfort in them; she felt as though she belonged there.

"Did you hear?" Was that toneless voice hers?

"Not everything, but enough."

"Then you know. Not that any of it is true. He didn't know Mother. If he did, he couldn't say those things. I hate him for saying them." She tore herself away. How ironic. Julian had proven trustworthy after all, but now it was too late. "Excuse me. None of this could matter to you. I understand your position. Not even Grandfather would hold you to the contract now. However, I might need your help in getting to London, if you don't mind?"

"London?" He was leaning on the banister, watching her.

"Surely you can see that I can't remain here."

"Certainly. That's why I came for you."

"But you heard what he said."

"My dear, he told me all that long ago." He opened his arms again and she gratefully fell into them. "Ah Katy. Poor, poor Katy. Cry if you want. Don't worry. I'll deal with your grandfather."

"But . . ."

"None of this makes the slightest difference to me. If you swear that your mother was innocent, I believe you. You would know best. But I'm not marrying your mother. I'm marrying you."

"How can you want to?"

He smiled down at her. "Let's just say I like to keep my word, even if it is the word of a scoundrel. And thank you for defending me, Katy. It means a lot to me."

Staggering to his feet to discover the source of the noise, Farley joined them. "What in blazes is going on out here? Ah, Warwick. Took your time about arriving, didn't you?"

Julian put Katy to the side of him, shielding her from her grandfather. He sounded almost jovial. "Sorry, sir, I'm afraid there was some business to detain me. It's not every day that a fellow gets married, eh what?"

"Hmmmph! Tried to tell the girl, but you know women. Can't be happy unless they're fretting about something."

Furious, Katy was about to blurt out a denial when she caught the look in Julian's eyes. He spoke quickly before she could manage a word. "Forgive my intrusion at what must be your dinner hour, but as you see, I've been riding all day to get here on time. There's been a complication. When I went to make the arrangements, I discovered that the only ship sailing for America is departing sooner than I thought. I'm afraid I'll have to take Katherine with me tonight."

"Tonight?"

"Oh, I know it's frightfully short notice and not altogether proper, but we have no other choice."

"What about the guests I invited?"

"I've considered that. Why not tell them I was so anxious, I eloped with Katherine and took her off with me to America. It's such a romantic notion; they're sure to love it. And you will save all that wine."

That appealed to him. "Splendid idea, Warwick. Should have thought of it, myself."

Julian turned to Katy. "Darling, can you manage, do you think?"

The muscles of her mouth twitched as she struggled not to laugh. "I'll certainly give it a try. Darling."

"Good girl. Now run on upstairs and do your woman-things while I make the necessary arrangements with your grandfather. Oh, and Katy? Wear something suitable for riding."

Riding? She thought he was afraid of horses. "Aren't we taking your carriage?"

"Not tonight, love. Too long a distance to cover."

"But what about my trunks?"

"That's what I wish to discuss with Lord Whitney. Don't worry, between the two of us we'll manage to have them delivered to the ship." He took her arm and gently propelled her to the stairs, whispering in her ear, "Still trust me?"

This time she didn't hesitate. "Yes, Julian. I trust you."

He flashed a dazzling smile and said, "Good girl." Then he grabbed Farley's elbow and led him into the dining room. By the door, he looked back at her and winked. Impulsively, she winked back. As she flew up the stairs, she could hear him chuckle.

It was hardly possible, but Julian had done it. Somehow, he had defied her grandfather and now was going to take her off into the night. Perhaps not quite in the manner of her dream, but what did it matter? It was an adventure; it was wonderful. There had been more than ample time to run off without her, but he had done as he had promised.

Hurrying into her riding habit, she stuffed toilet articles into a reticule. The riding habit was a bit soiled from her ride this afternoon, but there was no help for it. What a garment to be married in. Thank heavens Aunt Judith need never know that the lovely lace gown would remain packed away in her trunk. No, she decided, this was not quite the fairy tale she would have designed for herself, but it was close enough.

When she joined the men downstairs, they were waiting in the hall. Julian smiled, but he was all business. Now what kind of a game was he playing? Was Farley the victim, or she? Oh, what did it matter? She had already put herself in his hands and she had no choice but to walk out of the house with him.

Outside the horses stood ready for departure, the white stallion impressive in the moonlight. With a jolt, Katy realized that she was saying good-bye not only to Whitney Hall and England, but it was time to leave Midnight, as well. In a moment of despair, she halted at the steps. As if he read her thoughts, Julian stopped, too. "Why, Lord Whitney. I thought you promised to fit Katherine with a proper mount. That nag won't last the night."

"Nonsense, Warwick. That horse was bred for endurance."

"But I distinctly remember that Katherine rides a black horse. This isn't her regular mount."

Katy held her breath. What was he up to, now?

"My good man, I simply can't have my future wife stumbling about in the dark on a tired old wretch that she's not in the least familiar with." He sighed deeply and peeled off his gloves. "That settles it. I suppose we'll have to stay. There will be other ships. Though not for weeks, I'm told." He draped an arm over Farley's shoulder. "I guess you'll be having house guests for a while. I don't suppose you play whist, do you?"

Farley was caught. In his befuddled state, he wasn't sure how, but he knew and resented it. But he was stubborn and not about to give in easily. "That mare is the only horse of value I have, Warwick. I think you have taken me for enough."

"Good heavens, is that all that's the problem? I don't wish to take advantage of you. Here, take my stallion. Pound for pound, he's every bit as valuable as that mare of yours."

Katy gasped. "Julian, don't. It's all right. I don't mind riding Margaret."

"Your life is more important to me than any horse, my dear. What say, Lord Whitney? Are you satisfied?"

Farley had been inspecting the stallion. Warwick was a fool to part with such a fine piece of horseflesh, but his loss was Farley's gain. Especially since the mare wouldn't let him touch her anyway. Turning to the groom, he gave instructions to fetch Midnight.

Katy was soon mounted and Julian was astride the poor belittled Margaret. It was an awkward departure and she couldn't help but compare it to her fairy tale.

In many ways, it had come true but reality had a way of adding little touches to spoil it. How perfect if Julian had looked the part of the prince and if he could have ridden the stallion to carry her off. Instead, here they were, politely wishing Farley their best before sedately trotting off. Annoyance bubbled up and she found herself remarking to Julian. "I thought you were afraid of horses?"

"Did I say that?"

"You know you did. And why on earth did you give him your horse?"

"You ask too many questions. When I can, I'll answer anything you might possibly want to ask, but for now, you and I have a ship to catch and a considerable distance to cover. Are you up to it?"

"If you can do it, I can."

"Then let's go." He was off and Katy had no choice but to follow. The pace was set and for the rest of the night she struggled to keep up with it. There was little time to wonder about his considerable ability to manage his horse. In fact there was little time for thought of any kind. It took all her concentration not to fall behind.

When night finally relinquished its hold on the sky and the first stirrings of dawn could be seen in the distance, Katy was exhausted. Midnight was foaming and short of breath while Julian and Margaret appeared ready to ride all day. Looking over, Julian drew rein. "It's not much further. Hold on a bit and I promise you can sleep all day."

"But I'm sure we can make it."

"Now you can see why I let Farley keep the stallion. After the wild ride yesterday, he'd have dropped by the wayside. And I doubt your poor mare could have

70

handled the two of us."

"But you insisted that I take Midnight."

"Whatever else I am, I'm not an ogre. I saw the look on your face. Do you think I would separate you from your horse? Here now, do you think you can both keep on a bit more?"

She threw back her shoulders. "Of course we can. And Julian, thank you."

But he wasn't listening. He was back at it, riding furiously, and she was forced to follow or be left behind.

An hour later, they approached a seaside town. Katy, virtually imprisoned at Whitney Hall, didn't recognize it as Bristol. Julian rode through, past the tall ships lying quiet in the early morning sun. One of these, she hoped, must be ours, but they were past the last of them and on the outskirts of town before he dismounted. Helping her down, he said, "Well, love, here we are."

Katy looked around, confused. "Here we are? I thought you were taking me to a ship?"

"I thought it might be more convenient and appropriate if we were married first."

"Married? Oh Julian, I forgot all about that."

"How flattering. Ah, here's Sam. Have you made the arrangements?"

"The parson will be honored, he says." Sam was watching her in a queer way. "Did you tell her?"

"Not now, Sam." Julian's voice had an edge to it.

"Tell me what?"

He took her by the shoulders but his touch was gentle. "I've asked you to trust me, Katy, and I'll answer your questions when the time comes. Do you still trust me? If not, there's no sense going through that door."

Looking into those eyes, she believed him. She didn't altogether trust him, with his quick changes of character, but she realized she was already linked somehow with this man and she had no choice at all. So she took his hand and led him to the door. "I'll trust you, Julian, but if you let me down, there'll be all hell to pay."

Whatever would have been his reply was lost in the excitement that ensued. The parson and his wife, an elderly couple, were delighted to entertain such a romantic pair. Providing flowers for Katy and drink for the men, they made it as festive an occasion as possible. Katy was ushered into a private room where she was fussed over until the older woman had her believing that she was indeed a beautiful bride, despite the riding habit. With a yellow rose in her shining hair, she was received into the parlor by an appreciative audience. Julian took her small hand in his comparatively large one. There were blisters on those once smooth hands, but she merely added that to the ever-growing list of questions to ask her husband.

All too suddenly, he was her husband. They spoke their vows without facing each other, in hushed voices. When the parson told him to kiss the bride, Julian turned to her with a question in his eyes. Unable, or maybe unwilling, to understand his question, she lowered her lashes. Hesitating slightly, he squeezed her hand and brushed her lips with his own. Was that all there was to it? Oh, it was nice, but not exactly paradise.

One moment she was being kissed, the next she was back on Midnight. Making his apologies, Julian explained their need for haste. With tears and wishes for a safe journey, the elderly couple sent them on their way. Katy, struggling with emotions she couldn't define and fatigue that she could, ignored the bickering of her companions. Most likely, she would have kept riding if Sam hadn't stopped in her path. Just managing to avoid a collision, she slid off her horse in front of one of the smaller ships. Vaguely, she noticed it was clean and seemingly seaworthy. The *Sally Ann*. It would be her home for the next few months, but all she could think of now was finding a bed. Any bed. With Julian's guidance, she found herself being hustled off to a comfortable cabin where she undressed and fell immediately off to sleep.

PART
TWO

Chapter 6

Katy was crying, happy to be home. For five long years she had held in the tears but today the sun was shining and the grass was so green it broke her heart. Only at Clonmara could the grass grow that green and only on her wedding day could the sun shine as brightly. By the doorway her mother was smiling, as beautiful as ever. Katy flew to her open arms with the joy of coming home. Holding her daughter close, Maureen wiped away the tears. "Ah, Katy me love, is this the way to be acting on your wedding morn? What will they all be athinking, seeing you carrying on so? Such a fine man you'll be marrying. If only your Dad could be here to see. It would make his dear heart sing with pride."

Yet as she spoke, her voice grew fainter and fainter until slowly, Clonmara faded away leaving a half-awake Katy struggling to hold onto it. As she opened her eyes, it was gone. She felt empty. The dream had been so real, so satisfying. Pulling herself into a sitting position, she noticed the rose on her nightstand. When had she taken it out of her hair? It all came back in a rush; the wild midnight ride, her wedding, Julian.

Smiling, she reached for the flower. It was a pale yellow rose, delicate and soft, but the rough treatment had left is marks. The flower's condition did nothing to lighten Katy's growing sadness. I suppose it needs water, she thought to herself without enthusiasm. But she had a love for natural things that would not let them die if she could possibly prevent it, so she dragged her weary body from the bed to go in search of water.

It was in the action of so doing that the thought first struck. My God, we're at sea! There was no mistaking the roll of the ship. Julian had left her with the impression that they would be at the dock waiting for supplies for a few days, at least. How long had she been asleep? And where was her husband? A wave of panic swept over her. Could he have left her on board and taken off for the gaming halls? Cold sweat collected at the nape of her neck. She groped blindly for her clothes. I've got to find him, she kept telling herself, forcing herself to believe that she would. All she could find in the way of clothes, was her dirty riding habit. Undoubtedly, her trunks were still on deck. Come now, she chided herself, get control. You said you trusted him; do so. Most likely, he's topside having one last look at England. Just dress and go up to join him.

A simple solution but harder to accomplish than she realized. Except for the confused crossing from Ireland, she had never been at sea. On the previous occasion, grief and shock had kept her in her cabin, so she was ill-equipped to find her way around the ship. Following the corridor to its end, she found a short flight of steps. To one side was a doorway and she peeked inside. Who could tell? Julian might be in there, whiling

78

away the hours at a card game. All she found was a rather long room, lined with tables, a dining room, apparently. While she was surveying the room, a large, burly man crept up behind her.

"And what do you want?"

"Excuse me, I was looking for my husband."

He addressed her with a deliberately insolent glare. Vaguely uncomfortable at the close scrutiny, Katy attempted to back away. Putting a filthy hand on her shoulder, he blocked the exit.

"And what would a pretty thing like you be doing aboard this ship?"

The look in his eyes made her shiver. Damn that Julian for leaving her alone. Resentful that this crude man felt he could treat her this way, she fixed him with her Farley glare.

"I suggest, sir, that you take your hand off my shoulder or you will have to answer to my husband."

"Harry McGee answers to no man. Be a good girl, now, and give old Harry a kiss."

With something close to nausea, she struggled in his arms. She could smell the liquor on his breath. Oh, she'd have him hung by his thumbs for this. Breaking away, she flew down the hall. All she could hear on the way back to her cabin was his coarse laughter.

What a mess. She was stuck in her cabin because of that foul beast and she couldn't leave until Julian came for her. What was he doing? A thousand possibilities crowded into her brain during the next hour until, finally, she decided to take her chances with Harry McGee. If she stayed in her cabin, she would go mad.

It proved easy enough to slip by him. Harry was far too busy with his bottle of whiskey and his lusty ballads to pay attention to what went on in the corridors. Careful not to repeat her mistake, she avoided the room and took the stairs two at a time. With the smell of fresh, salty air in her nostrils, she knew she had reached the deck.

She didn't have the slightest idea what to do next. All about her were sailors, busy with their work. As she passed by, they stared long and hard, adding to her uneasiness. It could prove most unpleasant if she didn't find Julian soon. Her anxiety increased as she noticed there was no sign of land on either side of the ship. They were in the middle of a vast and empty ocean with miles and miles of open sea and sky. Her sense of isolation grew. She was scared and it was all Julian's fault. Was this how he repaid her trust, by leaving her all alone in this new and terrifying world? Where was he?

Betraying teardrops were collecting on her cheeks when she saw Sam Culligan. It was as if a lifeline had been thrown to her. Reaching for it, she approached her friend. Somewhere in the back of her mind, the fact that he was not alone registered and her attention was drawn to the second man. Though his back was to her, it was evident that he was a fine specimen of his sex. Legs spread apart, he stood on the deck as if he owned the sea he sailed on. As she moved closer, she could see the firm muscles on his bare back and legs. Fair hair glistening in the sun, he bent over to hear what Sam was saying. He moved with a slow, fluid motion, further enhancing the aura of strength and power that exuded from every pore in his body. Katy felt herself being drawn to him like iron to a magnet. Then, as he threw back his head and laughed, deep and clear, she felt a thrill. There was a momentary

80

glimpse, the recognition that this was the hero she had dreamed of. With conviction, she knew there would be no brotherly kisses from this man. And with a pang, she remembered Julian. Lost in regret, she stood watching her hero with sensuous pleasure, afraid to make contact. For she knew instinctively that once she did, her life would never be the same.

He was shouting orders. The voice was vaguely familiar, but the wind carried it away, teasing her memory. She marveled at the way they rushed to obey his commands. This must be the captain, and therefore just the man she ought to see. Breaking out of the spell, she approached him.

Sam spotted her first. "Katy! What the devil are you doing up here?"

The captain whirled around. Flustered, Katy stared at his bare chest. Slowly taking courage, she followed the line of his throat, up to the clean-shaven face, past the strong mouth. All his features were gathered in an expression of exasperation but not until she reached the eyes did she know the cause. Those eyes!

"Oh no! It's you!"

"You seem to specialize in flattering remarks, my dear. Would you please tell me what you are doing wandering around my ship?"

Too shocked to answer, she could only stare. It couldn't be Julian, yet who else could it be? She'd know those eyes anywhere; the eyes that had promised so much. "*Your* ship?"

"Excuse me, I suppose I should say *our* ship. After all, it was your dowry that purchased her."

"Julian," she started. "I don't understand . . ."

"Not Julian. Please. It's Christopher."

"Christopher?" It was little better than a squeak.

"Or Kit, as my friends call me. Take your pick."

"Then where is my husband? Where is Julian?"

He laughed, but this time she didn't enjoy the sound. This man was making her angry and she was all too conscious of the smirks as the crew gathered around them to watch. He also noticed. "All right, men, get back to work. None of this concerns you. And you, my love, had better return to your cabin."

"Not until I have some answers."

Gone forever was the ineffectual Julian. In his place stood a man who expected to have his every order obeyed without question. Katy flinched at his stony glare.

"Now is hardly the time for a chat. I have a ship to sail. You are a distraction to my crew and I will not tolerate that. Haven't you any sense? These men aren't used to having women on board and certainly not one as scantily clad as you." He glanced meaningfully at her clothes. "Kindly remove yourself from my deck and I'll see you at dinner, where I can answer your questions without interruption."

Acutely aware of her appearance, she nonetheless resented his attitude. He made her feel like a child, making a fool of her in front of his men and then rudely dismissing her. There was this curious sensation that the world had dropped out from underneath her and she was falling deeper and deeper into confusion. She was angry and scared and lost, all at once. To her horror, she could hear herself shrieking, but she was beyond control. "I won't go back in that cabin. I demand you turn this ship back to England. As soon as my grandfather hears of this . . ."

His tone was irritatingly cool. "You seem to have forgotten how we left Lord Whitney. He will do nothing. Be a good girl now. Go back to your cabin and I'll see you at dinner."

With that, he swaggered off, leaving her gaping after him. His reminder about her grandfather left her defeated and more alone than ever. With heavy feet, she retraced her steps back to the cabin. Groping for the knob, she let herself in and collapsed on the bed.

Now what? Julian was no longer Julian. In his place stood a stranger. Who had she pledged her life to anyway? Stifling a sob, she cursed him. She had trusted him and he had betrayed that trust. How ironic. To finally escape Farley's control only to replace it with another. What a fool I am, she thought. I deserve him.

Her eye caught the faded rose. Was it only a few hours ago that she had thought she could turn to Julian? Painfully, she remembered her dream. How would her mother react now to the man she had married? Would she still be happy, knowing him to be a cheat and a fraud?

Her mind raced with speculation for the rest of the afternoon. Who was he? What did he want? What was to come of her? Though she wanted to refuse his dinner invitation, she knew she had to go, if only to get some answers. Not until she had all the answers could she make a decision about her future. Not that she'd do him the honor of dressing, though. She'd show him how little she cared for his opinion. No one had seen fit to deliver her trunks, anyway, and she'd rather wear her riding habit for the rest of the voyage than ask anything of this man who was somehow her husband.

In this frame of mind, she greeted the cabin boy who came to escort her to dinner. Katy was barely civil. In her anger, she hardly noticed him. With the patience of Job, he waited while she made one excuse after another to delay their departure. When she brushed her hair for the fifth time, however, he coughed lightly. "Begging your pardon, ma'am, but the captain's waiting."

It was the worst thing he could have said. All her indignation rose to the surface and she swung around to face him. "Let him wait. What do you think I've done all afternoon? Let your Captain, uh . . ."

"Warwick."

"Then let your Captain Warwick wait a while longer; it will do him good. Warwick? Then that part of it, at least, is true?"

"These are questions you should be asking the captain, ma'am."

"I suppose you're right. Well, what are you waiting for? Lead me to him."

He really was a remarkable boy. Without so much as a shrug, he led her to Kit's cabin. Ushering her inside, he discreetly took his leave.

Katy, still angry, was unprepared for the sight of her husband. If she had taken little care in her appearance, he had taken less. Completely naked from the waist up, he was in the process of shaving. This brought an unconscious gasp from Katy.

"Never see a male body before?" He was grinning behind all that soap and Katy longed to pull every hair out of that magnificent chest. But she wasn't going to let him provoke her this early in their conversation. She was going to get her answers.

"I'm sorry if my naïveté offends you, sir, but I assure you the male bodies with which I am accustomed to dining are, for the most part, fully clothed. I *am* correct in assuming it was a dinner invitation?"

Holding a towel in his hands, he smiled appreciatively. "I stand corrected. I must apologize. I seem to be running behind schedule. We had to put out sooner than expected and it's caused some unforeseen complications." He wiped the soap from his face. "Please find yourself a seat. I'll be with you in a minute."

"I can return later."

"Nonsense." To her relief, he was donning a shirt. "I'm afraid I can't treat you to my previous splendor, but I threw all of Julian's things overboard. Thank God Farley was such a tartar. Another week in those clothes and I'd have gone mad. I don't know how Julian can stand it."

She was startled. "So there really is a Julian?"

"Most assuredly. My elder brother, in fact."

"Do you mind informing me, then, too whom I am married?"

"Have no fears on that score. You and I are legally wed."

"I'm ecstatic. What about the contract? Didn't you sign his name?"

"I must confess—I'm a genius. I ran off with it before Farley could get a good look at it, not that it would make much difference to him, I suppose. But if he should ever check the signature, he'll find mine. Not my brother's."

"But the marriage license?"

"You never looked, did you? But then again, you weren't expecting such treachery."

She knew he was teasing and it irked her. "So you are a genius. But I still don't understand. Why impersonate your brother?"

"I suppose you have a right to know, but I warn you, it's not a pretty story. Why not forget it and we can start from scratch."

"I'd prefer to know what I've gotten myself into."

"I rather thought you would. Can't say I blame you, but you just might discover you'd have been happier not knowing."

"Let me hear your story."

There was a knock at the door. With the air of a condemned man who has just received a reprieve, Kit went to answer it. Carrying steaming trays, each laden with food that made Katy's eyes swim, the cabin boy entered. Her last meal had been so long ago and the aroma from those trays was sweet torture.

"Since this is probably the last meal we will be able to enjoy until we reach Charleston, I suggest we endeavor to do justice to it and save my confession for dessert. Can we call a truce?"

Unable to keep her eyes from the table where the boy was setting out the plates, Katy was tempted. Pride wrestled with hunger and lost. Later she could worry about her future; now she would eat. Greedily, she watched as he filled her plate with seafood: shrimp and lobster and a fish in a creamy white sauce. Not ever, even at Whitney Hall, had she seen such food. Barely concealing her impatience, she waited for Kit to take the first bite. Instead, he filled her glass with a deep, red wine and proposed a toast. "To my beautiful bride. May she find in America the fulfillment of her dreams."

Putting his glass to his lips, he saluted her. She couldn't tell whether he was teasing, but she didn't much care. At the moment, she was concerned only with the food. Applying herself with gusto, she more than did justice to the meal. Her husband, she noticed, drank far more than he ate.

In a somewhat mellower mood, she rose from the table. "Life must be comfortable for you with such a fine chef."

He laughed. "Sam will be pleased to hear that."

"Sam Culligan? Your groom?"

"One and the same. Only he's the first mate, not my chef or groom. Long ago he worked as a cook. He insisted that I had no right to make such a mess of our marriage ceremony. He seemed to think it should be special, especially for you. So he came up with this wedding feast, as a surprise for you."

"It was delicious."

"Then it was worth his effort. I'm glad you enjoyed it."

It was an awkward moment. In the ensuing silence, Katy was suddenly aware that she was in close quarters with this stranger, her husband. She was acutely conscious of him as a man, a very attractive one. With his eyes on her, she felt unsure of herself. Yet she knew instinctively that she would be off to a bad start if she didn't take the initiative. "It was a wonderful dinner. I thank you both. However, I have been repeatedly promised an explanation and you've proven quite adept at putting me off. Do you have any intention of ever enlightening me?"

He drained his glass and refilled it. "The day of reckoning?"

"All I need is the truth."

"Ah yes, the truth. I must admit I've strayed far from it in the past months. But it was all necessary. I swear to you, if there had been any other way..."

He shrugged and suddenly looked tired. "That is neither here nor there. I'm having difficulty getting started. You know so little of the world. What can I say? I am the second son. In South Carolina, that's every bit as useless as it is in England. Though we were raised as equals, by law, everything went to Julian. That part was true. Julian Warwick has the name and position to tempt the most reluctant parent. Unfortunately, somewhere along the line, my brother developed the curse of the aristocracy, a lust for gambling. In the ten years since my father's death, he's managed to go through most of the family fortune. It is well known that he needs to find himself a rich bride, making my task so much easier. Your grandfather was an answer to a prayer."

Glass in hand, he stared at a spot on the wall. "My mother always told me that honesty was a necessary part of being a man. Believe it or not, I've been accused of being too honest for my own good, at times. This whole affair has been distasteful; I could hardly wait to be done with it."

"Nevertheless, you did it quite well."

He grinned sheepishly. "Yes I did, didn't I? I wish you could have seen Farley when I tricked him out of that money. I don't think he ever suspected. Though I must admit it's frightening to know I could so easily be taken for my brother."

"Surely he isn't so . . . so, er, vivid a character?"

"I did overdo it a bit." He chuckled. "Julian would be furious if he knew what I did."

"You mean he has no knowledge of this?"

"No. If it's to have any degree of success, he must never know."

"You expect me to take part in this little deception? Without knowing why? I think you expect too much."

His eyes narrowed, as if assessing her. "You may be right. Very well, if you want the whole sordid mess, I'll

88

give it to you. Up until last February, my sole source of income was from a salary my brother paid me to captain the family's ship. You see, a great deal of the Warwick fortune came from our ability to ship our goods to England, dispensing with the middle man. But Julian, in his infinite wisdom, saw fit to use my ship as collateral for one of his gambling debts. Like everything my father worked so hard for, it was lost. I found myself without a ship, without a job, without income. Nothing could be more repulsive to me than being dependent on my brother."

"Surely he would have employed you elsewhere in the family business?" Katy wanted him to hear the scorn she felt for him.

"The family business? It's just about gone. All that's left is Oaks, our plantation, and even that is in sorry shape. I would have been more than happy to return there, but long ago Julian and I fought that battle and since he holds the purse strings, I don't stand a chance."

"So you just gave up and turned libertine?"

He refilled his glass again. "How reassuring to learn my wife holds such a high opinion of me! Don't sit there and judge me, madame. You know nothing of what is at stake here."

"And that is my fault? You seem remarkably able to forget how I've been used and deceived."

"Don't be so melodramatic. You knew you were taking a chance when you married me."

For a second, she was speechless. The callousness of this man! How could he sit there, so self-righteous, when because of him, her world was crashing down around her? Men! They were all alike. They believed the world revolved around them, and them alone. "I took a chance, all right, though I seem to remember being told all you had to offer me was your name. Now I find out that it's not even yours to give. How many other lies did you tell me, you who find it so hard to lie? How can I be certain you're telling the truth now? That this isn't another of your marvelous roles?''

He drained another glassful in a gulp. His eyes were beginning to blur and she could see his temper rising. But she was past caring what she said. What more could he do to her?

''You say you want the whole truth? Here it is, then. Your loyal Tory grandfather has dedicated both his granddaughter and his money to the rebel cause. I must say, I enjoyed taking him for all I could. Don't look so surprised, my dear. Surely treason isn't beyond my realm. I have absolutely no interest in selling Julian's damned cotton. I bought this ship to smuggle in supplies to the militia.''

''You're a traitor!''

''Why stop there? I'm a liar and a thief, as well.''

''And you're proud of it?''

''Pride doesn't enter into it at all. I merely do what I have to do. If it means looting the British fleet, then by all means, that is what I do.''

''Piracy too?'' It was too much.

''That 'piracy' will keep you dressed and fed.''

''I want nothing to do with it. Nothing at all. Do you really think I would be party to such a thing?''

''Your sense of morality is admirable but I'm afraid you have no option.'' He moved to stand in front of her, his eyes locked with hers. ''You are my wife, now, and you will go where I go.''

She felt his absolute power over her. As if she was drowning, she struggled to break free. ''This marriage

90

was a farce from the beginning. Why continue? All I ask is passage back to England. You can keep the stupid dowry."

"But remember, I can only give you dishonest money."

"I will find some other way to earn my passage, then."

"You forget yourself. You are my wife. I won't have you making a fool of me."

"You've gotten what you want. You have your ship. Can't you just leave me alone?"

Grabbing her wrist, his eyes traveled over her body, lingering for a moment on her breasts before coming up to meet hers. There was a leer in them as he spoke to her. "On the contrary, my dear. I haven't gotten what I want. Yet."

She was only a tiny bird in the claws of a cat, so she struck out at him in the only way she could. She laughed. "Are you trying to frighten me? I've already had a taste of your lovemaking and I must say I found nothing in it to frighten me."

"You little bitch."

There was fire in his eyes now, but she couldn't stop. She had discovered a vulnerability and she wanted him to suffer as much as she was. Taking Farley's hints, she chided him. "I'm in no danger from you. Now your cabin boy, perhaps he should be careful."

His grip tightened. "I'll show you what to be afraid of."

"You're hurting my arm."

"Don't tell me you're frightened?"

She was, but not for the world would she let him know it. Though it cost her, she kept her eyes even with his and held her head high. There was another knock on the door. With an oath, Kit released her and walked over to answer it. Rubbing her arm, she let out a sigh of relief. It was the cabin boy, returning to clear the table. Kit walked over to his bottle of wine and as he refilled his glass, Katy sneaked out of the room. Hurrying down the corridor, she let herself into her cabin and locked the door after her. Her heart was pounding. For the first time in her young life, she had known real fear. Her husband was a dangerous man when he was angry and she had provoked him to fury. Still, she had to admit to a certain satisfaction. She had gotten her revenge for the way he had treated her this afternoon.

Her satisfaction was short-lived. She had barely lit her candle when she heard him bellowing down the hallway. Rushing to the door, she made certain it was bolted. As he jiggled the handle, she shouted through the door. "Go away."

"You little bitch. You've locked the door."

"And I won't unlock it. You might as well go away and calm down."

"You're not going to unlock it, eh? Then I suggest you stand back while I unlock it for you."

About to refuse, she heard him throw his weight against the door. It split in a few places but the hinges held. She laughed. "Hah! The great and mighty Christopher Warwick loses to the door. Go away."

He didn't bother to answer. He applied his weight to the door once more and Katy had a moment of misgiving. Backing away in time for the third assault, she found she had reason for worry. Unable to withstand the pounding, the door finally gave way to come crashing off its hinges to fall at her feet. In the doorway stood a red-faced Kit and he looked awesome. "Are you scared yet? Then why do you cringe like a cornered animal?"

Backing away slowly, she kept her eyes on his face. What she saw there brought her no comfort. "You wouldn't!"

"I'm afraid you don't know me very well." He was approaching steadily.

"No gentleman would consider this."

Laughing, he grabbed her roughly and pulled her to him. "And haven't you already decided that I'm no gentleman, anyway? Besides, I'm well within my rights as your husband to do whatever I wish."

"You're drunk!"

"Have no fear, love. It's never stopped me in the past."

"I'll fight you."

"Whatever for? Wasn't it you that said there was nothing to fear? I'll just kiss you, first on this cheek and then on this one."

His breath was hot on her smooth skin. Holding her in a viselike grip, he continued to kiss her face, light butterfly kisses that made her tingle. On another occasion, she might have enjoyed it, but she was infuriated that he could treat her with such contempt and expect her to welcome him in her bed. When their lips met, she spat at him.

Too late, she realized her mistake. He was angry, again, and far too drunk to listen to reason. In a flash, he had her by the bed. "I think it's time, once and for all, to establish that I am indeed your husband."

With that, he tore the clothes from her body, leaving her standing there, humiliated in her nakedness. As she strove to cover herself, he watched her intently.

93

Innocent as she was, she could recognize desire in his gaze. There was a stubborn streak in her and a pride that was not about to let this happen to her. Determined not to give in, she reached out to slap his face, but he caught her arm and spun her around. With a quick movement, he had her on the bed underneath him. Really frightened now, she wiggled and squirmed, but it was no use. He was stronger and they both knew it. Somehow, he held her down while he undressed himself.

"You animal," she hissed.

He laughed at her, making her angrier than ever. With one hand holding her securely by her hair, he moved down to kiss her throat. His kisses were warm and moist, mingling with the tears that streamed down her cheeks. Her mind kept repeating *no, no, not this way* until she thought she would scream. She sensed the total maleness of him. Her body burned where he touched her and in spite of everything, Katy could feel her young body responding to his loverlike caresses. Struggling now, not only against him, but also her own traitorous body, she tried to pull away. In answer, he tugged her hair, pulling her head backward. Suddenly his tongue was in her mouth, reaching deep into her, and something within exploded. His tongue was everywhere, on her face, flicking her taut nipples, caressing her throat. Strong warm hands stroked the curves of her body. Coherent thought was gone. She was conscious only of a need to be closer to him. Her breath was coming in gasps. He entered her and she hardly felt the pain. There was fire growing and leaping within her. Without realizing it, she was kissing his throat, urging him on. There was a salty taste to him and she couldn't seem to get enough. Then their mouths met again. He was groaning. With every thrust of his lean body, she arched herself closer.

When they reached the climax, it jolted them both. Katy felt herself falling, as if from a great height, in slow motion. Her body, no longer under her control, was quivering. The silence was intense. Aware, finally, of the sound of the waves splashing against the side of the ship, she returned to reality. She opened her eyes to find him staring down at her. It seemed he was immensely pleased with himself. "Well, my dear, that should just about settle any ideas you might have about an annulment."

Sick with self-contempt, she looked away. Slowly, his words began to penetrate. As the enormity of the situation struck, her Irish temper flared and she put every ounce of loathing she could muster into her voice. "Get out!"

The words seemed to hang between them for a few minutes before he shrugged and rolled off the top of her. Bending over to retrieve his clothes, he tried to apologize. "I'm sorry for the way it happened." He grinned sheepishly. "But I'll be damned if I'm sorry it did happen."

He was looking at her in that little boy way but she was not moved. "If I live to one hundred, I'll never forgive you for this. Never! You've had your way. Maybe there won't be an annulment but I promise there'll be a day when you'll wish there had. If it takes the rest of my life, I'll repay you for what you've done to me."

He seemed surprised. "I said I was sorry."

"That excuses your behavior? I neither need nor want your lame apologies. You've taken what you wanted. Now get out!"

His body stiffened. "Very well. I beg your pardon. It

was never my intention to force my presence on you. Rest assured I won't ever again enter your room without permission. Your precious body is safe from me. However"—he glared at her—"please don't expect me not to seek my pleasures elsewhere." With a sweeping bow, he left the room.

Sick with humiliation and disillusionment, Katy surveyed the damage to her room. Like a hurricane he had stormed in, wreaked havoc, and without a moment's regret, departed, leaving her to pick up the pieces. She hated him. To think she had once thought of him as the man of her dreams. She despised him. And she wasn't altogether happy with herself, either. Farley was right; she was a slut. That Kit was her husband didn't enter into it. She had no feeling for the man, just lust. Yanking the soiled linens off the bed, she cursed herself for being every kind of fool. He had applied a little pressure and she had yielded like a bitch in heat. In that moment she hated herself as much as she hated him.

Near tears, she picked up what was left of her clothes. They were ruined. Rolling them into a ball, she threw them on the pile of linens. There was nothing she could do about the door and she felt too tired to worry about it now. She wrapped a blanket about her bruised body and crawled into bed. Curling into a ball, she cried herself to sleep.

Chapter 7

The sound of waves woke her in the morning. Her head was throbbing. It took several seconds to remember why. For a moment or two, she held onto the possibility that it had all been a bad dream, but the door lay accusingly on the floor. Slowly rising, she groaned.

She heard a slight cough. "Begging your pardon, ma'am, but the captain sent me."

Kit's cabin boy stood in the open doorway, trying hard not to look around the room.

"What do you want?" she barked at him.

"The captain was thinking you might be needing help."

Sitting upright, she tried to be her haughtiest. "You can tell your captain that I don't need any help from him."

The boy blushed to the roots of his very red hair and quickly turned his head. Too late, she remembered her state of undress. Covering herself with the blanket, she tried to regain her dignity. "I'm sorry. I'm in no state to be entertaining a gentleman."

Still looking the other way, he shuffled his feet. He

looked so comical that, surprisingly, Katy wanted to laugh.

"Then if there's nothing you need, I'll report back to the captain."

Though he seemed to want to escape, Katy needed his company. "No, please wait. It's all right now. I'm decent. Or at least as decent as can be expected under the circumstances."

He turned his head slowly, as if afraid of what he might see. "Do you think you might be wanting some breakfast?"

"I'd love some." She realized that she was starving. But before she could eat, she would need some clothes. With the door off its hinges, she had no desire to be caught in this state by some less gentlemanly member of the crew, its captain included. "First, though, I'd like you to bring me my trunks."

He was shuffling his feet again, obviously ill at ease. What was the matter now? She was properly covered. "Are you deaf? I asked for my trunks."

"I heard you, ma'am, but I'm afraid I can't get them."

What was this? Was it her husband's idea of a joke, keeping her in her cabin by any means possible? Her temper, never exceptionally stable, was on the rise. "What do you mean, you can't get them? Is this your captain's order?"

"Not exactly."

She heard herself shrieking again. "Not exactly? I need those trunks. What kind of a ship is this? What kind of men are you?"

"The fact is, ma'am, we haven't got your trunks."

Something snapped in her head. "What are you saying?"

His clear eyes refused to meet hers. "We had to leave port before they arrived from your grandfather's house. They never came on board."

This was worse than she thought. "You mean I have nothing?" Blanket clutched around her, she jumped out of the bed. "I can't believe that man. What does he expect me to do without clothes?"

His grin told her what the captain expected. Fury exploded within her. Every oath she could remember hearing came pouring out of her mouth and the astonished boy could only stare in disbelief. The indignities of the last two days had pushed her past caring what anyone thought. Close to tears, she turned on him. "And where is your precious captain through all this? Hiding in his cabin? Does he hope to avoid me by sending you to take care of all the unpleasant details? I want him here immediately."

"The captain is a busy man."

"Too busy for his loving wife? I think not. I think it's time he started taking care of his responsibilities instead of acting like a little boy playing at war. I need my clothes and he'd better do something about them. Don't just stand there gaping at me. Go get him!"

"That won't be necessary, Josh." Kit's shoulders blocked the doorway. "You can return to your duties. I'll deal with Mrs. Warwick."

Josh slid out of the room, anxious to be gone. There was a storm brewing between those two, and he didn't want to be caught in the middle of it. Arms folded across his chest, Kit lounged in the door frame, watching her pace the room. "Now suppose you tell me what is so important that you have to scream at the boy and interrupt me from my work?"

"Don't you dare be condescending with me, Captain

Warwick."

"Lower your voice. Sound carries aboard ship. Let's not create any more of a scene than necessary."

"You mean you could hear me up on deck?"

"I wouldn't be here, otherwise."

As the implications of this hit her, the color rushed to her face. "Then everyone heard us last night?"

"I wouldn't doubt it. But come now, what's your problem?"

He was unruffled and it drove her to a frenzy. "It doesn't bother you that everyone on board knows you raped me?"

"Not so loud, love, or you'll have the boys laughing at us." He grinned at her. "Besides, I could hardly call it rape."

She reached out to slap his grinning face but in so doing, the blanket fell from her shoulders. Mortified, she groped with it to cover herself. If he was any kind of a gentleman, he would turn his head. But then, if he was, she wouldn't be in this mess. How could he remain so calm when she was seething?

"Are you going to tell me what is bothering you or are we going to spend the day glaring at one another?"

Katy struggled to regain her composure. "I was informed by your cabin boy that we left England without my trunks."

"So?"

That left her speechless. So? Was she really that unimportant to him? "What am I supposed to wear?"

"What's wrong with what you have on?"

"Are you serious? Do you expect me to stay this way for the rest of the voyage?"

"Why not? I find it quite charming." Still grinning,

he took a step closer.

"If you touch me again, I'll scream."

She watched desire become disgust. Turning his back to her, he started for the doorway.

Desperate, she grabbed his elbow. "Isn't there anything from my grandfather's?"

"There was no time to wait."

She thought about all those things from Clonmara, lost to her. "Are you telling me that you were so anxious to be out with your new toy that you couldn't wait for my trunks? All I have in the world was in those trunks."

There was ice in his words. "If you were inconvenienced, I am sorry, but it couldn't be helped. The lives of the men on this ship were in jeopardy and I could hardly justify the risk for a trunkful of clothes that can easily be replaced. At present, I have far more important things to do with my 'toy' than to stay here discussing your wardrobe. And a word of advice, my dear. The men aboard this ship are as human as anyone else. I would hate to hear that my wife has proven to be too much of a temptation to anyone. I recommend you stay here to avoid any difficulty. I will see to it that your every need is taken care of."

"And what about clothes?"

"Damn your clothes!" He turned on his heel and stomped out of the room. Shaking with indignation, Katy could follow his progress down the corridor and up to the deck. Tears that had threatened erupted, dripping down her face. Standing in the middle of her cabin with nothing but a blanket to cover her, she felt an utter fool. What was she going to do?

Josh found her in that position when he returned. "Excuse me, ma'am. I don't mean to be adding to your troubles but I was thinking that maybe my old trousers and this shirt of the captain's might just see you through until you get something of your own to wear. I promise they're clean." He held up the articles in question for her inspection.

It was all too much. His thoughtfulness proved her undoing. The tears were falling in earnest now.

"I'm sorry. I guess I shouldn't have come. If you want, I can leave the clothes in this chair and you can look them over later. They're nothing special, but I thought . . ."

"Why are you being so nice to me? I was perfectly awful to you."

"I know what it's like to be putting out to sea for the first time. I knew it wasn't me you were mad at."

Trying to control herself, she took the clothes from his outstretched hands. "I'm so grateful. I don't know what to say. These clothes are a great idea."

He was pleased. "You think so? It seemed so to me, too, but when I came in here I got to thinking that maybe you wouldn't like them, them being hand-me-downs and you being British and all."

"Even the British like to be clothed."

He blushed again. "I didn't mean it that way. I guess I meant because you're such a fine lady, maybe these old clothes wouldn't be good enough."

"I hope I never become such a fine lady that I can't appreciate a fine gift like this. Thank you, Josh."

"Don't go thanking me yet. You haven't looked at them."

Obediently, she looked them over. She and the boy were close in size but the shirt would need alteration. "They're splendid, Josh, especially compared with my current attire."

"I was thinking, if you'd like, I could stand watch by the door while you put them on. I promise I won't look."

Smiling, Katy watched him take his position at the door. As she slipped into the clothes, he continued talking. "When you're done dressing, I'll go see if I can get you some breakfast. And while you're eating, I'll get some tools and see what I can do about fixing the door."

He was too good to be true. Katy's spirits began to revive. She was already planning how she could pull down some of the draperies to fashion some sort of a frock for herself. Katy wiggled into the pants. They were a bit tight around the hips, but the shirt managed to hide any indecencies. "You can turn around now," she told the boy. "I'm decent. Or at least as decent as can be expected."

Facing her, a little grin began to play around the corners of his mouth. With considerable effort, he managed not to laugh. Puzzled, Katy went to the mirror and what she saw there soon had her laughing as well. The shirt not only covered the indecencies, it virtually covered all of her. She was lost in it. Kit had never seemed that large to her, but in his shirt she looked like a dwarf. Katy, making the most of it, began to dance around. After the confusion of the recent past, it felt good to laugh. Finally subsiding, she rolled up the sleeves and tucked the hem into her trousers, allowing ample material to hang over her hips. The shirt was still yards too big, but it would have to do. On a whim, she rolled all of her hair into a large knot at the base of her neck and pinned it there. Raising her hand in a mock salute, she addressed Josh. "Seaman Katherine Farley, uh, Warwick, reporting to duty, sir."

Josh looked at her in surprise. "Begging your pardon, ma'am, but you sure look different."

Sitting on the bed, she tried to fit her feet into her boots. "Am I to take that as a compliment?"

Blushing, he stammered. "I reckon so. I'm not much for words, but I think you could manage to look like a lady, no matter what you wore."

Now it was Katy who was blushing. "Why, what a nice thing to say. I wish there was some way I could thank you for everything."

"Aw, don't go talking that way. You just sit there and wait for me. I'll be back in a second with some food."

He disappeared, leaving Katy alone in her cabin. She really should do something with those dirty linens. Her first choice would be to throw them all overboard, but as this was an all-male ship, she seriously doubted that there would be any replacements. And there was the business of creating a wardrobe for herself. These clothes were fine, but they would not do indefinitely. Ocean breezes could be quite chilly, she had been told, and despite her husband's wishes, she had no intentions of freezing.

When Josh returned with the coffee and a piece of hard bread, he found her ripping the drapes off the wall. "Excuse me, ma'am, but what are you doing? The captain isn't gonna like this."

"The captain doesn't have to know. I need clothes and these drapes seem to be all I have to work with. He'll never enter this cabin, as long as I'm here, and what he doesn't know won't hurt him. Or me." She surveyed the pile. "Can you get me thread? And needles?"

Before the journey's end, Josh would be better

equipped to understand his captain's wife's bursts of energy, but at present, he could only gape at her. "But, ma'am, It's gonna make this cabin awful drafty."

"Better the cabin than me. Here, hold this a minute. I want to measure this piece. Can you find scissors, too?"

"I reckon so. This ship used to belong to a merchant with three daughters. They left all kinds of things behind."

"Really? I wonder why."

"I reckon because they had to leave the colonies in a hurry, being Tories and all. In fact, they were in such a rush to get to England, they didn't think to bring much money. Lucky for us, I mean for the captain, that they needed money so bad. Else he might never have gotten this ship."

"Let's hope part of the deal included needles and thread. Oh, you've brought my breakfast. Good lord, what is it?"

"Guess you're gonna be initiated into sea life real quick. We don't carry the kind of food you're used to. The fare's simple here, and Harry, that's our cook, isn't fancy."

"I think I've met the man."

"Then you know what I mean. He wasn't too happy this morning and he didn't like the idea of fixing anything special for you. I had to grab what I could. The captain's the only one who can handle him when he's like this. Sorry, maybe lunch will be better."

"This is fine, Josh. You must think I'm an awful nuisance. I don't really expect any special treatment."

"But you're a lady. You're used to things being different."

"I don't know what your captain told you about me,

but I doubt any of it's true. For heaven's sake, I can't be much older than you and I'm certainly not in the habit of being regarded as a lady of quality."

"But your grandfather had so much money."

"Oh, so that's it. The dowry. The sad truth is that the only reason there was such a large dowry is because my grandfather was so anxious to be rid of me. I grew up on a farm in Ireland. There were many times when I wore clothes similar to what I have on now. It was a simple life and, I must admit, I enjoyed it far more than the false life I lived at my grandfather's, for all his money. So you can stop thinking of me as a grand lady. I'm just Katy. Stop calling me ma'am; it makes me feel ancient. Katy will do just as well."

"Oh, I couldn't do that. The captain would skin me alive."

"Your captain is a tyrant. It happens to be my name and right about now, it seems that it's all I own. I'd consider it an honor if you'd use it."

"But . . ."

"Please? It would make me far more comfortable."

"Well, if you're sure?"

"When your captain's around, which I doubt will be often, you can always return to the ma'am, if you choose."

"I guess so, ma'am, uh, I mean Katy. It's going to take some getting used to, though."

She looked around her. "I suppose there's a lot to get used to. You've been a great help, Josh, and I know I don't deserve it. No, you know it yourself. I was mad at your captain and I took it out on you. I'm sorry for that."

"You don't have to go apologizing to me."

"You're wrong. I do. And I want to explain. I know I

106

sounded impossibly silly and spoiled, carrying on so about my trunks. The trouble is, I was so upset that I just didn't think about what I said or who I said it to. I guess I went crazy. My life has changed so in the past few weeks. I feel as though I'm caught up in a hurricane, being blown helplessly here and there. Every time I think I have myself headed in the right direction, something new happens and I find myself blown off course again. Those trunks undid me. I don't care so much about the clothes, but your captain didn't seem to care whether I froze or not. He led me to believe he cared a little about me, that I could depend on him. When I learned otherwise, I felt so alone."

"The captain would've thought of something, sooner or later. His mind is on the ship and all of us now. He's always a bit short-tempered when things go wrong."

"Me too, I guess. Anyway, my complaint was with him, not you."

"Aw, Katy, I knew that. I sure am sorry about your clothes."

"Thanks. But the clothes don't bother me, not really. I can always make do, somehow. No, Josh, I was upset because there was one trunk that held all the things my mother had given to me. They were silly things, of no real value to anyone but me, but they were all I had left of her. To tell the truth, it just about breaks my heart to think of them rotting on that dock."

"Don't you worry. When your grandfather discovers the mistake, he'll just send them along on the next ship."

"I'm afraid you don't know him very well. He'd

rather throw them into the water than spend another penny on me. No, I doubt I'll ever see them again." Her voice began to tremble.

"Katy, don't cry."

"I don't know what's wrong with me. I haven't cried in years, but since I've been on this ship, it seems that's all I do. I'm not usually so silly, even though I'm a girl."

He regarded her shyly. "I reckon you're entitled to a good cry after all you've been through. But it won't do any good to be sitting down here all alone in your cabin, thinking and brooding. Why don't you go on up and get some fresh air?"

"Like this?" She gestured at her clothes.

"Sure, why not? Here." He pulled a cap from his back pocket. "Put this on your head and nobody'll bother you. And when you get back, I'll have the door fixed for you."

The thought of fresh air was tempting. She remembered Kit's warning about his crew, but in this outfit, who indeed would bother her? She wouldn't stay long, and she'd be certain to stay out of her husband's path. "Yes, Josh, I think I will go up on deck. And I'll take this tray back to the dining room for you."

He laughed. "You've got a lot to learn about sea life, mate. We don't have a dining room; it's called a galley."

"Yes, sir! Then I'll take this tray to the galley. Is it the room at the end of the hall?"

Her terminology was off, but he figured her heart was in the right place. Indulgently, he smiled at her. "Yes. Just listen for Harry's grumbling and you should find it easy enough."

"Thanks." Picking up the tray, she slid past him.

"Just a warning, though. Harry can be a mean one. Don't get in his way."

"Don't worry about me. I can handle Harry McGee."

A few minutes later, she was to regret that boast. With all that had happened since, she had forgotten what a large man he was. The sight of his sweaty body both alarmed and repelled her. He was already well into a bottle of whiskey when she arrived. His grimy back was to her, so she laid the tray down as quietly as possible and tried to escape. He must have had eyes in the back of his head. Without turning, he bellowed at her. "And what do you think you're doing? Haven't I got enough trouble without you bastards bringing me more work to do?"

"I'm sorry, I was just returning my breakfast dishes."

At the sound of the feminine voice, he spun around. The leer on his unshaven face made her vastly uncomfortable. "Ah now, if it isn't the captain's pretty wife."

She was beginning to regret her impulsive gesture. In sparing Josh the extra work, she seemed to have landed herself in trouble. "I don't see that it's any concern of yours, Mr. McGee."

"A saucy one, eh? Leave it to the captain to find himself a scrapper." He circled around her. "Heard you giving him a damned good fight last night."

"I think you'd better be careful how you speak to me."

"Don't go putting on airs with me. I heard you cussing at him. Tell me now, what's the captain got that old Harry doesn't?"

Teeth, for one thing. His lecherous smile turned her

stomach, none too settled after that breakfast. Katy glanced around for a way out of the room, but for a man who was inebriated, he moved quickly. Before she realized what was happening, he was between her and the doorway, and was rapidly closing in on her. Oh no, she thought to herself, not again. She spotted a knife on the table. With surprising agility, she darted over and grabbed it. "Mr. McGee," she said, brandishing the knife, "I am in no mood to play a game of cat and mouse with you. If you so much as touch me, I'll put this in your gut. I suggest you move aside and allow me to leave. If you do so, I promise this incident will be forgotten. Neither of us need discuss it with my husband. However, if you don't get out of my way, I will personally deliver your stinking carcass to the captain. Make your choice."

Warily, he watched her. There was indecision in his eyes and Katy said a silent prayer. She kept the knife poised, ready to strike, and Harry sensed she was in earnest. He moved backward, out of the doorway. "You win this time, little lady, as long as you have the knife. But there'll come a time when you don't have it, and, then, you and me will have some reckoning to do. I don't take kindly to being bested by a girl."

Trembling, she dashed out of the room. From the hallway, she put on a show of bravado. "You listen to me, Mr. McGee. I intend to carry this knife with me wherever I go. If you ever lay a finger on me, for any reason at all, I won't hesitate to use it."

As she fled, she missed the toothless grin. Licking his lips, Harry returned to his bottle. "A real lively one, all right," he muttered to no one in particular. "Someday that little filly is gonna show me a real good time."

110

Chapter 8

Up on deck, it was a glorious day. Fresh and clean as new laundry, the breeze brushed against Katy, making her want to open her lungs to catch as much of it as possible. Breathing deeply, she tried to forget the horrid scene below. There was no way to know if she would have used the knife or not, but she was grateful she hadn't been forced to make the choice. Now if only the cook would keep quiet about it. If Kit found out, she'd be locked in her cabin for the rest of the voyage.

On a day like today, it would be a prison. Above her, the sky was clear and the waves below sparkled with sunshine. Legs firmly planted, she opened her body to the salty air, feeling exhilarated. For the first time, she had an inkling of why men spent a lifetime on the water. This was freedom. It was like riding, only instead of a horse beneath you, there was an entire ship. How would it feel to control it? To ride the waves with its great sails catching the wind? It was not a live thing, like a horse, but she sensed it would respond in the same way.

Her imaginings came to an abrupt halt as she remembered Midnight. She had forgotten all about her, with all that had happened. Where was she? Katy hadn't seen her since they had left the dock; the poor horse would be frantic. Feeling a bit frantic herself, Katy left her spot on the deck to go in search of the mare. On her way to ask directions from Josh, she didn't watch where she was going and she bumped her full weight into a sailor that was passing by.

"Look where you're going, mate," a gruff voice warned. "You looking to kill a body?"

"Sam! I'm sorry. I guess I wasn't thinking."

"Katy? What in tarnation are you doing up here? Your husband told you to stay in your cabin."

"Oh, Sam, not you too. You know perfectly well that I could go insane locked up in there on a day like today."

"Never mind, lass. On board, a captain's word is law."

"I'm not hurting anyone. He only objected to me distracting the crew. Even you thought I was one of them."

"Where did you get those clothes?"

Katy grinned. "Josh brought them to me. It was his idea to get fresh air. I just can't stay cooped up in that cabin." The mention of Josh reminded her of her mission. "I was trying to find Midnight. I've got to see her, Sam. She won't understand what is happening to her if I don't explain."

"Don't go worrying about your horse. I fixed up a nice spot for her down in the hold. She won't be getting much exercise, but she'll be as comfortable as can be."

"Sam, I love you! How is she? Can I see her? Please?"

Sam was weighing it in his mind. The captain would

be mighty angry to have his orders disobeyed, but then, he didn't understand this girl like he did. It was a big mistake to confine her to her cabin and a bigger one yet to keep her from her horse. Well, he'd disobeyed orders before, and for a lot less reason. Guess he'd have to take his chances with the captain. He was rewarded for the risk by the look on her face when they reached the hold.

Tears streaming down her face, Katy hugged her mare. "Forgive me, Midnight. I would have come long ago, but things have been so mixed up. Are you all right?"

Sam coughed discreetly. "I imagine you know your way back? Since you don't need me any more, I'm gonna trust you to get back to your cabin without getting into trouble."

"Of course, Sam. Thanks for understanding."

"Just don't give me any reason for regretting it."

After he had gone, Katy told Midnight everything. Whether or not the horse understood didn't matter; Katy was happy to have a sympathetic listener. The mare was the only creature on board, besides herself, whose loyalty didn't belong to the captain. Making certain that Midnight was well cared for and relatively happy, Katy said good-bye. Apparently, the horse had adjusted better than her mistress because she took the sugar lumps and the good-bye with the same good grace. Katy was no such stoic. But Sam's words were tugging at her conscience. Not for anything did she wish to cause him trouble, so she made her way as unobtrusively as possible back to her cabin. Luckily, most of the crew were up on deck and the few she encountered paid no attention to her.

The door was back on its hinges and all traces of the

scuffle last evening were gone. In a pile on the bed lay the draperies. Now seemed as good a time as any for starting her new wardrobe, but unfortunately, there was still no sign of the needles and thread. Debating the merits of waiting for Josh to arrive with them, Katy decided to ask Kit for them herself. It was time to set things straight with her husband. Surely, if she was polite and kept a civil tongue in her head, he would be willing to meet her halfway. She was saving him a great deal of trouble and expense by making her own clothes. What could be his objection? It was time to stop being afraid of him. Why not just admit that she was tied, as he so accurately phrased it, to him for life and however much she might resent the fact, it was up to her to begin some kind of working relationship between them.

With these lofty intentions, she made her way down the hall. On passing the captain's cabin, she heard voices. It would be better to confront him in the privacy of his room. She raised her hand to knock. A nervous twitter in her stomach made her hesitate. It was just as well, for in the next minute she heard Kit's voice raised in anger. "Of all the stupid females, Sam. God, what a mistake I made. If I had known she was going to be this silly, not even that dowry could have made me marry her."

"Give her a chance, Kit. She's only a girl."

"I don't have time to be taking care of a child. I have a war to fight. I'm responsible for a great many lives. For God's sake, Josh isn't half her age, but he has double the sense. Can you believe it? All the trouble we've had and she's crying about her clothes? Of all the empty-headed, ungrateful brats. I rescue her from that bully of a grandfather, risk my neck carting

114

her all over England with that horse of hers, and she yells at me for not bringing her clothes."

"It's all new to her. Give her time."

"Time is one thing I don't have, Sam, and you know it. Just keep her out of my sight. Every time I get near her, I get the urge to strangle her."

"That's not the way it sounded last night."

"Last night never would have happened if I wasn't so drunk. I can assure you it won't happen again. Just keep her out of my way."

Out in the hallway, Katy heard footsteps cross over to the door. Fearing discovery, she fled down the corridor. Ears still ringing she closed herself in her room. What a little fool she was. When would she ever learn? Though she denied it to herself, she actually believed there had been something between them last night when they had made love. But he had said it would never have happened if he wasn't so drunk. Was he that indifferent to her? Farley's words echoed in her brain and she wondered if she would always have that effect on men. What chance was there for a marriage if he couldn't stand the sight of her? He was right about one thing; they had both made a mistake. After only two days, their marriage was in shambles. Had it only been two days? It seemed a lifetime. And if two days seemed a lifetime, then the rest of her life stretched into a nightmare.

If she had remained to hear the rest of the conversation, however, she could have saved them both a great deal of trouble and heartache. By the time Sam had crossed the room to leave, Kit had finished with his tirade and was ready to listen to reason.

"No, Sam, don't go. I know what you say is right. The girl's not to blame." He sounded tired. "I've acted like every kind of fool. It seems I don't know how to act around her. She's so different from any other female I've ever known. I honestly tried last night, but she kept getting me riled up, teasing and taunting me. It's no excuse, I know, but I was drunk. I forced her, maybe but I could've sworn she enjoyed every minute of it. Yet she turned on me, accused me of rape. God knows I feel guilty enough about it but she'll never give me the opportunity to apologize. I tried, last night, and she ordered me out of the cabin. Every time I see her, we fight. It's better if we avoid each other. At least as long as we're on this ship."

"And what about when we dock?"

"You know this war will go on for years. I'll hand her over to Julian, who, once he learns who her grandfather is, will care for her like a sister, at least. She'll be safe, and relatively happy with all his Tory friends. Maybe with the passage of time, she won't hate me as much."

"You're taking a chance, boy."

"Sam, you and I have been friends for a long time, but I won't have you telling me what I should do. You know damned well I won't be my own man until this war is over."

"And the girl? Is it fair what you're doing to her?"

"Don't you think I've thought about that? Over and over? The only fair thing that I can do is leave her alone. I've asked Josh to keep an eye on her and I'm asking you. I trust you both to see that she's taken care of; it's the best I can do. And later, Julian will do his best for her, whatever his motives. Especially since she's my wife." His voice was bitter.

"I won't question you, boy. I reckon you're old enough to know your own mind. Only I'll tell you something now and I won't bring it up again. That girl of yours is special to me. She's had an awful lot of heartache and if I find you've been adding to it, I won't hesitate to do what I can to help her. Even if it means going against orders."

Kit's eyes narrowed. "What do you mean?"

"I took her to see her horse today."

"I gave orders that she was to stay in her room."

"So you did and you were wrong. Caging her up is the worst thing you can do. She's like a wild cat, lovely to look at but shut them up and they turn vicious. She won't hurt anybody visiting with her horse. That animal is all the family she has."

"You win, Sam. She can go to the hold if you go with her. But I won't have her wandering around the ship alone. And I won't have my orders disobeyed. Not even by you."

"You just be careful with your wife. She's the one who doesn't understand about orders."

"She's just a girl, innocent and painfully naive. She doesn't realize how men can be. Any one of them could corner her and she would be helpless. I should know." He picked up a dart and threw it at the target on the far wall.

"So you do care about her?"

He looked up in surprise. "That will be enough, Sam. Don't you have some work you should be doing?"

Sam grinned. "All right, boy. When you're ready to talk about it, you know where to find me."

After he left, Kit picked up another dart and inspected it carelessly, his mind concentrating on Sam's question. Did he really care about her? But that was nonsense. He had a war to fight; this was no time to be

117

getting involved with an eighteen-year-old girl. Sighing in frustration, he tossed the dart over his shoulder. As he left the cabin to return to his duties, it was still quivering in the center of the target.

Chapter 9

Over the next few days, alone in her cabin, Katy had time to consider her situation. She was a prisoner and not once during that time did she see her jailer. Though she begged and pleaded with Sam to let her go up on deck, on this issue he was adamant. Three times a day she could go with him to visit Midnight, but that was the limit of her travels. Occasionally, Josh would stop by to see if she needed anything and sometimes these visits would include a chat, but it still left her with hours to occupy herself. Desperate for activity, she set to work on the draperies with the materials that Josh had managed to get for her. But although her fingers were busy, her mind was free to wander where it would.

All too often, it chose to dwell on the man she had married. Over and over she replayed the scene where she had yielded to him, but even in her thoughts, the outcome was always the same. If he was to walk into her room this minute and demand she submit to him, she would probably do so. Farley was right; she was a slut. No, she was worse than a slut; she was a fool. She continued to lust after a man who couldn't stand the sight of her. She had no reason to fear, or hope, that he would take advantage of her again. He avoided her with dogged determination. To him, she was nothing more than an empty-headed chit he had made the mistake of marrying.

Grandfather was right; where was her pride? She didn't respect, she didn't even like the man. So why was she mooning over him like a lovesick schoolgirl and hoping every time there was a knock on the door that it would be Kit, coming to talk things over? She could waste the rest of her life this way, waiting for him to discover that she was important to him.

When she woke on the fifth morning of her incarceration, as she termed it, she decided that if she stayed one more second in her cabin, she would go mad. More than anything else, she had to have some fresh air. She hadn't slept well the night before. A commotion in the hallway had disturbed her. It was quiet enough now, and she figured she could sneak up to the deck and back again without discovery. It would be worth the risk to feel the cool breeze on her skin and to see something more than the bare walls of her cabin. Slipping into her trousers and the now altered shirt, she surveyed herself in the mirror. With her hair tucked under Josh's cap, who would know who she was, except possibly Sam and Josh. There was a remote chance that she'd run into old Harry, so she slid the knife into her belt. Lord, she looked like a pirate.

Her face was aglow with anticipation of the morning's adventure as she stole out of her cabin. She thanked the stars for providing her with men that never thought to provide a maid or companion for her. A female, now, would be an encumbrance, especially one whose duties would be to report to her husband.

She hurried past the galley, gripping the knife. No one was about. Stealthily, she climbed the stairs and rose to find the sun breaking over the horizon. It was enough to take her breath away. After the enforced captivity, the sight of the sun climbing out of the tranquil water was a gift. Surrounded by muted reds and oranges, the golden orb was magnificent. To Katy, it was more than the beginning of a new day; it would be the start of a new life for her. It gave her hope, inspiration. Somehow, she vowed, she would spend every morning on deck. Renewed, she turned to sneak back to her room when she caught sight of motion on the other side of the ship. Without thinking, she moved closer to investigate. A large man was stripped to the waist and was being tied by his shipmates to the mast. He wasn't submitting without a struggle and it took ten of them to subdue him. At last he was secured and the crowd drew back. Katy saw his face. It was Harry McGee and he was black with rage. She wondered what was happening, but just then the men grew quiet, and with a feeling of dread her mind begun to register the implications of the scene before her. At this moment Kit made his appearance. Also stripped to the waist, his face was grim. After not seeing him for five days, Katy was amazed at how tanned his body had become. Her eyes took in every line of him with pleasure, halting at his right arm. To her horror, poised in his outstretched hand was a whip that whistled menacingly through the air until its tip had connected with the bare and tender skin of the cook's back. Harry's scream rang out in the still morning air.

Reacting instinctively. Katy screamed with him. Up until now, she had been protected by her anonymity but her outburst had separated her from the crew and

Kit whirled around to face her. The silence was terrible. Looking down from the platform, he glared at her in disgust. She would willingly have shrunk from sight but she was powerless to move under his unrelenting gaze. He pointed at her. "Will someone get that female off my deck?"

While he went back to beating his cook, Katy ran for her cabin. She could hear the screams all the way back, though she covered her ears. With every shriek, she saw again the way his body had twitched when the leather lashed his back. His agony was her own. She had no particular liking for him, but no one deserved to be treated in that manner. What kind of man was her husband?

There were ten screams before the awful noise ceased. A wave of nausea threatened. She longed for the stuffiness of Whitney Hall, where life was dull, but at least civilized. She would never adjust to this new life; these men were savages. Her husband was a man who beat his crew and raped his wife. His men couldn't even be trusted to allow her to walk on deck unmolested. Why did she waste time making clothes? She would spend the rest of the voyage in her room anyway. She'd be happy to; at least she'd be safe from those animals. In a fit of desperation, she grabbed the dress she had been sewing and ripped it into shreds.

Someone was at the door. Katy stared at the ruined dress in her hands and dropped it as if it was alive. There was another knock. Automatically, she opened the door and without so much as a greeting, she stepped aside and let Sam into the room. Expressionless, she walked over the mess on the floor and fell onto the bed.

"What's going on here?" asked the bewildered Sam.

When she didn't answer, he picked up the remains of her dress. Whistling softly, he took it all in. His gaze rested on the inert figure on the bed. It was a bad sign; she wasn't even crying. Damn! Whatever had possessed her to come up on deck today, of all days? Ah well, the damage was done and he'd better set to work putting things back together again before it was too late. He moved over to touch her gently. With a start, she looked up at him, her eyes focusing narrowly. "Oh, Sam, it's you. Please go away."

"Not yet, young lady. I've a few words to say to you and I want you to listen."

"Please, no lecture. Just leave me alone. Don't worry, I won't go near that deck."

"Aye, lass, that's what we have to talk about. I know what you saw up there has you frightened. You don't understand it. Believe me, the captain did what he had to do."

"That includes beating a defenseless man?"

"You know nothing about it. Out at sea, every man knows the captain's orders are to be obeyed without question. If you weren't a woman, you could be up there tomorrow for going against orders."

"He's an animal."

"No, lass, he is not. Captain Warwick is a fair man. When a man breaks the law, he has to be punished. If he isn't, he, and the others who see him getting away with it, will only break the law again. It's the captain's duty to maintain order. Your husband is one of the rare birds who carries out the punishments himself. He doesn't like it, any more than you or I, but he does his job."

"How noble of him. Tell me, what was the dreadful crime?"

"As a matter of fact, Kit was protecting you. He discovered Harry was trying to take advantage of you."

"Oh no. I thought he'd keep quiet about that."

Sam was puzzled. "What are you talking about?"

Katy explained the scene in the galley, including the bit about the knife. "So you see, Sam Culligan, I can take care of myself. I have no need of a husband to fight my battles for me."

Sam chuckled as he heard her story, but he was suddenly stern. "Remember one thing, lass. You're a babe compared to these men. They've seen things I hope to God you never have to see. Don't underestimate them. They won't respect you for it and it will land you in a heap of trouble. For your information, Harry wasn't being punished for that episode. He was found, dead drunk, trying to break into your cabin last night. He attacked the captain and would have made it into your room if a few of us hadn't happened by. And I'll tell you something else. When a man is in that condition, no kitchen knife is going to stop him. Screaming either. You should be grateful you have a man to look after you. No matter what he's done, you married him of your own free will, for better or for worse. He has enough troubles without you adding to them."

Katy was staring into space, as if she hadn't heard a word. In utter frustration, Sam threw his hands in the air. She was in no state to listen to reason; he'd come back when she was. Giving no indication that she noticed his departure, she lay listlessly on the bed. But whatever her outward appearance, her mind was in turmoil. She had been in the wrong again. Sam was right about one thing; she wasn't tough enough for this sort of life. However innocent she might be, she

124

somehow managed to always say or do the wrong thing. Kit was disgusted with her and now she had lost Sam, too. Undressing slowly, she burrowed under the blankets. With any luck, maybe she could sleep all the way to America. Once they landed, she would lose herself in a crowd and Christopher Warwick need never be bothered with her again.

For two days, Josh brought trays to her room, and for two days, carried them out, untouched. By the third day he was worried. He was reluctant to approach the captain, sensing it would make matters worse. He groped about in his mind for some way to bring her out of her depression without success. Being a simple boy, he was not experienced in the moods of females. But there was something in the way she had given up that made him sad. He wanted to see her smile again. A real smile that lit up her face, not this wistful imitation.

By dinner of the third day, Josh knew he had to get her to eat somehow. Face to face with her, he knew it wasn't going to be easy. Katy glanced at the tray without enthusiasm, promising him with that sickly smile that she would try later. Having been through all this before, he knew better than to trust her. She had also promised to try sewing, but the drapes he had risked stealing from the captain's cabin were still in a heap on the floor. Nothing seemed to work. In desperation, he pulled up a chair and lifted her spoon.

Katy stared at him without interest. "What are you doing?"

"I'm going to feed you. Seeing as how it takes up all your energy just lying around in bed all day, I figured I'd help out by lifting your spoon for you." He grinned.

"Leave me alone. I'm not hungry."

"Being hungry has nothing to do with it. Keep on this way and before you know it, you'll be real sick. There ain't no doctor, either, to make you better."

"Who would care."

"I would. Maybe I'm only a cabin boy, but I thought we were friends."

"This has nothing to do with you."

"Then why are you quitting on me? You used to be a fighter. I admired that. Why let a little thing like a whipping get you down?"

"You don't understand. For one thing, I caused that little whipping. If it wasn't for me, there wouldn't have been one."

He snorted. "That's silly. You can't help being pretty. Harry knew what would happen but he did it anyway. Nobody blames you 'cept maybe yourself."

"Well, I do. And it's not just that. It's everything."

"I think you're just feeling sorry for yourself. Let me tell you something. You're not the only one to lose your home and family. My folks were killed in an Indian raid when I was ten. The place was burned and there was nothing left but a batch of graves on the Carolina countryside. I had nowhere to go; no family or friends to take me in. No, I ain't looking for pity so don't go looking at me like that. Why it's so long ago, it feels like a whole different life. We all got troubles, Katy. At the time, I thought I'd go crazy. I was so lonely. But I found that as you go along, you make your own family and friends. It's only when you give up that you're alone, but, Katy, you have me, and you have Sam, too."

There were tears glistening in her eyes. "Josh Randall, you're a very special friend." Then she was sobbing and the poor boy was at a loss to know what to do.

"I didn't mean to make you cry. I just wanted to cheer you up so you'd eat."

"It's all right; really it is. It's something that's been building up for a long time. I know you think I'm only feeling sorry for myself, but I swear, you're the first person to care what happens to me since my mother died. You and Sam. Very well, you little tyrant, hand me the spoon. I'm still not hungry, but if it makes you feel better, I'll eat."

Beaming, he handed her the spoon. Not totally trusting her, he watched until the last morsel was safely tucked away. "I've been thinking. You've been in this bed for three days now, with no company but your thoughts. From the looks of you, they haven't been much company. How about coming up on deck with me for a walk?"

"Josh, please. I've eaten your food like a good girl. Let's leave it at that. If I stay in my cabin, I won't get into trouble and I won't get anyone else into trouble, either."

"You still worrying about that? You're in worse shape than old Harry. Couldn't you tell by that awful dinner that he's back on the job?"

"The more reason to stay where I am."

"You mean to tell me you're afraid of him?"

"Wouldn't you be?"

"Aw, Katy, he's only a bully. The way I hear it, you didn't used to be scared of him. You made him back down once."

"Who told you that?"

"The story's all over the ship. The men think you're great, pulling that knife on him. Nobody will try any-

127

thing on you."

"How can you be so sure?"

"When I first put out to sea, I wasn't lucky enough to have a master like the captain. If there's no women around, a lot of the men go after the boys. There was no one to protect me so I had to do it myself. The secret is to make them believe you can do it; you have to act tough. Look 'em in the eye and let 'em know they ain't getting nothing without a fight. Sometimes, it comes down to a fight, but most times, a man will take your measure and leave you alone. Build yourself a reputation and then you're safe."

"But you're a boy. I'm only a girl."

"Doesn't matter. You just gotta go about it different. And remember, on this ship, you can always count on the captain. If there's one thing he can't stand, it's a bully. He once risked his life, defending me from one. Without knowing who I was, he stepped in and knocked that swine off his feet. That's how I got to be his cabin boy. Don't worry about Harry, not with the captain around. Besides, you always have your knife."

She laughed, a real laugh. "Oh, I wish you could've seen his face. I think it was surprise, not fear, that held him back."

"Maybe. But it worked and now you have your reputation. Believe me, there's nothing scarier to a man than a woman waving a weapon around. Can't deal with it. The men will leave you alone."

"I wish it was all that simple. It's a whole new world for me. I'm not sure I can get used to it, much less like it."

"I don't want you to think I'm unfeeling, 'cause it ain't so, but you've got no choice. Sure, you can hide away in your cabin till we land, but what then? Sooner or later, you're going to have to come out fighting and I say the sooner you start, the easier it's going to be. There's always going to be somebody to knock you down. The trick is not to let them keep you down."

Leaning over, she kissed him on the cheek. Flushing with pleasure, he lifted the tray. "Don't worry about that new life of yours. Take each day as it comes and learn all you can. I'll teach you what you need to know and so will Sam. All you've got to do is ask. And for your first lesson, I'll give you a word of warning. I don't want to alarm you but we may be hitting some bad weather tonight, by the looks of the sky. If we do, we can't be having fires. Whatever you do, don't light your candle. I'll do what I can about nailing things down for you."

"Will it be that bad?"

"Hard to tell, but it doesn't hurt to be prepared."

"Thanks for the warning. I'd have been scared if I didn't know what was happening and the first thing I would have done is light my candle to see. With the way my luck has been going, I would have started the ship on fire and then I'd really be in trouble."

"We all would. The Atlantic, in rough weather, is no place to be without a ship."

"Could it actually happen?"

"This ship is all wood. One small fire, undetected, would spread in no time to the entire ship."

"Then thanks again for the warning. I guess it's another of those things your captain expects me to know."

"Aw, Katy, the captain's a busy man."

"Don't be so sensitive. I won't criticize your precious captain. And I won't light my candle."

"Good."

"And now, Mr. Randall, get back to work. You've done what you came to do and I'm grateful. It's high time I got to work, too, on my sewing. I'll need a dress to go up on deck with you."

Grinning, he left her to her sewing. Out in the passageway, he bumped into a worried Sam. "How is she?"

"She ate her dinner. And she's working on her dress."

Sam's weather-beaten face broke into a smile. "That's good news. I must admit, she had me worried. You'd better get up on deck, lad; the captain's looking for you. It's looking bad up there. Should be hitting rough weather soon. Did you warn Mrs. Warwick?"

"Yes, she'll be fine, Sam."

"I certainly hope so."

Six hours later, Sam would have good cause to be worried. Katy woke to the sound of something banging around in the cabin. In his haste to report to duty, Josh had forgotten to secure the articles in her room. She had gone to bed blissfully unaware of what a storm at sea could be. Opening her eyes to the darkness, her first impulse was to light her candle, to investigate the noise. But the room was heaving back and forth, making it impossible to get her balance. She remembered Josh's warning. So much for the candle, even if she could find it. But if the ship was going down, she wanted to be dressed. If it wasn't, she fully intended to find out what was happening outside her cabin. Groping about in the dark proved more difficult than she imagined. Each time the ship heaved, she had to fight to maintain her position. Nausea threatened. With only the greatest concentration, she got to her chamber pot in time, pouring her entire insides into that pot. So much for Josh's meal. When she was done, there was no energy left to make the return trip to the bed. She lay on the floor, sick and exhausted, until she lost consciousness.

Nature was in a foul mood that evening and wouldn't allow her the luxury of oblivion. Katy was unconscious for only a few minutes before the ship made a lurch over the crest of a mammoth wave, tossing her the full length of her cabin into the opposite wall. She woke. Fortunately, the major extent of her injuries were centered in her posterior, but Nature heaped insult upon injury by sending the chamber pot after her. Contrarily, it was the mess that gave her the strength to get up off the floor. That Irish backbone, that many mistake for stubbornness, would not let her lie there and take any more. Josh had told her to start fighting and now seemed like a damned good time. With righteous indignation, she dared the ocean to knock her down. And though it tried, again and again, Katy had found her sea legs. She was far from feeling well, but she found a cloth and wiped herself off. Then she searched for her clothes. When she finally gathered enough to make herself presentable, she ventured into the hallway. It was colder out there but she wasn't going to stay in her cabin with a storm raging. Stifling a shiver, she realized how dark it was. By now, fortunately, her body had grown accustomed to the irregular motion of the ship and by anticipating the direction in which she would be shoved and shifting her weight accordingly, she was able to counteract it. It was slow going, but she enjoyed it.

Midnight! Suddenly she remembered the horse, down in the hold, the bottommost and darkest part of the ship. How could she ever understand what was happening; she would be panicky. Saying a silent prayer that Sam had remembered the mare, she ran for the hold.

With growing apprehension, she reached the bottom of the ship and started to fumble about in the dark. There was an awful stench but she was too worried to think about it now. The quiet was ominous. The horse should be stomping and screaming at the rough treatment she was getting.

When she reached the stall where the mare was stabled, her worst fears were justified. Close up, she could see the ruined mess of the makeshift stall. Pieces of wood were all over the place and there was a heavy beam on the horse itself. In her panic, Midnight must have tried to escape, bringing the lumber down on top of her. Calling softly, Katy despaired at the lack of response. Desperately, she tried to move the beam that pinned the animal, but it wouldn't budge. Placing a hand on her flank, Katy slid down next to the injured horse. With a burst of hope, she saw that she was still breathing. Midnight looked up then and whinnied.

"It's all right, Midnight. Katy is here now. I know it hurts, but I'll get help somehow. Hold on for me and I'll get Kit, or Sam; they'll know what to do. We'll have you up and around and as good as new. Just don't be scared. I'll be right back."

The horse looked up with pain in her eyes. Haunted by that look, Katy flew up the stairs in half the time it took her to descend them. Reaching the stairs that led to the deck, she was forced to slow down. The wind was blowing so hard, it nearly blew her back down the stairs. But she was frantic and nothing short of a can-

132

non was going to stop her. Fighting the wind, she gained the top of the stairs. What met her there was worse; she had to clutch onto the railing. The wind and water were beating the deck with such ferocity that if she stepped out, she would be washed into the sea. Her eyes searched for another human being, but it was impossible to see through the grayish mist. She tried to shout but her voice was soon carried away. Just as she was admitting defeat, she saw a rope, thrown carelessly at the bottom of the stairs. With fingers that trembled from cold and urgency, she tied a knot to the railing and attached the other end of the rope to her waist. Thus secured, she ventured out onto the deck.

Many a time in England she had been caught in a storm and she had always enjoyed the experience. Nothing in her past, however, prepared her for the fury of this weather. It literally took her breath away. All she could do was cling onto the rope and slowly edge her way in the direction of the wheel. Instinct told her that there would be the greatest likelihood of finding someone to help her. Before too long, she collided with her husband. Predictably, he was angry. "What the hell do you think you're doing up here? Haven't you got any sense? I can't afford to lose anyone stupid enough to try to save your life."

Katy was too preoccupied to let his words penetrate. Barely listening to him, she blurted out. "It's Midnight. A beam's fallen on her and I can't get it off by myself. I think she's hurt bad; she's not making any noise."

He reacted instantly. Calling to Sam, he barked out an order and two men materialized out of the mist to take their places. Kit grabbed Katy by the arm and dragged her to the stairs. Once in the shelter, she broke free. "I've got to untie this rope. Go ahead; I'll catch up. Please hurry."

With an appreciative glance at the rope, they hurried off. Katy fumbled with the rope and within minutes ran after them. Reaching the hold, she saw that they had already assessed the situation. Each had a grip on the beam and were straining to lift it. She added her weight to theirs and together, they freed the horse. In a flash, she was on her knees next to Sam, who was examining Midnight. In the darkness, the silence was deafening. If only the mare would make a sound. Unable to bear it any longer, Katy swallowed hard to keep her voice from shaking. "How bad is it, Sam?"

He pulled his eyes from the wounded animal and looked at her. He groped in his mind for the words to make it easier to take. Then from the silence, Kit put into words what the other two couldn't say. "She'll have to be put out of her misery. Sam, take the girl up to her cabin. I'll join you later."

Katy hated him in that moment. His cold, emotionless voice had pronounced sentence, condemning her horse to death. Was he satisfied? She would lose her childhood friend; she would have nothing left. No, she wasn't going to let him do it; she'd do it herself. And there was no way on earth he would ever know how much it hurt her. She stood up to face him. "No. She is my responsibility and I'll thank you to let me deal with it. You can return to your duties, Captain. If you'd be so kind, I'd appreciate the use of your pistol."

"Do you know how to use it?"

Her voice matched his in hardness. "I won't blow a

hole in the side of your precious ship, if that's what's worrying you. Sam can stay, if he wants, to see that I don't use it on anyone else."

Sam didn't need to see to be aware of the tension in the air. It was a shame. The girl was too proud to let her husband see that she needed the comfort that he alone could give her. And who could understand Kit, who was old enough to know better, letting this poor little slip of a girl break her heart in half without raising a finger to help her. He sighed as he heard Kit say, "Very well, Sam, take care of it."

They heard his footsteps echo up the stairs until eventually, they were drowned out by the sounds of the storm. Katy turned to Sam and sobbed. "I just couldn't let him do it. He'd kill her without feeling anything for her. I couldn't stand that."

"Do you want me to do it?"

For a moment, she was tempted. "No. It's something I have to do. Are you absolutely certain there's no hope?"

"I'm sorry, lass, but it'll only be a couple hours more, at most, and it will only mean hours of pain for her."

"It's all my fault." She dropped to her knees. "Oh, Midnight, what have I done to you? If I had left you where you belonged instead of dragging you with me . . ."

"You're wrong, Katy. No one could've predicted this and there was nothing you could've done to prevent it. I told you before; life has a way of rearranging things. Midnight knows this and she wouldn't want you spending the rest of your life feeling guilty for something that wasn't your fault. You both had good times. Think of those times now, and it'll make your job easier."

Katy felt the warmness of her horse and her heart screamed at the injustice of it. But time was passing and with every second, Midnight was suffering. Katy knew what she had to do and she was going to do it in the least painful way she knew. She began to sing; a slow, haunting ballad, with all the pain they both felt in every note. Sam could feel the hair on his arms begin to raise and he felt pride in this girl.

Katy said good-bye, softly, and put the pistol to the horse's head. The sound of the shot ripped through the air, echoing its finality. Both humans flinched, but the mare, as if she understood, died without another sound.

Katy stroked her pet's neck and whispered again, "Good-bye, my friend." Standing up, she brushed off her clothes. She was soaked and she was shivering. Turning to Sam, she handed him the smoking pistol. "I hope you're right, Sam. I hope she understood. I suppose she'll have to be buried at sea; please make Kit understand that I have to be there." She sighed. "Right now, though she's gone from this place and if you don't mind, I'd rather be someplace else."

Wrapping his coat around her slender shoulders, Sam helped her out of the hold. There was nothing for either to say so they made their way back to the cabin in silence. It wasn't until they reached her door that Katy felt the blood begin to flow in her veins again. With something close to panic, she grabbed the front of his shirt. "Oh, Sam, don't make me go back in that room."

Her eyes were wide and Sam felt helpless. "Ah, lass, you know the captain's orders."

"I'll go crazy if you lock me up in there."

136

"I'm sorry but a ship in a storm is no place for a lady."

"Look at me. Do I look like a lady to you?"

Katy stood in the hall, dripping water from Josh's hand-me-downs. She was right; she looked more like a drowned rat. "Katy, you're a scrapper, but have pity on me. The captain would have my hide if I let you anywhere near that deck. You were smart about that rope, but you're still a landlubber. If you didn't get in the way, you'd be washed overboard in no time."

"That would solve a lot of problems."

"Katherine Warwick, if I ever hear that kind of talk from you again, I'll take you over my knee, captain's wife or no."

She held her ground. "I promise you, if you send me back in there, I won't be in any condition for spanking when you come to get me out."

"Are you threatening me?"

"Of course not. Only I can't go back in there, not the way I feel. If you make me, I won't promise to stay. Isn't there anywhere else I could go, just for a few hours?"

For a while, he looked at her as if he was weighing the possibilities. Deciding finally that she was in earnest, he made up his mind. Captain's orders or not, this girl had gone through enough. "If you can stay out of trouble, I suppose you could stay in the galley."

"What about Harry?"

"All hands are up on deck and likely to stay there awhile."

"Is the storm that bad?"

"Don't go worrying about this ship, lass. Your husband knows these waters better than some know their name, and take it from me, there's none better to get

137

us out of this. Between us, we've logged a lot of hours on this ocean and old Mother Nature hasn't gotten the best of us yet. C'mon." He reached for her hand. "Let me take you to the galley. You can wait out the storm in there. And I'd better get back up on that deck and back to work."

Wordlessly, she followed him to the galley. Fear gripped her as he was about to leave. For the first time in her life, she was afraid of the dark. In every shadow, she found menace. She clutched at his sleeve, "Please don't go. Stay and talk a little while longer."

"You don't know what you're asking. My place is up there with the captain; I can't stay. As soon as the storm lets up, I promise to sit all night with you, if you want. But I've got a job to do now. Don't go looking at me like that, child, you're only making it harder for the both of us."

Katy took a deep breath. "I'm sorry. You're right, of course. I don't know what's come over me. I'll be fine. really I will. You go on up there and try to keep us all out of trouble."

It pulled at his heart, the way she smiled up at him. He wanted to stay, but he knew his duty. Placing a hand on her damp head, he tried to thank her. "You're a good lass and a mighty strong one, too. You do an old man proud. I only wish you were my own."

In her heart, she knew that no matter how scared and lonesome she might feel, it wasn't fair to worry him. He'd be in danger if he didn't keep his mind on his work. Selfishly, she didn't want to lose him too. "I don't know what's wrong with you, Sam Culligan. Sitting here gabbing with the likes of me when there's work to be done. Go up to your captain and I don't want to see your face until you've sent this storm back where it came from. Go on, get out."

With a strong sense of guilt, he took the opportunity she offered. He was still worried, though. They all expected too much from her. After all, she was a girl, not a seasoned sailor. So he made arrangements with Kit to send Josh down to sit with her. Kit was happy to comply. The boy had been doing a man's work all night and though he did it uncomplainingly, the strain was beginning to show. And Sam was right. Katy should not be alone with her grief. Friendship had sprung up between the two, and at present Kit was grateful for it. He summoned Josh and requested he join his wife in the galley.

Meanwhile, Katy faced the desolation of the room. Apparently, the never-too-efficient Harry had forgotten to secure his supplies, resulting in an assortment of debris on the floor. Katy had to step over countless undefined objects to find a place to sit. She chose a wall bench, as it was the only place she could be reasonably certain to stay put. Watching the clutter roll from one side of the room to the other, she sat down to wait out the storm.

It was on the bench, with hands folded across her lap, that Josh found her. She was staring off, at nothing in particular. He was dismayed to see that look on her face again. Only today he was so tired he honestly felt incapable of dealing with her. Like a coward, he considered turning around and heading back up to the deck. But Katy had noticed him and called out. "Josh! What are you doing here? I thought all hands were needed topside."

"They say I'm too tired to be of much use to them."

"He sent you to the galley to rest? Is he afraid I'll do something stupid? Can't he trust me to be alone?"

"It's not like that. We, I mean I, well I thought you might like some company and, besides, I really am kinda tired." He slumped into the nearest chair. Water dripped from his coat, forming a puddle on the floor.

Katy was all contrition. She had missed the lines of exhaustion on his young face, being absorbed in her own problems. "I'm sorry, Josh. I feel a bit upside-down, but I shouldn't have snapped at you. I'm glad of your company. I must admit it was a little scary all by myself. Why don't you get out of that coat; it's soaked. You'll be catching a fever and we don't have a doctor, remember? How about something to eat?" She looked around the room. "There must be something in this mess that's edible."

Surprised by the sudden change in her voice, he glanced up at her. "I guess I am hungry. Working up there, you forget about things like food. If you can find anything, I'd be grateful." As an afterthought, he added, "Don't forget—no fire."

She was already sorting through the debris. With something to do at last, she set to work organizing the galley. At his reminder, she jumped up in a huff with an angry reply on her lips, but he was sitting, as if in a trance, still in his wet coat, and the words died where they were. "Josh Randall, you've got to get out of that coat. Here, let me help you. What's wrong with that captain of yours to work you to the point of exhaustion? No don't answer. I know, every man has to do his share. I hate to think what the rest of them must feel like. If only I could light a fire, I'd make some coffee."

"You don't need a fire for coffee. It's not the same, but I've seen Sam and Harry do it lots of times."

So here was something useful she could do. They could all do with something in their bellies. She helped

Josh with his coat and settled him at the table. Telling him to rest, she promised to have something for him to eat in no time at all.

It took considerably longer than anticipated to sort out the confusion to determine exactly what was in stock. The boy needed solid food so she sliced off a chunk of ham and two slices of bread. Experimenting a bit, she found she could grind the coffee beans into a mush that would mix with water. Not by any means the best brew she had ever tasted, but it was drinkable and it would do the job. Proud of her accomplishment, she brought the meal to Josh. His head rested on the table. Realizing he was asleep, Katy felt a strong maternal feeling come over her. She had the urge to cuddle him in her arms. Instead, she pushed the soft red hair from his eyes and thought that a woman could be proud to have a son like Josh. It was an odd thought, with him not three years her junior, but she had done a lot of growing up in the last twenty-four hours and she felt as old as the sea itself. He had been right, last night. She had been feeling sorry for herself, getting herself and everyone around her, absolutely nowhere. If Josh could handle what life dished out, then surely so could Maureen's daughter. It would be wonderful if life was like it was in novels and daydreams, but it wasn't. If it was determined to knock her down, she was going to give it a good fight. Midnight was gone, and it hurt like hell, but she could begin again, being responsible for no one but herself. And maybe, just maybe, that poor boy sleeping at the table.

Letting him sleep, she drank his coffee herself. While sipping at it, she had an idea. She found what she was looking for, searching through the cabinets. Perhaps it was not of the same quality as the stuff that appeared on Farley's table, but Harry McGee's whiskey would put a kick in this coffee that would warm the insides of the coldest sailor. She liberally doused the insipid brew and took a taste. Oh, it had kick, all right. Splashing the improved beverage into containers, she felt a thrill of achievement. Stuffing some food in a sack, she appropriated Josh's coat and took her prizes up to the deck. She found the rope where she left it. This time her fingers were steady and she tied the knot quickly. Once again that day, she ventured out on the deck. Luckily, she ran into Sam first.

"I told you to stay below, lass. I won't have you disobeying the captain's orders."

"No need to bellow. If he hears you, we'll both be in trouble. Here, take these. I made coffee." She handed him the sack. "Here's some food, too. Pass it around and if you need more, let me know."

Not giving the astonished Sam time to question her, Katy hurried away. Staring after her, Sam wondered what was going on. He looked at the bags in his hands. Food, eh? Tasting the coffee, he chuckled. That girl had spunk. There would be the devil to pay when Harry discovered the shortage in his supply, but it was the best coffee he had ever had. Sam covered the deck, distributing coffee and food. By the time he had reached the last of them, they were waiting anxiously word having spread more rapidly than the coffee. Sam was a hero.

Meanwhile, Katy was busy in the galley. The storm wouldn't last forever and she was determined to have the galley in tip-top shape before the cook returned. He would be furious about the whiskey, so she hoped to forestall his anger by presenting him with a clean galley and a prepared meal. It would give her something to do, to keep her mind off other things. Josh, oblivious to the world around him, was still asleep. Humming softly, Katy set to work. By the time she sat back to view her accomplishments, the ship was rocking less severely. If the storm was abating, she had better make more coffee before they all descended on her.

Sam watched her work from the doorway. Noticing the sleeping boy, he understood why Katy had brought the coffee. So the girl had been working alone. Apparently, she no longer needed his company. He felt another bubble of pride and it made him laugh.

Katy whirled around at his chuckle. "Oh, you startled me. You're just the man I wanted to see. I've got a fresh batch of coffee. That is, if you think anyone is interested."

"Interested, lass? If I show up without it, there'll be mutiny."

Katy reached into the closet. "This is the last of the bottle, I'm afraid. I hope Kit can replace it or I'm in for a heap of trouble."

Sam laughed again. "I'll deal with Harry; he won't be bothering you." He nodded in Josh's direction. "Has he been sleeping long?"

"Poor Josh. Thank you for sending him, but he was exhausted. I told him to sleep."

"Are you feeling better, then?"

She flashed a quick smile. "Yes, I am. It hurts, deep down inside, but I don't feel as alone as before. Both you and Josh have gotten me over the worst and I'll be forever grateful for that."

"Don't be forgetting your husband."

Katy snorted. "Him! As if he cares."

"Aye, lass, he cares, in his own way."

"He has a strange way of showing it. But it doesn't matter. What I meant was that though it helps to have people caring about you, no one can make you get a grip on yourself. That has to come from within. I'm not altogether sure where it came from, but it's there inside me now. To answer your question, yes, I am feeling better, Sam. About myself."

Sam wanted to hug her but he grumbled instead. "Fill up those mugs. They'll be screaming for their coffee and we've had enough of that storm without trouble from the crew."

Katy grinned. "Aye, aye, sir. Let me know when it's safe enough to light a fire and I'll see what I can do about a real meal."

He grumbled a bit more as he shuffled out of the room. "Go on ahead, lass, if your mind's set on it. The wind's died down. Start your fire, but be careful."

An hour later, there was a pot of Irish stew simmering on the stove. Leaving it to cook itself, she sat down with a cup of coffee. It felt good to be useful; it was a satisfaction that was new to her. She had a proprietary feeling about this kitchen (no, it was a galley); and she would hate to give it up. For a few leisurely moments, she mused over her coffee, mentally rearranging things.

Some time later, she walked over to Josh and gently shook him. "Josh, wake up. It's time to put some food in your stomach before you spend the rest of the day fighting that storm in your dreams."

He jumped up and looked at her in confusion. "Mother?"

She had a queer feeling in the pit of her stomach. "No, Josh," she said gently. "It's just me, Katy. I hated to wake you but the crew will be coming soon

144

and I didn't think you'd want them to find you asleep."

He rubbed his eyes. "Storm's letting up. Have I been asleep long?"

"A couple of hours or so. You needed it. You'll undoubtedly have to take over for the others later, so they can sleep."

"Thanks. I reckon you're right. And thanks for waking me up. They'd never let me hear the end of it; me sleeping while they fight the storm. Mmmm, what's that smell?"

"That's your dinner. Wash up and I'll fix you a dish."

"No. They'll be accusing me of special treatment, for sure."

"Let them come to me with their complaints. Until Harry comes back, I rule this kitchen and I say who eats when. Hurry along and do as you're told or maybe you won't get anything at all."

"Yes, ma'am. Who'd a' thought you'd turn into an ogre while I was sleeping." But he dutifully washed his hands while she fixed his plate. Still grinning and teasing, he sat down to eat. His tune changed when he took the first bite. "This is delicious. Where'd you learn to cook like this?"

"You forget; I grew up on a farm. With no cook, a nontalented mother, and a busy Nanny, most of the meals were my responsibility. We had a lot of stew in the beginning, since it was easiest."

"This sure is good. Can I have more?"

Josh was mopping up his second bowl with a crust of bread when the first of the tired crew trudged down the stairs. Katy pointed to the bowl of wash water and soap, while Josh watched in amusement. Although re-

145

luctant, at first, to be ordered around by a girl, once they caught a whiff of the stew bubbling on the stove, even the more obstinate of them were washing their hands.

When the captain and his mate straggled into the galley, an unusual sight met their eyes. Cozy in the candlelight, it seemed a refuge. Tired sailors lingered over their coffee, contented to sit and talk. Never had the room seemed so warm, or clean. Katy was at the sink, mopping up dishes. When she spotted them, she rushed to fix their plates.

"Hey!" one of the sailors shouted. "How come they get special treatment? We wasn't allowed to eat till we washed our hands."

Laughing, Katy admitted he was right, and showed them the basin. When they reached the table, she had their food, warm and aromatic, before them. "So, Captain, can we relax a bit now?"

Kit looked at his wife in undisguised amazement. "Madame, not only can we relax, but I personally plan to sleep for three days. That is, after I eat this stew."

Sam was looking at her too, amusement pulling at the corners of his mouth. "Irish stew, Katy?"

"What else?" She poured steaming coffee into their mugs. "Here's some decent coffee to warm your bellies."

Kit shook his head. Here was his wife, whom he had left suffering in the hold, looking like one of his crew and working just as hard. Had she done all this? With an uncomfortable feeling that he had misjudged her, he took his first bite. He was in love. Food had never tasted this good and for the first time in days, he felt warm inside. Yes, it was quite likely that he had misjudged her.

146

Katy, for her part, was too busy for such speculation. Still, her eyes had a way of straying over to where her husband sat so obviously enjoying her meal. She had been pleased by the praise of the others, but his had special meaning. Shyly, she approached him. "How is the ship? Did we sustain much damage?"

Again she surprised him. Who would suspect with her own trouble, she'd be concerned with the ship? "Not too bad, considering the storm. Sails are torn, but they can be mended. The ship itself is in fine shape but we're afraid we might have lost one of the crew."

"How awful! Do you know who?"

"Not yet. Cummings heard a yell, as if someone was being swept away, but with the fog, it was hard to say who. I guess it's not something I'm anxious to know."

Sam spoke up. "We think we know, now. It must've been Harry, Kit. Everyone else is accounted for."

The color drained from Kit's face. "You're sure of that?"

"I know what you're thinking and you can just wipe it out of your head. That man was as fit as you or I to be on that deck. If he went over, it was because he was drunk, not because of anything you did to him."

Kit was not to be convinced. "Poor Harry. Damn! He had the makings of a good sailor. Still, I shouldn't have signed him on, I guess." Slowly, he rose from the table. "I'll be holding services in the morning. Spread the word, will you, Sam?" He started for the door.

Without thinking, Katy blurted out. "If you've got the time, Captain, I'd like to talk to you."

Lost in guilt, he looked at her, expressionless. Interpreting it as annoyance, she went on the defensive. Typically, he wasn't going to make this easier for her.

147

Trying to keep her need from showing, she sounded haughtier than she intended. "I know you think me intolerably silly, but if you could spare one of your crew, I'd like to bury Midnight tomorrow, also."

"Your horse?" It was only a question, but she was certain he was mocking her.

"Some of us are capable of feeling, Captain Warwick, even if it is only for a horse."

Now he was annoyed. She was deliberately trying to provoke him and he was too damned tired for any nonsense. "Don't get yourself into a state. Do whatever you want with your horse; only don't bother me with it. Sam, take care of it please. Now, if you'll both excuse me, I've got to get back to work."

"Are you insane? You're so tired, you'll be the next one going over the edge. You need sleep."

Kit glared at her from under raised eyebrows. "I am grateful for your concern, my dear, but unfortunately, this ship cannot sail itself. As its captain, I have a job to do, whether or not I need sleep. You're one to talk; you look terrible. Get some sleep yourself. And for God's sake, find something decent to wear. I won't have my wife appearing in rags."

She stared at the retreating form in disbelief. As if it was her fault she was wearing these clothes! She looked terrible, did she? Of all the ungrateful wretches. Let him catch pneumonia, then; see if she cared!

Sam marveled at the way these two never understood what they were doing to each other. "Don't mind him, lass. He's got a lot on his mind."

"Don't we all?"

"Aye, that we do. But he's responsible for the lives of each and every one of us and it just about kills him

148

to have lost one. He thinks it's his fault we lost Harry and there'll be no talking him out of it. That's a heavy burden for a man to bear."

She knew he was right, but it didn't stop her resentment. Why should he be permitted to take out his problems on her? "I've tried to be understanding. I thought I was helping him, trying to make things easier. I should've saved my energy for all the thanks I'll get."

"The boy can't easily show his emotion. Somewhere along the line he was taught to hide it well. So don't you go thinking he doesn't feel it just the same. Take my word for it—he's mighty grateful and what's more, he's proud of what you've done here. Just don't ever expect him to tell you so."

Katy sighed. "Forgive me, Sam. I guess it was a relapse into self-pity. I didn't do it for praise, anyway. I wanted to be useful. Everyone else was doing something, and feeling sorry for myself was a waste of time. Marrying Kit may have been a mistake, but it's done now and there's no sense wishing it was otherwise. Only I'm not going to allow him to push me around any more. Don't worry—I'll live up to my vows the best I can, but I have a life to live, too. I'm too young to settle for what is given to me. And Mr. Warwick will just have to get used to the idea."

Sam threw back his head and laughed. "You're a treat for my old age. Poor Kit has met his match, I fear. But he was right, it's time to take off that apron and get some sleep, lass."

"No, I'm too worked up to sleep. I have these dishes to finish and then I thought I'd bake some bread . . ."

"Bread? You're to follow orders. On board . . ."

". . . the captain's word is law." She laughed. "Very

149

well, Sam. Maybe you're right. No sense making him any angrier and I guess I'm a little tired. But what about you?"

"I think I'll head topside and see what I can do to convince that stubborn jackass that he'd be of more use to us if he was rested."

"You're an angel. I hope he knows how lucky he is to have a friend like you. Good night, Sam. You won't forget about Midnight?"

"I'll take care of it. Go get your sleep, lass."

On tiptoe, she kissed his forehead. "God bless you, Sam Culligan. And thank you. Thanks for everything."

Chapter 10

It was with a feeling of deep peace that Katy found
herself back at Clonmara. The aura of contentment
was broken only by a hammering, far off in the distance. Once again, the sun was shining warmly, sparkling on the tiny seed pearls Aunt Judith had
fastened to the ivory lace. Maureen was smoothing
the gathered folds of the gown while giving her worried daughter advice. "Be careful, love. He's a hard
man, but he's strong and loyal and he'll make a fine
husband if you can learn how to handle him. It will
take a woman, just as strong and loyal, but if you use
the brains God gave you, I haven't a doubt but that
you're just the woman."

She tucked a stray curl under Katy's veil and with
love shining in her eyes, whispered good-bye. The finality was there, but no sadness. For Katy was running to Kit's open arms, feeling peace and great joy
when she reached them. Clasped together, they
watched as Maureen faded slowly into the mist. Katy
turned to her husband, the doubts and questions in
her eyes, and he answered with a long and passionate
kiss.

The dream melted as the constant hammering became a knock on the door. Katy opened one eye. There it was again. With the taste of the kiss still on her lips, she hurried to the door. She wasn't altogether certain who she expected to see, but she experienced a sharp disappointment to be facing Josh. "Oh, it's you. Come in, Josh. I guess I was sleeping."

"Time to be up, sleepyhead. I brought water for a bath."

She rubbed her eyes. "A bath? What time is it?"

"Just a little after dawn."

She was awake now. "Dawn? Oh, Josh, they haven't done anything with Midnight, have they? Sam promised."

"Easy, Katy. They wouldn't do anything without you. The captain told me to bring some water so you could wash up. Then, if you feel up to it, you can go up on deck."

So he was going to make sure she didn't disgrace him by appearing in public like a hoyden. Perversely, she decided to forego the bath. He would learn to take her the way she was. "Forget the bath, Josh. I'll go the way I am."

"I don't think that's a good idea."

"And why not? If these clothes aren't good enough for your captain, then tell him to find me some that are."

"It's not the clothes. It's just that they're having services for Harry in a few minutes."

Harry. In her fit of temper and anxiety about Midnight, all thoughts of the poor cook had fled her mind. They came back, filling Katy with an uncomfortable feeling of guilt. She, too, felt vaguely responsible for the man's death. She would go to the services; it was

152

the least she could do. But Josh was right. She couldn't go to the service in the clothes she had slept in. Her only other choice was the dress she had been sewing the night of the storm. Looking it over, she decided it would have to do. It wasn't finished but she could tack it together where it wasn't. Against his protests, she hurried the boy out of the room, telling him she would meet him on deck. Gingerly, she fitted the dress over her shoulders. It felt strange to be in skirts again. With a silent prayer that the seams would hold, she made her way up to the service.

When she joined the others, Kit raised an eyebrow but made no effort to remove her. It the others were surprised to see her there, they gave no sign. Quite likely, they had grown accustomed to expecting the unusual from their captain's wife. All heads were bowed, solemnly listening to Kit's emotionless voice reading from the Scriptures. It was a sad occasion, made sadder still by the obvious fact that no one truly mourned the passing of the cook. Each was doing his duty, but Harry had been a loner and an unpopular one at that. Katy thought of her grandfather. Who was there, actually to mourn James Farley's passing? What a waste it was, to live a life and then to pass from it without having one single soul miss you when you were gone. Katy shivered. Her own life was far from ideal, but she wouldn't trade it for all the wealth and power of Farley's empty existence. He had his pride intact, perhaps, but at what price?

Kit's somber voice ground to a halt and there was only the gentle breeze to accompany everyone's private thoughts. Irreverently, Katy thought of the morning's beauty and the welcome warmth of the sun. As the crew was dismissed, she crossed over to the railing to look out over the ocean. Poor Harry, she thought. To be swallowed up in the vast darkness of it, never to feel the sun again. She was shivering when Kit joined her.

"I thought you might prefer the deck empty. Still, if you don't mind, I'd like to stay."

She looked up in surprise. As usual, his eyes were guarded and she couldn't begin to guess what he was thinking. Yet, it was a kind gesture and she responded to it. The feeling of dream returned and she knew she trusted him. "I'd appreciate that. I'm not sure I can face it alone. I know I'm probably silly, but Midnight was my best friend, my only friend, in fact. The water is so cold. It's not that I imagine she'll feel it, but it seems so impersonal somehow."

"It's all in how you look at it, I suppose. Death is impersonal. It doesn't much matter where you put the body; not as much as how you go about it. Think of it as sending her peacefully to the bottom, letting her drift to her resting place, instead of sticking her in a hole in the ground. And you'll be sending a part of you with her. I doubt that even a human could ask for more."

"So you do understand?"

"I said good-bye to my mother this way so I know how you feel."

Disarmed by his consideration, a small tear formed in her eye, leaked out and dripped down her cheek. Seeing this, he covered her hand with his own warm one. The tears were pouring now and she was unsure what emotion she was fighting. All she knew was that she needed that hand to support her, to say good-bye to her childhood friend and all she represented. As Midnight was heaved over the side, Kit squeezed her

154

hand and she returned the pressure.

Kit dismissed the men and opened his arms to her. Soon, she was sobbing on his shoulder. He held her gently, but close to him, leaving her strangely at peace. It was her dream, all over again. Having ended a chapter of her life, she was ready now for a fresh start, a new beginning with this man who stroked her hair and murmured words of comfort. Pulling back to look at him, Katy was surprised at the depth of emotion in his eyes. "Thank you," she said softly but she meant so much more. His grip tightened and he was kissing her, gently at first, and then with a growing urgency. Her blood began to race through her veins. She groaned softly with the pleasure of it, and suddenly Kit broke away.

He wouldn't face her. "Forgive me. I seem to have lost all sense of decency. As I said, I know how you feel, but I can promise that it won't hurt as much after a while. Except, perhaps, at times like these." He shrugged. "I'm sorry for the way I acted; it won't happen again. Are you all right, now? I have to get back to my ship."

His brusqueness all but took her breath away. Just as she thought they had reached an understanding, she woke as if a second time from that dream to discover they were as far apart as ever. His mother had been occupying his thoughts, not her. She meant nothing to him. "I'm fine," she told him defiantly. "I'd like to stay here awhile."

She turned her back on him and thereby missed his look. There was longing in every line of his body. He reached out, as if to touch her. For a suspended moment, it seemed he would reach her, but he hesitated a fraction of a second too long and the moment was gone. With another shrug, his eyes were veiled again and the glimpse of vulnerability disappeared. Turning on his heel, he left her there, to lose himself once more in his work.

Katy was in turmoil. He stirred up emotions in her she wasn't aware existed and, typically, left her alone to deal with them. She missed the comfort of his arms, however irrational it sounded. It was as bad as if he had raped her again, for that was exactly how she felt. Twice now she had opened herself to him, and with disastrous results. Never again! Grandfather was right; where was her pride? From now on, she would build a barrier between Kit and her foolish emotions and never would she allow him to penetrate it. If he could so casually dismiss her, she would have to learn to do the same with him. Though she was all too susceptible to his great charm, she had acquired a new strength now. The next time she faced her husband she would be in control of herself. With a thrust of her shoulders, she marched back to her cabin.

The promised bath water had arrived. Slipping gingerly out of the dress, she slid into the warm water. Ever so slowly, her cares seemed to melt with the soap, leaving her with a sense of well-being. She soaked her tired limbs until the water cooled far beyond the point of comfort. With shriveled skin, she pulled herself out of the water.

What was she going to wear? She had lived, day and night, in those trousers and she couldn't bear to put her clean body into them. But she couldn't wear the unfinished dress. She laughed at herself. Here she was again, sighing for the loss of those trunks. Unwilling to be accused of being silly, she set to work washing her trousers. They would dry in an hour or two in this breeze, and she could sew on the dress while they did. It meant changing her clothes a number of times, but what choice was there?

Some time later, she stood in the still-damp but clean trousers and shirt. She remembered the ship was without a cook and she wanted the job. After all, she was the most qualified and she doubted there would be a rush of volunteers for it. That Kit would fail to see the logic in this she didn't doubt, but it only served to strengthen her resolve. For the first time in this crazy marriage, Katy knew what she wanted and she was going to get it. She almost felt sorry for Kit.

In the galley, Josh was struggling with the pots and pans. "I should have known he would stick you with kitchen duty." Katy rolled up her sleeves and donned an apron. "Move over, Josh. This is my kitchen and I don't want any ham-fisted sailor messing it up."

He couldn't keep the gratitude out of his expression. "The captain's not going to like this." Somehow, his protest lacked conviction.

"The captain is going to have to get used to it. Since it was my dowry that purchased this ship, by right it is half mine. That entitles me to make some decisions. My first is that I can cook better than you. If the captain complains, send him to me and I'll tell him myself. Now get out of here and let me get to work."

In no time at all, Josh was scrambling out of the galley, all too anxious to be convinced. With an efficiency she thought she had forgotten, Katy soon had the fire going and food on the stove. Singing softly as she set the table, she heard heavy steps stomping down the stairs.

"What the hell are you doing?"

With a lurch of her heart, Katy realized it was far

157

easier to defy Kit in the solitude of her thoughts than in person. She had forgotten the overpowering presence of the man. And there was no question that he was angry. Blue eyes that made her want to squirm dared her to find an excuse for her behavior. But the more she thought about it, the angrier she herself felt. Without facing him, lest he see the shaking hands, she replied, "I'm setting the table." With a gulp she turned, all innocence shining from her eyes.

"Never mind the evasions. I gave this job to Josh."

"And I took it away."

"And by what right do you assume to do that?"

"Because I can do the job better."

"No wife of mine will be a cook."

She forced her voice to stay calm. "Be realistic. You need a cook. I need something to do. I am the only one qualified that can be spared to do the job. Why should I vegetate in my cabin and why should Josh do the work of two men because of your silly pride? And just because I'm a female."

"That's just my point. I have enough to worry about without adding you to my list." He, too, was fighting his temper.

"How flattering. Do you suppose that if I'm kept from sight, I'll cease to exist? That I can be summoned when you have further need of me? No, Captain Warwick, you're going to have to make up your mind about me. Am I the milk-and-sugar miss, to be pampered and protected, or am I the strong woman that can take whatever you thrust upon me without complaining? I can be one or the other. When you make up your mind, suppose you let me know and I'll act accordingly. In the meantime, however, I intend to keep busy." Katy whipped the knife from her belt.

"And don't worry, I know how to take care of myself."

He glared down at her scornfully. "I could take that out of your hand in a second."

She matched his glare. "I doubt that. Perhaps you'd win eventually but not before I made you wonder whether it was worth the trouble. I'm not a green girl anymore—thanks to you."

Katy regretted the angry words before they left her mouth. She watched the color drain from his face. For a moment, from his expression, she thought he would attack her, but she refused to let him see her fear. Without another word, he turned on his heel and quit the room.

Her body was shaking as Katy let out a sigh of relief. It wasn't exactly a victory but she had stood up to him and made her point. She had forced him to view her as an individual, with needs and rights of her own. And for whatever it was worth, she still had her pride.

Chapter 11

Uneventfully, the weeks slipped by. Katy kept her job, nervously waiting for something to go wrong and for Kit to appear with that I-told-you-so expression on his face. Nothing happened. Apparently the crew had far too much respect for their captain to mistreat his wife. And they were beginning to respect their new cook in her own light. They were no fools. They were eating better than ever before. Their constant show of appreciation made Katy smile, remembering Nanny's advice that the way to a man's heart was through his stomach. And since she always wore trousers, it was easy to think of her as one of them, leaving her free to come and go as she pleased. She loved this new freedom.

She took full advantage of it. No day would pass without her presence on the deck, badgering the crew with questions. In this way, she learned more and more of how the ship was run. It fascinated her. She came to admire the lives of these men. There was a dignity to the job, in the lifting of a sail, of battling the elements, of mastering a skill. Thrilled to be part of it, she begged them to teach her. First she learned to handle the ropes and, in time, she learned the hows and whys of raising the sails. Without the restrictions imposed on most females, she became part of this male world and she liked it.

Of her husband, she saw little. Kit seemed to take special care to avoid her and on the rare occasions their paths crossed, he was stiffly polite. Katy told herself it suited her just fine.

But as the days passed, she found herself wishing there was more to their relationship. How nice it would be to go to him with her doubts and fears. Instead, she turned to Sam. Each evening, after the galley had been scrubbed and closed for the night, Katy would take her sewing and two mugs of steaming coffee to join her friend at the wheel. It was her favorite time of the day. Grateful for the appreciative audience, Sam would entertain her with stories of his adventures.

The days had been growing steadily warmer and at the end of a particularly fine day, Katy settled into her favorite spot by the wheel. As she handed Sam his mug, she remarked on the weather.

"That's because we're headed for the Caribbean."

"Is that near to America?"

"Didn't that grandfather teach you anything?"

"I had some formal education and I read a lot, but at Whitney Hall, it was as if anything west of Ireland didn't exist. My grandfather didn't have much patience with the colonies."

"Then it's time for a geography lesson. You do know about Africa? Good. If you head west, from the north of Africa, across the Atlantic, you'd hit the West Indies in the Caribbean Ocean. South Carolina and the colonies are a bit north of there. To answer your first question, we're moving toward the equator and that's why it's getting warmer."

"But I thought we were going to South Carolina?"

He took his eyes off the wheel to glance at her, speculatively. "That's something I can't talk about, lass. All I can say is that we have a date with some Frenchmen and we've got to keep the appointment before we can head home."

She was just as happy not to know their business; she had no desire to become involved in their treason. She watched Sam over the rim of her mug. Staring straight ahead, he was an extension of the wheel he was steering. She envied him. Sam knew who he was, and where he was going; he belonged here. Would she ever belong anywhere? "Sam, whatever made you decide to go to sea?"

"That's a funny question."

"I'm serious. You were once a farmer, tied to the land, and yet here you are, living on the ocean. Why?"

"I guess it's something I've asked myself from time to time. When I was young, the land, my land, was all I needed from life. But it was taken away and I knew I could never be a slave to anyone else's land. That left the sea. I found the life suited me." He paused, thinking back. "I signed up as a cook, you know, my first trip out. I worked for the elder Mr. Warwick. That's how I met your husband."

"Have you known him long, then?"

"Close to sixteen years. He was ten when I first met him. You should have known him then, when he didn't have so much on his mind. A bright boy, he was, always asking me questions, like you. He was the joy in his father's life. That is, next to his mother. Too bad the missus had to die that way."

"Kit never said how she died. What happened?"

Sam seemed lost in the past. "You would have liked her, lass. You couldn't call her a real beauty but she had a way of making everyone feel worthwhile, important. A kinder, nicer woman, I've never met. They were going to London, on the new ship, for Kit's birthday. Old Mr. Julian had the idea of training Kit for a career at sea. He always felt bad that the boy would inherit nothing from the business. Young Julian raised a holy fuss, said he wouldn't go. He was going to school in England the next year anyway, he said, but I figure it was because he hated the sea. Always got seasick. He was trying to spoil things for Kit and nobody paid much attention to him.

"It was a fine April day when we set off. I can still remember it. Everybody was excited, it being the first voyage for most of us. Kit was running from one side of the boat to the other, dragging his poor mother with him. I guess we were all caught up in the excitement. That's why we never noticed now pale she was. She didn't complain. How were we to know?"

"What was wrong?"

"Don't know, exactly. The doctor figured she must've fallen and hurt herself, somehow, back on shore. Being who she was, she'd never say anything to ruin Kit's trip. Three days out, she fell down the stairs in a faint and never recovered. By the time the doctor got to her, there was nothing he could do. The infection had spread too far. Poor Kit took it real bad. Always felt guilty about it. His father didn't help. With his wife gone, he couldn't bear to look at his sons. He ordered the ship to return home and he never took another step off his plantation."

"How terrible. What about Kit?"

"It was a hard time for him; his whole life changed overnight. I couldn't do anything, though I thought about him many a time. I went to see him when I was in port. For the most part, he was left to run free. So was Julian. That boy managed to get himself into one scrape after another until he finally found himself in so much trouble, he was glad to leave for England to go to school. I was glad to see him go. Without a mother or father to intervene, he made Kit's life a living nightmare. How one boy could be so vindictive is beyond me. Kit used to sneak off into the swamps for days. He said it was the only place he could think."

"Swamps? What is that?"

"Marshes, in a way. A man could go into them and no one would ever find him if he didn't want to be found. And Kit didn't."

"That poor boy."

"Aye, lass, that he was. Still, it wasn't all bad. As I said, Julian left. And there was a man in the neighborhood that also liked the solitude of the swamps and he understood Kit. They would go hunting together for days at a time. Sometimes I think that if it wasn't for Francis Marion, Kit wouldn't have turned out any better than Julian."

"I'm not so sure he has."

Sam looked at her sharply. "Don't be making a rash judgment, lass. Mr. Marion was a fine man and he taught Kit that there's more to life than just survival, though he taught him that, too. He was more of a father than Mr. Warwick was. The old man finally gave up pretending he was still alive when Kit reached sixteen. Nothing had been done to provide for the boy; everything was left to Julian, who wouldn't return from England. Kit dealt with his brother's responsibilities and a good job he did of it, too, until he refused to pay one of Julian's gambling debts. That's when the lord and master decided to get off his carcass and come home. Staying at the plantation with him was impossible, so Kit came to me, signing up as a cabin boy at first. He was a hard worker, earning his way up the ranks. When the previous captain retired, he asked his brother for the job. Relieved of the bother, Julian was delighted to give it to him. With a hand-picked crew, Kit soon had the ship running at top efficiency, for the first time in years."

"The same crew as now?"

"All except Josh. Kit discovered him being knocked around by some bullies, one of which claimed to be his captain, and decided then and there he needed a cabin boy. It was a wise decision; that boy is worth his weight in gold."

"How well I know. But I don't understand. If everything was going so well, why did you all turn to treason?"

"Ah, I have to think a bit to answer that one. Remember how you felt about your grandfather? How you hated his petty rules and regulations because they robbed you of your dignity? Imagine a thousand Farleys. We all decided that no stiff-necked lobster-back, sitting comfortably over in England, was gonna tell us where and when we could sail. Everyone of us owed our jobs and some even our lives to Christopher Warwick and if he said it was time to fight the British, then that was what we were going to do. His friend, Colonel Marion, came up with the idea of using the ship to go after supplies for the militia. When they attacked Charleston, we ran in behind them. Mainly, we've been playing hit and run, attacking their ships at night and under cover, so the captain wouldn't run the risk of recognition. It's been hard on him."

"I would imagine it's been hard on everyone."

"Sure, that it has. But Kit has a full time job of it. The rest of us can go home as heroes, but he has to pretend that he's as loyal as the best of them. Lying doesn't come easy to him."

"Hmmmmpf!"

"That's the truth and you can take my word for it. I've been up many a night while that boy drank himself into a stupor, fighting off his worries and loneliness. Can't you understand how it's been? And for what? There's nobody to come home to, to pat him on the back, to tell him he's doing a fine job. Fellow patriots despise him for being a loyalist and the people he's forced to associate with, Julian's friends, think him a fool. If he wants to be successful, he had to keep them thinking that way. His brother is only too willing to consider him stupid. I cringe when I watch them in public. I know that boy's pride. I know how much it costs him."

"Are you trying to have me believe that there is no one waiting for him in Charleston? There's no girl? A man like him?"

"That's been the hardest on him, I'm afraid. At first, he made the mistake of bringing them home. Women find him attractive, I guess, but he didn't have a chance with Julian. If Kit showed interest in a particular girl, Julian would do his best to charm her. Compared to his wealthy and powerful brother, Kit would seem a poor prize. Of course, once he succeeded in making a fool of his brother, Julian lost interest in the girl."

"Every girl?" She was skeptical.

"You don't know Julian. This last one was the worst. Rachel Worthington. I never liked her much, myself, but I think Kit had plans of marrying her. Julian discovered this and stepped in. It was just about this time that Julian lost one card game too many and came up with the scheme of using Kit's ship as collateral. You can't know what it was like for the boy, with nothing to do, forced to go to party after party with those people, watching his girl on Julian's arm. When they announced their engagement, Kit took to drinking, a binge the likes you've never seen. It took weeks to dry him out. I was glad to go when he decided to leave for France. Most of the crew was there and I figured it would be good to be with his own kind for a change. That's when he concocted this ridiculous scheme and I couldn't talk him out of it. Said he had to have a ship. He never meant to hurt you, lass; he wasn't thinking of anything but his own hurt. And your grandfather made it all so easy."

"He used me, Sam."

"You forget I was there. You weren't marrying him out of love either. Has it all been so horrible? You're free of your grandfather, aren't you? Kit's a good man; you could've done worse."

In the days that followed Katy found herself thinking about their conversation. Now that she knew some of Kit's background, she would watch him covertly while he worked. Despite all that had happened, she wanted to offer him comfort to make up for all he had suffered. But she had seen at firsthand what interest he had in the comfort she could offer. Her softening heart would freeze back into place and the barrier between them would remain intact.

The captain wasn't as oblivious to her presence as she imagined. Under his orders, she was allowed free access to the deck, and he received daily reports about her. He, himself, would watch carefully, to ensure her safety. Often, he would listen while she was caught up in conversation with one of the men. In a lot of ways, he admired her. There were times, especially late at night, when he longed to go back in time to when she had trusted him, to see those soft, blue eyes looking innocently up at him, to be filled with the desire to do anything to protect her. But those same eyes were now frozen in hatred.

What kind of woman did he want her to be? This fiercely independent woman was what he needed at the moment, but in his heart he knew he wanted her to lean on him a bit more. As each day passed, though, he knew he was becoming less necessary, leaving him empty. It's just as well, he told himself sharply. It would certainly make it easier to leave her with Julian when they reached South Carolina.

Chapter 12

It took some time to locate the captain. He had been in the hold with Sam, inspecting the cargo. By the time they reached the deck, the British ship was bearing down on them. Katy, catching the mood of fear, grabbed at Sam's shirtsleeve. "What's wrong?"

"Good God, Katy. I forgot all about you. You'll have to be getting below, lass."

"I don't understand. They said it was a British ship."

"It's not just a ship; it's a man-of-war."

"What's the problem. Just raise the flag."

Sam laughed, without humor. "Every man on this ocean flies the Union Jack when he spies a man-of-war. It won't promise us immunity now. This ship isn't registered. We'll have some explaining to do if they try to board us, especially with those French guineas we're carrying in the hold."

Kit, ignoring Katy's presence, turned to Sam. "What do you think? Should we run?"

"It's too late for that now. If we'd spotted her an hour ago, maybe, but we've a full cargo while she's riding mighty high in the water. She'd overtake us, easy.

169

As it is, she'll be on us within the hour."

"What the hell is a man-of-war doing in French waters, Sam? I was a fool to relax. Is she heavily armed?"

"Sure looks it."

"Can you make out the name?"

"It's the *Olympus,* captained by Joshua Pitts."

"No, I heard something about a change of command while I was in London. It's a young man, now— a Cecil Lawrence. It's his first command. Maybe we can take advantage of that."

Katy's ear picked up. Cecil Lawrence? Why, he was one of Farley's proteges. She had met him a number of times on his visits to Whitney Hall. Not that she had ever been included in the meals or discussions, but she knew he had looked at her with unconcealed interest. So he was a captain, now? Because of Farley's patronage? With a start, she caught Kit's next words.

"We've got no choice, then. We'll have to stand and fight."

"Think carefully, boy. She'll blow us out of the water. You're forgetting we've a woman on board."

"Damn!"

"And what possible difference could I make?"

Apparently, from their expressions, they had forgotten she was there. Slowly, surprised was replaced with exasperation. "You were told to go below, lass."

"Not until you answer my question. Why do I make a difference?"

"I'm in total agreement with you, but Sam, here, would rather risk a prison sentence than risk your life in battle."

"That's absurd. But are you certain we have to fight?"

170

"At another time, perhaps, I can explain the intricacies of war with you, but at present, I have a lot on my mind. Sam, tell the men to prepare for a fight. We'll try to outmaneuver her but let's be ready for any contingency. Pete, come here a minute. I've got to talk to you about this."

Katy, her question still unanswered, stared after him as he moved away. Sam tried to follow but she had hold of his sleeve. "No, wait a minute, Sam. I have an idea."

"Katy, you heard the captain. I've got work to do."

"First tell me the truth: do we stand a chance if it comes to a fight?"

He looked her straight in the eye. "No."

"I thought as much. Then you've got to listen to me. I think I know how we can bluff our way out of this."

He regarded her suspiciously. It was against all rules of nature to be discussing strategy with a female. Yet, it was Katy, and for some reason, that made a difference. "What's on your mind?"

"We've got a few things on our side. One is the Warwick name; another is my grandfather's influence in the Admiralty."

"This is a war, lass, not some parlor game."

"I don't know about that. Granted, we're playing for high stakes, but it is a game. And I just so happen to be holding the trump card."

"Go on."

"You know how the British navy works. There are few men brave enough to risk the disapproval of an admiral, a powerful man like my grandfather. Especially one who has just acquired his rank."

"But Farley is retired."

"Perhaps, but he still has influence. You forget my trump card. I happen to know Cecil Lawrence and I'm willing to bet he received his command through my grandfather's efforts."

Sam gave a low whistle. "So what is your plan?"

Excited by his interest, she told him what had been formulating in her mind. "The way I see it, we have to make the first move. If we head in their direction, instead of running away, we'll catch them off guard. Especially if we fly a distress signal."

"A distress signal?"

"To keep them from blowing us out of the water. Then, just before we get too close, so they can't see too much, we drop anchor. And a boat."

Sam was suspicious again. "What for?"

"You said yourself it would be disastrous if they boarded us. We'll have to board her first. Take the initiative."

"We?"

He would have to focus on that word. Katy explained patiently. "It's too late to be protective of me now, Sam. Of course I'll be in that boat. It will stop them from firing on it. If I know a British captain at all, I know he's a gentleman, first, last, and always. Besides, I know Cecil Lawrence. If my plan is to work, I'll have to deal with him directly."

"What happens after we board her?"

"I'll demand to be taken to the captain. I have every reason to believe that he'll be sympathetic to my tale of woe."

"What tale of woe?"

Her eyes were glittering in secret amusement. "My poor, dear husband is too ill to continue the journey. If I don't get proper medication, he will in all likelihood die of this hideous disease, and then where would I be? Adrift in the ocean, alone, carrying the seed of death."

"Enough, enough. You'll have me crying. Katy, that's the most muddle-headed, cock-eyed, crazy scheme I've ever heard."

"Since our only alternative is certain death, I can't see how you can be so critical. If my plan doesn't work, we can always fight. Be reasonable; we've got nothing to lose by trying and I honestly believe I can pull it off."

"Supposing they still want to board?"

"With our contagious disease? I wouldn't dream of exposing Captain Lawrence to it. But if it becomes necessary, we'll let them. I think I can convince him not to disturb my poor husband who will, by the way, be tucked in bed with the French guineas." She glanced nervously at the approaching ship. "Sam, you know it's our only chance. We've got to at least try."

"Even if I agreed, Kit would never go along with it."

"So you are considering it? You've got to convince him. Let him think it's your idea. Make him see reason. Only we've got to hurry. Once she catches us, it will be too late."

"You win. I'll do what I can with the captain. But you stay out of sight. Do what you can to make yourself look more like an admiral's granddaughter."

She looked at her clothes and laughed. Impulsively, she hugged him. She could trust him to convince Kit. She ran below. With trembling fingers, she hurried into one of the dresses she had recently completed, grateful, now, for the shortage of buttons. In her excitement, she couldn't have handled any more. Managing as best she could with her hair, she hoped

173

Lawrence would see her as the worried wife who was too busy nursing her husband to spend much time on her toilette. Within ten minutes, she was ready to join the others. Her heart skipped a beat when she passed two sailors carrying a strongbox to Kit's cabin. He had accepted her plan. Now if only she could do her part. So many lives were at stake, she had to do it.

Heads close together like conspirators, Sam and Kit were deep in discussion when Katy reached them. Whatever resentment she might have felt at their adopting her plan as their own had to be suppressed. In the distance, the gap between the *Olympus* and themselves was rapidly diminishing. If she had any misgivings, now was the time to tell them. She remained silent. All too soon, Kit gave the order to drop anchor.

"You'd better get below, boy. If they were to spot you . . ."

"I'm not leaving this deck."

"If they board . . ."

"I thought it was her job to see that they didn't."

"Katy'll be doing her best, but anything could happen. We've got to be prepared. You're supposed to be a sick man. In bed."

"Now you listen to me, Sam. I'm still captain of this ship. I've gone along with this crazy scheme on your recommendation, but don't push me too far. I'll remain where I am until I see the boarding party and then it will be my decision, and mine alone, whether or not I choose to hide in my cabin."

"Don't be a fool."

He glared at her. "I'll thank you, madame, to mind your own business. Take care of your end and leave me to mine. Believe me, if there was anyone else to send, it would be you who was locked in her cabin."

"Thanks for the vote of confidence." Stung by his implication, she was unable to say what was on her mind. How could she wish him well, when he thought so little of her?

"I seem to remember a vow of revenge for robbing you of your virtue." He spoke so low that only Katy caught the words. She had forgotten that vow. It had been uttered in a moment of anger and she never supposed he would remember it, either. Could he believe her to be so vindictive?

Contrarily, she refused to deny it and hissed back at him. "When the time comes, Captain, I'll be happy to see you pay. In the meantime, trust me not to risk the lives of innocent men just to see that you receive your just reward."

Eyes locked, they glared at each other. Before either could have a change of heart, it was time to board the boat that was to take Katy to the *Olympus.* A wave of panic threatened to engulf her. If not for Sam's comforting presence, she wouldn't have been able to move her feet off the ship that had become her home. He handed her down into the small craft, then jumped in beside her and headed for the man-of-war.

As they approached the vessel, Katy was impressed. No matter what her loyalties of the moment, she had to admit, with a certain pride, that the British navy had the finest fleet in the world. The *Olympus* towered over them, glistening in the late afternoon sun. She rose out of the water like a magnificent beast in search of prey. There was, indeed, something of the predator in her sleek lines. At least twice as large as the *Sally Ann,* it was clear that she could devour them, if she so chose. Katy's plan was their only hope for survival. Sam was right; the *Olympus* was too heavily armed for a fair fight. As they boarded her, Katy realized that she was just as heavily manned. Taking a deep breath, she tried to clear her head of the rising hysteria. Remember your mission, she commanded herself. You are Katherine Farley Warwick, with all the power and influence of those two high-placed names.

Wasting no time, she asked to see the captain. To her relief, her name was recognized and she was led to his cabin immediately. Sam, close on her heels, was amazed by this new Katy. If he didn't know better, he too would be convinced she was the spoiled, arrogant granddaughter of the aristocracy that she pretended to be. As he watched Lawrence greet her, he saw the spark of interest in the man's eyes. If she played her cards right, this just might work.

Captain Lawrence, having just finished his tea, was feeling more than a little bored with his new position. When he had first taken the assignment, he had expected to see action. Instead, he was saddled with the dreary job of escorting merchant vessels across the Atlantic. It was with the greatest discontent that he was sailing to New York for the sole purpose of convoying one such vessel. He was ripe for diversion and Katherine Farley, here in the middle of nowhere, was a balm to his sore spirits.

"Miss Farley, what a pleasant surprise."

Face to face with the man, Katy was almost jolted out of her composure. At one time, she had considered Lawrence in the role of her rescuing prince, so tall and forceful had he seemed. But today, compared to Kit, he seemed less the hero and more the dandy. If there were any qualms about using him, they were dispelled by his soft hands which grasped at her own. When he placed a wet kiss on them, she had to squelch her shiver of annoyance. "Captain Lawrence, the pleasure is mine, as is the surprise. I had no idea you had achieved such an exalted position. And so fast, too. May I congratulate you. How comforting to learn the Admiralty recognizes quality when it sees it and makes the proper promotions."

He absolutely beamed. "Tell me, how is your grandfather?"

"You would know better than I. It's been months since I've been home."

"I regret that I, too, haven't been home recently. But what could bring you so far from England, Miss Farley?"

"I'm afraid it's no longer Miss Farley. I'm Katherine Warwick, now. My new husband and I were on our way to Charleston, South Carolina."

"Indeed?"

"There was a storm that blew us off course and now we seem to be lost." She crossed her fingers, hoping it didn't sound contrived.

He couldn't suspect anything. "Then that explains what you're doing in enemy waters."

To feign shock, she opened her eyes wide. "Enemy waters? Surely you must be mistaken." At the shake of his head, she forced a tear or two. "I knew we were hopelessly lost. Oh, haven't I been through enough?"

He leaned over to pat her hand. "There now, don't cry. Tell me, where is your husband through all this?"

Katy allowed a fresh crop of tears to slide down her cheeks. "Captain Lawrence, I'm at my wit's end. I don't know where to turn."

"Can I be of assistance?"

"I couldn't possibly impose on your friendship with Grandfather. If I had known this was your ship, I'd never have asked those colonials to flag you down. But I was so alone and so desperate."

"Let's not quibble about my friendship with the admiral; you obviously need my help. Never let it be said that a Lawrence failed to come to the aid of a woman in distress."

Katy winced. He was making it almost too easy for her. Men could be such fools sometimes. The courageous Cecil Lawrence was melting like butter in her hands, just because she cried a little and fluttered her eyelashes. If Sam had tried the same story, he would have been thrown off the ship. For the first time, she was happy to be a female. No man could resist the temptation of protecting a weak woman, especially one who was trying so valiantly to be brave. Heartlessly, she continued to use him. "Captain, you can't know how wonderful it is to find help. I was ready to give up when I saw your flag. I told those colonials that here was one of my grandfather's men. All I would need do is ask for help and I would receive it. But do you know? It was exceedingly difficult to convince that fool of a captain that his ship was safe."

"Why was that? Does he have anything to hide?"

She had gone too far, been too cocky about her abilities; she had underestimated the man. It was a shrewd question; she should have anticipated it. Now she had to talk her way out of a possible trap. "Hide? Certainly not. That ship belongs to my husband and I won't hesitate to tell you that the Warwick name is highly regarded in both the colonies and in England. No Warwick vessel would ever feel the need to hide from a British man-of-war."

Warwick? So she had married that fop. Lawrence had met Julian Warwick in London years ago and nothing he had seen in the obnoxious young man could explain why the pretty granddaughter of his sponsor would choose him for a husband. It must have to do with the name, well known to any commander who visited Charleston. A little less sympathetic now, he regarded her cautiously. "You haven't answered my question. Where is Mr. Warwick?"

Katy was sensitive to his change in tone. "Oh, Captain, I'm so afraid that he's very ill." She groped around for an imaginary handkerchief. "My goodness, you can never find a hankie when you need one." She punctuated it with a sniff.

Ever the gentleman, he handed her one of his own. Katy flashed a bright smile of gratitude at him as she daintily dabbed at her eyes and touched the end of her nose. "I must look a positive sight."

"You're no such thing. You're absolutely charming."

Now that she had him back where she wanted him, she continued. "Captain, you're so kind to me. I almost wish I could remain here on your ship where I know I'll be looked after, but my duty is with my poor husband. He's never been strong and the doctor warned him to be careful. But he insisted on seeing all the sights, especially at the docks, and now he's caught this dreadful disease."

"Come now, it can't be as bad as that, now can it?"

"If he doesn't recover, what shall I do? I'm all alone, in enemy waters you tell me, with no one but foreigners for company. And what if I catch the disease? I'm told few recover from smallpox."

There was an audible gasp. Slowly, all color drained

179

from his face. His fingers itched to touch his smooth skin, to make certain it was as unblemished as ever. Those dreadful marks! In his line of work, he had seen too many faces scarred by the disease—those who were fortunate enough to live through it. Good God, what had he gotten himself into? Katherine Farley or no, he could hardly wait to be rid of the girl.

Some of his depression escaped into his voice. "Mrs. Warwick." He faltered. "Mrs. Warwick, you are in luck. We have more than an adequate supply of medications on board. If you'll follow my aide, Lieutenant Perkins, he'll take you to the surgeon. I'd accompany you myself, but I'm sure you can understand that I am a very busy man. Let me wish you all the luck in the world for your husband's recovery and the successful completion of your journey."

Inwardly thankful that she hadn't needed to depend on Lawrence to rescue her from her grandfather, Katy rose to go. But unfortunately, this Lieutenant Perkins seemed to have a strong sense of duty. "I beg your pardon, Captain, but regulations require us to search their ship."

"Don't be absurd, Perkins. I can vouch for their loyalty. I know Mrs. Warwick, personally."

"I would not dare to impugn the lady's loyalty, sir, but it's not hers that is in question, after all."

"Yes, I see what you mean." Damn Perkins and his blasted interference. Not only had he made him appear the fool in front of these people, but he gave him no choice but to board that diseased ship. As he considered all the germs he would be exposing himself to, he shuddered. If he contracted the pox, he'd have Perkins court-martialed.

At the same time, Katy was fighting the urge to

stick out a foot to kick the self-righteous Perkins in the shins. No doubt he was displaying his superior knowledge of regulations to his young captain, but it could cost them their lives. Reluctantly, she addressed Lawrence. "By all means, search the vessel, if necessary. I quite understand your obligations." In the corner of her eyes, she could see the horror in Sam's expression. "All that I ask is that you don't disturb my poor husband unduly. You can conduct a search quietly, can you not?"

Lawrence felt the beginnings of a migraine. "Perkins, I am certain we can satisfy regulations with a two-man boarding party. Get me Simpson and Smithe. And that medicine."

"But Captain . . ."

"May I remind you that I am captain of this ship and I give the orders here. Get those men immediately!"

"Yes, sir!" Perkins gave a brief salute and stomped out of the room.

With Perkins gone, Katy's relief allowed her to feel some gratitude to Lawrence. "Captain, how can I ever thank you? As soon as I reach Charleston, I'm going to write to my grandfather. He'll be so pleased to learn of how you came to my rescue. And I'm certain the Warwicks won't soon forget, either. We'll see to it that you're properly rewarded."

Lawrence saw his first ray of hope. Perhaps something good would come of this yet. Next to his looks, his career meant a great deal to him. Katherine seemed to be transformed from the angel of death into an angel of mercy. It was little enough to do for her to ensure that her husband was not bothered. He gave orders to Smithe and Simpson to conduct the briefest of searches.

When the medicine arrived, he magnanimously offered to escort her to the deck, reasoning that in the open air, the fear of contagion would be less. After all, why quibble over a few germs when through this girl he held the possibility of seeing action? But when Katy tried to return his handkerchief, he drew the line on self-sacrifice. Looking at it as if it had sprouted two heads, he insisted she keep it as a reminder of the generosity of the British fleet.

Katy wanted to tell him what to do with his generosity, and his handkerchief, for that matter, but they were far from safe. Instead, she showered him with gratitude before descending to the small boat. Using the handkerchief, she waved to his diminishing form. So he was going to watch them from the deck. Had Perkins insisted upon that, too? Katy prayed silently that Kit would have the sense to go to his cabin. To the sound of the oars rhythmically splashing in the water, she began to prepare Smithe and Simpson for what they were about to face—the ship at sea, doomed to sickness and suffering, shadowed by the ordeal of her husband's disease. Sam's stern face warned her not to overdo it, but by the time the sailors reached the *Sally Ann,* they could hardly wait to leave. Their inspection, under Katy's supervision, was perhaps even briefer than Lawrence intended. Taking a chance, she led them to Kit's door. Both insisted they would rather not wake him and Katy gushed with gratitude. Bidding them good-bye, she told them she would go in now, to see what she could do with their wonderful medicines to save her husband's life. Filled with admiration for this courageous young woman, they nonetheless were anxious to put the maximum distance between her and themselves in the shortest time possible. As Katy slipped through the door, they ran topside and made a hasty departure. Sam, wisely deciding to be cautious, instructed the crew to carry on as normal. Lawrence, realizing the smaller ship would stay put, felt the sudden need to be in New York. On his orders, the *Olympus* hoisted sail and started in a northerly direction.

Meanwhile, Katy stood in Kit's cabin for the first time since that horrible night. Glancing around, she decided the room suited him, with its dark wood and masculine furnishings.

"Have they gone?"

She jumped. Up until now, she hadn't realized that Kit was in the room. As he popped out of the bed, she saw the money underneath him. "Not yet, but I think they believed us. They couldn't wait to get off the ship."

"I heard. Didn't you overdo it somewhat?"

"I'm new at this. All I had was you for an example."

"Need you bring that up every time we talk? And I never overplayed my role as Julian. It's a wonder they believed you."

"They did, and so did their captain. I wouldn't be at all surprised to learn that they're headed north by now."

"You actually enjoyed it, didn't you?"

He was right. She had enjoyed herself, once over the initial fright. But the fact that she had saved the ship hadn't escaped her notice, though it had certainly escaped his. "Yes, I did. It was pleasant to be among civilized men, for a change. No matter what you think about the British, our men know how to treat a lady."

There was a strange glint in his eye, sparkling in the

intense blue. "We Americans know how to treat our women. You see, we know what they really want."

From his look, she knew what treatment he had in mind and she backed away from him. Part of her welcomed what he had to offer, but the more rational part warned her to keep her distance. Instinctively, she knew this man had the power to hurt her like no other, if she gave him the opportunity. "Apparently, Captain Warwick, you don't know me very well."

His voice was soft, coaxing. "What's the matter, Katy. Can't you trust me?"

"Trust? How many times are you going to use those words on me? You must take me for a fool. I've tried to trust you, but you always make me regret it. No, Kit, I am not a fool."

Her words dangled between them. Having uttered them, Katy would have given her soul to take them back, struck by the hurt that registered on his tired face. Again, she had spoken in anger and given too much meaning to the words. Something turned upside-down in her mid-section.

Sam burst into the room. "They're gone, running with their tails between their legs. And all because of you, lassie."

Kit recovered quickly, once again the captain. "Are they out of sight?"

"Not yet, but they're making good speed, northward. We should lose them in an hour."

"They didn't suspect anything?"

"If I hadn't helped load those chests myself, your wife would have had me convinced all we were carrying was smallpox."

"Smallpox? Are you joking? Who picked smallpox? How am I supposed to explain that in Charleston?"

"I'm sorry if I picked an inconvenient disease. At the time, I was more concerned with saving the ship than worrying about what you would tell your friends. Don't worry, I have a feeling Cecil thought you were Julian anyway. He'll be so confused by this whole episode that a small matter such as which disease you recovered from will be beyond his consideration."

"Cecil?"

"Captain Lawrence. He was one of Grandfather's favorites."

"Now we've brought Farley into it. Didn't your Cecil get suspicious, knowing your relationship with Farley?"

"He's not my Cecil. And contrary to what you may believe, my grandfather didn't try to marry me off to everyone he met."

"Oh, I'm the only lucky one?"

"What's wrong with you two? We just beat a British man-of-war, without firing a single shot, and all you can do is fight? Why are you criticizing her? You should be on your knees thanking her."

"Thank you, Katy."

"I mean it, Kit. It was all her idea. She knew you wouldn't listen to her so we pretended it was mine. She was great. If you could've seen them falling all over themselves to do what she wanted. I wish you could've been there."

"So do I." He was studying her, speculation in the steely blue of his eyes. "And you're wrong. I do appreciate the effort. Will you accept my apology, Katy?"

What was he up to now? "Don't be silly. You have no reason to apologize and nothing to appreciate. I only did what anyone else on this ship would have done. I happened to know Captain Lawrence, that's all." She

185

yawned. "Excuse me. I seem to be worn out from the afternoon's activities. If you gentlemen will excuse me, I think I'll leave the rest of the war in your capable hands while I retire for the night."

Lifting her skirts, she swished out of the room. But before she reached the door, Kit grabbed her hand, his touch sending hot sparks through her body. "You're wrong, Katy, I have a great deal to thank you for. After all I've done to you, you alone saved my ship. I can't expect you to forgive me, but I want you to know that I consider myself in your debt and if there's any way to repay you, I'll do so willingly."

Oh, she wanted to believe him. His eyes were holding her, burning through the barrier, frightening her. "Then give me an annulment."

He flinched. "I thought I made it clear that it was impossible."

"Then it would seem there's nothing you can give me." Roughly, she pulled out of his grasp, knowing that if she didn't, she would surely drown in the deep blue of those eyes. With every ounce of dignity she could summon, she walked out of the room.

Kit watched her go, still holding out his hand. "Damn!" he muttered under his breath. He was a fool to keep trying. Spinning around, he remembered, with a start, that Sam was still in the room.

"Boy, how you manage to say the wrong thing every time is past comprehension."

"Stay out of it, Sam. Mind your own business."

"I am minding my own business. That girl is like a granddaughter to me. Somebody's gotta look out for her."

"I'd say she was more than qualified to take care of herself."

"Which proves you don't know the first thing about her."

"I do know she can't stand the sight of me. I just can't figure her out. She's so damned tough and independent, there doesn't seem to be any way to reach her. And yet, there's something in her eyes that invites me. When I reach out for her, she lashes out at me. There's no predicting what she'll do next."

"She's a woman."

"I've known plenty of women, but never one like her."

"All the more reason to hold onto her."

"And how do you propose I do that? Whenever I walk into a room, she makes any excuse to leave it."

"She's scared. She left England as a sheltered little girl and we've forced her into being a woman too early. This is a whole new life for her and it's gonna take a lot of gentleness and patience to unscare her. You've got to prove she can trust you."

Kit laughed, a dry, mirthless sound. "Trust? How do I teach her to trust me when I'm not sure I trust myself? I never meant to hurt her. I don't know what came over me that night."

"You did a stupid thing and it's gonna take time to undo it. You'll never accomplish anything hiding here in your cabin."

"I'm not hiding."

"Sure you are. Even Katy's noticed."

"She has?"

"She has. No wonder she's afraid you want to rape her. She never gets to see the other side of you."

"And which side is that? The traitor? The imposter? The pirate? Oh, she's seen enough to make up her mind."

187

"She hasn't seen the man who guides this ship and her crew. Take time to show her your ship. Her money bought it."

"She wouldn't be interested."

"You'd be surprised at how much she already knows. She doesn't waste her spare time; I've even let her take a turn at the wheel. But I'm sure she'd prefer to learn about her ship from her captain."

"Her ship?"

"She likes to think of it as half hers. What's the harm? I think she proved what a valuable asset she can be. Show her you care. Give a little of yourself."

"There's no time for that. We'll be reaching port soon. I have to concentrate on getting those supplies to Marion."

"Go on, make your excuses. Keep so busy with your work and forget about your wife. One day, boy, you're gonna wake up and find it's too late. You're gonna lose that girl and I'm telling you, victory ain't gonna amount to a hill of beans aside the loss of your wife. Believe me, I know. And that's all I've got to say."

With that, Sam, too, was out of the room, leaving Kit alone to brood in the darkness. As he carelessly tossed the darts, Sam's words echoed in his brain. Oh damn, how could he lose something he never had? It was too late from the beginning. Way back in England, when she had burst into Farley's study, fresh from her ride and exploding with indignation, he had cursed the fates that had forced him to deceive her. Sam was right; she was special. But little good it did him. Cecil. Huh! She had spoken of him with more affection than she had ever shown her husband. She probably would have been happier with Julian.

He moved to his desk. From the bottom drawer, he

grabbed a bottle of brandy. Maybe it wasn't his wife's warm body, but it was the only warmth he'd get for a long time. Not bothering with a glass, he held the bottle to his lips and took a long, healthy swallow. Yes, he'd always understood why poor old Harry drank so much. When you're lonely, there's no other choice.

Chapter 13

The following day, Katy was ordered to stay below. None too happy with the restriction, she was unable to maintain her standards in the galley. To her surprise, no one complained. Something was going on and she was to be kept in the dark. How typical! She could risk her neck on a British man-of-war but she still couldn't be trusted with their silly secrets. Let them play their stupid war games; she'd bake bread. It was going to be a tough loaf, judging by the way she was pounding at it.

As she was putting away the dinner dishes and the virtually untouched bread, Josh came to request her presence on the deck. The captain had finally gotten around to renaming the ship and he wanted all hands present for the announcement.

"Even me?"

"Sure, you're one of the crew, ain't you?"

She looked in dismay at her dirty trousers. "I can't possibly go up there like this. I need time to change. And to fix my hair."

"I could probably stall them for about twenty minutes. Is that enough time?"

She kissed his cheek. "Josh, you're really a friend."

The boy blushed. "Aw, go on, get out of here. You've only got twenty minutes, remember?"

She needed no reminder. Ripping off the apron, she was already pulling the pins out of her hair. Before Josh finished speaking, she was flying out of the room and down the corridor. Josh chuckled and went up to inform the captain that she would be there in twenty minutes.

Actually, it took twenty-five, but the extra time was worth it. When Katy stepped out on deck, she moved with confidence. She hadn't the finery of a London beauty, but she was a vision to the men. Kit's draperies had made an elegant gown, cut in simple, direct lines that complemented her figure and matched the blue of her eyes.

Sam let out a whistle as he moved forward to take her hand. "The captain's gonna have his hands full trying to keep the crew out of the galley from now on."

She smiled, enjoying every moment. "Don't worry, I still have my knife."

He threw back his head and laughed. "Katy, you look beautiful. Come, the others are waiting."

He led her to where the crew had assembled. The deck was cleared, except for a pair of chairs. Sam took her to one of them. Then Kit was at her side. His gaze of undisguised admiration nearly unnerved her.

Suddenly, he was standing on the other chair, ignoring her. Damn him, she thought. He all but makes love to me with a glance and then forgets I exist.

He started to speak. "Gentlemen, we are here tonight for a special reason, or should I say, a special person. I know you're planning a celebration afterward, to pay your own tribute, but if you'll bear with me for

191

a few minutes, I've got my own words to say." He reached down for a bottle of champagne. "I know the *Sally Ann* has already been christened, but with her new name, I figure she deserves another. And I'm sacrificing my best bottle for the purpose." Laughter broke out at the look of reluctance on his face. "I figure it's for a good cause. In honor of my beautiful wife, from this day on, the *Sally Ann* will be known as the *Irish Lass.*"

Stepping down, Kit handed the bottle to an astonished Katy. She could only stare, stupidly. His smile was genuine enough—but why was he doing this?

"You're supposed to take it and break it over the bow."

"I know. But why me?"

"For one thing, it's half your ship. For another, it's been named in your honor. But mainly, it's because tonight, you're a hero. You helped save our ship and our lives and we all want to thank you. Now hurry before I change my mind and give you claret."

Katy did as she was told and the bottle smashed in a thousand pieces. A cheer went up from the crew and she felt suddenly shy. Before long, she was besieged with gifts. Josh presented her with a cap with the words, Irish Lass, written across the top. Salty had carved a spoon for her, out of wood. Others had dug into their private supplies. Perfumes and trinkets, that were no doubt meant for wives and sweethearts, found their way onto the pile. Lastly, Kit approached her, smiling.

"I shouldn't have to give you anything, seeing as how you are wearing my drapes." He raised one eyebrow. "I must admit, though, they never looked that good on the walls." The men chuckled.

"You don't have to give me anything; no one does. This is all wonderful but I only did what anyone else would have done."

"No, Katy, most women would have hidden below until the worst was over. We admire you for your courage and for your sacrifice. It hasn't escaped our attention that you could easily have gone over to the *Olympus* and asked for refuge while they dealt with us. Knowing where your loyalty lies, there's not a one among us that would have blamed you. But you didn't and we're all alive today because of it. We're not only grateful, we're proud of you. Me included. That's why I want you to have this. I was going to wait until we reached Charleston, but I want you to have it now." He was holding out a bag, jingling with coins.

She stared at it in puzzlement. "I don't understand."

"It's what's left of your dowry; it's that extra bit I tricked out of your grandfather. I always planned it for you, as a settlement, especially if something should happen to me. In my line of work, I wouldn't be able to provide for you if anything went wrong. If you count it, you'll see there's some missing. I took the liberty of putting it away. As soon as we reach home, I'll buy a horse for you. I know I could never replace Midnight, and I wouldn't try, but I am known to be a good judge of horseflesh."

The tears were there again, straining at the back of her eyes. But she no longer cared if she made a fool of herself. It was such a thoughtful gesture that if she hadn't had an armful of gifts, she would have hugged him. Instead, she managed a feeble thank-you. Kit seemed to understand.

"Aw, Captain, now see what you've gone and done. You've got her crying and we wanted to have a celebration."

"I'm not crying." She sniffed. "And I'm more than ready for a party so don't go using me as an excuse not to have one."

"You heard the lady. Pete, where's that fiddle of yours? I think we need some music." Executing a deep bow, Kit addressed his wife. "Madame, may I have the pleasure of the first dance?"

Katy was caught off guard. He knew very well that she had never danced with a man before. Was he trying to embarrass her? To be held in his arms, in front of all these men, was a terrifying thought. About to plead exhaustion, she caught the challenge in his eye. Oh, so he thought he could tease her, did he? No colonial clod was going to get the best of Maureen Farley's daughter. Assuming her haughtiest tone, she spoke as she curtsied before him. "You are too kind, sir, to take your chances with such an inexperienced partner, but I would be honored to make an attempt."

Her mock humility was not lost on Kit and he smiled in appreciation.

"Good girl," he told her. His arms encircled her waist and he was sailing off with her. Katy, as unworldly as she was, knew that this was not a proper dance, nor was Kit supposed to hold her this closely, but she had to admit she enjoyed it. At first, it was difficult to coordinate her steps with his, feeling awkward with an audience that cheered them on, until Kit whispered in her ear to relax. Lost in the lively music of Pete's fiddle, it was as if she and Kit were the only people in the world. The touch, the smell, the very nearness of him excited her. There was no need for her

194

barrier now; in the rhythm of the dance, they belonged to each other.

All too soon, the music ended. Kit continued to hold her close and she felt a thrill as he stared down at her. Then someone tapped his shoulder, demanding the next dance with the lovely lady. With no choice but concession, Kit relinquished his hold and Katy whirled off with the sailor. Kit moved over to the rail to watch. He was scowling when Sam approached him.

"Good idea, Kit, to start off the dancing. These men haven't had an opportunity like this in a long time. Mighty generous of you to share your wife."

"Did I have any choice?"

"Don't be such a poor sport. Look at them, especially Katy. This is her party, her first, in fact. Don't spoil it for her. One look at your long face and the party will break up."

"Am I that obvious?"

"You are to me."

Kit faced the sea. "Is that better? Now nobody has to see me."

"What's the matter with you, son?"

"I guess I'm tired of sharing her with the crew. While we were dancing, I could have sworn she was mine, all mine. If Hutchins had played a little longer, or if I could have had another dance . . . Ah, what's the use."

"I've never known you to give up so easily."

"What would you have me do? There's not much time before we reach port and I was counting on tonight. By the time she's danced with everyone else, she'll be too tired for me."

"Do you have to dance? Why not try a little conversation?"

"Because every time we talk she turns on me like a wild she-cat."

"Did you ever stop to think why? You've got a lot to learn about how to treat women, boy."

"I have *no* trouble handling women!"

"Katy isn't that kind of woman. She's a lady. She deserves special treatment."

"I've told you before, Sam. I'm a busy man. I don't have time to be strutting around like a dandy, putting on airs."

"It's up to you, of course, but personally, I think that girl's worth a minute or two of putting on airs, as you say. She's seen you at your worst; it wouldn't kill you to show her you know your manners."

"Dammit, Sam. Don't I have enough with Julian, always telling me to mind my manners, without having to hear it from you? I spend most of my time in polite society and their hypocrisy bores me to death. If that's what Katy wants, then I'm sorry; she asks for more than I can give."

"Calm down, boy. No one is asking you to make a fool out of yourself. You can be polite and charming, if you want, without any effort at all. I've seen you with Colonel Marion and Miss Videaux; you don't have any trouble being a gentleman with her. So why should it be so hard with your own wife? Who knows? She may have less use for hypocrisy than you. But it's only fair you give her a choice. So far, all she knows is that you can imitate your brother to perfection and that you can act like an animal."

Kit had the good grace to color, but his voice betrayed his annoyance. "Exactly what do you expect me to do? Kneel at her feet and beg forgiveness?"

"Don't get so riled up. Why can't you just think of her as a new girl that attracts your attention? Court her as if you've just met."

"Things have gone too far for that, Sam. She'd never believe I was sincere. She'd be suspicious, thinking I had an ulterior motive."

"Why are you always arguing with me? You're giving me excuses; I'm giving you good advice. A woman likes to be treated special, as if nothing's too good for her. Spoil her for just one night. It's not gonna kill you."

"I don't know."

"Go on, boy. Go get your wife."

With a shove in the back, Sam propelled him in the direction of Katy. She was standing in a crowd of men, laughing. For a moment, Kit held back, feeling strangely shy. Katy looked up then, and her look renewed his confidence. "Excuse us, men, but I believe Mrs. Warwick needs a rest. Perhaps after she's had time to catch her breath, you can continue dancing." He turned to Katy. "If you let them, they'll dance all night. They seem to forget there's only one of you."

Katy was panting, finding it difficult to breathe. The draperies made a beautiful gown, but it was a heavy one. Perspiration was collecting on her neck and back, and little beads were forming on her forehead. Thoroughly embarrassed, she tried to search for the handkerchief Cecil had given her, as inconspicuously as possible.

"Here, use mine. It's exceedingly warm, tonight, isn't it?"

Katy had to accept it, though she felt an utter fool. This new Kit made her uncomfortable. She was all too conscious of her appearance, with the perspiration

197

dripping down on her new dress. What must he think, he who had known so many sophisticated women? "I think I'd better go to my cabin to freshen up a bit."

"I don't think that's such a good idea. The minute the men see you go, they'll blame me and I'll have mutiny on my hands. I have a better plan. I have a second bottle of that champagne. We could sit for a while and share it. In this fresh air, you'll feel more like yourself in no time."

"I don't think . . . I mean . . . I . . ." Oh no, she was stammering.

"I would be honored."

For some reason, the situation struck her as being suddenly comic. It was too silly that she and Kit, of all people, should be standing here, nervous, acting as if they were meeting for the first time. After all they had been through together, why should she feel flustered just because she was sweating? She couldn't help it. It made her laugh.

Kit, ignorant of what he could have done this time, looked at her questioningly. "Did I say something funny?"

That made her laugh harder. His features darkened and she tried to sober up. Taking a deep breath, she struggled to control the spurts that threatened to bubble out of her mouth. But her body was shaking and she was unable to keep the amusement out of her eyes. "I'm sorry, Kit. Really I am. Please don't be angry with me. I wasn't laughing at you at all. It was myself that struck me as being so funny. There you were, treating me like I was a girl at her coming-out party, and all I could think of was a way to wipe the perspiration off my face without you noticing. I felt so young and silly. It was your handkerchief that finally set me off. Remember when you proposed to me and you took out that handkerchief to wipe off the bench? You put it back in your pocket. That filthy thing in that immaculate jacket. It was funny then, but knowing you now, it's even more laughable."

To her relief, he was grinning. "I guess my true character showed."

"Mine, too."

"It's clean now, though."

That set her giggling again. It was contagious and Kit was laughing with her. Taking the handkerchief from her hand, he mopped off her forehead. "There now, you don't have to worry about your perspiration and I can act more like myself."

"Not quite. My back is still wet."

"You don't do things halfway, do you? Well, lift up your hair and I'll see what I can do."

"I'm not sure that's proper."

"Out at sea, the captain determines what is and is not proper. As I am conveniently the captain, I suggest we get you dried off before you attempt another round of dancing."

Giddy with the excitement of the evening, she obediently lifted her hair. Gently, he dabbed at her bare back. The temptation to kiss the base of her neck was strong, but he restrained the impulse and concentrated on the job at hand. Spinning her around to face him, he gave her a boyish grin. "We are left with only one problem."

"And what is that?"

"Please tell me what to do with this handkerchief?" The article in question hung limply in his hand, starting Katy on a fresh set of giggles. "I hope you don't expect me to put it in my pocket."

"Do you have another?"

"You see? I'm not a gentleman, after all. A real one would have been prepared for any emergency. A second handkerchief. I'll have to remember that one."

"Why don't we hang that one up to dry? If I'm to do another round of dances, I'll need to be wiped off again."

"Will I have that honor?"

She blushed. "It's your handkerchief and you're the captain."

"Quite so. I tell you what. You can go back to your dancing and when you've had enough, give me a signal. I'll be waiting with my trusted handkerchief and a bottle of champagne."

"That sounds good. What's the signal?"

"I liked the way you winked at me when we were getting ready to leave your grandfather. Can you do it again?"

"Like this?"

"Perfect." He gestured at the crew who were watching from a discreet distance. "I think your friends are waiting."

Katy blushed, only just now remembering the others. But tonight it didn't matter what anyone else thought, herself included. Kit was everything she had ever dreamed of him being and she was going to hold onto every minute of it. Smiling, she glided off to join the others.

Kit, true to his word, hurried off to find the champagne. He gave an order to Josh to bring up some of his private stock for the others. Might as well make it a real party. Whistling, he rushed back up to the deck with the bottle and two glasses. He stood at the rail, waiting for Katy's signal, and watching her dance.

She was glowing. Kit couldn't remember when she had looked so alive, so happy, except maybe that night when they had run down the hill like children. Something warm stirred within him at the memory of her shining eyes, inviting him to kiss her. How he had longed to, but respect for her innocence had stopped him in time. He was just going to have to learn to ignore that look in her eyes; at least until she knew what she was saying with them.

As she danced, Katy's thoughts were all of him. Was she really going to let him seduce her? She knew enough, now, to recognize that look. Was it enough to know that he only wanted her body? Was it worth sacrificing her pride to hold him in her arms, to feel his warm body next to her own? If she wanted, she could neglect to give him the signal and he would leave her alone for the rest of the trip. Yet she was no longer sure that was what she wanted. Glancing recklessly in his direction, she saw him lounging on the rail. The sight of him made her feel warm all over. When he smiled and waved his handkerchief, she realized there had never been any choice. Laughing, she winked.

Trying his best not to appear overanxious, Kit sauntered over to her. He tapped her partner on the shoulder. "Excuse me, Abe, but poor Pete is about to quit. I'm sure you'll understand if I dance the last dance with my wife?"

Abe smiled, knowingly. He handed Katy to Kit, who danced off with her. Breathlessly, Katy struggled to keep up with him. "Wait a minute, Captain Warwick. I thought you were rescuing me. I can't possibly keep this up."

Kit slowed the pace. "Sorry. I guess I wasn't thinking. Pete, don't you know anything slower?"

"Sure thing, Captain." He was a genius with the instrument. He played softly, a sweet, haunting sound, the music of the gypsies. They were barely moving now, but like her husband, Katy hated to have the moment end. When Pete reached the last chords, he asked if they wanted him to keep playing.

"No, thanks, Pete. It'll be dark soon and you deserve a rest. Josh has some of my whiskey. Why don't you join the others?"

Katy echoed his thanks and followed him over to the chairs. When she tried to sit, Kit held her back. "This time, Madame, I am more than prepared. I've brought an extra handkerchief for your fevered brow and I will use the original to dust off your chair."

Katy giggled while he busied himself with the motions of dusting. Keeping a straight face, he changed cloths and mopped her forehead and back. Only after both jobs were finished did he allow her to sit. Then carefully, he filled the glasses with champagne, handing one of them to Katy. "Mrs. Warwick, may I propose a toast to the prettiest cook I ever had serve under me?"

"Only if I can propose one to the prettiest gentleman I ever had propose to me."

"Flattery will get you nowhere."

"I'm sorry, Kit. I'm in a mood tonight. How about toasting to the successful completion of this war?"

"Ah yes, I can drink to that." He raised his glass and touched it to hers, keeping his eyes on her as he drank. "But it would seem we must have a different opinion as to what constitutes a successful completion."

Flustered by the close scrutiny, she groped for the right thing to say. "I don't know if they're all that different, actually. I would like to see the seas safe for travel and both countries free of this bitterness. Which side wins isn't that important to me."

"It is to me. There can be only one outcome—an American victory. We won't give up, you know, until we have our freedom."

His vehemence startled her. "Freedom? Can you justify the loss of homes and lives for such an abstract concept?"

He studied her. "You're right, in a way. I'm sure freedom means something quite different to each one of us. As a whole, I guess it's more a matter of pride. A man has to be able to live with himself. We are not being governed by your Parliament; we are being used. The government continues to impose stricter regulations and stiffer controls and all so we can pay for their war with the French. How long can a man maintain his pride and dignity if he is continually pushed into a wall. Eventually, his back will be against that wall and he must either fall in defeat, or stand and fight. We have chosen to fight. Having made that commitment, we will continue to fight until we win or until we are destroyed."

"But you are Englishmen."

"Tell that to Parliament. They like to overlook the fact. Besides, we have virtually governed ourselves for over a hundred years and we've done a good job of it, too. Once you've tasted freedom, it's not likely you'll give it up. We won't. Certainly not to be treated like naughty children sent to bed without their suppers. Can you blame us for resenting their highhanded treatment? How can they presume to govern us, to know what is best for us, when most of them have never stepped foot on American soil? We know;

203

we've worked and sweated over that land for over a century."

He had been gesturing with his hands but he suddenly dropped them to his sides. "Sorry, I didn't mean to sound so fierce. But this is important to me. I want you to understand why I lie and cheat and steal. If there was any chance of a fair fight, believe me, I'd take it. Unfortunately, however, England has the resources to crush us. All we have is cunning. And spirit."

Katy was quiet for a time. "You said before that everyone had their own idea of what freedom meant. What is yours?"

He took a deep breath and let it out slowly. "It's not easy to put into words. I've never had the knack of finding the right ones." He reached for her hand. "Come over to the rail with me a moment. I want you to look at the sun."

Bewildered, she followed his pointing finger to where the sun was setting on the horizon. The sea had taken on the hue of the sky, reflecting its fading light, melting and fusing until it was hard to determine the line separating them. Sliding over the waves, moving closer and yet, never close enough, the *Irish Lass* seemed to be paying homage to the grandeur of the spectacle. It was so beautiful, so peaceful, that Katy sighed.

Kit had been reading her face. "By your expression, I can see that you sense what I'm trying to tell you. There's something about all that beauty, so intense, and yet, so available to everyone. It inspires even the most hardened of us to imitate it, to be just a little better than we are, to begin again, if necessary, to make something of ourselves. I suppose life is full of such moments; the song of the morning bird, a rainbow, the birth of a child, but for me it is the setting sun. It reminds me of a promise I once made." He leaned over the rail, watching the waves.

"I was with my mother right before she died. She was so weak she could hardly talk but she had something to say to me before she could die in peace. She kept saying, over and over, that I must protect my birthright. I tried to tell her that it wasn't mine, it was Julian's, but she wouldn't listen. As long as my name was Warwick, she told me, it was my duty to ensure the continuation of the family's heritage. I promised, so she could die in peace, but it took me years before I understood what she had been trying to tell me. Do you know, I can still remember the sky that evening. It was so vivid, so awesome." He was silent, lost in the past. Katy was content to study his profile, pleased by the angular lines of his face.

Coming out of his trance, he glanced over at her. "Sorry, I've been rambling. I warned you I'm not very good with words."

"You're doing splendidly. Tell me more."

He smiled. "I guess you could say it's more like a dream I have. Over a hundred years ago, my ancestors came from Britian. Warwicks have always had money, but not an ounce of noble blood flowed in our veins. In the days of the Carolina Commonwealth, it was a handicap. But they had a dream, shared with the countless others that made the journey with them, that with a little hard work and maybe a touch of luck, they would be able to carve out an empire for themselves and for the generations to follow. They worked, they suffered, and with dogged determination, they succeeded. My brother and I received the bounty of that success, but with it went a responsibility. The Warwick line doesn't end with us. At least it shouldn't. There must be future generations so we can pass the legacy down to them. Every furture Warwick is entitled to the advantages we have had. Do you see, now, why I am so resentful of my brother's gambling? I tried to keep the plantation going; I did the best I could. But failing that, I went to work for the purpose of passing down a more important legacy. Freedom. There's that word again. Oh Katy, I wish you could know what it's like in America; the vastness of it, the overwhelming possibilities. Imagine it. A brand-new country, wide open with opportunity, with a future that has its roots in its own soil. I will do whatever it takes to achieve its freedom so I can have something of my own to pass on to my descendants. Then, when I'm too old and tired to fight any more, I can look up at the sun with contentment, knowing I've done the best I could'"

Katy was moved by his quiet words. He had given her a glimpse of the real Kit, his inner strength, his buried emotions. His was a dream she could under-stand and share. For the first time in their relation-ship, Katy felt respect for this man who was her husband. The attraction she had always felt had deeper roots now. There was no longer any denying that she loved him; her body ached with it. Watching him, she felt the emotion overpower her. Hatless as al-ways, Kit's fair hair caught the fading light. Golden strands, bleached by long days in the sun, rippled like waves in the evening breeze. She longed to touch it, to touch every part of him. To hold him now, to make love to him, would have meaning and fulfillment.

Kit spoke and Katy was startled out of her

thoughts. His voice was low and husky, causing her to catch her breath. "I've been so busy with myself tonight that I haven't taken very good care of you. Here I am, rambling on, keeping you out in the chilly night air. Sam will have my head."

"I'm not cold."

"I saw you shiver. Come, give me your hand and I'll take you to your cabin."

Short of telling him how badly she wanted him, Katy could think of no way to explain her trembling. So she took his outstretched hand and followed meekly. It was painful to be so close. Somehow, he would have to know she wanted him to stay with her tonight, for every night for the rest of their lives. Wasn't it obvious? But when they reached her door, he merely kissed her lightly on the lips and whispered, "Sweet dreams, Katy."

She prayed for the courage to grab for his retreating arm but it never came. Too young and artless to know the way to keep him, she could do nothing. Helplessly, she watched him saunter away, never once looking back. With a heavy sigh, she let herself into her room. She could have wept with disappointment. Listlessly, she removed the dress, folded it, and carefully put it away. She didn't need it; he found her no more enticing in that gown than he did in the trousers. As a woman, she didn't exist for him. He had only been nice to her because he felt he owed her something and his stiff pride wouldn't allow that.

She jumped into bed but sleep was as far away as her husband. Tossing and turning, she tried everything she could think of to quiet the stirrings of her body. Each time she closed her eyes, the vision of him standing at the rail came back to taunt her.

At the same time, Kit was having similar problems. Damn those eyes of hers. He was positive they had invited him with a desire to match his own, but he had already made the mistake of paying more attention to them than the rest of her, and with disastrous results. It had taken all his concentration to ignore the urgings of his senses. It had nearly broken him to leave her with only a kiss, yet he knew he would never have stopped if he had attempted anything more. No, he wasn't going to take chances. Tonight had been the beginning of an understanding between them and he wasn't about to let his lust destroy it. He would wait until she was ready for him. Then he'd show her how wonderful it could be.

What was he going to do in the meantime? The memory of her soft body, pressed closely to his own, was torturing him. Twice already, he had almost allowed his senses to trick him into going to her room but rationality had returned in time. Sam had said to go slowly and he was going to do this thing right if it killed him. And the way he felt tonight, it just might.

It was stupid to sit around moping. What he needed to do was get so drunk that he'd kill whatever lust lurked within him. With enough whiskey, he could blot her image out of his mind. Hopefully, there was enough whiskey left on the ship. Good old Sam would help; always there to watch out for him, to see that he didn't do anything he might regret in the morning, and to put him to bed when he could no longer stand by himself. Gratefully, he set out to find him.

Katy, still unable to sleep, heard them both some hours later. Kit was right; noise certainly carried aboard ship. Their loud shouts could be heard miles away. Worried that something might be wrong, she dressed and ventured out into the hall. The disturbance seemed to originate in Kit's cabin. Were they quareling? With an overactive sense of guilt, she hurried down the hall. When she heard a crash, the tinkle of glass, and then a low moan, she barged in on them without thinking.

The scene that met her eyes was far from the one she had been imagining. Both men were kneeling over a broken bottle on the floor. Brown liquid was seeping through the floorboards as they frantically tried to save it.

"What on earth are you two doing?"

They looked like two little boys caught in the act of mischief. Their eyes were glazed, and Kit was having noticeable difficulty in maintaining his balance. He grinned sheepishly. In spite of herself, Katy had to laugh. "You're dead drunk, the two of you. Here I am, expecting catastrophe from the noise you were making and I find you in this condition."

Kit made a feeble attempt at dignity. "But you're wrong, my dear. It is a catastrophe. This was our last bottle of whiskey and now it's gone."

"And whose fault is that? If you hadn't been so damned stubborn, it never would have happened. But now, you had to prove you were sober enough to carry it on your head. Now what are we going to do?"

"You know I can do that trick with my eyes closed."

"All I know, boy, is that the only time you try to do that trick is when you're too damned drunk to know better. You never seem to remember in the morning how many bottles you break."

Katy left them arguing. She had remembered something in the galley and hurried to find it. When she returned, they were still kneeling on the floor, but the belligerence was gone. They looked lost.

"It's not exactly vintage stuff, but I found this bottle in the galley and I thought, under the circumstances, you might be able to adjust your tastebuds accordingly."

Kit's face brightened. "Hell, we haven't got any tastebuds left. Katy, my love, you're an angel of mercy. Sam, make a note of that. That's twice, now, she's saved our lives."

Sam was grinning too. "I always said you were a girl after my own heart. That's some wife you've got yourself, boy. We wake her in the middle of the night with our brawling and instead of giving us the scolding we deserve, she fetches us another bottle. I say, the least we can do is drink the stuff after she went to all that trouble."

Licking their lips, they took the bottle to the table, leaving Katy standing at the door. After Kit filled two glasses, he seemed to realize he had forgotten something. In an attempt to remember, he surveyed the room. When his bloodshot eyes came to rest on his wife, they seemed to come to life. "Whadda ya say, Katy. Wanna join us?"

It was her turn to brighten. She stepped forward as Sam blurted out. "Don't be ridiculous, boy. Ladies don't drink whiskey."

"This one does. Pour one for me." She pulled a chair up to the table, excited and happy to be included. Kit poured another glass, slopping whiskey over the sides. The men raised their glasses and she followed their lead. Kit belted his down in one shot. Sam did the same. With dismay, she saw their eyes turn to her. She had planned to sip it slowly. But if she was to continue playing the hero, she would have to toss it down or lose face. With the air of a condemned man heading to the gallows, she drew a deep breath and raised the glass to her lips. One, two, three; she poured it down her throat. For a moment, she was paralyzed. When feeling returned, she had to struggle not to make a fool of herself. Her throat was on fire and the urge to choke was overwhelming. It was some time before she could breathe. She steeled her body with fierce concentration. All the men saw was one little tear that she had been unable to control. Not trusting herself to speak yet, she smiled at them both and brought the glass down to the table with a bang.

They stared at her in astonishment. Sam found his voice first. "Damn, Kit! Did you see that?"

"I'm not sure. I don't think it's possible. Katy, you never cease to amaze me."

A warm glow was spreading through her body. Whatever its origin, his words or the whiskey, didn't much matter. It was enough that she was here, with her two favorite men, basking in their approval and acceptance. She held out her glass. "I'll have another, please."

"Hey now, young lady. You go slowly. This stuff can be dangerous if you're not careful."

"Practice what you preach, Sam Culligan. Besides, it's my bottle."

"She's got you there, Sam." Kit filled the glass. "I doubt she'll feel any worse than we will in the morning."

Katy smiled at him gratefully. She had already proved herself; she would sip this one. The taste was quite pleasant, actually, once you got used to it. Too bad it wasn't considered proper for ladies to drink it.

Kit and Sam were arguing again; this time over the

propriety of permitting her to drink the whiskey. Katy
watched them silently while she poured herself a third
drink. This stuff was good. By now, she was feeling a
little light-headed, but it was a remarkably delightful
sensation. Then, from somewhere in her throat
popped a hiccup, and then another, and another. Sam
pointed to her. "See there, you've gone and gotten her
drunk. You should be ashamed of yourself."

"Nonsense, Sam," she squeezed in between hiccups.
"Nobody got me drunk. I'm as sober as a babe. Want
me to prove it?" She lifted the bottle and balanced it
on her head.

Kit threw back his head and laughed. Katy joined
him. Sam, alone, found nothing funny. Exasperated,
he left the table. "I wash my hands of the two of you.
Take care of yourselves tonight. Sam Culligan is going
to bed."

True to his word, he quit the room. Katy stared
after him, hiccups all but forgotten. Suddenly, she was
left alone with her husband, in his bedroom. The glow
was replaced by intense heat. In spite of the slug-
gishnes of her brain, the rest of her body quickened its
pace. Shyly, she turned to look at him. "I guess Sam is
mad at us."

He mumbled some sort of answer. Katy was unable
to make out what it was because his head was resting
on his arms on the table. As she moved over to investigate, she could see he was sleeping. Sleeping? Was he
that disinterested? Here she was, ready for the taking, and he couldn't bother to stay awake!

Her first thought, in her frustration, was to leave
him there. It would serve him right if he fell on the
floor. But he called out in his sleep and when she heard
her name, something melted in her heart. She could

212

never sleep, herself, unless she managed to get him into bed. Swallowing that useless commodity, her pride, she whispered in his ear. "Kit, we've got to get you into bed. Sam has gone so it's only you and I. I'll do what I can, but I'll need your help. Here, I'm going to slip your arm over my shoulder so you can lean on me. I can steer you to the bed but you'll have to get up from the chair first. Do you hear me? I said I need your help. Kit?"

Still, he didn't respond, so she tried to move him by her own efforts. Something must have registered in his brain, finally. He stirred and tried to stand. The sudden motion took Katy totally by surprise; it proved to be too much. They toppled on the floor, with Katy on top. The entire situation was ridiculous and with more than an ample supply of whiskey inside her, Katy's giggles became even more uncontrollable than her hiccups.

Kit's hazy eyes stared at her. "You're beautiful when you laugh. I wish I could always make you laugh."

That stopped the giggles. Was she dreaming? Kit's gaze grew in intensity, penetrating deep into her. His voice was husky and she had to strain to catch the words. "I can't help it, Katy. I love you."

It was inevitable that he should pull her to him. Heart thundering, Katy could no more refuse him than she could make her silly heart stop beating. His kiss was slow and tender, and she was melting into him. She was his—mind, body, and soul.

Responding, she returned kiss for kiss, touch for touch, marveling in the joy of it. As always, their bodies moved to an identical rhythm, as if learned in a prior time, a prior life. The symmetry was broken only

213

by the fumbling with buttons and laces until at last their bodies were naked and free.

Kit eased her over and rolled on top of her. She held him tightly. In the back of her mind was the fear that he would reject her at the last minute, and that she couldn't bear. She became the aggressor, giving him no opportunity to reconsider. Her tongue was like fire, darting here and there, with a will of its own, teasing, burning. Kit groaned and repeated her name, over and over.

Then he was inside her and they moved with the same fluid grace as before. Gasping, Katy clung to him; she couldn't seem to get close enough. Tension was building, building, and her body seemed to be spiraling upward. I love him, she kept saying to herself, oh, God, how I love him!

It was a heady, giddy, almost dizzy sensation that carried her back down to earth. So this was love; it had been well worth the wait. She held onto him, afraid to loosen her grip, afraid to have reality come sneaking back. He's mine, she repeated; he's mine. In the peaceful silence, she held him tenderly, possessively, her love for him like a steady companion. It was part of her now, as vital as her heart or brain, as important as the blood that coursed through her veins. She loved him, and that, more than anything else, was her reason for living.

But even love could not compensate for the smothering feeling his weight soon became. What was he thinking? No doubt she had shocked him with the easy conquest. Loosening her grip, she felt suddenly bashful. She opened her eyes to look at him.

He was asleep. Dear Lord in heaven, how could he be asleep? She had given all she had to give; couldn't he stay awake long enough to thank her? Disillusioned and heartsick, she slipped out from under him. While she was dressing, Kit moved and reached out for her. Softening, she took his hand. He seemed so helpless; how could she leave him to freeze on the floor? There was no use in denying it mattered what happened to him. Like him with his war, she had made her commitment and she would see it through to the end. That it was hopeless didn't make the least difference. She pushed the hair out of his eyes. Ah, those eyes! If only, when she faced him in the morning, they would shine with the same love and desire she had seen tonight. Sighing, she pulled a blanket off the bed and covered his shivering body. Tucking the edges in, she fought the urge to stay with him. Diminished as it was, her pride would not let her be found as an unwelcome guest in the morning. Feeling tired, and so much older than her eighteen years, she left him on the floor to go to a room that more than ever seemed her prison.

Chapter 14

In the early hours of the morning, when Katy wrenched her head from the pillow, she was certain that she was going to die. Too late, she realized why it was that ladies didn't drink whiskey. Kit had said they would feel bad in the morning, but, oh lord, *this* bad? There was a lump lodged in her throat, gravitating between the base of her tongue and her stomach, undecided as yet which direction to take. Not since the night of the storm had she felt so ill, and that had been merely a prelude. She swore she would never drink again. For it was the memory of her behavior last night that made her feel the worst. What had come over her? She had all but raped him! How was she going to face him today? Oh, she still loved him, more than ever, but she was sick at the thought of that knowing smile, the smug grin. Would he make light of it? But, a little voice told her, he said he loved you. Common sense argued back that he was more than a little drunk at the time. So was she, for that matter. It was entirely possible that she had heard what she wanted to hear. But he said you were beautiful; you didn't imagine that. And how many girls have heard

216

that before they were seduced? But he didn't seduce you; it was the other way around. Well, all the more reason to doubt him. Be sensible, for once. Where's your pride? Who cares about pride; that one night was worth all the pride in the world. And what about this morning? Does it still feel so wonderful to know he didn't bother to stay awake to kiss you good night?

So it went until she thought she would scream. What was the sense in arguing with herself; she had to see Kit. She would know when she saw him how she felt. All she needed to do is watch his eyes. If they were closed to her, she would know the worst. Teasing she could handle and maybe give back, but if he avoided her eyes, she would be forced to listen to her common sense. But until that time, she preferred the little voice.

The men would be wanting their breakfast. That, and the hope of seeing Kit got Katy up and dressed. Her head still ached but she was determined to make the best of things.

Although she waited a full hour after the last man had left, Katy was compelled to consider the possibility that Kit wasn't going to arrive for breakfast. Should she wait longer? Go up and find him, the little voice nagged. Pride or not, she had to see him.

He was up on deck and judging from his tone of voice, not in the best of moods. He looked awful. If not for a feeling of dread, she would have pitied him. He looked worse than she felt. At the last minute, she decided that she didn't want to see him after all, but it was too late; he had already spotted her. "What do you want?"

She stiffened. "I'm sorry, I didn't realize you were so busy. I can come back later."

"I'm always busy. Now's as good a time as any. What is it?"

He stood above her, looking down, making her feel awkward and foolish. This was the other Kit, not the one she had held and loved last night. She searched for something sensible to say. "I only wanted to see how you felt this morning. You didn't look well when I left you last night."

Kit stepped down from the platform, looking puzzled. "What do you mean? What happened last night?"

She couldn't help it; she blushed. "You don't remember?"

Kit looked horrified by now. "Did I do anything I should regret?" He rubbed the back of his hand across his face. "But Sam was there. He always makes sure I behave myself."

"Sam left. He was angry. You really don't remember, do you?"

"I remember you bringing the bottle from the galley, and then you slugged it down, but it gets hazy after that. Sam left, you say? I don't remember anything else. Should I?"

It was worse than she thought. Bad enough to have forgotten it all, but was it necessary to look so horrified? Cursing that little voice, she put him out of his misery. In as casual a tone as possible, she called a halt to the foolish dreams she had been spinning. "No, of course not. You fell asleep. I tried to get you into bed but you fell on the floor and I couldn't get you up so I grabbed a blanket and covered you up." Oh no, she said that too fast.

"Then who undressed me?"

She had forgotten that. She squeaked, "I did."

"You?" It was his turn to color.

"I wanted to make you comfortable. It's what Sam would have done."

Kit was embarrassed. Damn, why couldn't he remember? She was acting strangely; could he have done something to upset her? But no, she'd be locked up in her room or at the very least, avoiding him. If only his head wasn't so foggy. How could he concentrate on what she was saying? Something of the pain he was experiencing showed in his expression. "Thank you. I was fairly useless last night. Please accept my apologies; it won't happen again."

Was he going to say that every time they made love? "No apologies are necessary." She glanced around, anxious to be anywhere else. "As long as you're all right, I guess I'll leave now. I, uh, have some work to do in the galley and I can see you have work of your own. Maybe I'll see you later."

Knowing he mustn't see the tears that had been threatening all morning, Katy ran to the stairs. She heard him call out but pretended otherwise. Bewildered, Kit watched her disappear down the stairs. Now what was wrong? Oh damn; he'd have to deal with it later. The pounding in his head kept him from doing anything more than the work at hand.

Still, if he had seen her, he would have left his work. For Katy was locked in her room, with every intention of avoiding him for the rest of the voyage. Sobbing, she dredged up all the heartache and disappointment until she could cry no more. Drying her eyes, finally, she told herself sternly that it was time to grow up. Dreaming silly fantasies was fine at Whitney Hall, but she was married now and it was time to look at life realistically. A man like Christopher Warwick would

219

never be interested in a silly, little girl who cried all the time. All he needed her for was to feed his crew. Her strength was in the kitchen, not the bedroom. Face facts, her common sense commanded. He doesn't need you. Forget him; forget all about last night. Go to the galley and do your job. And for once, she agreed with it. Still, all the while she could hear the little voice crying inside her.

There was some consolation in banging around the pots and pans. When Kit didn't arrive for a second meal, she was glad. So he thought he could avoid her again, did he? That was just fine with her. There were other things in life besides Captain Christopher Warwick.

Yet, when she received the summons, later in the evening, a heavy weight seemed to lift from her heart. See, the little voice chirped, I told you he cares. He's remembered and he wants to make it up to you. She tried hard to be rational, to listen to what her common sense had to say, but she found herself hurrying into her gown, brushing her hair until it glistened, and splashing the new perfume in all the strategic locations. All that mattered was that he wanted to see her. She danced around the room, putting the finishing touches on the vision she planned to be. When the flurry of activity was done, she pulled in her midsection, took a deep breath, and in a deceptively calm manner, arrived at Kit's door.

She was a vision; his expression told her so. But his look of appreciation soon faded into determination and Katy was left with the uncomfortable premonition that she had misunderstood his intentions. There was a tense silence. She tried to think of something terribly clever to say, but as usual in his presence, she was out of her depths.

It was Kit who finally spoke. "Would you like a seat? I'm sorry if I interrupted something"—he glanced meaningfully at her gown—"but I promise to get this over with as quickly as possible."

Feeling overdressed and extremely foolish, Katy went on the defensive. "Get what over with?"

He winced. "Please, sit down. I'm not feeling well, which I readily admit is no one's fault but my own, so bear with me. You and I have to talk about your future."

The vague premonition turned to fear. No, this was not going to be a romantic evening. Katy took the seat he offered her. Waiting for him to continue, she watched him. He looked a little better than this morning, but not much. If she had been older, wiser, and a bit more sure of herself, she would have taken him in her arms and told him that tonight was not the night to worry about the future. Gently, she would have eased the lines of worry that marred his handsome face and given him the comfort he so badly needed.

Save your pity for yourself, warned her common sense; he doesn't want it. Look at him. Can't you tell by now when he's angry? "Am I about to be lectured?"

"What?" Kit came out of his preoccupation to stare at her blankly. "I beg your pardon?"

"It's the only reason I can think of for you to be standing there scowling at me."

"Was I scowling? I'm sorry; I didn't mean to. I'm searching for a way to begin. I don't need to tell you that every time we talk we seem to fight."

"I'll try to keep my temper in check."

"Good girl."

Good girl, indeed! Why didn't he just pat her on the head? She wasn't a good girl; she was his wife. But he was unaware of her anger as he paced in front of her. He had something to say.

"Katy, what can I say? There is no way to excuse myself. When I first thought up this crazy scheme, I was desperate. I needed a ship, for more reasons than I care to go into now, and I wasn't thinking of the consequences. I hadn't thought about how I was going to botch up your life. I wasn't thinking of anything but myself." He tried to choose his words carefully, all too aware of those alert eyes examining him.

"By the time I realized what I was doing to you, it was too late. We were married. Evidence to the contrary, I am not an insensitive lout. I know how much I owe you. If we were to set up a tally sheet, I'm afraid I'd be sadly behind. Yet, in spite of all this, I have more to ask of you. I know I'm in no position to ask another favor and believe me, if there was any other way. . . oh damn, Katy, I need your help."

He paused, as if afraid to go on. Glancing over, he checked for her reaction, but her noncommittal gaze told him nothing. Drawing a breath, he plunged in. "If all goes well, we shall reach the West Indies tomorrow."

"So soon?"

"Not soon enough, I'm afraid. You know about the money we carry. There's a gentleman in port who will trade arms and munitions for that money. We can waste no time getting those arms to the militia. There is talk of a British attack on Charleston; they've already taken Savannah. The *Irish Lass* must set sail immediately, as soon as she receives the goods. But you and I won't be on her."

222

Her dismay was all too evident. "Oh no."

"We will go to Charleston on a separate ship, one whose log will make no mention of the stopover in the Indies. As far as anyone else is concerned, we made our honeymoon voyage on her. The existence and whereabouts of the *Irish Lass* will be kept secret."

"Does that mean I won't see her again?"

"I'm afraid that's a possibility. I'm sorry! I know how you feel about the ship, but it can't be helped. But while we're in port, we'll have some time to do shopping. Maybe I can replace those clothes I lost for you."

"You mentioned a favor?" Trying to hide her hurt and disappointment, her voice was hard. Kit had no way of knowing this and he thought she was merely trying to make things difficult for him.

"I'll be blunt. When we reach Charleston, it is important that we act as man and wife. They will be expecting a happily married couple and if we wish to keep up this charade, I will need your help."

Charade? Steeling herself, she vowed not to let him know how she was hurting inside. "And how do you propose we go about being this happily married couple?"

Annoyed, he moved away from her. "Have no fear; I won't hold you to anything in private. I promised I wouldn't touch you and I'll keep my word. In public, however, we will have to deceive a number of people. Julian is clever, make no mistake on that score, and he would never approve of what I did with your dowry. Better he doesn't know about it; let him think it was a love match."

"Love match?"

"I know I'm asking a great deal, but I'm prepared

223

to strike a bargain with you if you will agree."

"Do you mean I am going to get something out of this? How novel."

He flinched. In his heart, he had never believed it would come to this. If only there had been more time . . . But no, his time was gone. She was right. It was only fair that she be given something. His words, when he offered, were clipped, hard, and unyielding, nonetheless. "In return for your cooperation, I promise that I will see to it that you are delivered to England, or any place in the world you want. I can't end our marriage, but I will provide you with whatever money you need to set up your new life and I will offer no resistance or interference with whatever manner in which you choose to spend it."

To Katy, his words were like a slap in the face. He would use her and when he had no further need of her, pack her off to some remote corner where he need never see her again! So much for the little voice. Clenching her fists to stop her hands from trembling, she told him defiantly, "Very well, Mr. Warwick, we have an agreement. I doubt you could have found yourself a better partner. I pride myself in being able to make anyone believe what I want them to believe about me. Between the two of us, I daresay we can fool all the American colonies. Only, I warn you. I'll make you pay, and pay dearly, when that war of yours is over."

"I made you a promise."

"Fine. I gave you a warning. It's so much better, don't you think, when we understand each other? Now, if there's nothing further to discuss, I suppose I might as well leave."

"I'll take you back to your cabin."

224

"That won't be necessary. Tomorrow will be soon enough to play the devoted husband." The truth of it was that she was going to start crying again. With a swish of her skirts, she turned and hurried for the door.

"Katy, wait."

With one hand poised on the knob, she waited, holding onto her last feeble hope. Kit, too, wanted to keep her there, to break down the wall that had sprung up between them again, but what could he say? There was nothing left; it had all been said. "Never mind, it was nothing."

She didn't trust herself to speak. Silently, she slipped out of the room. Left alone. Kit kicked his chair. Damn! Damn! Damn! Did she have to be so anxious to leave him? So desperate to be out of his reach? Last evening, it had been so different. God, if he lived to be one hundred, he'd never understand women.

PART
THREE

Chapter 15

Charleston was nothing like she thought it would be. Not that she had expected wigwams, actually, but the early morning's activity on the busy docks came as quite a surprise. Nothing in Farley's derisive comments had prepared her for this bustling city.

Kit, uncommunicative at her side, stared at the approaching wharf. For a second, he smiled stiffly at her before resuming his vigil. It was a nice gesture; it reminded her of the last few weeks. Forced into each other's company, they had kept a truce, managing a pleasant, if not passionate, relationship. Yet, the closer they came to his home, the farther away he seemed to drift. She felt suddenly afraid. It was his home, not hers. Not only was she a stranger here, she was the enemy. If only she could reach out and cling to him, like a child. But she was no longer a child. She was his wife, and besides, his remoteness made such an action impossible. Instead, she smoothed the ruffles of the pretty new dress Kit had bought for her. It was her first new dress and touching it now gave her confidence.

Kit went suddenly rigid, his eyes riveted to a spot

on the end of the dock. Katy could see a carriage, elaborately decorated by a coat of arms. From her husband's behavior, she could only assume it was the Warwick vehicle.

When the ship had docked and was secured to the wharf, Kit took her hand and led her to the carriage. He squeezed it tightly before relinquishing his hold, a gesture of encouragement, but whether it was for her or for himself, she would never know. Grateful, nonetheless, she squeezed back.

Stepping down from the carriage was a man every bit as elaborate as his conveyance. It could only be Julian. His resemblance to his younger brother was uncanny. Except for the tiny lines of dissipation around the eyes and a barely discernible softness under all those ridiculous clothes, he could easily be mistaken for Kit. Katy looked from one to the other. Laughing indulgently, Julian spoke to her with an incredibly annoying voice. "It takes everyone by surprise. You can't imagine the problems it has created throughout the years."

Katy, who could only too well imagine, turned her attention to the woman he was assisting down from the carriage. Without a doubt, she was the most beautiful female her inexperienced eyes had ever seen, and she carried herself regally, as if fully aware of the fact. She glanced at Katy, with a flash of green eyes, and as if finding nothing worth her attention, turned to the men. Bristling, Katy had to admit the impossibility of competing with such a female. She had that reckless kind of beauty that men found so fascinating, with the age-old knowledge of how to use it. And she was using it now on Kit. The soft, cool voice, charged with sensuality, caressed him, hinting at an intimacy that effectively excluded everyone else. "Kit, darling, where have you been? We've been frantic, waiting for you to return to us. I was so afraid something dreadful must have happened."

Katy could feel Kit stiffen. Something intangible passed between this gorgeous woman and her husband and she felt like an intruder, embarrassed to have witnessed it. Typically, however, Kit's voice was under control and if there was an inward struggle, only Katy seemed aware of it. "I'm flattered that you noticed my absence, Rachel. I assure you I had no intention of causing anyone alarm. But you must have gotten my message. Why else would you be here to meet us? But that reminds me—Rachel, Julian, I'd like to present my wife, Katherine."

It should have been a special moment for Katy, but with the three pairs of eyes suddenly upon her, she felt so foreign and alone. They stood, like judges, and she couldn't blame them for finding her wanting. Whatever they had been expecting, she obviously was not it. The dress of which she had been so proud seemed so childish compared to Rachel's. Perhaps it was not altogether proper, but Rachel's gown, which fit her like a glove, revealed far greater attractions than Katy could ever hope to possess. Shifting her weight from one foot to the other, Katy mumbled the carefully practiced speech and just as mechanically, they uttered their welcome. Then, as quickly as she had become the center of attention, Katy found the conversation drifting away from her to local matters, in which she had neither knowledge nor interest. Feeling as if she had been tried and found wanting, she stood dejected as the three of them wandered toward the carriage. Only genuine fear that they would forget all about her, leaving her there on the dock, spurred her into scurrying after them, ignominiously lifting her skirts so that she would be spared making a complete fool out of herself by tripping.

A little out of breath, Katy was lifted into the carriage and deposited, not next to Kit, as she expected, but rather beside his brother. Rachel, undoubtedly responsible for the maneuver, snuggled next to Kit, taking every opportunity to grab his arm to point out people and sights they alone knew. Clenching her teeth, Katy vowed revenge on Kit for not warning her about this woman. Julian, to give him credit, tried to involve her in conversation, but feeling grossly inadequate, Katy could only answer in monosyllables. The journey passed in uncomfortable silence for her until they were stopped momentarily by a rather ragged-looking group of men, marching in disorganized fashion, down the center of the street.

Not one to miss an opportunity, Rachel touched Kit's shoulder, lingering there longer than necessary. "Look, Kit, the militia." As she leaned over, supposedly for a better view, she gave the men a glimpse of hitherto concealed parts of her anatomy. Katy's eyes met Kit's as they moved away from Rachel's chest, and they both turned away in embarrassment. To draw attention from the deep red that must surely cover her face, Katy asked quickly. "The militia? Here in Charleston? Does that mean we are in danger?"

Julian patted her hand. "Certainly not. You are not to worry your pretty little head about danger."

Rachel laughed derisively. "Especially with the militia to protect you."

"Those men? They are your army? They can't expect to win?"

232

"Rachel was teasing you, my dear. No one with any sense takes the militia seriously."

Katy, knowing how seriously Kit took it, glanced up at the words. Kit was laughing with Rachel, sharing a joke at the soldiers' expense. He was more a stranger, someone she had never known, and quite honestly, he seemed someone she would never care to know. Alone and alienated, she kept to her corner of the carriage. Not that they missed her company.

It was with great relief that she greeted the dwelling to which Julian referred as his town house. It was as impressive as his vehicle. If the Warwick fortunes were suffering, it was not evident here. Without thinking, Katy jumped down from the carriage, not waiting for assistance. Months of being one of the crew had encouraged independence, but it was not fitting behavior for a lady. Rachel's sharp look of reproof made her want to hide. She was not to be spared. With the help of both gentlemen, Rachel demonstrated how it should be done and she made a pretty job of it, too.

Inside, Katy's discomfort grew. There was something oppressive about the ostentatious display. As she was presented to a long line of slaves, she found she couldn't blame them for their suspicious, if not hostile, glances. She wondered briefly why Rachel was doing the presenting, until Julian explained that Rachel was visiting with them for an indeterminate amount of time. It seemed the elderly aunt with whom she had been staying had suddenly decided to return to her family in England and there was nowhere for poor Rachel to go. Of course, with the newlyweds to provide propriety, nothing could be considered amiss. Katy could have laughed at the thought of being a chaperone for the headstrong beauty, but truthfully, she could find little humor in her situation at the moment. All she could think of was that Kit's arm should be supporting his wife and not his brother's intended.

Julian, God bless him, was the only one concerned with her welfare. Summoning one of the slaves, he instructed her to take poor Mrs. Warwick to her room so that she could rest after the taxing journey.

"Just a minute, Julian." Kit now seemed more like himself. "Where is Rosie?"

"Rosie? For heaven's sake, Chris, what a ridiculous question. It this another of your childish games?"

"I want her for Katy."

"Katy? Oh, you mean Katherine. Don't be absurd, if you can help it. Rose hasn't worked upstairs since you came out of the nursery."

"Nevertheless, I want her for Katy."

Julian was annoyed and somewhat surprised by his brother's stubbornness. "She's far too old for the work."

"She's as fit as you or I. And Katy doesn't need a maid as much as she needs a companion. This is a whole new life for her. Rosie will take care of her."

Rachel's green eyes were speculative. "Why Katherine, where is your own maid?"

Kit cut in quickly. "The silly chit refused to come to America and there was no time to find another. I want Rosie for her; at least until someone more suitable can be found."

The brothers stared at each other for a full minute, neither seeming to like what he saw, until Julian shrugged and looked away. "Very well, if you insist. I don't understand what all the fuss is about, though. Honestly, Chris, I had hoped the time abroad would have done you some good, but it seems you're as

234

brash as ever. Are there any more demands?"

Maddeningly, Kit grinned at him. "No, Julian, that should just about take care of it. And now, Rachel, my dear, where is that brandy you promised me?"

As he walked off, Katy caught herself with her mouth falling open. Did he think by shoving her off on his childhood maid, his responsibility for her was at an end? No wonder Julian was exasperated. Well, she wasn't going to stand here gaping after him. He was welcome to his brandy. And Rachel. She was going to her room.

That is, if she could find it. Apparently, nobody remembered that she didn't know her way around yet. Julian had left in a fit of temper, abandoning her to the empty hallway. Goodness, it was huge. No doubt the stairway wound up to the bedrooms, but which one was hers?

"Child, what are you doing? Where is that boy?"

"I beg your pardon?" Katy, poised midway between the first and second step, turned guiltily at the sound of that commanding voice. She faced the largest woman she had ever seen. "I'm sorry, I was just trying to find my room."

"And where's your husband?"

"I believe he and Miss Worthington are having some brandy."

"I oughta take that boy over my knee. What's wrong with him, leaving a pretty little thing like you waiting and taking up with that hell cat? Would've thought he had more sense. Well, girl, don't just stand there; get on up those stairs. We'll get you some bath water and having you feeling better in no time at all."

"Excuse me, but I'm a little lost. I take it you are Rose?"

235

"Child, call me Rosie. Everybody does."

"Thank you, Rosie. I hope you don't mind having to alter your schedule to take care of me. I hate to disturb the household's routine."

Hustling her up the stairs, the black woman snorted in contempt. "Routine? It could use some stirring up. Child, I been taking care of Master Kit since he was born and I consider it an honor to be watching out for his bride. Though what's wrong with him, bringing a babe like you to a place like this, I'll never know."

"What's wrong with this place?"

Rosie stopped when she did and looked her in the eye. "There's sharks in these waters, child, and a little thing like you could get eaten alive."

Katy's eyes went round with surprise and then she laughed nervously. "You're trying to frighten me." Then, with false bravado, "I don't scare easily, you know."

Rosie's terrible expression vanished. "Just warning you to be careful, that's all. Come along, we'll get you settled. This is your room, here, and Master Kit has the one next to it. That over there is the door that joins them."

"Oh, how lovely," Katy remarked with forced gaiety. She hated her room, hated this house. It was attractively decorated, she supposed, but it was much too dark and heavy for her tastes. As Rosie chatted on, she crossed to the door that joined with Kit's room. Curiosity got the better of her and she twisted the knob. It was locked. Well, what did she expect? He had told her they wouldn't carry on the farce in private, hadn't he? It depressed her further to realize she was truly alone in this awful place. Warily, she followed the slave's movements as she unpacked her

236

trunks. What had he been thinking of when he requested this fierce old woman for her? Was she meant
to be a protector or a jailer?

She shook herself. What fanciful thoughts! Rose
was her maid, nothing more. It was merely the atmosphere of this dismal house, combined with the quite
natural fear of never belonging in it. It had been this
way on the *Irish Lass,* at first, and look how happy
she had been there. Katy squeezed her eyelids, but the
tears insisted upon erupting. Try as she might, she
couldn't stop them. Spilling over onto the lovely vel-
vet bedspread, they formed a wet spot. Rosie saw,
mumbled something unintelligible and tactfully left.

Truly alone now, Katy sank down on the bed, un-
mindful of the damp spot. From down the hall came
the sound of laughter, a deep, throaty sound. They
were wasting no time getting reacquainted, it would
seem. No wonder Kit hadn't warned her about Rachel.
How he must regret, now, the impulsiveness that had
tied him to his silly, schoolgirl wife. Innocent though
she might be, Katy could read the messages the beautiful woman sent to her husband. Kit was a hot-
blooded young man, and no man in his right mind,
married or otherwise, would turn down an invitation
from a siren like Rachel Worthington. She could see,
now, why he was so anxious to pack her off to England.

Rosie returned, leading a troop of slaves armed with
soap, towels, hot water, all the articles necessary for a
bath. Directing them, shouting orders, she soon had a
tubful of hot water ready and waiting. Gratefully,
Katy sank into the sudsy water, feeling its warmth
penetrate her brain. Her cares and worries melted into
a hazy, lazy indifference. With the slaves to supply a

237

steady source of hot water, she could remain in this state indefinitely.

But her skin was beginning to shrivel and it was just not in her nature to remain idle for long, Sighing, she dragged herself out of the bath. As if by magic, two slaves appeared at her side, holding soft, thick towels. She should have been pleased with all the attention, but the impersonal nature of it made her uncomfortable. These girls would be far more useful, and probably happier, working in the kitchen as opposed to being at the beck and call of their mistress. It was impossible to think of herself in the role. With a weak smile, she dismissed them and set about deciding what she would wear this evening for dinner.

When she joined the others in the drawing room, she discovered her choice was a poor one. Rachel had chosen her gown with far more intelligence than taste, and even Katy had to admnit the effect was stunning. Her long, black hair was piled high on her head, cascading in curls and tendrils that framed and softened the striking features of her face. Perfect white skin gleamed, radiating an excitement that was at the very least compelling. In her pale, blue frock, Katy looked and felt like a child.

Once again, Rachel proved adept at manipulating the conversation. By some chance, Kit was placed at her side at dinner, while Katy was left with Julian. Not that he paid attention to her. The three of them spoke of matters that were foreign to her and Katy began to believe that her wish to become invisible had come true.

Only at the end of the meal did anyone address her. Rachel suggested coyly that they retire while the gentlemen discussed business. It sounded like they were going to have a cozy, little chat, but nothing could be farther from the truth. Katy spent the next half hour under the older woman's careful scrutiny, watching a sly, little smile that she didn't much like, but was powerless to erase.

When the men finally joined them, Katy vanished into the woodwork again. With an audience, Rachel was at her best, showing them (or showing off) her many talents. Having no real accomplishments of her own, Katy sat in uncomfortable silence while Rachel played one boring tune after another. But when Kit rose to turn the pages, at Rachel's request, she could take no more. Muttering her apologies, she begged to be excused.

Frowning, Kit offered to escort her, but was gently pushed aside by Rachel. "No, Kit, this is your first night home. You stay with Julian, I'll take care of Katherine. Another woman is always better for these things."

Katy couldn't keep the irritation out of her tone. "Don't be silly. I hardly need an escort to my room. I thank you all for your concern, but it's just a little headache, not my decline."

Rachel sniffed prettily, skillfully hiding the secret smile of triumph. "I'm sorry, Katherine. I hadn't meant to offend you. I was only trying to be helpful."

They had to see through her act, but somehow, they seemed to think that Katy was in the wrong and she was forced to apologize.

"I'm sorry if I was sharp, Miss Worthington, but . . ."

"Oh, Katherine, surely you can call me Rachel. Why, we're almost sisters!"

God forbid! "Very well, Rachel. I appreciate your offer, but I would hate to spoil your evening. I'll be fine after a good night's sleep. Please, go on as you were."

As if it mattered whether she was there or not. As she trudged up the stairs, she heard Rachel's sensual laugh. It hadn't taken too long to forget her. What did she expect? They belonged here, she didn't.

While Rosie turned down her bed, Katy sat at her dressing table, vigorously brushing her hair.

"You better slow down, missy, if you want to have any hair left in that head of yours."

Starting guiltily, Katy focused on the slave's image in the mirror. "It's a bad habit I have. I find I do it whenever I'm upset." Grinning sheepishly, she set the brush down.

"What's that witch been up to now?"

"Witch?"

"Don't roll them eyes at me, child. I've lived in this house too long not to know when something's brewing. And if there's trouble on the way, you can bet Miss Rachel's at the root of it."

Turning in her seat, Katy faced her. "Oh Rosie, is there anything she can't do? She's so beautiful and poised and talented. She makes me feel like a child."

"And that's just what she wants, though it ain't like her to show her claws so soon. Must be feeling threatened."

"I doubt it. I've never seen anyone so in control of everything in my life."

"Don't let them airs of hers get to you. I bet she did her best to make you think she was mistress of this house, and not you."

"Me, mistress?" The thought of being responsible for this vast hulk of a home filled her with something close to horror. "Oh no, Rosie. Not me."

"Fact is, you should be running this house and not leaving it to someone who shouldn't even be here."

"But, Rosie, I can't. I wouldn't know where to begin. I've never done anything like it in my life."

"Child, it can't be anything more than your granddaddy's place over in England."

"The closest I ever came to running his house was arranging the flowers. And even that I did badly."

Rosie viewed her suspiciously. "Is that how they teach young ladies in England? To be useless?"

In the hopes of forestalling the question that was on everyone's mind, why had Kit married her, Katy rushed on. "To tell the truth, my grandfather never believed it worth the time and trouble. But I'm not useless," she added with a defiant note of pride. "I can cook, sew my own clothes, and given a plot of land, grow anything under the sun."

Rosie's snort told her what she thought of her accomplishments. "You sound more like kitchen help than a lady."

"Maybe I'd be better off in the kitchen."

Now Rosie was angry. "Don't talk that way to me, girl. I made a promise to my mistress, before she died, that I'd raise her son to be a gentleman, fit to be called a Warwick. I ain't about to see his wife make a mockery out of my life's work."

"It's not that I won't; I can't."

"It's your responsibility, child. You want people laughing at your husband, pitying him behind his back because the girl he married won't do what's expected of her?"

"No, of course not."

"You plan to sit back and let that she-devil take your rightful place and maybe your man in

241

the bargain?"

The barb struck home. Katy gulped, trying to swallow the tightness in her throat. "What can I do? It was too late before I came. All she has to do is say the word and he'll go running to her."

Some of the sternness left Rosie's face. "So you do love him?"

The lump in her throat loosened, slipped upward and became a tight little knot behind her eyes. She struggled to hold it there, but once the first betraying drop slid out, others followed in alarming proportions. Oh no, she was going to cry again.

Silently, Rosie opened her arms and Katy felt the overwhelming relief of belonging, of being young and innocent again, as she sank her tired head on the massive breast. As she had done with Nanny, all those years ago, she cried; convulsively at first and then with diminishing urgency as gentle hands stroked her hair. "Hosh now, child," she softly crooned. "That boy made you a promise and I know him. He'll keep it."

Katy had the vision of an angry Kit, framed in the open doorway, promising never to touch her again and warning he would seek his pleasures elsewhere. Thinking of the availability of that pleasure, she could find no comfort in Rosie's words. "I've watched them, Rosie. He still loves her."

"Don't you go confusing love with lust. That woman, she might know all the tricks of making a man think he wants her, but all they are is tricks. Tricks any woman knows."

"I don't know them. I can't seem to make him want me."

"Then maybe you ain't going about it right. Child, don't go wasting your time wishing you was her. She's

242

bad, through and through. I'm an old woman. In my time, I've seen plenty of her kind, feeding their vanity off of men too stupid to know better. My boy ain't stupid. Someday he's gonna wake up from that spell he's under and see her as she is. If you're smart, you'll be waiting. But not in the kitchen. He's gonna need a lady at his side."

Katy broke away in exasperation. "Oh, Rosie, please."

"Never you mind, missy. I may be old, but I ain't blind. I can see it's hard for you, in a new country with people that don't hardly give you a welcome at all. But there ain't gonna be nobody noticing you if you don't give them reason. I ain't gonna hound you. You're tired out tonight. You take your time to get used to us, but use your time wisely. Ask questions. Watch. When you feel ready, you come to old Rosie. I'll help you run this house. I've been doing it for years, and without the help of Miss-know-it-all Worthington."

"But . . ."

"Never you mind. You heard what I said. Now you think on it." She fluffed the pillows and patted the bed. "In here now. Time I stopped sitting here gabbing and got back to my chores before I have that she-dragon breathing down my neck."

"I'm sorry; I didn't realize . . ."

"One thing you're gonna have to learn is to stop saying you're sorry for everything. You're the lady of this house and you don't have to apologize to anyone. Now go on, hop up in that bed and get some sleep before you get sick."

Katy knew better than to argue. As she sank into the yielding luxury of the mammoth four-poster, she felt nothing but gratitude for the gentle bullying.

There was something to be said for being the lady of the house, after all. All this fuss and spoiling, she could certainly enjoy a bit of it for a change. Still under the wonderfull illusion of being pampered, she drifted off into a deep and untroubled sleep.

Chapter 16

However much she might have enjoyed her pampering, it was only an illusion, one which was to die a slow and painful death in the days that followed. Rachel was not about to relinquish her control over household matters and Katy did not challenge her, as she had neither the knowledge nor courage to make the attempt. Yet, it was hard to accept that Rachel did the job with an efficiency that took her breath away. Katy's life was ordered and managed, without her realizing how or when it had been done. It was Rachel who decided where and when she should eat, where and how she should spend her day, and when and if she would see her husband. Admittedly, Kit rarely put in an appearance. Julian kept him busy with family business during the day and Rachel occupied his nights— though how far into the night that occupation continued, Katy preferred not to consider. On the few occasions they were thrown together, there was awkward silence. Tortured by the conviction that guilt kept her husband tongue-tied, Katy could think of nothing to say. But of course, there would only be a few minutes of this discomfort before Rachel invariably glided into the room to draw his attention to her.

Slowly, they all settled into a routine. It was a routine of Rachel's making and, predictably, Katy's position in it was obscure. Volunteering her services, hoping to be useful, she was rewarded with a pile of mending, obviously Rachel's opinion of her worth. So much for being the lady of the house. Dinnertime was worse, if possible. Katy could have been another piece of furniture in the already overcrowded room, for all the attention she received. Once or twice, she blundered into their conversation, but the glances were enough to call a halt to such reckless behavior. Apparently, she was a child whose privileges at the adult table did not extend to conversation. They were quite convincing, actually. Katy began to believe it herself.

One afternoon, when she was again left to her own devices with a pile of mending, the oppressiveness of the house became too much for her. Lonely and bored and altogether tired of mending linens, she knew she had to be outdoors. Kit's vague promise to show her the sights had never materialized and she had a deep curiosity about this new land. Slipping on a light shawl and a new bonnet, she stepped out onto the street. It never occurred to her to tell someone where she was going; she was accustomed to being left alone to fend for herself.

Outside the house, Katy felt the cool, fresh air fill her lungs. Oh, glorious spring. Even in this foreign land, the sun was her old friend and the gentle breeze her faithful companion. Life was beginning again after the heavy incarceration of winter. As if tasting their freedom, tiny buds unfolded tentatively, suspicious of the sudden warmth. Katy, not the least bit suspicious, reveled in it. Her feet, acquiring a life of their own, took her farther and farther from the house that had imprisoned her.

It wasn't until those same feet began to drag a bit that she noticed how the vibrant colors were beginning to fade. In the enjoyment of her freedom, she had neglected to watch where her feet were leading her. She realized with alarm that the sun had lost its warmth and was well on the descent. She wasn't afraid, yet, but she was confused. In the failing light, nothing looked the same. Which way was the Warwick house? Retracing her steps, she followed a path that should have led her home, but with each step, she became more and more hopelessly lost. At first, she thought with satisfaction that they would be worried about her back at the house. But as she grew more weary and discouraged, she knew they wouldn't notice her absence until dinner, if then. Self-pity gave way to apprehension as the sun slowly disappeared. What if it was dark and she never found the house? She knew no one; she had nowhere to go. Shadows took on an ominous significance and her footsteps echoed loudly on the empty street. Insidiously, panic began to creep into her brain, slowly taking possession of her normally logical thinking processes until, at last, it gained control of her feet, sending them in a hurried flutter down the street. In a tangle of skirts, Katy fell to the ground with a thud.

The panic ebbed away. In its wake was a feeling of extreme foolishness. Realizing how ridiculous she must appear, she dragged her aching limbs into a sitting position and examined the bruise on her right hand. Her new dress was ruined. She knew there would be some explaining to do when and if she reached the house. But she was unlikely to reach that goal by running like a wild animal or by sitting in the street, feeling sorry for herself.

As she reached the decision to move, she heard a horse. Reacting instantly, she was on her feet in seconds, much to the distress of her sore knees. The urge to flee was strong, but instead, she carefully leaned over to retrieve her crumpled bonnet and held her ground. As the rider approached, she could have wept with relief. A rather stern Kit pulled up beside her, atop a dancing, white horse. Though not as grand as the stallion he had left with Farley, the horse made him seem like her gallant knight, once more to the rescue. A tiny smile, almost timid in nature, curled at the corners of her mouth.

Kit, unfortunately, was in no mood for humor. "What in God's name do you think you are doing? Wandering around these streets by yourself? At night? Are you insane? Where are your brains?"

All at once, she was a child again, defending herself. "It wasn't night when I started out." Realizing the inadequacy of her reply, she tried, "Really, Kit, must you treat me like a child?"

"As long as you continue to act like one. Now give me your hand so I can get you home."

She was ready with an argument but his icy glare silenced her. Reaching out with her right hand, she winced as his rough one scraped the bruise. He didn't notice; he was far too angry. Katy sat in front of him for the slow, humiliating ride home. This time she had ruined everything. Would she never do the right thing where Kit was concerned?

Julian and Rachel were waiting in the hallway when they entered. Predictably, Rachel saved all her sympathy and concern for Kit. Forced to resort to trickery,

Katy fainted. It was silly and cheap, but it worked. A very concerned Kit lifted her as if she weighed nothing at all and carried her upstairs. On the way, Katy fluttered her lashes in what she hoped was a becoming manner and sweetly apologized for causing such a fuss. He looked at her with such worry that she felt a little guilty but not enough to let him off the hook. She deserved the attention and the longer it lasted, the better.

Kit kicked open her bedroom door and waited while Rosie drew the blankets. Then he gently lowered her and tucked her in. "Are you all right now?"

Katy knew she could keep him her slave all night this way, but she had lost her taste for the game. "Aside from a bruise or two, there's nothing much damaged but my pride."

"But you fainted."

She couldn't suppress the giggle. "What would you have done if everyone was looking at you as if hanging was too good a punishment? I just couldn't face their questions. It would mean I would have to admit what a silly little fool I've been. I didn't mean to trick you."

"And the touching scene on the stairs?"

She grinned, defiantly. "So I was pretending again. But you were so angry at me."

"As I had every right to be. That was an incredibly stupid stunt, Katy." His words were severe but there was a twinkle in his eyes. Katy wanted to hug him.

Of course she did no such thing. "I'm sorry, Kit, it won't happen again. I needed fresh air. I didn't expect to get lost."

"Ladies do not go out unescorted in Charleston."

"No, I suppose I should have realized that. It's not at all like Whitney Hall, is it? But I was so bored and it was such a gorgeous day."

"Were you really that bored?" He seemed surprised.

"I shouldn't have put it that way. It's just so quiet after the *Irish Lass*. There's no one to talk to here."

"But there's Rachel."

And they thought she was naive? "Yes, but Rachel is always busy. Like you and Julian."

"I thought I explained that to you. I have business to attend to; I can't be with you every minute, making sure you don't get into trouble."

"I didn't mean it that way. I know what you have to do. I won't get in the way. I'll be a good girl, like I promised."

"What's wrong, Katy? You're not yourself lately. Aren't you happy here?"

Any irritation she might have felt disappeared. How could she burden him with her problems when he looked at her like that? She longed to touch his face, to smooth away those lines of worry, but he was still too far away. So she tried to ease his mind. "Don't mind me; I'll adjust. Everything's new and unsettled still, but give me time. I'll be fine."

She was rewarded by the smile that lit his handsome face, but her moment was quickly snatched away as Rachel slipped into the room. "I hate to disturb you two lovebirds," she said mockingly, "but it is soon time for dinner and, Kit, darling, you really must change if you don't want to listen to Julian's complaining all through the meal. Don't you worry, I'll sit and chat with Katy to keep her company." She flashed a bright smile, full of perfect white teeth, for Kit's benefit. "I nursed my father on many an occasion, so I can surely handle your wife."

Kit glanced at the door and then at Katy. Low

250

enough so only she could hear, he whispered, "If you need me for anything, I'm on the other side of that door." His eyes strayed in that direction.

"But it's locked," she whispered back.

There was surprise in his eyes and then, determination. "It won't be." It was a promise. He placed a brotherly kiss on her cheek and changed into that other Kit right before her eyes. "Rachel dear, you're right, of course. Where would we all be without you to keep us in line? Duty calls. If you ladies will excuse me . . ."

Bowing low in their direction, he marched out of the room. Katy squelched the desire to laugh. If there had been mockery in his tone, Rachel didn't seem to notice. Indeed, that smug smile of triumph denied any knowledge of being any less than perfect in Kit's eyes.

As soon as he was gone, the smile was too. With a businesslike air, Rachel placed a cool hand on Katy's head and viewed her with scorn. "You don't have a fever and I seriously doubt there's anything wrong with you. Don't you think you'd better tell me where you've been?"

It would seem the sweet, concerned nurse routine was reserved for Kit. "I went for a walk and lost my way."

"A walk? By yourself?"

"There was no one about. I had no idea it would cause such a fuss."

Rachel's eyes narrowed. "I wonder."

Katy sat upright. "And what is that supposed to mean?"

"You seem remarkably recovered, all of a sudden."

"I went for a walk and lost my way," Katy repeated stubbornly.

"Save the innocent airs for the men. If you hoped to call attention to yourself, it was a very childish and futile gesture. You see, now I will have him all to myself at dinner."

Astonished at the blatant admission, Katy could only stare at her stupidly. Fortunately, Rosie chose that moment to waddle into the room. "Miss Rachel, what you doing here? You go on and make yourself pretty for the gentlemen. I'll take care of Master Kit's lady. You don't wanna be getting those pretty hands of yours dirty now, do you? The sickroom's for the sick, not the likes of you."

The appeal to her vanity was too great a temptation. Rachel couldn't resist a glance at her well-groomed hands and then at Katy's bruised ones. With a self-satisfied smirk, she addressed the slave. "Thank you, Rose. Sickrooms are so depressing. Though I doubt we need lose sleep over Katherine. I'm sure she'll live."

After she was out the door, Rosie winked at Katy. "That woman sure has her nerve."

"That woman, Rosie, is a bitch."

Rosie chuckled. "Child, you know better than to talk that way. T'ain't fitting. You sure is right, but t'ain't fitting."

"I don't understand how you could be so polite to her."

"That's just years of experience, missy. I know better than to make an enemy of that one. I'm only a slave. If his brother wanted to sell me, there's be nothing Master Kit could do about it. So I bow low and do what she tells me and save my grumbling for the kitchen. And when I can, I see she gets her tea cold and her breakfast late."

"Oh, Rosie, not really?" Picturing the imperious Rachel waiting for her breakfast made Katy laugh. "And she never suspects what you're doing?"

"She expects me to be stupid and I try not to disappoint her. Her way of looking right through me, as if I don't exist, suits me just fine. As long as she doesn't think I have a brain in my head, I can do as I please."

"What a wonderful idea. I should try it."

"Oh no, missy, it's not for you. That woman is watching you like a cat stalking a mouse and don't you think otherwise. You've got something she wants and she ain't about to let you keep him. Sooner or later you're gonna have to fight if you want your rightful place in this house."

"Oh, Rosie, not again."

"You can't hide in this room forever. And what about Master Kit? You plan to abandon him to her?"

"You promised not to hound me about this."

"So I did, child. I'll keep my promise. But if you're ever gonna change your mind, I sure hope it's soon."

That caught her attention. "Why? Do you know something?"

Rosie seemed to realize that she had spoken out of turn. "Sakes, child, you jump on everything I say. I only meant you should take your rightful place, that's all. And we ain't talking about that no more, remember? C'mon, let old Rosie look at them hands and see what she can do about them."

Was Kit leaving soon? Was that what Rosie had started to say before she thought better of it? With the British approaching closer every day, it was quitely likely. Katy wanted to tease the slave for more information but, by now, she could tell when Rosie couldn't be budged. So instead, she allowed herself to

be bandaged, fed her dinner like a baby, and then bundled in the big four-poster.

Rolling on her side to go to sleep, Katy sighted the
door to Kit's room. A sad smile touched her lips. It
was comforting to know that it would no longer be
closed to her, that Kit would be there if she needed
him. He'd be there, but for how much longer?

Chapter 17

"Don't you think you've slept long enough?"

Opening heavy eyes, Katy found it hard to focus on where she was. With sudden intensity, the early April sun was streaming in her windows and striking her face. Startled into consciousness, she watched Rachel wak to the other window to pull the drapes. Who did this woman think she was, barging into her room without invitation, intruding on her privacy? Did her household duties include determining how long she could sleep? Swallowing her irritation, though it left a bad taste in her mouth, Katy remarked in what she hoped was a pleasant tone, "Ah, I had a wonderful night's sleep. I had no idea it was so late. What time is it?"

"Time for your breakfast."

It wasn't as easy to master her annoyance this time. "What's the hurry, Rachel? I have nothing more pressing than some mending to do."

Shoving a tray under her nose, Rachel glared at the girl. "Eat your breakfast. You and I have to talk."

Moving the tray to the side, Katy motioned to a chair. "Very well. Sit down."

Rachel ignored the chair, preferring the advantage her height gave her. "Katherine, we are all trying our best to understand the difficulties you are facing here. We are trying to be patient. But after yesterday..."

We? Who did she mean by "we"? "I told you what happened."

"Please don't interrupt. Kit has asked me to talk to you about this."

That traitor. What a cozy little dinner they must have had, deciding what was to be done with "poor Katy." "Go on Rachel."

"We're certain you don't do these things intentionally, but surely you must see that a man in his position cannot afford to have his wife making a fool of him. No, don't interrupt. We have tried to be patient but we have friends that want and deserve to meet the girl Kit has married."

"Fine. I'd enjoy meeting his friends."

"My dear child, you obviously don't understand. Until you can learn how to behave in polite society, I am afraid we can't risk introducing you to our friends. Your eccentric behavior may have seemed quaint to him at one time, but it's become a nuisance."

"Thanks for the advice, but I think I can conduct myself properly in your "polite" society."

"I'd like to believe that, Katherine, but experience tells me otherwise."

"Experience?"

"For example, that little display yesterday."

"How many times do I have to explain?"

"You're interrupting again. Anyone with any sense at all would have known better than to go out on the streets alone. What you choose to do with your life is your affair, but when it affects Kit, I must step in. No matter how embarrassing it is for both of us."

Irritation gave way to anger. "I think you are taking a bit too much upon yourself. What happens between Kit and me is our affair and no one else's."

The green eyes glittered. "Let's get this clear. Whatever affects Kit is my affair. It always has been and always will be. Take this as a warning: the Warwicks are my property, both of them. I won't tolerate usurpers."

"Usurper? Kit married me."

"You are a silly child. It's obvious to everyone that he merely married you to spite me."

So there was something mightier than Rachel's nerve—her conceit. "However obvious it may be to you, it's not true."

"Then tell me why he did marry you."

The real reason was hardly any better than her suggestion, but she didn't have to know that. "Whatever his motives, the fact is, Kit belongs to me."

"When you've grown up a bit, you'll learn that it takes more than a few lines on a piece of paper to hold a man. Marriage, if it's to be binding, requires more of a man-and-woman relationship."

"Did you and Kit discuss our relationship, too?"

"We didn't need to. I've been aware of his needs for longer than you've been able to fill them. And I know they can't be filled by locking your door to him."

"How dare you!"

"Once you get to know me better, you'll realize that I dare do whatever I please. It pleases me to have your husband and I doubt there's anything you can do to stop me."

"Kit is my husband." Katy wanted to sound firm, but even to her own ears, it sounded childish. She might just as well have stuck out her tongue.

Rachel smiled. "Try not to be incredibly naive, if you can help it. Your marriage, for what it's worth, has nothing to do with me. I plan to marry Julian but I could hardly be faithful to him. Like your husband, I have my needs, too."

"You're contemptible. I'll have Kit ask you to leave."

Rachel laughed. "So the babe has teeth? Just remember, before you try using them, that I've had mine years before you started cutting yours. And there wouldn't be much sense asking Kit; I doubt he's as anxious for me to leave as you are. And I would so hate to cause a marital spat."

The fine thread that held her temper in check finally snapped. "Get out!"

"But, Katherine," she purred. "We haven't finished talking."

"I neither require nor desire any advice from you, Rachel. For my part, I would just as soon pretend this conversation never took place. However, unless you leave immediately, I will open my lungs and scream with every ounce of energy in my body, and you can do the explaining."

"Don't think your tantrums frighten me. I'll leave because it's quite plain that there's no sense trying to talk to you now. Poor Kit. He'll be so disappointed when he learns how poorly you took my advice."

With a swish of skirts, she glided out of the room. Katy was up in an instant, with a pillow to throw after her.

"Child, what are you doing?"

Katy felt suddenly foolish, standing on the bed with a limp pillow dangling from her hand. "I let her get me angry again, Rosie."

"That's plain enough. What ain't is why? Suppose you c'mon down from there and tell me what she's done now."

Making the humiliating descent from the bed, Katy recounted the conversation. "She thinks she has a right to everything."

"Seems to me she's scared."

"Rachel, scared? I've never seen anyone so confident in my life."

"If she wasn't feeling threatened, she wouldn't bother warning you. She's just trying to scare you into thinking the way she wants."

"Then she's made a mistake. You were right. It's high time I showed Miss Worthington who's in charge here." She marched to her closet and flung open the doors. "Let's start in here. This dress will be fine if I tear away some of the lace."

"Lawdy, child, what are you doing?"

"This is war and I'm going to need some weapons. What was it Kit said? Cunning and spirit. A few alterations, here and there, and perhaps I can compete with the alluring Rachel. What do you think?"

She held the lace-free gown to her chin and paraded around with it. "I'll teach her to think twice before challenging me."

Rosie chuckled. "That poor girl. What do you plan to do?"

"What I should have done long ago. Become the mistress of this house. Oh, Rosie, you will help me, won't you?"

"Can't think of anything I would enjoy better. Fact is, I've been waiting for this for a long time."

"Then let's get started. There's a great deal to accomplish if I'm to present the new Katherine at dinner this evening."

"Tonight? Child, you sure don't waste time."

She couldn't afford to waste it, not when it seemed there was so little left. When her husband left for his war, he would be certain to return to the right girl. She would leave nothing to chance. If necessary, she would make the decision for him.

Chapter 18

Unbuttoning his shirt, Kit sank into his chair. Lord, he was tired. Julian was running him into the ground with his petty errands. Today, he had been sent for the fourth time to inspect the cotton. Julian and his damned cotton; he hoped it would rot. He knew this cotton business was a blind, that there was more serious business underfoot, but, as yet, he hadn't discovered what it was. As long as it must be kept such a carefully guarded secret, why didn't Julian dispense with this needless work and just send him home.

At least then he could be with Katy. He had seen so little of her and until last night, he had assumed that was the way she wanted it. Kit smiled as he remembered her faint and then the laughing confession. God, he had been scared out of his wits when Rachel had come to him with the story that Katy had run off. He had been frantic, but she had been standing there as if she knew he would come for her, obviously frightened and so determined not to let it show. She had been lonely, she said. Would she welcome his company? She seemed to be saying so last night. Before Rachel came.

Damn Rachel. What was she up to, anyway? Whatever had been between them was long since dead, by mutual consent, yet she was behaving otherwise. Just what he needed. It was hard enough to keep up this facade without having to deal with his brother's fiancée. It seemed every time he had a chance to be alone with Katy, Rachel would happen along. He tore off his shirt. Ah, to be back on the *Irish Lass* again, where you didn't have to dress for dinner or conform to silly rules; to be free of this pretense, of suffering through Rachel's insipid music night after night, of playing the fool for Julian, of being so far away from Katy. He looked longingly at her door. If only he could come home after a long and frustrating day, and just once, find her waiting for him.

He shook himself. Damn, he was getting soft. He'd played this charade too long to let a little thing like fatigue get to him. Pouring himself a brandy, he took a deep breath. It was just one more boring dinner to get through. And get through it he would, just as he had all those countless others.

On the other side of the door, Katy was putting the finishing touches on her new image. Not wishing to risk any comparisons, she had kept it simple, but her gown borrowed heavily from the style of her opponent. With a few changes, Katy could expose as much skin as Rachel, and to her delight, with as much flair. Yes, she was going to enjoy this. Sitting on the bed, she forced herself to be patient. She would wait for the prearranged signal from Rosie, timing her entrance until after everyone else had arrived.

It was a full half hour before it came, and Rosie delayed her another ten minutes, fussing with her hair and smoothing her dress. At the top of the stairs,

Katy sucked in her breath, trying to draw courage from the air. Facing Rachel in battle was far more alarming than anything else she had ever done, even boarding the *Olympus*. But she had been challenged and a Farley did not turn and run.

At first, only Kit noticed her entrance, as his lifeless eyes awoke at the sight of her. Katy's eyes were on Rachel, who was deep in discussion with Julian. It took Kit to bring Katy to the attention of the others. "Katy, you look wonderful tonight." His gaze emphasized the words and her confidence grew.

Julian, not to be outdone by his brother, kissed her hand. "Indeed, you're positively radiant. I find it impossible to take my eyes off you."

Rachel, alone, showed the surprise they were all feeling. She stared, barely able to conceal her displeasure. "What a lovely gown. Though I'm sure I've seen it before. Have you done something with it?"

Katy smiled just as sweetly. "How clever of you to notice. Yes, I hope you don't mind, but I wanted to be like you. Everything you wear looks so lovely and I did so want to fit in here. Is it suitable, do you think?"

Her question was skillfully directed at the men, who hastened to assure her that it was. Still focusing her attention on them, Katy continued. "Rachel was thoughtful enough to point out that I was doing things all wrong. And she was right. I offer no excuses. Homesickness is no reason to forget all I've been taught. I'd like to apologize to you all."

Kit was clearly amused. "None of us had any complaints."

So that conversation this morning had been Rachel's idea, not his. "You're a darling, Kit. All of you are. Thank you for being so patient with me. But all

263

that is behind me now. I must forget my beloved England and my dear grandfather, because I have a new home and family now. And I have responsibilities. Oh, I know Miss Worthington—I'm sorry, I mean Rachel—has been doing an admirable job filling in for me, but I simply cannot impose on her good nature for a second longer. After all, she is our guest. No, Rachel, don't interrupt. I just couldn't sleep at night, knowing I was taking such advantage of your generosity. From now on, I will assume my duties as Julian's hostess. You are to take a well-deserved rest and enjoy your visit with us. Isn't that right, Julian?''

He was assessing her, surprised and yet pleased with what he saw. "Quite right, my dear. How uncomfortable it could be if anyone should learn that Rachel was running my household. What would they think?''

"And since when do you care what anyone thinks, Julian?''

"Careful, Rachel, your fangs are showing.''

There was an awkward silence, with Rachel glaring and Julian ignoring her, before dinner was finally announced. Kit rushed to Katy's side to escort her and was rewarded by a dazzling smile. "Careful,'' he whispered to her. "Don't ruin it by overplaying your part.''

"Thanks for the advice,'' she hissed back, "but I no longer need coaching from you. I was born into the part.''

It seemed it was no idle boast, as Kit soon learned. With an ease that surprised him, Katy managed everything from the slaves to the conversation. To Julian's questions about her background, she answered skillfully and evasively, providing just enough information to whet his appetite financially. As for Rachel, she was far more charitable than the woman deserved.

But then, she could afford to be.

Kit was beginning to relax and enjoy himself for once, when Katy jarred him out of his complacency with a casual remark. "Why is it, Julian, that none of these friends of yours come to call? At Whitney Hall, people were stopping by at all times of the day."

Rachel sneered. "It may have escaped your notice, but we are fighting a war here."

"How silly of me. Of course. It's just that you don't talk about it. I began to assume it was being fought elsewhere."

"I think what Rachel was trying to say, Katherine, is that the best families have been divided. Those that support this ridiculous patriot government no longer associate with us loyal Tories. Still, though we have been reduced in number, there are some of us who entertain. Most, like myself, are waiting for the British liberation."

"The British, here? What exciting news! But I was told that we had already been successfully repelled."

"This time, we will be better informed and better equipped. Lord Cornwallis won't easily be rebuffed a second time. And General Clinton himself is on his way from New York. I'm told we can expect his arrival at most any time."

"That is quite a bit of news, Julian. However did you come by it?" Kit's tone was casual, almost bored, but Katy could recognize the sudden attentiveness.

"I can't see how it matters, Chris. What does matter is that Katherine is correct. We have been remiss in introducing her to our friends and neighbors. War or no, we cannot neglect the amenities. We certainly can manage some sort of affair."

"Oh, Julian, do you think so? I'm so excited. Why, I

haven't met anyone socially since leaving England. That ship was dreadful and I was so sick all the time. Can we have dancing? I adore dancing."

"Of course, if that's what you want. After all, it is your party."

"You're wonderful. Can I help plan it? I was always my happiest when planning a function for Grandfather, wasn't I, Kit?"

Though he knew better, Kit readily agreed. Now what was she doing? Was she still acting or was this the real Katy? She played the part so well, it was impossible to tell. He remembered how silly she had been about those trunks. A party, for God's sake? Didn't she know what Julian's friends were like?

Since she didn't, Katy was able to enjoy the next few days. Each morning she spent with Rosie, going over the intricacies of household management. The staff, bowing to Rosie's authority and grateful to be rid of Rachel's intimidating presence, did their best to cooperate. If Katy wasn't as efficient as her predecessor, no one was the wiser.

In the afternoon Katy would join Julian in his study where the two of them would sit like school children over lists and menus. Kit would return later to hear the sound of her laughter but, for once, it gave him no joy. Funny, but he was a jealous beast. Why couldn't she see through that veneer of charm, to know that Julian was merely exploiting her grandfather's connections? Surely she was far too intelligent to be misled like all the others. Still, why couldn't she have remained quiet and shy and out of the focus of attention? Especially his brother's.

Eventually, the night of the party arrived, and none too soon, to Kit's way of thinking. Swallowing his pride, he went to Katy's door with words of encouragement. He knew, if the others did not, that this was her first social affair, and invitation or not, he planned to be at her side to help her through it.

He could have spared himself the effort. Julian answered his knock, looking every bit the sophisticated man-about-town. Next to him, Kit felt big and awkward and thoroughly ill at ease.

"Chris, you're late, as usual. But come in. You can give us your opinion. What do you think?"

Katy, in a filmy, white creation, was a dream. "She's beautiful."

"Of course she is, but that's not what I meant. The jewels, stupid. What do you think of the jewels?"

"The Warwick diamonds, Julian?"

"Certainly. They are, after all, hers by right until I marry. I hope you realize that it was painful for me to have to present them to her in your place. I can't believe you were prepared to allow your wife to face all those people without a single jewel to her name. Really, Chris, your carelessness becomes too much to bear sometimes, especially when it extends to the neglect of a beautiful woman like your wife. Katherine, we must try to be patient with him. I must say, those diamonds are exquisite with that gown. You'll be the envy of every woman in the house."

He chatted on while an uncomfortable Katy stood on display. She hated the diamonds. They didn't suit her at all and they ruined the image she had tried to create. One glance at Kit's face confirmed her suspicions; she looked like an overdressed snowflake. If only she could throw them back at Julian, but she was trapped in the role she had designed for herself.

Kit, meanwhile, fingered the single ruby that lay in

his pocket. Its warm, red glow would have suited her better than the gaudy display that glistened on her soft, white throat. But who was he to challenge them? Julian was showing off for Katy, at his expense, and years of experience had taught him not to argue with his older brother. Besides, he had a role to play. Grinning cheerfully, and feeling like the village idiot, he fell in behind them to go down and greet their guests.

If he resented Julian's proprietary air upstairs, it proved near unbearable as the night progressed. Who exactly had she married? It galled him to watch his wife dangling on the arm of a man who was so obviously using her to ingratiate himself with these overdressed, overstuffed fools? How could she like these people? She was certainly enjoying herself, laughing and joking with every man in the place except her husband. Well, he for one wasn't going to stand in line to beg a dance from her. She was welcome to all her Tory friends; this was where she belonged. If he had any sense at all, he'd leave her to them.

Unaware of his fuming, Katy searched through the crowd for him. Once, he danced past with Rachel, but other than that, he was nowhere to be seen. The party, which Julian assured her was a huge success, had lost its flavor. She had expected something different; it was hard to believe these were Kit's friends. What was the sense in proving her capabilities as a hostess when the person she sought to impress wasn't there to see? Why struggle through another dance if it was never going to be with him? All pretense of gaiety was gone. Her feet throbbed and her jaw ached from smiling and she absolutely refused to dance again with that fat little man in the blue coat. Before he could approach her, she ducked through the door and slipped outside for a breath of fresh air.

Outside, Katy forced herself to face the facts. As bitter as it might taste, she must swallow the truth and put an end to this self-delusion. All her plotting and scheming, all her hoping and dreaming, all her efforts had been in vain. The closest she would ever get to Kit was when he glided past with Rachel. No doubt that was where he was this minute, clandestinely meeting with his mistress while she, like a fool, pined away for him in the chilly night air. From inside, she could hear the instruments tuning, the beckoning of music. Sighing heavily, she resigned herself to her fate. She had started this farce, she might as well see it through to the end.

"What's wrong? Didn't he show?"

Kit was leaning against the wall, half in shadow, glaring at her. The shock of seeing him, as if he had materialized out of her thoughts, caught Katy stammering. "I, uh, Kit, I don't, I mean, well, what are you doing out there?"

"Watching you. Tell me, who were you rushing out here to meet?"

"What are you saying? I came out here for fresh air." All at once, the implication of his quiet words hit her and her temper flared. "You! You have the nerve to accuse me of some sordid meeting? You are accusing me of infidelity? You? I think you have your nerve!"

In the face of her anger, he remained intolerably cool. "Then perhaps you will explain what you were doing out here."

"I told you already that I came out for fresh air."

"And were disappointed to find the air not so fresh. Is that your explanation for the tears?"

How long had he been watching her? Who did he

think he was, making vague accusations at her? As she had so often in the past, Katy struck out at him blindly. "In the event that you are entitled to an explanation, Mr. Warwick, which I personally do not believe you are, they were tears of disappointment. I have rarely been more bored in my life. If I had to smile one more time, I think my jaw would lock into place. I've done my best to show your tiresome friends that you could be proud of me, but to tell the truth, I could not care less what they thought of me. And you, my husband, abandon me to them. Instead of supporting me through this ordeal, you're sneaking around, spying on me."

Kit straightened, eyeing her cautiously. "I was not spying. Dammit, I'm your husband!"

"Ha! You've shown remarkably little evidence of that fact. You haven't spoken a word to me all evening. You could at least have asked me to dance." She tried to keep the pleading note out of her voice, to regain her fading anger, but her lower lip began to tremble and she had to bite it. "You found time to dance with Rachel. Couldn't you have spared time for me?"

He had never expected this. All along she had been waiting for him and he had been kept from going to her by his pride. Sooner or later, he would have to learn not to compare her to the other women he had known. She was no scheming Rachel; she was Katy, sweet and good and oh, so beautiful when she looked at him like that. On impulse, he took her in his arms.

"Kit, let me go. What do you think you are doing?"

"You asked to dance, did you not?"

"Out here? Don't be silly."

"Be quiet. You're ruining my timing."

"But . . ."

He stopped, put a finger over her lip and said softly, "Are we going to argue or are we going to dance?"

Katy couldn't have spoken another word if she had wanted to. What was the sense in protesting when this was what she wanted? Out here, in the open air, with only the stars to watch, their bodies moved as one, floating across the lawn. How could she have ever thought her feet hurt? She felt reborn.

Oh no, was it over so soon? Why was it that the dreadful times dragged on and on, but when she was truly happy, truly alive, time chose to speed past, taking her happiness with it?

Kit didn't want the moment to end, either. Without releasing her, he looked down. "Did you mean it? Did you want to dance?"

Suddenly bashful, Katy lowered her eyes. "Yes."

"I was afraid to ask you."

"You? Afraid? But why?"

"You seemed happy enough, doing what you were doing. You didn't lack partners."

Her shyness forgotten, Katy rushed to reassure him. "I know. As Julian would say, 'I was a crashing success'. But I was so bored. I kept thinking back to that other party on the *Irish Lass* and how much fun we had then. Do you remember?"

Kit smiled. "As I remember, you took my handkerchief."

"I did not!" She laughed when she saw his expression. "Oh, you're teasing me, aren't you? You see, one night with those people and I can't even tell when you're teasing me. Do you understand, now, why I needed you to rescue me?"

"As flattering as it sounds, I'm afraid I can't believe it. If ever there was a one who could take care of

271

herself, Katherine Farley Warwick, you've got to be it. You put on a fine performance, tonight. You certainly had me fooled.''

"It was a wasted effort. They know less than I about the whereabouts of the British."

He tightened his grip on her arms. "Is that what you've been up to? I won't have it, Katy. You little fool. They hang spies."

"I was only trying to help."

He drew her to him, holding her gently. "Ah, Katy, I know what you're trying to do and I appreciate it. But it's not your fight. And for God's sake, don't underestimate these people, especially Julian. They're far more ruthless than you ever could be and you can get hurt." Putting a finger under her chin, he lifted her face up to his. "Promise you won't try anything like this again?"

"If you want. I was just trying to be useful. I spend day after day in this house with nothing to do. I wish I was back on the *Irish Lass.*"

"Yes, I know. So do I. It was much easier then, even if you didn't speak to me."

"Now I know you're teasing me."

He smiled down at her. Warwick diamonds or no, she was beautiful. For a second, he wondered if she would let him kiss her but before he reached a decision, another couple stepped outside. He gestured in their direction. "It's getting crowded. I suppose we should go in."

"Yes, I suppose so. The performance isn't over yet. Will you dance with me again?"

"Lady, I'm not going to leave your side."

True to his word, Kit remained with her for the rest of the evening. The fat little man, with one glare from

Kit, ceased his attention. Now it was a party for Katy. She could enjoy the dancing, knowing that wherever she was, Kit would be watching for her, and smiling. At the very last, he took her hand, remarking to anyone who cared to listen that it was a tradition for him and his bride to dance the last dance together. Laughing, Katy followed him, determined to make the most of this night, to store away the memories like a squirrel with its nuts, for she knew, with sudden clarity, that it might as well be winter when he had to leave. Tonight had taught her that Kit was the color in her life; without him, it would be a dull and drab existence.

After the last guest had departed and a sullen Rachel had bid them good night, Julian walked with them to their rooms, chatting constantly about this person and that. When they reached Katy's door, Julian stepped in front of Kit to kiss Katy's hand. "Katherine, you were marvelous. We must do this again, soon."

"Thank you, Julian. I'd love to stay up and talk about it all, but I'm rather tired. All that dancing, you know. I must say good night."

He made no move to leave and finally Kit had to say, "Do you mind, Julian, if I say good night to my wife?"

"Your thoughtlessness knows no limit. Didn't you just hear Katherine tell us she was tired? If you had any consideration for her, you would know better than to bother her with your amorous advances tonight." He grabbed his brother by the elbow and propelled him down the hall. "Come along and give the poor dear a chance to rest."

As she let herself into her room, Katy couldn't help but grin. Poor Kit. Amorous advances, indeed!

In his room, Kit paced the floor. Given half a chance,

he would have talked, really talked, with Katy tonight. Damn, he had to talk to her tonight. Determined, he marched to her door. With his hand on the knob, he realized he had absolutely no idea what he was going to say. All he could think of was how lovely she had looked and how soft and warm she had felt when he held her. To be truthful, it wasn't conversation that was on his mind. No, if he went in that room now, it would be for one reason only. With painstaking control, he pried his fingers off the knob and went, instead, to his bottle of brandy for the warmth and comfort he needed.

Chapter 19

Rachel haunted her dreams, flitting in and out, smiling, laughing, beckoning to an eager Kit. Over and over, Katy would shoo her away and Rachel would disappear, only to pop up again somewhere else.

Katy finally woke to the sound of whispering. It could have been another dream, but something nagged at her consciousness, forcing her to sit up to hear better. Oh, it was whispering, all right. Did he think her so gullible? A couple of dances, a few nice words, and a carefully placed hug and then he could safely entertain his mistress? Under the same roof, with only a door separating them? Fury engulfed her in a hot wave. Without thinking, she threw on a wrapper and thundered into his room, prepared to tell them both what she thought of their morals, if they had any.

Before going far into the darkened room, Katy was grabbed from behind. As she clawed and scratched to free herself, she heard someone curse softly. There was a scratching sound and a flame appeared out of the darkness.

"For God's sake, let her go, Billy. That's my wife."

The arms that held Katy were dropped. Giddy with

relief that it was the mysterious Billy and not Rachel that Kit entertained, she faced her captor. In homespun breeches and ragged shirt, he was a far cry from the men she had met this evening. His chin sported a rough and dirty beard while in his hands was an equally disreputable hat which he twisted and turned. "Begging your pardon, ma'am. Hope I didn't harm you. We can't be too careful, these days."

Katy turned a bewildered face to Kit, who was lounging against the door frame, obviously amused. "Katy, Billy Harden. We used to hunt together in the swamps. He's still hunting, though he's changed his quarry somewhat. He serves under a mutual friend, Colonel Marion, in the militia."

I should have recognized the uniform, Katy thought wryly. "I'm pleased to make your acquaintance, Mr. Harden. I had been told I was to meet Kit's friends tonight, but I hardly expected it would be under such extraordinary circumstances. Could you please tell me how you got in here?"

Kit laughed at Billy's equally bewildered expression. "It's quite all right. I know her accent is British but she can be trusted. It's too late now anyway, she's already seen you. You might as well tell me why you're here."

Ill at ease, he glanced from husband to wife and then back at Kit again. "All right, then. I'm afraid it's bad news. General Moultrie wants to see you."

"Why Moultrie? I thought I was supposed to report to Francis?"

"He's been relieved of duty."

"Whose ridiculous idea was that? We don't stand a chance without him. Didn't they learn that in '76? Why, Francis Marion was responsible for that victory."

"Calm down, Kit. Nobody knows that better than I, or Moultrie, for that matter. It wasn't a matter of choice. He fell and broke an ankle in a stupid accident. He's not getting any younger. Moultrie has him under orders to rest and recuperate until it's mended, regardless of what happens here in Charleston."

"This is bad news. How's he taking it?"

"You know my brother-in-law. He's so afraid he'll be missing something. To my way of thinking, he's better off out of it."

"What do you mean?"

"It looks real bad. Clinton is coming from one direction, Cornwallis from another, and the fleet from yet another. And Benjamin Lincoln refuses to budge. Says he won't leave the city unprotected."

"But he'll be trapped."

"Yes, that's what we all think, but he's in charge and we have to follow orders. That's why Moultrie wants to talk to you."

"Does that mean I'll finally get some active duty?"

Little pinpricks of fear stabbed at Katy's insides. War was a necessary evil until its grasping tentacles snatched at somebody you love; then it was just plain evil.

"I doubt it, Kit. Sorry, but Moultrie knows better than to waste you in a losing effort. You'll be needed later on. Now you'll only be needed to get certain people out when the British finally arrive. You and your ship. But I'm not the one to be telling you this. You've got to see the general."

"Does he expect me tonight?"

"He figured it would be the best time for you."

"Yes, I suppose it is." He seemed hesitant, watching Katy.

She was so relieved to learn that he wouldn't be involved in the fighting that she spoke without thinking. "Do you want me to cover for you?"

"Damn, Katy, I don't want you involved in this."

"I think it's too late for that."

"But it would mean sleeping in my room, keeping everyone out until I returned. It would be all over the house tomorrow—about us sleeping together, I mean. Are you prepared for that?"

Thinking of Rachel's reaction, Katy was more than prepared. "I don't mind, really. Besides, is there any alternative?"

"No, I suppose not. Damn, I hate to put you in this position, but I must admit I could use your help."

"Then it's settled. But how are you two going to get out of here without being seen? Someone is bound to hear you, Kit, especially when you return."

Taking her hand, he led her to the closet. "See this knob? It may seem an ordinary doorknob, but if you pull it toward you, like this, it opens a sliding panel at the back of the closet. You see? My father did little enough in his last days, but I applaud the inspiration that made him decide to bequeath this suite of rooms to me for the rest of my life. It enabled me to have this secret passage built, early on in the war, as soon as it became evident that I would need to come and go without my brother's knowledge. This has worked out better than anticipated. That's how Billy got in, incidentally. What do you say, Billy?" Kit called over his shoulder. "Shall we go see Moultrie?"

"Yes and we'd better hurry. It'll soon be sunup."

"You go on ahead. I've a few things to say to Katy."

Billy grinned. "Sure enough. Only don't take too

long. Nice meeting you, Mrs. Warwick." Tipping his hat in her direction, he disappeared into the closet.

Kit turned a serious face to her. "Are you certain you want to do this?"

"I'll be just fine. It matters little to me where I sleep. I think you're just afraid Julian will scold you in the morning for bothering me with your amorous advances."

He chuckled. "Trust Julian to make me appear the fool."

"Not to me, Kit."

He looked at her, long and hard. Then he whisked her up off her feet. "You're shivering; let's get you into bed." With a gentleness that surprised her, he set her down on his bed and tucked the covers under her chin. It reminded her of bedtime, long ago, when her mother would settle her down for the night. She knew, with sudden intensity, that she couldn't bear to lose him. She wanted to grab him, to beg him to stay, but all she said was, "Be careful."

He pushed the hair from her face. "Don't worry about me. I've been doing this sort of thing for years. I should be back by dawn, but if I'm delayed, just tell Julian we had a fight and I went off in a huff. He'll believe that."

"Because I wouldn't welcome your amorous advances?"

"Are you ever going to forget that? I think you're the tease, not me. Tell him whatever you think best." He added as an afterthought, "Only try not to make me look like too much of a fool."

"Aye, aye, Captain."

He grinned. "Thanks for everything. Sweet dreams, Katy."

Sighing, she watched him make his way to the closet. Once there, he put a hand in his pocket. He lingered for a full minute before returning to her bedside. In his fingers dangled a ruby pendant, its warm color capturing the magic of the candlelight. Fascinated, Katy watched as he presented it to her tentatively, almost shyly.

"I almost forgot. This is for you. I planned on giving it to you to wear tonight, but Julian was so insistent on the diamonds. I figured this would seem so insignificant compared to them." He hesitated and when she said nothing, he continued. "If you don't want it, I understand. If you wish to give it away, that's fine."

He shrugged and dropped it in her lap. "I'd better be going."

Katy finally found her voice. "No wait! Please. I don't know what to say. It's beautiful; it must have cost you a fortune. I've never had anything like this in my life. And it's mine, not on loan until Julian and Rachel marry. Oh, I wish you had given it to me earlier! It would have been so much nicer than those awful diamonds. I still don't know what to say—but thank you."

She was half sitting, half kneeling on the bed. In the flickering candlelight, she presented a lovely picture. Her long hair hung loose on her shoulders, barely covering the creamy breasts that were revealed by the flimsy gown she wore. Desire burned in him so strongly that he couldn't trust himself to speak. As she struggled with the clasp, he fought the fire that threatened to consume him. He took the ruby pendant from her trembling fingers and placed it about her throat. With the greatest difficulty, he kept himself from kissing the soft flesh of her neck. The ruby glowed against the satiny smoothness of her skin. Innocently, she glanced up at him, tears brimming in her eyes. He would need to put distance between them or it would be harder and harder to resist this overwhelming temptation. Though he yearned to stay with her, he knew he must leave.

"It's perfect on you, Katy, as I knew it would be." His voice was level, betraying nothing of his inner struggle. "When you wear it, perhaps you'll think of me. But I've got to go now or Billy will be coming back after me."

Fingering the jewel, she watched him go. How could he be so thoughtful and considerate one minute, and then, without warning, so cold and distant? Blowing out the candle, she wondered for the hundredth time if she would ever succeed in making her husband love her.

Chapter 20

When Kit slipped back into their room, it was nearly daylight. The events of the past twelve hours made him feel far older than his twenty-six years. Not for the first time, he wished there was someone else to do his job, leaving him free to take Katy away from all this. Left to themselves, he was certain they could have a good life together. But it was not to be. He would have to leave her in the hands of his unscrupulous brother, who would no doubt do his best to convince her that her future was not with Kit. He crossed the room to stand by the bedside. Curled in a ball, Katy seemed so young that his hand moved automatically to pull the blankets over her. But she moved in her sleep, rolling over onto her back. This was no child who lay exposed before him. What was left of his will crumpled and he reached out to cup one breast in his strong hands. She groaned softly and moved closer to him. Gently, he stroked her, feeling the tightness grow in his belly. Her soft body was warm to his touch and his hands grew more insistent as they traveled over her. There was a ghost of a smile on her parted lips and Kit lost all sense of reality in his need of her.

All at once, her lashes fluttered and she opened her eyes wide. He was quick to recognize the flicker of fear and he cursed himself for the fool he was. Reluctantly, he pulled his hands away and tried to make light of it. "Sorry, love. You made an attractive picture. Far too attractive for me to resist. I was going to take you to your room, but those," he pointed to her breasts, "got in the way."

To his surprise and delight, she laughed. Still, she was quick in covering herself. "I see I should have listened to Julian."

Perhaps it hadn't been as bad as he feared. She was blushing but she wasn't angry. If he were any less exhausted, he might be tempted to test how far she would let him go, but he was in no mood for rejection. Wearily, he sat at the edge of the bed and tried to pull off his boots.

"Here, let me help you." Katy jumped to the floor and had hold of a boot. It was a scene he had imagined often, coming home tired to a solicitous Katy. Pulling at his boots, in that flimsy gown, she was better than his imagination. The familiar feeling began to boil in his belly and he was forced to look away.

Katy, seeing him turn his head, was suddenly embarrassed to be standing half-dressed in front of him. She grabbed for her wrapper. "It seems to me that we're lucky you were, uh, distracted. You're exhausted. If you had tried to lift me, we would both have landed on the floor. Here, let me help you undress and we'll get you into bed."

He waved an ineffectual hand in the air. "I can undress myself."

"That's highly unlikely. Don't worry, I'm not embarrassed. I've done it before, if you remember." Busy with the other boot, she missed the horrified expression. "How on earth do you get into these things?"

Suddenly, the boot gave way and both it and Katy went crashing to the floor. Kit looked down at her sitting in a very undignified position, and had to laugh. To his delight, she laughed too. He reached down to help her to her feet and she took his hand gratefully. But when he pulled, one or the other of them overexerted themselves, sending her crashing into his chest. Her face was dangerously close and he could feel her heart pounding against his ribcage. The laughing had ceased and for a full minute, they stared hungrily at each other. Despite his good intentions, he pulled her to him and poured his soul into the kiss they shared. She responded with an eagerness that amazed and excited him.

Reality reimposed itself on them with a commanding knock on the door. With an oath, Kit started to rise. Katy whispered softly into his ear. "No, get under the blankets. I'll get rid of whoever it is."

Kit kissed her on the forehead, murmuring "good girl," and without arguing, burrowed into the bed. Katy pattered over to the door. Before opening it, she glanced backward to see him grin at her before laying his head on the pillow to feign sleep. Katy jumped as their impatient caller knocked again. Recovering, she pulled her wrapper tighter and opened the door.

"Katherine! I hardly expected to find you here. Where's Kit?"

Did she have a sixth sense that enabled her to tell when Katy was alone with her husband? Or had this been prearranged? She felt betrayed as she faced a composed and lovely Rachel. It was barely morning and she contrived, somehow, to look as if she had spent all day preparing for this visit. It must have been prearranged. It caught her like a blow in the stomach. Her suspicions had been, after all, only suspicions, but to be face-to-face with Kit's beautiful mistress filled her with an anger that was hard to control. "Rachel. You're certainly up and about early this morning. I'm afraid Kit is still asleep. We had rather a late night, last night. Perhaps I can help?" Oh no, she was not going to make it easy for them.

Green eyes flashed their dislike before Rachel hastily recovered. She smiled sweetly, but it never reached her eyes. "No, my business was purely personal. I'll catch him when he's not quite so tired. Good morning."

That bitch. How she would love to scratch those green eyes. With some effort, Katy managed not to slam the door. Her hands strayed to her hair, to put it in some order to face Kit. She was a fool to try to compete with Rachel, but she knew she'd keep trying.

But he was asleep when she reached him. She was relieved not to have to risk an argument over Rachel, but how she wished they could go back to what they were doing. Working carefully, so as not to disturb him, she slipped off his clothes. Except for when she couldn't resist touching the golden curls on his chest, he never stirred. She folded the clothes and put them in a neat pile on a chair. If one of the slaves should come in, Kit wouldn't need to explain why he slept in his clothes. With one, last, wistful glance, she returned to the cold emptiness of her room.

Breakfast wasn't easy, but she was determined not to let the others suspect a thing. She blushed prettily when she told Julian that Kit was still sleeping and was gratified to see Rachel's eyes narrow. When he expressed a hope that Kit hadn't bothered her, she muttered some nonsense about her wifely duty. Rachel looked at her with ill-concealed disgust, but Julian clucked like a mother hen. Poor Katherine, indeed!

Making her excuses, she left the table as soon as it was politely possible and made her way to her room. Locking the door behind her, she went to the door to Kit's room. She planned to wait by the bed, until he woke, but when she entered, Kit was nowhere to be found.

He arrived, finally, five minutes late for the noonday meal. Smiling, he slipped into his seat and into the role Julian had designed for him. Katy hid her amusement and even encouraged him to appear the fool, deriving an almost sadistic pleasure at having someone besides herself in the role.

Kit surprised them all. "I say, Julian, what would you say to Katy and I stealing away to Oaks for a few weeks. It's spring and I have a yen to show her the plantation. That is, if you can spare me . . ."

"Naturally I can spare you. Perhaps we can all go."

"I had thought of it as a honeymoon trip."

"Of course. How thoughtless of me. I can spare you for a few days, I suppose. That is if Katherine wants to go."

Kit looked at her. "What do you say, darling. Shall we go to Oaks?"

Katy couldn't contain her excitement. "Oh yes! How soon can we leave?"

"That depends on you. How soon can you be ready?"

She jumped out of her chair. "Immediately. I'll go pack." Impulsively, she kissed his head and ran from the room.

When Kit joined her later, she was ready to leave. As she fastened her cape, he watched her thoughtfully. "You seem very anxious to go. Why?"

How could she tell him? Could she say she was excited at the prospect of being alone with him, of not having the beautiful Rachel to outshine her, of leaving the interfering Julian behind? Could she explain that she longed to see the house in which he had been raised, that he loved so? Could she tell him that she loved him so much that any time he could spare for her was like a gift? Sometime in the future, maybe, she could say those things, but not yet. Today, she could merely tell him that she was looking forward to the ride and to the change of scenery.

"I'm afraid I'll only be able to stay a few days with you. Rosie will come along later, but otherwise you'll be alone. Do you mind?"

"Not at all. How long shall I stay there?"

"I should return in a week or so. If I don't, I want you to return to Charleston. If the British do take the city, as everyone anticipates, they won't stop at that. I don't want you alone and unprotected at Oaks."

"I can take care of myself."

"Sometimes I wish you weren't so damned independent, Katy."

"And what is that supposed to mean?"

"Ah, nothing. Don't listen to me. I'm thinking too much about this damned war and it has me on edge. I know you can take care of yourself and it's a comforting thought. But I don't want you taking any unnecessary chances, do you hear?"

"Aye, aye, Captain."

"Come on, then. Let's go."

When they reached the hallway, Kit put his hands

over her eyes.

"What on earth are you doing?"

"It's a surprise. Just walk straight ahead. Don't worry, I won't let you bump into anything."

"Why are you doing this?"

"I'm making good on my debt. Here, what do you think? Can you manage her?"

Katy blinked up in the sunlight, trying to focus. In front of her stood a cream-colored mare, proud and haughty. Slowly, hand outstretched, Katy approached her. Though the animal watched her carefully, she allowed Katy to stroke her mane.

"What's her name?"

"We've been calling her Dawn, but since she's your horse now, you can name her whatever you want."

Your horse. He had remembered. Once again, the tears came unbidden, but she didn't try to stop them. His subtlety wasn't lost on her. Knowing that no horse could ever replace Midnight, he hadn't tried. Everything about her was different and Katy would be free to love her. "Dawn's a perfect name for her. She's beautiful, Kit. I never expected this."

"I gave you my word, didn't I?" Embarrassed by her gratitude, he spoke more abruptly than he intended. "Now hurry up and mount before Julian changes his mind and comes with us, after all."

"Thank you, Kit. Promise or not, it was a very nice thing for you to do. But I'm afraid we're too late. Here comes Julian now." Rubbing her eyes, she did her best to hide all traces of tears.

If he had noticed that she had been crying, Julian didn't mention the fact. Rather, he delayed their departure with a detailed account of what Kit was to do at Oaks. If he kept on, it wouldn't be much of a honeymoon trip. So with a skillful play on the reins, Katy convinced Dawn that she was restless. As the horse skitted and danced, a terrified Julian was only too happy to let them go on their way. Yes, she and Dawn would be good friends.

Both horses were strong animals and they made good time, aided by the fact that they wasted none of it in conversation. More than once, Katy opened her mouth to speak, but his look of grim determination made her bite back the words. He was in a rare mood, it seemed, and she wasn't about to spoil her adventure by arguing with him. Besides, it was a gorgeous day and she was happy just to be riding again.

The sun was going down as they reached the drive to Oaks. It was that magic, going-home-time-of-day, when everything is touched by a special light, its clarity lending a sense of unreality to everyday sights, making them seem almost achingly beautiful.

Kit was sitting forward in the saddle, his horse motionless, gazing wistfully ahead. With one hand, he gestured feebly in front of him. His voice was bitter. "And this, my dear, is the ancestral home of the Warwicks—Oaks, empty and falling into ruin."

Her eyes followed the direction of his outstretched hand, taking in every detail. Rising from a small knoll stood a large, white house, badly in need of a coat of paint, yet commanding attention in spite of it. Katy thought it a splendid house, remaining tall and proud amidst its fading grandeur. To her, it was the embodiment of Kit's dream; it was Kit himself and it filled her with pride. Its gracious lines spoke of a continuity, a legacy of the countless Warwicks that had lived and loved here. An air of hospitality beckoned to her, welcomed her as one of them, and for the first time

289

since leaving Clonmara, she felt as though she had come home. Unaware of Kit's eyes on her, she slipped off her horse and walked slowly to the door.

Kit watched her with pleasure, a slow smile spreading across his face. "You like it?"

"Oh, Kit, why didn't you bring me here first?"

The scowl returned. "As my brother would quickly point out, Oaks does not belong to me."

"I'm sorry, I hadn't meant to upset you. It's just that I think . . . no . . . I know I could be very happy here."

He was staring at the house with a faraway look in his eyes. "When I was younger, I had such dreams for this place. I liked to imagine bringing my bride home and filling the rooms with children's laughter. Now look at it. One laugh and the walls would collapse."

Timidly, she placed a hand on his arm. "It's not that bad. Oh, Kit, I know I'm not the bride you would have imagined, but I love this house. A spot of paint, a little love and care, and it would be as good as new. Let's pretend, just for this short time, that I am that bride, that you're bringing me home. Just this once?"

Slowly, he dismounted. "Well then, ma'am, it's a custom in these parts for a man to carry his bride over the threshold. If you will permit me?" Without waiting for her reply, he swept her up and carried her through the doorway. As he kicked the door behind him, he shouted into the semidarkness. "Lilah? Jeremy? Where is everybody?"

There was a shuffling sound and a middle-aged black man appeared. "Master Kit! This sure is a surprise. We thought you was in England."

Kit laughed. "So I was, Jeremy. And I brought someone back with me. I'd like you to meet Mrs.

Warwick."

Katy felt extremely foolish. "Kit, please let me down."

"Sorry, my dear. You're so light, I'd almost forgotten I was holding you." Still laughing, he set her on her feet. "Katy, this is Jeremy. If there's anyone in the world that knows Oaks better, I haven't met him."

Katy smiled at the beaming slave. "Hello, Jeremy."

"Master Kit, that sure was a mean trick to play on us, bringing your wife and not letting us know. There ain't no place for you to sleep. And there ain't no dinner, either. This ain't no place for your lady."

"Nonetheless, my lady insists upon staying. Besides, there was a problem with staying in Charleston. Mr. Warwick was beginning to entertain, again." As Jeremy nodded knowingly, he continued. "We won't need much. Perhaps Lilah could fix up my suite and we could have a cold dinner up there."

As if hearing her name, a woman appeared. "Master Kit, is that you? Who's the lady?"

Kit grinned. "Katy, this is Lilah. She was just on her way upstairs to prepare my suite, weren't you?"

"Are you up to one of your tricks?" She glanced meaningfully at Katy.

"Excuse me, I should have explained. This is Mrs. Warwick. We've ridden all the way from Charleston, so if you can also manage hot water for Katy and then some food, I'd be forever grateful."

"There's no need to go to all that trouble."

"Never you mind, missus. Me and Jeremy will see to it all. You go on up to Master Kit's room. I keep it ready for him all the time 'cause he's always surprising us with these visits of his. We'll have a fire going and everything fixed up in no time."

Kit shrugged his shoulders in a gesture of helplessness. "Once you've lived here awhile, you'll learn not to argue. Just do as she says. Personally, I'm not up to arguing; I doubt I can handle much more than my fork tonight. Come, I'll take you upstairs."

His room was much as she expected. Its masculinity denied the touch of a feminine hand, with its comfortable rather than lavish furnishings. It suited him far better than the room in Charleston. Kit soon had a fire going and as Katy drew up to it to warm her hands, she again experienced that feeling of belonging. Reluctantly, she followed Lilah through another room, a dressing room of sorts, into her own room. It was a hastily thrown together assortment of well-used furniture, but Lilah assured her there would be plenty of time later to arrange it to her taste. Not that she would be in much of a hurry, being on her honeymoon and all. Lilah giggled as she glanced over at Kit's room. Oh lord, Katy thought, they'll be expecting us to sleep together. Not that she'd mind, but would Kit be willing to take pretense that far?

She was startled out of her imaginings when Jeremy arrived with the hot water. Though it tempted her, she insisted the first bath go to Kit, who needed it more. With an appreciative grin, Jeremy assured her that he would take care of it. Katy did her unpacking. Rummaging through her clothes, she found what she wanted. Tonight, for sentimental reasons, she would wear the blue gown she had sewn from Kit's drapes. And her ruby, of course.

Bathed and dressed scarcely a half hour later, she entered his room. He was standing, hands in pockets, staring into the fire, looking lost and lonely. I love you, she thought tenderly, and I hate to see you this way.

He turned then, and abruptly, his expression was one of pleasure. "Here, let me look at you. Do you know, that gown has always been one of my favorites." He touched the ruby. "I'm glad you're wearing it."

Katy felt a thrill of excitement, but did her best not to take him too seriously. It was her suggestion, after all, that he play the adoring husband. He was charming, but she mustn't make the mistake that it was real.

Kit, on his part, did his utmost to charm her throughout the romantic candlelit dinner, but not for the reason she suspected. Yet, he was not blind to the fact that she was conspicuously quiet. Her wistful smiles did little to encourage him and eventually, he, too, fell silent, brooding that she found it so difficult to enjoy his company.

"Are you very tired?" She spoke quietly, gently.

He looked up, startled by the concern in her voice. "No, not very. Why do you ask?"

"It's just that one minute you were talking and then you grew so quiet. I know you didn't get much sleep last night. If you'd like to retire, I'd understand."

"I'm not that tired."

"Then what's wrong?"

"I thought I was boring you."

"Oh, Kit, no. Nothing could be farther from the truth."

"You've been rather quiet yourself. I've said some very funny things and you haven't laughed once."

"Yes, I did. Here, inside. I loved the story about the rabbit."

"Then why so quiet?"

"You'll laugh at me."

"No, I won't." He took her hands. "Tell me, I want to know."

Katy stared at their hands. "I know it sounds silly, but I guess I'm still shy. In all the time we've been married, we haven't spent much time together, alone. Here we are, finally, and I'm afraid I don't know how to act."

Kit thought he understood. What an idiot he had been not to realize. "Relax, Katy. I won't try to take advantage of you, I promise. I'm enjoying this, just being alone with you, talking with nobody interrupting us. It's as if we really are happily married and it's a memory I'd like to take with me when I leave."

Yes, that was bothering her too. At any moment this wonderful pretense of theirs could be over and he would be snatched away. But she would give him a memory he would never forget, of a happy Katy, a laughing Katy, a loving Katy. And maybe, just maybe when he came home, he'd no longer be satisfied with only pretense. Determined, she forced a smile. "Very well. I'll relax if you promise to finish that story about the rabbit."

"Then may I suggest we move over to the fire? I think we'd be far more comfortable over there."

Sipping her brandy, Katy listened to him, forgetting her shyness. Soon she was telling him things she had never shared with another human being before and time passed all too quickly.

Much to her dismay, Katy let a betraying yawn slip out and Kit was adamant. Tomorrow was another day. If they planned to enjoy it, they would need sleep. Pulling her to her feet, he led her to her room.

As she reached for the doorknob, his hand moved in

the same direction, for the same purpose. They met. At his touch, a tingling sensation sped through her veins. He must have felt it too, for his voice was husky. "Here, let me do it for you."

Katy stepped back while he opened the door. He executed an exaggerated bow, sweeping his hands in the air. In like manner, she curtsied prettily, and tried to glide past him.

"Not so fast." He grabbed her arm and drew her to him. "I want to thank you for a wonderful evening. No, dammit, that sounds so trite."

Gentle fingers played with her hair and his eyes searched hers. Something like pain settled in her chest. With excruciating slowness, his lips approached. They touched her own, warm and tender, and when they were withdrawn, Katy was left weak and shaken. His voice was barely a whisper. "Thank you for a memorable evening. I won't soon forget it."

Alone is his room, Kit felt proud of himself. Even Sam couldn't complain. Another brandy and he'd never have left her with just one kiss, but he'd watched his drinking carefully. He was sure she had enjoyed tonight. If he could keep his patience, the day would soon come when she'd willingly sleep with him in that big mahogany bed. Oh, he'd be patient, for as long as it took, even if it killed him.

Chapter 21

Instantly awake, Kit jumped to a sitting position, his heart pounding madly. It was some time before reality and reason reimposed themselves.

Katy was sitting on the edge of the bed, looking pretty in a red and white flowered dress, holding a tray. "I didn't do that at all well, did I?" She sighed. "I'm sorry. I hadn't meant to startle you; it's such a beautiful day and I hate to see you waste it in bed."

He tried to wipe the fogginess from his eyes. "What time is it?"

"Ten or so. I've waited and waited, honestly I did, but I'm not very patient. You promised to take me riding this morning and I began to fear there would be no morning left." She held up a tray. "I've brought your breakfast."

With both sleep and panic gone, he could smile. "Good girl. I'm famished."

"Then you're not angry?"

"Not at all. I'm glad you came for me, I don't usually sleep this late. And I did make a promise."

Visibly, she relaxed. "Oh good. Enjoy your breakfast, then, and I'll meet you downstairs."

"What's the hurry? Can't you sit awhile and talk to me? I'm told that's what married people do."

Sitting down again, she grinned. "As a matter of fact, I suppose I should warn you. I've planned to make a day of it. I took it upon myself to ask Lilah to pack a picnic lunch."

"What?" He pretended horror. "Can you honestly plan to take the day off when there's so much to be done? What would Julian say?"

Crossing over to the windows, she laughed. "I'll take care of the chores after you've gone. But," she said as she drew open the drapes, "tell me you care what Julian says on a day like this."

"I can't see anything from the bed. If you would be so kind as to turn your head, I'll, uh, try to make myself decent."

Not long ago, his nakedness would have embarrassed her, but today she felt very wifely. Nonetheless, she turned her head obediently and looked out the window. Oaks, by morning light, was even more impressive. Its dark fields stretched on and on, and little bits of green sprouted from the cultivated rows.

"What are they growing?"

"Our crop, known to the locals as Warwick's folly, is cotton. Julian refuses to plant anything else and unless he gets some sense in that thick skull of his, he's going to complete our ruin."

"But what's wrong with cotton?"

"Nothing. Warwicks have always grown cotton, as Julian would point out. But with the war on, there's no market for it. My brother refuses to admit that we've severed ties with Britain. Our cotton has rotted on the docks for three years now, but in his infinite wisdom, Julian continues to plant it."

"What should he plant?"

"Any number of things. Tobacco, vegetables, rice. If you'll look over to the right, to the Videaux place, you can see how well Esther has done. And my friend, Francis Marion, has been doing experiments with indigo. He seems to think it should do well in our swamplands. But of course, he had to put it aside for the war."

The war. Could she really have forgotten how close it was? Continuously creeping up on them, it waited out there to make its claims on her husband. Staring at the peaceful fields, she shuddered. Would the fighting come close enough to rob them of their dignity and beauty? Would it require the life of the plantation's second son?

She jumped as Kit touched her shoulder. "Why so glum? I thought we were going to enjoy today."

With an effort, she willed herself to smile up at him. The war and all its viciousness would have to wait. Today, Kit still belonged to her.

On Katy's request, the tour began in the fields. Their vastness filled her with pride. Curious fieldhands stepped over to see the Master's woman and quick on the heels was a weasley little man, cracking a whip which disappeared as he realized it was Kit, and not Julian. When Kit introduced him as Silas Wharton, the overseer, Katy refused to shake his hand. It was impossible to hide her dislike. Realizing this, Kit laughed and hurried her along before she lost her temper and said something they would both regret.

They had their picnic on a grassy knoll in a meadow that was not, as Kit explained, strictly part of the property. Not that Esther would mind them using it.

Katy waited until after the lazy meal, when Kit settled his head on her lap, to let her curiosity get the better of her. She wanted to know more about this Esther.

"Why, my dear, I do believe you're jealous!"

"Don't be absurd. You all speak of her so often, and with such respect, that naturally I'm curious."

"Naturally. There's no mystery, love. Esther is a neighbor and a good friend. She's more or less promised to another friend you've heard me mention, Francis Marion, so there's no need to be jealous. Stop scowling. I'm only teasing you. Say, I've got an idea." He jumped up, pulling her to her feet. "I'll take you over there to meet her."

"Now? Oh, Kit, I couldn't. Look at me, look at these grass stains. I'm in no state to be visiting."

"Don't worry, Esther won't mind. She'd be far more upset if I failed to bring my new wife over to meet her."

Later, in Esther's garden, Katy was glad that he had insisted. Esther put down her tools and rushed to welcome them both. Even in her old workclothes, she retained a sophistication and worldliness that Katy envied, yet admired. Now here was a woman who could teach her how to be a lady. Katy liked this Esther, with her keen sense of humor and her obvious affection for Kit.

"What is the matter with me? I got so excited at seeing you that I've forgotten my manners. Here I am keeping you out in the hot sun when I know you're just dying for something to drink. Let's go in. Only I must ask you not to mention anything about Charleston to Francis. He gets so worked up about it, I've had to restrict his visitors. The way things are going, I'm so afraid he'll try to get up and walk, and further damage that foot."

"Francis is here?"

"I thought that was why you came. How flattering. You mean you came to see me?"

"Katy wanted to meet you. And it's been far too long since I've had any of your famous biscuits."

"You're in luck. I baked this morning. Come, Katy, you can help me with the tea and we'll let the gentlemen talk about their war."

Katy was comfortable with Esther and it was nice to be herself for a change. Talking of trivial matters, it was evident that Esther accepted her as Kit's wife, for whatever reason. There were no speculative looks, no sly questions, and no allusions to Rachel. It was a thoroughly enjoyable experience.

When they joined the men, Katy was surprised by Francis Marion. He was not at all what she had expected. From the way Kit and his men talked about him, she had been anticipating a huge bear of a man. It seemed strange that this soft-spoken, courteous gentleman, propped up with pillows in the chair by the fire, was the military genius Kit claimed him to be. The only time he raised his voice was in reference to his "cursed ankle", and even then he apologized to the ladies. Though he was not quite like her expectations, as people seldom are, Katy liked him. As Esther had, he made her feel welcome.

Much too soon, Kit made their excuses and rose to leave. Katy would have preferred to stay, but she recognized the gratitude on Esther's face as she glanced from Kit to the colonel. Esther made Katy promise to come for a visit soon, as she'd like the opportunity to get to know her better.

They rode back to Oaks in companionable silence. It

was late. Already a rosy glow was spreading in the sky. Katy remembered Kit's dream; would she be with him in the future to help fulfill it?

He broke into her thoughts. "Tomorrow, I think I shall take you into the swamps. I spent a great deal of time there when I was younger, and even now I like to roam around in them. I think you'll enjoy the trip."

"Swamps. I like that word. Much nicer than bog."

"Much nicer looking, too. Well, here we are. Home, at last."

"I like that word, too. Home."

"It does have rather a nice ring to it." He helped her dismount. "Come along. If we hurry, we should catch the sunset."

Obediently, she followed him to a small hill behind the house. "So, what do you think?"

Like that other time, Kit's face took on the glow of the setting sun, making him seem part of it. Yes, she could understand his dream, his pride, his hope. Though he might never be aware of it, his dream would always be her dream; his hope, her hope. No matter what different paths this crazy war led them to, the sunset would mean Kit to her, and she'd never again enjoy one without him.

He slipped his arm around her waist and led her back to the house. Darkness was closing in around them, but she felt secure in his grasp. Near the house, someone stepped out of the bushes in front of them. Instinctively, Kit thrust her behind his back.

"Kit, it's me. Sam."

"For God's sake, Sam. What are you doing here, jumping out of bushes, scaring people half to death?"

"Sorry. Didn't know who was around. We've received orders. We're to sail on the morning tide."

"Already?"

"The British are here. We've got to get out before daybreak, if we want to get out. Our passengers are waiting."

"Damn! I'm not ready to go yet. I had hoped for more time."

"I know, son, but orders are orders. And there are people depending on you. I can give you tonight, but I'll need you in the morning."

"Tonight? Are you sure?"

"Go on with you, boy; you're not indispensable. I can take care of things on the ship. You just see to it your wife is settled before you leave. There's no telling when we'll be back."

Katy shivered at his words. "I'll be fine, Sam; don't worry about me. You take care of yourself. And my ship."

"Aye, lass, that I will. And I'll be watching out for that man of yours, too."

Blushing, she leaned over to kiss his cheek. "Thank you. Oh I hate this war, Sam. I hate it."

Folding his hands over hers, he gave them a squeeze. "Hold on, lassie, and we'll see an end to it sooner or later. Kit, you'd best get her in the house. She'll be catching her death, standing out here shivering. I'll see you in the morning."

Kit wrapped an arm around her shoulder and they watched Sam disappear into the night. Sighing, he led her into the cozy kitchen, but the pleasure of being home was spoiled for them both. There was little to say at dinner; the memory of the gaiety of the previous evening lingered like an unwanted ghost, making them feel suddenly like strangers, even to themselves. Shy and awkward with each other, they

302

stumbled through the polite phrases and meaningless conversation until it was mutually conceded that it was time to retire. After all, it had been a long day and tomorrow, well, tomorrow they would both need to be rested.

All the way up the stairs, Katy searched through her mind for the right words. Kit knew the words but lacked the courage. Then they were in front of her door and time had run out. It hurt too much to say good-bye. Not trusting himself to speak, and not altogether sure his voice would work if he made the attempt, Kit kissed her gently, drawing in the warmth, the very scent of her, and then quietly left her standing in the hall.

Katy was numb. Was it always going to be like this? Would she always come so close, so agonizingly close, only to find him gone? Had it all been pretense then? He was leaving in the morning and he hadn't bothered to say good-bye. Had she read too much into a relationship that probably didn't exist? While she had been giving and loving, had he been taking and laughing at the foolish little girl who should know better by now. You are a fool, she told herself sternly, to waste time worrying about it. It's quite likely you'll never know. He's leaving tomorrow and, in Sam's words, there's no telling when he'll come back.

Empty and defeated, she undressed. As she glanced at the useless nightgown she had packed, she laughed bitterly. Back in Charleston, anything had seemed possible. It was lovely, but its transparent finery would never be appreciated by anyone but herself. Sliding under the covers, she told herself to get used to sleeping alone.

There was a noise. Looking up, she saw Kit in the

doorway, barely distinguishable in the rosy glow of the dying fire. "Katy? Are you still awake?"

"Yes." She kept her tone flat, noncommittal.

"I couldn't sleep, either."

Katy sat up. In spite of everything, she found herself hoping again. "Did you want something?"

He shrugged, looking oddly vulnerable. "Katy, I can't just go away and not talk to you." There was silence as he waited for encouragement.

"Come in, then. You can sit here." She shifted her position to make room on the bed.

It took him three strides to reach her, but he hesitated at the bed. Up close, she could see he was clad only in trousers, but he seemed unaware of his state of undress or its effect on his wife. Something was obviously bothering him. Afraid to know, and yet reluctant to have him leave, she patted the bed. Absentmindedly, he sat, his back to her. "Funny. In my room, I had a thousand things to say, but now, the only words I seem to find are, 'I'm sorry'."

"Sorry? For what?"

"Sorry for everything. If it wasn't for me, you'd be safe in England. I should have left you there or at least sent you back the minute we landed."

She stiffened. So he was talking about England again. "I'm in no danger."

He turned to face her. "I hope not. But I have this terrible feeling about leaving you. You've got to promise that if Charleston falls, you'll go to Julian. At least he can protect you."

"I'll go, if that's what you want, but don't worry about me. I'll manage just fine."

"You're probably right. I suppose I'm being foolish. After all, you are British and as my brother would quickly point out, highly connected. I don't imagine you'll notice I'm gone."

It seemed almost a question and she answered automatically. "You could take me with you."

"What?"

"I won't get in the way. I can be cook. You still need one, don't you? Or I'll do whatever you need me to do. I'll be a tremendous help, I swear it." She spoke quickly, to finish before he could say no. If she was making a fool of herself, she was past caring. He leaned over and ran his lean fingers through her hair.

"You can't come with me, Katy, and we both know it. You're safer here. I've risked your life too often and I won't do it again."

"Don't patronize me. I'm not a child. If you don't want me with you, just say so."

He grabbed her shoulders and held her at arm's length. "Good God, Katy. All I want is for you to be out of this." He tightened his grip. "If anything happened to you . . ."

He halted as her eyes widened. Releasing her, he dropped his hands to his sides. "Oh lord. I didn't mean to frighten you. I'm sorry. I guess I always do the wrong thing where you're concerned."

"I'm not frightened." She spoke softly, her love and longing for him shining in her eyes.

Kit was lost in those eyes. Beckoning, beguiling, bewitching; he was powerless to refuse. Never before had he been so conscious of her as a woman. Kneeling before him in that filmy gown, she was more desirable than ever. He could feel the pulsing of her blood in his fingertips, his head was swimming with the scent of her. All he could think of was that he wanted to possess her, once and for all time. With all his might, he tried to summon the strength to put her from him, but when she looked at him like that, it was all he could do to breathe. For a full minute he stared down at her, storing the vision for the long, dry days ahead. Stroking the soft, white flesh of her arms, he was drawn closer, like a moth to a flame. Something new was kindled in her eyes and he couldn't take his own off her. All that existed was Katy. God forgive me, he thought, for she never will, but I can't be patient any longer. Part of him hungered to take her right there and then, but he wanted this moment to last forever. He held her tightly and she didn't fight him. His brain was on fire, but still he held himself in check. Caressing her slowly, gently, he felt her respond. They touched, hesitantly at first, and with their growing passion their lips sought each other. Kit would have willingly declared himself her slave, but he was afraid to speak lest he break the spell. His nerves tingled where she touched him; it was sweet torture to delay the moment when she would finally belong solely to him. As her touch grew more urgent, all rational thought was driven from his mind. His mouth was on hers, possessively, and his body was telling her all the things his lips refused to say. She was warm and alive and willing beneath him and he was lost in the wonder of it.

He took her, tenderly at first, but his need for her was mounting. As always, they moved as one. At the last moment, he tried to hold back, to prolong it, but she was moaning in his ear, driving all reason from his mind. Wave after wave of sheer pleasure assailed him. Katy gripped him tightly and called out his name. Slowly, still clasping each other, they slipped back to reality.

Kit opened his eyes and looked down at his wife. Never had she seemed so beautiful and never had he loved her more. His body still vibrated with the pleasure of that love and he swore he would do everything in his power to keep her from going to England. She belonged to him now and he'd never let her go. Her soft, brown hair spread like a fan on the white pillow. As he reached out to touch it, her lashes fluttered and she opened her eyes to look up at him. Small tears lingered at the edges of her lids.

"Did I hurt you?"

Her lips trembled and the tears multiplied, dripping down to the pillow. Kit watched helplessly, concern and remorse filling his features. "Oh God, I'm sorry. I know I promised, but you were so damned beautiful, I couldn't stop."

She placed a fingertip on his lips. "No, Kit. Please don't be sorry. I'm not."

"You're not? But you're crying . . ."

"I'm always crying. I try hard not to, but I can't seem to control it any more."

"But why are you crying? I don't understand."

"To tell the truth, I'm not sure I do either. I never used to cry like this, honestly. But it was so wonderful and then I thought, this is the last time. Tomorrow, you'll be gone. It doesn't seem fair. We could have had so many nights like this and we wasted them all, fighting over such silly things."

Kit didn't trust his ears. "Do you mean that? Will you miss me, Katy?"

"Kit, take me with you."

The appeal in her eyes almost finished him. Shutting his mind to it, he dragged himself off of her and flopped on the bed. "Katy, don't do this."

Oh lord, when would she learn? She must remember to keep it light, carefully avoiding pitiful scenes like this one. "I'm sorry. I guess I gave way to panic. You see, I've gotten to depend on you."

"Oh, Katy." He sounded tired, defeated.

"I've said before that I'm entirely capable of taking care of myself, if need be, so you needn't worry. I'm just being terribly silly, I'm afraid. I thought women were allowed to be silly sometimes. Indeed, I thought it was expected of them."

"No one wishes more than I that I didn't have to go."

"I know. I was being selfish, thinking only of myself. Will you be in any danger?"

"Danger? No more than usual. No, Katy, I'll be safe enough. You needn't worry about me either."

"You don't seem too happy about it."

"I'm not. I'm so damned tired of sneaking around, pretending to be someone I'm not. Just once, I'd like the chance to do some honest fighting."

Timidly, she touched his hand. "You will, Kit. Colonel Marion respects you; I could see it when he talked to you. He knows better than to waste your talents."

"But that's the problem. With Francis out of action, himself, I don't stand a chance of having any part in saving Charleston."

"Then I'll just have to talk to this General Moultrie of yours. Once I get done with him, he'll have no choice but to make you a colonel, at least."

Kit chuckled. "I pity the general. You realize, of course, that you're to do no such thing. Moultrie would have my head if I let you loose on him."

"I was only trying to cheer you up."

"I know." He rolled on his side, propped himself up

on an elbow and played with her hair. "And I appreciate it. This isn't going to be easy for either of us, I'm afraid. Oh, Katy, you're not going to cry again, are you?"

"Of course not." She sniffed, in a very unladylike manner. "I don't suppose you have a handkerchief?"

He grinned. "Afraid not. I didn't bring too much with me."

"It's just as well. You'll be accusing me of stealing it."

"You never forget a thing, do you?" Gently, he used a finger to remove the tears from her eyes. "Tell me, will you miss me?"

"Of course," she answered flippantly. "Who will I fight with?"

"I daresay you can always find someone."

"Probably. But there's nobody quite like you when you get angry. You can be so stern with me."

"Only when you do something stupid."

She popped up. "Christopher Warwick, you know I don't do stupid things. It's your interpretation of them that's stupid."

"Good lord. Let's not quarrel tonight."

"I have a foul temper. Grandfather always warned me that it would get me into trouble. I don't want to fight, either. Let's keep pretending we're like any other happily married couple, that you don't have to go tomorrow. Can't we?"

"We can at least give it a try."

"Will you stay with me? Sleep with me all night and kiss me when you leave?"

"Do you want that?"

"Yes."

"Then come here and let's get comfortable. No,

309

closer. Here. I want to hold you. There, that's better, don't you think?''

Nodding, she felt so much better that she felt like crying again. Even though he was going away, she had never been happier. Nestled in his arms, she was where she wanted to be, where she knew she belonged. Suddenly, her future was brighter; she had never known such peace. Kit's warm breath fell softly on the back of her neck and she sighed in contentment.

As Kit thought of the past two days, his mind also was at peace. He hated to leave her, but now he had hope. If it was still too soon for love, at least she trusted him. They could build a life on that. He wanted to talk about their future together, but she was breathing deeply. It hadn't taken her long to fall asleep. Did she always sleep so peacefully? Oh God, how he longed to stay with her. There was so much he wanted to know, so much he needed to learn about her, so much left unsaid and undone. Once again, he would need to force himself to be patient, but at least he had had tonight. The memory of it would make the long days and nights that stretched ahead of him seem more bearable. For the first time in his life, there would be a reason for coming home; this time, there would be someone waiting for him.

Chapter 22

Time, which seemed so short yesterday, now stretched endless and empty. Katy, habitually an early riser, felt no need to get out of bed. What was the purpose? What would she do? Breakfast held no attraction. Nor did reading, walking, or even riding. Nothing would be much fun alone.

But this was ridiculous. All her life she had done these things alone. Could one wonderful day change her life so drastically? Yet, was it just since yesterday? Or had Kit always been in her thoughts since the beginning? As long as she could remember, she had spent her mornings planning what she would do or say when she saw him. But today she wouldn't see him, nor tomorrow or the next day. It was clear that she would revise her thinking if she planned to survive this war.

She spent the morning wandering aimlessly about the house, unable to settle her interest on anything. There was none of Rachel's cool efficiency here. Aside from the kitchen and the parlor, dust covered everything. If steps weren't taken in the near future, valuable pieces of furniture would be ruined by neglect. A little dusting, scrubbing, and polishing, and this house could be quite a showplace. Faint stirrings of guilt pricked at her conscience but nothing penetrated the blanket of lethargy. It seemed to require too much energy to know where to begin.

In the early afternoon, she was roaming around on the second floor when Lilah informed her of a visitor. Surprised, Katy hurried down the stairs. It was Esther Videaux with an invitation for tea that afternoon. Uncomfortably, Katy led her into the parlor.

"Please excuse the condition of the house. I haven't had time to set things to rights yet."

"Please call me Esther. Otherwise, you'll make me feel quite ancient." She smiled pleasantly.

Katy felt compelled to smile, too. "Then please call me Katy. I'm not accustomed to the Mrs. Warwick yet, and Katherine seems so formal."

"Very well, Katy, will you and Kit come for tea this afternoon? Your visit yesterday was so good for Francis."

Katy struggled to find a reasonable excuse for Kit's absence, to avoid suspicion. Esther noticed the hesitation. "Of course, how foolish of me. You're honeymooning. Naturally you'd prefer to be left alone. Perhaps we can make it some other time?"

"Oh no, it's not that. We, I mean, Kit, well, Kit isn't here." She broke off feebly.

"Kit isn't here? I don't mean to pry, but it's important I know. It's the war, isn't it? The British have already attacked?"

Katy nodded. "Please, don't tell anyone. Kit must keep it all a secret. Not even Lilah knows."

"Certainly. I have reasons of my own to keep this quiet. If Francis were to learn of this, there's no telling

312

what he'd do. But, Katy, surely you're not considering remaining here alone?"

"I'll be fine. I've no intention of returning to Julian if I can help it."

"Yes, I can understand that. But you can't stay here alone. It's just not practical. Come and stay with us until Kit returns."

"I couldn't impose."

"Nonsense. I would be glad of the company."

"Oh, Esther, so would I, but you have enough to do with Mr. Marion without the added burden of a guest. Besides, how could we explain my presence to him without causing suspicion? No, as much as I'm tempted to accept your generous offer, I'd be better off here."

"What will you do? This house hasn't been lived in for years."

"I know. I have a lot of work, but then, they say it will be a long war."

"You can't mean to take this on by yourself?" She grinned. "But of course you do, I can see it in your eyes. You're already planning what to do next while sitting here talking to me."

"I'm sorry. I didn't know I was so obvious."

"Don't apologize. I quite understand. I'd be the same myself. I envy you your project. If I weren't so busy myself, I'd offer my services. But please, don't hesitate to stop by for a chat when this old house gets to be too much for you. I want to hear of your progress."

"I'd like to do that, very much. It's rather lonely here without Kit."

"Yes, that boy has a way of filling up a room, doesn't he?"

"It's certainly empty enough without him."

Esther placed a comforting arm on her shoulders. "This war can't last forever. Kit will be coming home soon. In the meantime, though, if you need someone to talk to, remember I'm available. I wish I could stay now, but Francis will fret if I'm gone too long."

"I understand." Katy saw her to the door, taking her hand and clasping it as she said good-bye. "Thank you, Esther. Your visit has cheered me more than you can know. It makes a difference to know you're here, that I'm not truly alone."

"Then don't be a stranger. Come to visit us, soon."

Katy laughed. "Don't worry, I will. I only hope I don't become a nuisance." She stayed in the doorway, watching Esther's buggy disappear down the drive. It was funny, but the visit had cheered her. In fact, she felt quite excited about the prospect of setting the house to rights. Calling to Lilah, she started making plans. The first floor required the most attention for the present, so she might as well begin in the receiving rooms. Speechless, Lilah followed her, listening as Katy spoke of her intentions. When she stopped for breath, Lilah broke in.

"Begging your pardon, Miz Katy, but I don't have time for all this work, and cooking for the fieldhands and all."

"I realize that, Lilah. I can see that you're doing the work of two women already. I was asking your advice, not your help. I have no idea where to find supplies and I hoped you might help me with that."

"I don't mean no disrespect or nothing, but are you crazy? How is a little bit of a thing like you going to tackle this monster of a house, all by herself? Miz Katy, I've tried. It breaks my heart to see Oaks going

314

to ruin, but it just can't be saved by one person alone."

Katy refused to be discouraged. "You're not telling me anything I don't already know. It doesn't matter. I have to keep busy until my husband returns and I doubt there's any way to keep busier, don't you agree? I'll start in here and work my way through the rest of the house. I may be old and gray before I finish, but I plan to enjoy myself immensely. Now, do you think you could tell me where to find some rags and soap?"

Lilah shook her head. "Miz Katy, you are crazy, just like that man of yours. Probably just as stubborn, too. Well, come along then, and let's see what we can find. We'd better open these windows if we want to breathe while we work."

"We?"

"You don't think I'd let you be crazy by yourself, do you? Jeremy can let those weeds go another day; we'll need him to do the lifting. That furniture's too heavy for us."

A slow grin spread across Katy's face. "It is rather a challenge, isn't it?"

"Seems like you and me understand each other, Miz Katy. Together, we just might get the better of this old house."

They spent the rest of the afternoon on that goal. With Jeremy's help, the floor was scrubbed and polished, heavy drapes were taken outside to be aired and even the dirty carpet came back to life. The slaves had to leave to prepare dinner, but Katy worked until she was satisfied with the results. It was only one room, but what a difference it made. Tomorrow, if she could ignore her aching muscles, she would tackle the dining room.

By the end of the week, she had reclaimed the parlor, the morning room, the dining room, and the spacious hallway. The library, with all its volumes, was too much of a challenge for now, so she chose Kit's apartments next. Supervising the moving of furniture, she heard a commotion on the drive. Anticipating that Rosie had finally arrived, Katy flew down the stairs. She had missed the black woman's gentle bullying, and she had to admit the extra hands would be welcome.

When she threw open the door, it was Julian, not Rosie, who stood before her.

"Julian! And Rachel. What a surprise!"

The green eyes raked her over. "Apparently."

"I was expecting Rosie."

"Katherine my dear. We hate to catch you off guard like this, but there was no way to warn you. We simply had to get out of that city before it was overridden with soldiers. The British have laid siege and no one knows when this mess will be over. I could see no reason to endanger our lives needlessly. Why, where's that brother of mine?"

Katy, feeling conspicuous in her dirty clothes, didn't hear half of what he said. But Rachel, pushing past her into the hallway, repeated his question. "Yes, Katherine, where is the happy bridegroom?"

She hadn't planned for this. Why weren't they in Charleston where they belonged? Mind racing, she mumbled what she had told the slaves. "Oh, Kit. He's gone. You know him. When I announced my plans to do a thorough cleaning of this place, he took to the swamps. He's been dying to go and since I was going to be so busy, I told him to go enjoy himself and to take as much time as he wanted."

Rachel was smiling, gloating. Julian was thoughtful. "In the swamps, you say? I never could understand his fascination for them, but I suppose it's just as well. I certainly have no need for him at the moment. But, Katherine, my dear, I don't understand. You are doing the cleaning? What can Chris be thinking of to permit this?"

"Kit had nothing to do with it. I could hardly live in this house the way it was and there was no one else to do the job. In fact, I'm afraid I don't have rooms prepared for either of you. It seemed more important to restore the ground floor first."

"You're quite right, of course." Katy bristled as he glanced distastefully around the cleaned hallway. "I had no idea how badly this place had deteriorated. I haven't been home in years. That drive is appalling. No matter, we'll deal with it. I've brought a sizable staff from town so there's no further need for you to dirty those lovely hands of yours, Katherine."

"I don't mind honest work, Julian."

Too late, she saw the raised eyebrows. In her annoyance, she had forgotten who she was supposed to be. But this was her project. Were they going to dance in, with their army of slaves, and take it away from her? Apparently, and she was powerless to stop them. Close to choking on frustration, she strained to be polite. She resented their presence, but it was her duty to arrange for rooms for them. Cursing like a sailor under her breath, Katy decided it had better be a short visit. Too much time in the same place with these two would drive her into insanity. One more knowing smile from Rachel, and it would be without teeth.

The days passed slowly. Repairs continued throughout the house, but Katy had lost control of it. Julian was insistent that she concern herself with domestic arrangements only, leaving the restoration in Rachel's capable hands. Oh, she could understand Kit's frustration with his brother. She knew she should be happy to see the house come to life again, but Julian made it all too plain that it belonged to him and that she and Kit were only guests.

Whenever possible, she would sneak out of the house. Dawn was a willing accomplice and they would escape together, if only for a few hours. Very often, Katy would visit Esther, to complain about Julian.

One afternoon, when she walked into the stable, she found Sampson with Dawn, treating a scratch on her hind leg. It was rather a deep cut and Katy winced when she saw it. "Sampson, what happened?"

"Miz Katy, you done scared me for sure. I was hoping to fix her up before you saw it. I know how you feel about your horse and I sure hate to cause you grief."

"How did you scratch her?"

"Wasn't me, Miz Katy. It was Miz Worthington. She don't know nothing about horses."

"What was Rachel doing on Dawn? She's my horse."

"Please don't be angry with me. I only does as I'm told, else I get whipped. When Miz Worthington tells me to saddle a horse, I gotta do her bidding."

"I'm sorry, Sampson; I didn't mean to scream at you. I was worried about Dawn and angry at Rachel. She has no right to touch my horse. I'm going to have to talk with Mr. Warwick about this. Do you know where he is?"

"Went out to the fields."

"I suppose I shall have to go after him. Can you prepare another horse for me? I think this situation must be dealt with immediately."

Sampson's smile stretched from one ear to the other. "My pleasure, ma'am. I'll have that horse of yours as good as new when I gets done with her, too."

"I'd appreciate that, Sampson. And I'll do my best to see that Rachel never again gets the opportunity to maul her."

Later, approaching Julian, Katy lost a good deal of her confidence. How like his brother he looked when he was angry. Apparently, something was wrong with his carriage because both he and Wharton were standing by it, Julian screeching and Wharton cringing. It was not a good time for her complaint and she would have turned and ran, like the coward she was, if Julian hadn't spotted her first. "Oh, Katherine, what on earth are you doing here? Some domestic crisis that only I can solve? As if I don't have enough problems. Well, what is it?"

The little boy pout dissolved whatever fear she had. "It can wait. Maybe I can help with your problem. What's wrong?"

With a derisive snort, Wharton showed his contempt of her abilities. "You go on home, Miss. This here is man's work."

"No, wait. She can at least get some fieldhands to help us."

"Begging your pardon, sir, but all the fieldhands in the world ain't gonna get that horse to budge if he don't want to."

"I hold you responsible for this, Wharton. You will find some way to get this carriage home; I refuse to walk another step."

"I'm trying, Mr. Warwick, the best I can. That horse is too scared to move."

Katy left them to their aruging and walked over to the horse in question. He stood absolutely still, eyeing her suspiciously. Huge welts were springing up on his back and hindquarters. Katy spun around, pointing an accusing finger at the overseer. "Have you been beating this horse?"

"Had to be done. The stupid animal won't move."

"I can have no idea how your mind works, but it would seem rather obvious that the horse won't move because you're beating him. The beating isn't doing any good, except maybe satisfying your sadistic impulses."

"Now you just wait a minute. It was that gunshot that spooked him, not me. I only whupped him to get him going again."

"He's right, Katherine. Something, I suppose it could have been gunfire, scared the beast and he went flying. We've been unable to convince him to go home. I've ruined a new pair of boots, a perfectly good pair of trousers and I'm not altogether certain there is anything left of my feet. If whipping will get the beast to move, then by all means, Wharton, do your best."

As Wharton raised his whip, Katy lifted a hand to stop him. "Please, Julian, give me a chance first. If I can't convince your horse to move, Mr. Wharton will still have ample opportunity to vent his frustrations on the poor animal."

"I admire your concern for the 'poor animal', but really, my dear, what do you know about horses?"

"Whitney Hall had a very fine stable and Grandfather encouraged me to spend whatever time I wished in it. I know a great deal about horses and I know I can convince this one to take you home."

Whitney Hall was the key word. "Certainly, my

dear. I had forgotten you lived in the country. Please, try your best."

"Aw, Mr. Warwick . . ."

"That will be enough, Wharton."

Katy was busy with the horse. She had spoken with a conviction she didn't feel, but she could hardly stand by while this poor horse was subjected to another beating. Why, he was trembling. Swallowing her anger at the injustice of it, she forced her voice to be gentle, calming, coaxing. As she stroked his mane, she spoke soothing, promising words. After several minutes of this, she could feel the horse relax. Whether he understood her assurances or whether it was merely her tone, Katy couldn't be sure, but to her relief, she was soon able to lead the horse to where Julian was standing. "I hope you don't mind, Julian, but I think it best if I lead the horse back to Oaks for you. He trusts me, I think, and in case another emergency arises, I'd better be there."

"I'll see that Mr. Warwick gets home."

"That horse won't let you within ten feet of him." As if to support her accusation, the horse snorted in Wharton's direction.

Julian laughed. "Let that be a lesson to you, Wharton. You take Katherine's horse and she can drive home with me in the carriage. You can drive a carriage, can't you?"

Though she had never done so before, she was not about to admit it. "Certainly, but we will need to travel slowly. And I want Mr. Wharton's word that he won't use his whip on that horse."

"That's reasonable enough. You heard, Wharton? No whip?"

"If you say so, sir." With a sneer for Katy's benefit,

he mounted and left in the direction of Oaks.

"It would appear you have made yourself an enemy, my dear. Wharton doesn't like being bested by anyone, especially a woman."

"I daresay I shall muddle through somehow, without his friendship."

Julian chuckled, reminding her suddenly of Kit. "I have this feeling that you and I are going to be such good friends, Katherine. What do you say, shall we start the drive home?"

"With pleasure."

Managing the carriage, even over the rough roads of the fields, was easier than she had anticipated, and she was able to converse with her brother-in-law. She listened while he spoke about his cotton crop, asking intelligent questions, impressing him with her interest.

"You're an unusual woman, Katherine. Most women would have been intolerably bored with this conversation."

"Farleys, despite their other achievements, have always been farmers. It's in my blood, I suppose. You're very fortunate to have a place like Oaks."

"A rundown, has-been plantation? Fortunate?"

"What happened, Julian? This was obviously once a fine place. And not too long ago, either."

"What happened? Oh, a number of things. The war, mainly, I suppose. If we had a market for our cotton, I might have kept the place up, despite its earlier mismanagement."

"Mismanagement."

"Yes, my dear. I hate to speak poorly of Chris in front of you, but I'm afraid the boy has no common sense. We were quite nearly ruined when I finally had

322

to take things out of his hands. To be fair, my father started the process. When my stepmother died, he fell to pieces and lost all interest in the place. Chris tried, but, well, you know Chris. He can be terribly irresponsible, like this trip of his into the swamps. He always disappears when you need him."

"He needed the rest, Julian."

"Don't we all? Still, he was a fool to go off and leave you alone. If I was in his place, I would never consider it."

His gaze was frankly admiring, and Katy blushed. To change the conversation's direction, she brought it back to Oaks. "If the British regain South Carolina, you will have a market for your cotton. Will you try to recoup your losses?"

"Not if, my dear, but when. Don't fear, it's merely a matter of time before we're all back under England's rule and I will be ready for that time. That's why I'm working so hard to get the crop in."

Working so hard? "But where will the money come from?"

He smiled a secret smile. "I'll worry about finances. I am still fairly comfortable. Comfortable enough to see to the restoration of my family home."

"I wish you'd let me help."

"Help, my dear? In what way?"

"The house needs redecorating, painting. The gardens need to be tended. Oh Julian, there's so much to be done."

"I made it clear that you are not to be bothered with that."

"But I'm so bored. You ride out to the fields every day and Rachel has her entertainments, but I have nothing to do. What if I promise only to supervise?"

"The social season will be starting soon; we will be returning to the city."

"But the war . . ."

"Trust me when I say that the war, for us, will soon be over."

"And what do I do in the meantime? I need something to do."

"Perhaps you are right. We can at least begin work on the outdoors. I will order paint, and you can get the slaves busy on the gardens. I might wish to entertain in the future, and that drive is a disgrace. Very well, you can be my assistant. Would that suit you?"

After she admitted that it suited her just fine, they spent the rest of the drive discussing plans for the house. She knew he was merely humoring her, but she didn't mind his lack of interest. All she cared about was the way Kit's face would look when he returned.

It was nearly dark when they pulled into the stable-yard. Not until Sampson came to lead the horse inside did Katy remember her mission. "Julian, wait a moment, please. I want to talk to you."

"We've talked at some length about this house and quite frankly, I'm tired of it. I told you to do whatever you think best. At the moment, I can't think of anything more important than removing these disgusting clothes, can you?"

"I'm sorry; I'm being terribly selfish. It's just that you know how I feel about the mistreatment of horses and I wanted to ensure that it doesn't happen again."

"I think you dealt with Wharton quite effectively."

"I wouldn't dream of interfering with your horses. I was speaking about my own. Dawn was a special gift to me, and I'd rather no one else rode her, especially if they mistreat her."

"Then give the order that no one may ride her."

"I'd like to, but I don't hold much authority here. My word against Rachel's?"

"Why do I have this feeling that you're trying to ask something of me?"

Katy laughed. "Probably because I am. Oh, Julian, you do owe me a favor, you know. Could you tell Sampson that only I may ride Dawn? I'll deal with Rachel, myself.'

"I suppose that's fair enough. I don't envy you, though. I'd rather deal with a rabid dog than with Rachel when she doesn't get her way."

Katy remembered his words at breakfast the following morning. To her dismay, she found herself alone with Rachel. Her catlike eyes were amused and Katy struggled not to squirm under their scrutiny.

"Poor little Katherine. It wasn't much of a honeymoon, was it? Only two days?"

Katy tried to appear smug. "It was enough."

"Oh, I bet it was. More than enough, for him. To do his duty to produce the heir, I mean. After two days of doing his duty, it's no wonder he left for the swamps."

"You sound terribly sure of yourself."

She laughed. "He never left me for the swamps."

"No, Rachel. He left you for me."

The beautiful face became vicious. "Believe what you choose. Shut your eyes to whatever you don't care to see. But I can tell you now that Kit has never left me and he never will."

Katy's stomach grew queasy, but she remained outwardly calm. She's lying; don't let her get to you, she warned herself. "I don't believe you. Kit loves me."

"Kit loves me," she mimicked. "There's a danger in being too innocent, Katherine. Did someone tell you

325

once that just because a man sleeps with you, he loves you? What do you know of love? You and your little girl airs. Oh, he might be kind and protective because he feels responsible for you, but has he ever said the words? Don't confuse obligation with love. Grow up, please. Or else it will be unpleasant for us all when you find your husband in my bed."

"Leave my husband alone."

"I may have to leave your horse alone, but only your husband can make me leave him alone and I doubt he'll ask it of me."

"I wouldn't be that sure of yourself."

Rachel was intimidatingly cool. "I'll play fair. Let's just see who he comes to when he's finished with his swamps, shall we? Knowing Kit as I do, I've no doubt that his already sizable appetite will drive him to one of our bedrooms. Let's see whose it will be."

With considerable effort, Katy kept her itching palm at her side. Whatever pleasure she might derive from the slap would be lost with Rachel's satisfaction. Better to let her think she wasn't worried; let Rachel do the worrying for a change. "Fine. We'll let Kit decide, then."

Rachel's confidence was not shaken. If anything, it seemed to grow with every day Kit stayed away. She fell into the habit of teasing Katy, and her insinuations began to gnaw at Katy's confidence. Not once had he ever mentioned love. Was she incredibly naive? He had said he wanted her, that she was beautiful, that he didn't want to leave her, but as Rachel so maliciously pointed out, that had nothing to do with love.

If not for the house, the insinuations would have driven her to insanity, but surprisingly, she found good company in Julian. He took to confiding in her at the end of the day, to boast of his accomplishments. In like manner, she would tell him of her progress. If Rachel felt excluded, she gave no sign. It was as if she was biding her time.

By early May, the cotton crop was in and the house itself was on the mend. There was still no sign of Kit, but then, the siege continued. Katy worried but she kept her fears to herself.

One morning, Julian announced his intention of closing down the plantation house and returning to Charleston. The cotton was thriving and the excitement of being home had lost its appeal. Serious work was fine for a time. It enhanced his role as a gentleman planter, but his soul was designed for the social life and he grew restless from the enforced captivity. Bored to the extreme, he decided to risk the trip back to town. Both ladies, he decreed, were to accompany him.

Katy searched frantically for an excuse, any excuse, to remain at Oaks. She had to be there when Kit returned, but she knew better than to let his brother know that. Instead, she told Julian that she couldn't possibly go until her apartments were completed.

"Katherine, I made the stipulation that you could work on this house until it was time to go back to Charleston."

"No, Julian, you said until the season began. The war is still going on, there won't be any season yet. As soon as my project is completed, I promise to join you, whether the siege is over or not. Don't make me stop when I'm so near to being finished."

Eventually, he relented. Rachel didn't want to leave either, but despite all her protests and tantrums, she was in the carriage when it pulled down the drive.

Katy felt absolute relief. As nice as Julian had been, Kit's continued absence had been impossible to explain and Rachel's smugness had been impossible to stomach.

After two peaceful days, she received a note from Julian. Charleston, he told her, was liberated. Benjamin Lincoln had finally recognized the inevitable and surrendered. The rebel army was disbanded and peace had come to the city. There were to be countless celebrations and he would need her. She was to drop whatever she was doing and come to town immediately. Dismayed, Katy wrote back, sending the only excuse she knew he'd understand. Her wardrobe was an absolute wreck and she would need a day or so to restore it. If Kit hadn't returned by that time, she'd have to invent another excuse.

Having sent off the note, Katy went to her room to pack. She and Lilah had added the finishing touches yesterday, so there was nothing to keep her here but Kit; she might as well be ready to leave when he arrived. Entering her room, she felt pride in what they had accomplished. With the money Julian had allowed her, they had repapered the walls and replaced the heavy draperies with curtains. The personality of the room had been altered to fit her own. It was now a cozy, pretty room and she was anxious to see Kit's reaction. If only he'd come home.

She was still packing when Lilah barged into the room. "Miz Katy, you in here? Jeremy just came back. Never got to Charleston, not with them soldiers on the road."

"What are you talking about?"

"Them Redcoats. They're on the march. Looking for escaped prisoners, they say.'

328

"I don't understand why Jeremy ran. Those men are British soldiers, my countrymen. They are only doing their job."

"Don't imagine their job has anything to do with burning down people's houses."

"What did you say? Burning? Where?"

"Pond Bluff, the Marion place, and without him there to defend it."

Katy remembered Esther, alone with Francis. They would need to be warned. He would have to hide, if it wasn't already too late. She couldn't send Jeremy; Francis's whereabouts must be kept secret. No, she must go herself. "Which way are they coming?"

"Charleston way. They should be here soon."

"That doesn't give me much time. Please have Sampson saddle Dawn."

"I don't think you heard me. Them British soldiers are coming."

"I heard you, but Miss Videaux will need to be warned. She's all alone. I, at least, will have the Warwick name to protect me."

"But you are a woman. You can't go out by yourself."

"Nonsense. I have nothing to fear from the British. Our officers are known to be gentlemen."

"But this is war, Miz Katy. Men don't bother with manners when they're fighting. And what about Oaks?"

"If the soldiers stop here, tell them I'm out riding. Let them search the house. In fact, encourage them to search thoroughly. The longer they remain here, the more time I will have to return. Do you understand?"

"Yes, ma'am, but I don't like it."

"I hate to put it this way, but it's an order. Now

hurry and tell Sampson; I want to leave immediately."

Dawn was ready for her when she reached the stable. Sampson wanted to accompany her but she wouldn't hear of it. When she reached Esther's, it was quiet. Saying a prayer that she wasn't too late, she went to the door. Esther opened it, with surprise and delight on her face, and Katy sighed in relief. Breathlessly, she told her friend of the imminent danger. Esther reacted instantly. Within two minutes, they were helping Francis out of the house and to a secret storehouse that he had constructed for Esther. He laughingly commented that it had been meant for far more precious stores than himself, but it would certainly make a fine hiding place. As they approached, Katy could see what he meant. The entrance was built into the side of a hill, concealed by bushes and undergrowth. Not until Esther parted the bushes could she be certain that a door did indeed exist. Thinking of Kit's secret passageway, she marveled at how the British underestimated the cunning and fore right of these supposedly backward colonials.

Inside, it was chilly and damp, but Francis reassured them that it was better than any jail he could remember. Armed with blankets, he told them not to worry; he had been far less comfortable in the past and would undoubtedly be less so in the future, as well. The difficult part was theirs; they would be dealing with the British.

With a quick hug, Katy left Esther to remove all evidence of Francis's presence while she hurried home to Oaks. The fear she had seen in both Lilah's and Esther's eyes was contagious. What if Oaks received the same treatment as Pond Bluff? Urging Dawn to hurry, she covered the distance in record time.

She almost wept with relief when she saw the chimneys of the old white house. Whatever else might have happened, Oaks was still standing. It would take more than a war to make that house crumble.

It was strangely quiet when she pulled into the stable, ominously so. Where was Sampson? Where were the horses? A fresh attack of fear assailed her. If those soldiers had harmed a single one of her slaves, she'd have every last one of them hung.

When she burst into the kitchen, fear evaporated. Huddled in a group before the fire were Lilah, Jeremy, and Sampson. Slowly, she pieced together their stories. The British had come, and finding the mistress gone, had taken advantage of her absence to loot the stables. In Lilah's trembling hands was a receipt for seven horses, one of them Kit's horse, confiscated for His Majesty's Royal Household Dragoons.

The fear became fury. Who exactly was this Colonel Banatre Tarleton? Horse stealing? British officers were supposed to be gentlemen, not thieves lying in wait for a helpless female. She would confront Julian with this treachery, and put to the test the alleged power of the Warwick name.

She sent Sampson to borrow a horse from Esther. This time she would take no chances; she would need him to accompany her to town. Delighted, he sped off to obey her. Katy paced the kitchen floor until he returned. Without a word, they were off for Charleston.

When they arrived in the city, it was much the same as she had left it, only now, the soldiers wore coats of vivid red and they were everywhere. A sentry was on guard and they were stopped for questioning. Apparently she had been expected for she had no problem establishing her identity. The sentry apologized for the delay and wished her a good day. Now that was what one expected from the British military.

In front of the Warwick mansion, Katy experienced a sudden foreboding. She was no longer sure that she wanted to go in there.

Bullying herself into opening the door, she heard the sound of laughter, Rachel's laughter. So she was entertaining already. With no desire to learn who the guest was, Katy tried to tiptoe up the stairs to her room. It was getting dark and in the failing light, she tripped on the first stair. She was rubbing a shin when Rachel came out of the drawing room. "Katherine! What a pleasant surprise. We weren't expecting you quite so soon." The smug grin was more firmly established than ever. Katy's foreboding increased.

"I have to speak with Julian. Is he home?"

Just then, Kit appeared in the doorway, as if his entrance had been carefully calculated to wound her. "Katy, what's wrong?"

What's wrong? She hated them, Kit worst of all for his concern and hypocritical kindness. Wasn't it a bit late to worry if there was anything wrong? He had come first to Rachel, hadn't he? No wonder the smugness. They had probably been laughing at her, her and her pitiful innocence. While she had been trying to save his friend, he had been satisfying his "sizable appetite" with Rachel. Oh no, they weren't going to laugh at her again, neither were they going to pity her. There was no way she would let them know how it hurt inside of her, how hard it was to even breathe. No matter that the earth had dropped out from underneath her, she still had the banister for support. Clinging to it as if it was a lifeline her knuckles growing white, she faced them. "My business is with Julian. Is

332

he here?"

A cloud passed over Kit's features. "He's at the wharf still. Can I help?"

"No, I think not." She added as politely as she could manage, "Thank you."

"Katherine," Rachel purred. "You look exhausted. Why don't you go upstairs and rest before dinner."

"Thank you, Rachel, I think I will. Please send Rosie up to me." With careful indifference, she turned on her heel and started up the stairs.

"Rosie isn't here."

The sound of his voice made her forget her careful indifference. "Where is she?"

"I sent her to Oaks, to help you pack."

"That was terribly considerate of you. Naturally"— she glanced from one to the other of them—"you hadn't expected me to return so soon. Very well, send Ruth, or anyone; it doesn't matter."

"I'll come with you."

That was the last thing she wanted. His kind, but impersonal attention would surely undo her. She needn't have worried; Rachel wasn't about to allow even that much. "Don't be silly, Kit. Your wife will want to bathe and rest after her grueling ride. She won't be needing or wanting you. Isn't that right, Katherine?"

The bitch was forcing her to admit defeat. Tightening her grip on the banister, she stared her in the eye. "That's right, Rachel. I won't be needing Kit. You can both return to whatever it was that you found so amusing and I'll take my well-deserved rest. Just inform me when Julian arrives."

Back stiff, she faced the seemingly never-ending stairway. Oh feet, she begged, just get me to my room.

"Katherine! How wonderful that you're finally home."

Julian stood in the open doorway. Conscious only that someone, even if it was Julian, was happy to see her, Katy rushed down the stairs and into his arms.

"My dear, what is the matter? Here, here, you must stop crying. I can hardly understand you."

As the tears subsided, she realized what an idiot she had made of herself. How could she explain her head-long flight or the desperate tears? She'd rather die than admit to Kit's treachery in front of the three of them. "I'm sorry, Julian." She sniffed. "It's just been such a strain, what with the burning and all."

"Burning? What burning?"

"Keep quiet, Chris; I'll handle this."

"The British came. They said they were looking for prisoners."

"What did they burn?"

"I won't ask you again to keep still. Can't you see you're upsetting your wife? Now tell me, my dear, what happened?"

"It wasn't Oaks; it was Pond Bluff. I was out riding when I saw the flames. I was so scared that I rode straight home. The house was untouched, but they took all the horses. All your horses are gone, Julian. Some man who calls himself a British colonel is to blame. He left this receipt."

Kit gave a low whistle. "So much for the power and influence of the Warwick name."

"I warned you to be quiet; now get out of my sight." Julian, in a temper, was not a pretty sight, nor a pretty sound. "Have no fear, I will deal with this Tarleton. How dare he steal from me! Rachel, where do you think you are going?"

334

Rachel stopped guiltily. "I was going after your brother. I think you made him angry."

"Leave him alone. I want a good, stiff brandy. Katherine, what about you? After your ordeal, you probably need something."

"Thank you, but no. I'd much rather go to my room and rest."

"Of course. You're not to worry about this. I will do the worrying for you from now on."

Perhaps he was right; where had all her planning and worrying gotten her anyway. How nice it would be to leave all her problems in someone else's hands. "Thank you, Julian. You're too good to me."

She trudged up the stairs as Julian dragged Rachel into the drawing room. As she heard his yelling and screaming, she silently thanked him for taking care of at least one of her problems. There was no room for pity. Rachel deserved all she got, and more.

To Katy's surprise, Kit was waiting for her outside her room. She tried to sidestep him but he grabbed her elbow. "Katy, I've got to talk to you."

"Not now."

"Not now? Then when do you suggest? Should I write and make an appointment first?" He sounded angry.

"Please spare me. I have no strength left for an argument with you. Just let go of me so I can take my bath and go to bed."

"What's wrong with you?"

"Let me go; you're hurting my arm."

"Not until you tell me what's going on. I'm not as easily duped as my brother. You weren't afraid of some British soldiers you never even saw, but something is bothering you. Tell me."

"I can't see that it's any of your business."

"Of course it's my business. Damn, Katy, it was hard enough explaining my presence here without you showing up like that. If you only knew how Julian badgered me about leaving you alone."

"I'm sorry to have inconvenienced you."

"I didn't mean it that way and you know it. If we don't want to get caught up in a lie, we need to be telling the same story. Katy, we've got to talk."

She sighed. "Very well, Kit, but not now. Perhaps after dinner, but not now. I'm really too tired."

Reluctantly, he let go of her arm. He seemed about to say something but someone was coming up the stairs. Katy slipped quietly into her room. Leaning on the other side of the door, she fought the weakness that made her long to beg him to hold her in his arms, hold her until all the doubts and fears were gone. But she couldn't fight it. Against her better judgment, she opened the door. Kit was gone.

With her pride intact, if not her heart, Katy strolled into the drawing room to wait for dinner. Rachel was there already, her lovely arm entwined with Kit's. Julian was as gracious as ever, though still quite angry about his horses.

He continued to complain throughout the dinner until Kit finally spoke out. "If you wish, I could stay at home and watch Oaks for you."

Julian's glance was indulgent. "Obviously, you have forgotten the last time I permitted that. No, I need you to go to England. I doubt even you could make a mess of that."

She couldn't help it. She blurted out, "You're going away?"

His voice was noncommittal. "With the blockade

lifted, someone has to take the cotton to England."

"Am I to accompany you?"

"Not this time."

He was leaving her again, and happy to leave her behind. Oh no, she wouldn't beg. She hoped she sounded indifferent. "What a shame. I suppose I'll have to entertain myself, unless your brother takes pity on me."

"But most certainly. I'm going to need you here more than ever. Our calendar is already filled for this month. Why, I'll wager that you'll be so busy, you won't even notice he's gone."

Rachel seized the opportunity to say the words Katy's pride prevented her from saying. "But, Kit, it won't be the same without you. It doesn't seem fair. You've only just returned and here you are, leaving again. We haven't even had time to talk."

Talk! Her mind was screaming but Katy remained outwardly calm. Somehow, she endured the rest of the meal but her tolerance stopped short of a cozy little hour with Rachel in the drawing room. Pleading exhaustion, she asked to be excused. Looking altogether too pleased with things, Rachel assured her she wouldn't be missed.

In her bedroom, her rage exploded. So he was going away tomorrow? He had never meant to see her; it would be far easier to avoid the tears and recriminations. With any luck, he might manage to steer clear of her until the war was over and then he could safely pack her off to England. Why had he come to Rachel? Couldn't he see that she was using him? If he was fool enough to love that lying bitch, he probably deserved her. She hoped they would be very happy together.

Sniffing loudly, she jumped into bed and burrowed under the pillows. If Kit and his mistress were going to carry on in the next room, she certainly didn't care to hear it.

She did hear a knock, barely five minutes later. She held her breath. The knob rattled. Knocking again, this time more urgently. Kit called her name. When she still didn't answer, he pleaded with her to let him in; he had to talk to her, he had to explain, and he couldn't do so in the hallway. Still, she kept silent. The knob rattled, and then there was silence. Katy strained her ears but she heard nothing until a door banged in the next room. Her breath came out, all at once. It hadn't taken much for him to give up; she could remember a time when a locked door had proved no obstacle for him. Irrationally or not, she felt he could have tried harder.

Much later, still flopping about in the huge bed, she had to admit she might be a bit unfair. Whatever commitment she might have made, he wasn't aware of it, nor had he ever promised her more than the protection of his name and a passage back to England. As he had said, they had made an agreement. To be honest with herself, she would have to admit that whatever excuse she might use, she had to see him again, to be with him one more time before he left. What good was pride when it left you with such aching loneliness? Abandoning what little was left of it, she crossed over to the door. Hesitating a moment to listen, she flung it open.

At least he was alone. Sitting before the fire, with an empty glass in his hand, Kit was staring blindly into the flame. He looked up in surprise when she entered the room. Jumping up, he nearly dropped the glass. "Katy! I thought you were asleep."

"I couldn't sleep."

The muscles of his mouth were twitching in an attempt to keep from smiling. Brown hair flying and blue eyes flashing, she was an avenging angel, seeking retribution. She was so typically his Katy that he felt a giddy relief. It had been so long since he had seen her, so long since he had held and loved her. He wanted to fold her in his arms now, not letting go until he was forced to leave in the morning, but he could see that she was very angry. By now, he knew her well enough to realize that no loving words would be believed as long as her temper flared. "Katy, I want to explain that confusion this afternoon. Don't think I'm not sorry for what you had to go through with the British; I only wish I could have been there to help you deal with them. But I thought you would be in Charleston. Wasn't that the arrangement? It was rather awkward not to find you here. I had a bit of explaining to do and then when you showed up today, before Rosie could explain to you, I was so afraid we'd get our stories mixed up." He hastened to add. "But I'm so glad you're here."

"Really?"

What was wrong? Was she accusing him of something? She was so cold, so distant; he wondered if he had only imagined that night at Oaks. His fingers itched to reach out for her unruly hair, to pull her to him. God, he wanted her so badly. Instead, he drew an uneven breath and tightened the grip on his glass. "I'm leaving in the morning, and this time I won't be coming back. I won't be going to England, as Julian plans. I'll set out with his damned cotton but Sam will see to it that we never reach port. I wanted you to know this so that when they tell you I've been captured by pirates, you won't worry." Unrelenting, she stood there, judging him. Slowly and deliberately he

339

set down his glass and approached her. "I won't be coming back, Katy, until the war is over."

Her voice was tight. "And you were going to leave without saying good-bye?"

Reaching out for her, he felt her body stiffen. "Of course not. I expected to find you here."

"Me? Or Rachel?"

"Rachel?"

"Don't play innocent with me, Kit Warwick. Don't lie out of pity. Do you think I'm blind? This agreement we made doesn't entitle you to make a fool out of me. Must you and your mistress carry on in front of my nose?"

He had to fight to control the laugh that threatened to overcome him. So that was it. "Why, Katherine Warwick. If I didn't know better, I'd think you were jealous."

"How dare you laugh at me!" On the verge of tears, she turned to flee, but he had hold of her wrist.

Towering over her, he pulled her close. "You little fool. Rachel means nothing to me." He put a hand under her chin and forced her to look up at him. "I could complain, myself, about the attention you gave my brother, if I didn't know it was all an act."

"You're awfully sure of yourself."

"Not at all. I can tell when you're acting. I was confused, at first, but now I think I know what it was all about. You were angry to find me with Rachel."

"Oh, I hate you!"

"Katy, please don't. Here we have another night to be together. I thought we weren't going to waste any more precious time fighting over silly things."

"I don't consider adultery silly."

"For the last time, Katy, she means nothing to me."

340

Looking into his eyes, she felt the old hypnotism taking control. She wanted to believe, she wanted to surrender the last threads of her pride, and she was very nearly convinced when, as if on cue, Rachel glided into the room. She certainly seemed to know her way around it. Clad in an outfit that left very little to the imagination, she made it clear what her intentions were. "Kit, darling, here I am. Oh! Am I interrupting something?"

Katy cried out and in his surprise, Kit lost his grip on her. Before he could recover, she was to the door. When he tried to follow, Rachel grabbed his arm and purred in his ear. "Let her go."

By the time he managed to break free of Rachel's cloying grasp, Katy's door was locked. He wheeled around to face Rachel, fury in his eyes. "What the hell do you think you're doing, barging into my room uninvited?"

"Oh, Kit, I hate to see you this way. She isn't worth it." She ran her slender fingers up his back, gently stroking the muscles of his neck.

Kit tossed those hands away. "I was with my wife, Rachel. Don't you understand that? My wife!"

"If you were so anxious to be with your wife, why did you come to Charleston? What you and I had isn't over yet, however hard you try to fight it. She's gone now, so there's no need to fight it."

"Get out! If I ever find you in my room again, I swear I'll choke the life right out of you."

Rachel backed away, disbelief in every line of her body. "You can't be serious. Why, one would think you were in love with her."

Kit looked at her in disgust. "Love? I doubt you know the meaning of the word. Yes, I love her and if you've ruined my chances with her, I'll make you pay for it. Now just get out of here before I do something I might regret!''

Rachel was scared. She knew him well enough to take him at his word when he was like this. Still, she couldn't resist adding, "I'll go, but remember, when she lets you down, I'll be there.''

When she had gone, Kit tried to get Katy to open her door, but he couldn't really blame her for not wanting to talk to him. How long would it take, this time, for her to cool off enough to listen to him? Damn Rachel! Damn the war! Damn the whole rotten world!

PART
FOUR

Chapter 23

Charleston, despite Katy's first impression, was indeed a new city. With the blockade lifted, trading resumed with the mother country. Except for the unescapable presence of the red and white uniforms, it was as if the war no longer existed. If it was a bad time for the rebel cause, it was a time for rejoicing for the loyalists. They opened their homes to the occupying army and social life resumed with a vengeance.

Katy readily adopted their attitude. Gone were the days of blindly following her husband, of listening to his lies, of letting her emotions get in the way of reality, of allowing him to use her for his silly games. Thanks to his brother, she would now have the social season neither her husband nor grandfather had seen fit to provide. Eventually she would be sent to England anyway, so she had better learn how to handle herself. If Julian was using her as well, at least she would be getting something in return. Flirting outrageously with lonely officers, she would show Christopher Warwick a thing or two. And she would show his lovely mistress, once and for all, that she could handle herself in polite society quite adequately.

Caught in the social whirl, Katy lost touch with the

reality of war raging around her. There was talk of battle, but it was always a British victory and always laughingly recounted. In South Carolina, the rebels were finished. Their militia had been disbanded and anyone not swearing allegiance to the Crown would be hung. The danger was past.

No one else took the war seriously so why should she? She was determined not to think of Kit. If she hid in her world of make-believe, of superficial pleasures, nothing could hurt her. She didn't laugh, but she didn't cry, either. To be considered beautiful, to be sought after by countless men, to be openly admired for her wit and charm was a novel experience. She would make the most of it while it lasted.

As her reputation grew, more and more men sought her company. One evening, she found herself being introduced to Banatre Tarleton, the arrogant young officer who had stolen Kit's horse. He was polite enough, but his assumption that she should be grateful for his apology grated on her nerves. Like so many of these men, he rarely found himself in the wrong. Apparently Lord Cornwallis's high opinion of his young officer was matched by the officer himself. Katy, alone, could not share it.

His manner of regarding it all as a silly misunderstanding, especially on her part, brought the war back into focus for Katy. No provision was made for the return of the horses; the apology would have to do. So when the colonel began to complain about the new folk hero, the Swamp Fox, Katy listened with interest. Intrigued by his open defiance of the British supremacy, Katy suffered more of Tarleton's company to learn about him. Fighting against impossible odds, this man seemed to be taking on the British army single-handedly. The patriots had given up, but it seemed this Swamp Fox of theirs would not let them.

Striking from the swamps, he would attack when least expected and disappear into the swamps, without a trace. Secretly, Katy applauded him, feeling very un-British. When Tarleton bragged that it was his responsibility to see to it that the impudent rogue hung, Katy hoped he would continue to outsmart him. It shouldn't, she thought uncharitably, be all that difficult. "Really, Colonel, you can't hang a man for impudence. What has he done that is so awful?"

Tarleton regarded her as if she was lacking in intelligence. "For your information, Mrs. Warwick, that man had the effrontary to insult one of our country's finest officers, General Cornwallis. He copied one of our posters, substituting the general's name for his own, and called for the apprehension of His Lordship as an enemy to American soil. And he actually had the gall to offer a reward."

"How ghastly!" Katy wanted to laugh, but she could hardly do so surrounded by British officers. "Tell me, do you have any idea who this Swamp Fox might be?"

"Certainly. He is not all that clever. We have been aware of his identity for some time. General Marion might have escaped my detection during the liberation of Charleston, but he won't elude me for long. He will pay for his bizarre sense of humor; he and all those who help him."

And what would you say, Katy thought, if you knew you were speaking to one of them, now? It was funny, but she was proud of the small part she had played. How gratifying to know she had thwarted this man just as he was in the act of stealing Kit's horse. That brought her painfully back to thoughts of her husband. Where was he? Had he finally found his action? Was he out there, in his swamps, with the colonel? (No, Tarleton had said he was a general now.) Was he well?

Katy shook herself. What did she care? She didn't really suppose he was wasting his time worrying about her, did she? Kit Warwick could take care of himself. Better save her energy for worrying about herself.

For worry presented itself in the person of Cecil Lawrence. Of all the people in the world she'd least like to see again, he would have to be at the top of the list. She had lied to this man, thinking she would never see him again. She began to tremble, all too aware of her precarious position, all too conscious of being alone. Her palms were sweating and her mouth was dry.

"Mrs. Warwick, I can't tell you how pleased I am to see you."

"Captain Lawrence, what a surprise."

If he noticed she had neglected to extend her hand, he chose to ignore it. Far too busy with thoughts of his own to give much consideration to her strange behavior, he continued. "When I heard that you were at this party, I rushed over to offer my thanks."

Katy stared at him dumbly. "Thanks? Whatever for?"

"You needn't be so modest. I know of the admiral's intervention. Thanks to you and your grandfather, I've been given new orders. At last, I'll see action. I can't say what it means to me."

Katy finally realized what he was trying to tell her. Saying a silent thank-you to Farley and deciding she might as well be hung for a large lie as a small one, she plunged in. "How splendid! I had hoped he might speak up. It seemed such a shame to waste your talents. And we were both so grateful to you for your aid."

"And how is your husband? He certainly seemed recovered."

348

Without thinking, she blurted out, "Kit is here?"

It was his turn to stare stupidly. "I don't understand. You did walk in with Mr. Warwick, didn't you?"

"Oh, you mean Julian?" Katy giggled nervously. "He's my brother-in-law."

"I think I'm quite confused."

"Yes, I can see that. Forgive me for laughing, but this often happens. I am married to Julian's younger brother, Christopher Warwick, but he isn't here tonight. He's on his way back to England on family business."

"He's well, I trust?"

"Oh yes, isn't it wonderful? It seems we were quite wrong about the smallpox." Something close to suspicion clouded his eyes and she hastened to add, "But I was so worried. If it hadn't been for the medicine you gave us, I'm not certain he would have recovered."

"I was happy to be of service."

"As I was happy to be of service to you. Tell me about your new position."

"You wouldn't be interested."

"But of course I'm interested. You spoke of action. Does that mean you will be fighting the American navy?"

Lawrence snorted. "Navy! These people have no navy, only a ragtag assortment of private vessels outfitted for war. The only thing saving them from being pirates is that their so-called government has given them sanction to loot and raid out ships. They are a nuisance and I am proud to say that I will be in the position to rid these waters of their menace. If I'm successful, as I stand every chance of being, I will be eligible for promotion."

Katy, thinking of the *Irish Lass,* hoped he was being overly optimistic. His speech reminded her suddenly of the difference between them. She must be careful;

349

she mustn't let him suspect her in any way. "This all sounds marvelous for you, Captain Lawrence, but does it mean that I won't see you again?"

Her voice sounded false to her own ears, but, once again, he seemed not to notice. "No, I will be operating out of Charleston harbor, so we'll be seeing a great deal of each other, I hope."

Katy did her best to return his smile. "How encouraging to know there will be a familiar face in this foreign land."

Foreign land? She could imagine Kit's reaction to that. Suddenly, irrationally, she missed his teasing. Trying to cover the unwanted nostalgia, she said brightly, "I can't tell you how I look forward to seeing you and speaking with someone from home."

"Then let's dispense with the formalities. I believe our previous acquaintance entitles us to be on a first-name basis, don't you agree?"

Katy was telling him how pleased she would be to call him Cecil when Julian strolled over to join them. This was even worse. One wrong word and all would be lost. Oh, Kit, she wondered, where are you? Ignoring sweaty palms, she introduced the two and waited while they exchanged pleasantries. Since only Katy knew there was anything to hide, the conversation remained trivial and when Julian, whose curiosity had been satisfied, lost interest, Katy knew the danger was past. They had little in common and it proved relatively easy, in the days that followed, to keep them apart.

Katy continued to play her role to perfection, but her heart was no longer in it. Where before she had avoided any mention of war, she now strained to catch the slightest bit of news. The Swamp Fox was always in the midst of it, as was his contemporary, Thomas Sumpter, called the Gamecock. How like children the

350

British seemed, with their nicknames for men who were fighting a life and death struggle to free their country. Laughing comtemptuously, they seemed to miss the seriousness of it all. How she resented their unfailing optimism, though she was forced to admit it was justified. By now, all of South Carolina was under British control; it had taken barely three months. Neighboring Georgia had suffered the same fate, and it seemed that soon the entire South would fall into British hands.

Victory might have been complete had they shown any sign of respect for their adversaries. Like all conquering people, the British were blind to their own vanity. Taking for granted that the backward colonials would soon break under a show of strength, they continued to heap insult upon injury. Before he departed for the comfort of New York, General Clinton revoked the parole he had already granted to the prisoners of the Charleston siege, requiring them to either sign loyalty oaths or be hung as traitors. He had forced them back into Kit's hypothetical wall. These men who had planned to stay out of the war now chose to defy Clinton and returned to the fighting with a vengeance.

As if that wasn't enough, men like Tarleton were sent out to enforce Clinton's decree. Burning and looting indiscriminately, he gained a reputation for cruelty. "Tarleton's quarter" was a phrase that would outlive its originator. Those who had resigned themselves to defeat now had a reason to fight. The war became nasty on both sides, and its presence became felt even in the drawing rooms of the elite. They never lost their arrogance, but the jokes had been replaced with a grim determination to teach these colonials a lesson.

In October, these same drawing rooms were cloaked in a somber atmosphere as the stunned British learned of the American victory at the remote frontier settlement of King's Mountain. It was mere luck, a minor setback, but it was plain that they were shocked that the ragtag remnants of the militia could defeat the prime of His Majesty's service. A note of doubt crept into the cocky self-assurance that it could never happen twice.

So bad was morale that Annabel Smithfield considered cancelling her annual costume ball. Thanks to Julian's constant efforts, the ball was held. Katy, for the first time in ages, found herself looking forward to the event. A patriot victory, no matter how small, was worth celebrating. She would design her own costume. From experience, she knew better than to compete with Rachel, who would be Helen of Troy. In complete contrast, she would be Joan of Arc, with breeches and brandishing sword. It was daring, but she had the confidence to get away with it. Julian's smug satisfaction and Rachel's glare of contempt assured her that she was right.

Her costume did cause a stir, but not nearly as much as the pirate. Katy was standing alone, momentarily deserted, when she saw him swagger in. Low murmuring spread throughout the room at the sight of the bare chest. Katy felt a queer feeling in her mid-section. Though his head was covered with a bandana and his face was masked, she knew that strut anywhere. How many times had she watched him prowl the decks of the *Irish Lass*? But it was impossible. Kit wouldn't take the chance of being seen, here, where he could so easily be recognized. But no one approached him. Could she be mistaken?

Her heart was still beating furiously when Cecil approached to request a dance. At the moment, it seemed easier to fall into the routine. After all, wasn't she here to celebrate? It was not her intention to fantasize about every male with a nice set of shoulders that happened to remind her of her unfaithful husband. Still, she glanced around the room at intervals. The pirate had disappeared. It must have been her imagination. Forget him, she told herself, and try to enjoy herself.

It was Kit. Lounging inconspicuously against a back wall, he watched her every move. He resented the dazzling smile she gave that fop, Lawrence. Not for one second did he doubt her identity. Oh, it was Katy, all right, but she had changed. She was lending herself to Lawrence's proprietary air and damn, she was enjoying herself. And why not? She was among her own kind. Everywhere he looked was the red and white of the British military. It was just a preview of the success she would enjoy in London, if she chose to spend her life there. Her colonial husband would hardly be needed; if anything, he would be an embarrassment. Once she had smiled at him like that. What had happened? Where was the sweet, innocent girl he had left at Oaks. This poised, sophisticated woman used Katy's body, but she was a stranger. The need to talk with her was strong, growing more urgent with each passing moment. The longer he remained, the greater the risk of discovery. Still, he lingered. Would she listen to him now, or would she hand him over to her friends?

Fists clenched, he watched Lawrence plant a kiss on her fingertips. How dare that overdressed clown fondle his wife! Straightening, he made his decision. Like a hungry cat, he circled the room, eyes on Katy, ready to pounce if anyone so much as touched her. He stalked her, waiting for the moment that she would be alone. When Lawrence left to fetch a glass of punch, he saw his chance and took it.

Katy's only warning was the sight of the golden

curls on that too familiar chest and she felt a tightening in her own. There was no need for him to speak. Wordlessly, she drifted into his arms, as if it was the most natural thing in the world. As he led her out onto the dance floor, her mind was dizzy with the knowledge that it was Kit. It was hard to get her bearings. He belonged to a different world, a different Katy. Finding her voice, she said the only thing that came to mind. "You're insane. What are you doing here?"

Typically, he laughed. "How gratifying. I risk my life to see you and for that I get insults."

She remembered her anger. How like him to sweep into her life, expecting to take up where he had left off. What favor would he ask this time? No, she wouldn't do it, whatever it was. She wouldn't even speak to him.

Meanwhile, Kit was trying to find the right words. This coldness was a bad sign. Still, he had risked a great deal and if he had to abduct her, she would listen. That gave him an idea. Deftly, he steered her to the large Fench doors to the garden.

"What do you think you are doing? Let go of me."

"Not until I get the chance to say what I came to say. Despite your performance to the contrary, you are still my wife. We made a bargain and I expect you to keep it."

Katy was speechless. Had he actually come all this way to chastise her for some harmless flirtations when his own guilt was so much worse? The unfairness of it made her want to lash out at him. "How self-righteous you are. I am expected to sit at home, playing the dutiful wife, but you can entertain your mistress under the same roof. No, sir, I think not."

He muttered an oath. "I have never entertained any mistress, under the same roof or otherwise. I swear to you I haven't so much as touched another woman since we took our vows."

"Last year I might have believed you, no matter what the evidence against you. But I'm not a silly schoolgirl any more. Thanks to you, I had to grow up fast."

He flinched. "Can you honestly believe that I have so little regard for you? That I hold you so cheaply? I had no idea Rachel would come into my room that night."

"Ha! Then why were you awake? Who were you waiting for?"

"Dammit Katy, I was awake because I was trying to find a way to make you listen to me." He tightened his grip. "I couldn't leave without explaining. Did you think I wanted to leave at all? Julian trapped me. I haven't forgotten that night at Oaks, even though you apparently have."

She blushed. "This is absurd. If you don't let go of me, I will bruise. If I promise to behave as is befitting your name, can you let me go? Thank you. Now that you've said what you came to say, I think you had best leave before someone recognizes you."

"No, Katy, I haven't said what I came to say. Not yet. I want you to know that there is a way to get in touch with me, should the need arise."

"I doubt it will be necessary."

"Please don't make this difficult. I've promised to protect you, and as strange as it may seem, you may be in danger."

Damn his sense of obligation. "Then how do I contact you?"

He seemed relieved. "On the edge of the swamps, on the western boundary of Oaks, there's a path. You won't be able to see it until you're practically on it. About a hundred feet down the path, there's a rather large cypress with a hollow at the bottom. If you put your hand inside, there's a niche, about six inches up. You can put any messages you might have for me, or any of the crew, in there."

"Messages in a tree? Isn't that awfully melodramatic? What if you're away at sea?"

"I can't explain how it works. I haven't the time, at present. If you need me, for whatever reason, I'll be there."

"Thank you for the thought, but I doubt I'll need you. I am surrounded by gentlemen who wish to protect me. In fact, I had better get back before one of them comes looking for me."

"No, wait. Please? Katy, you've got to be careful. Don't trust Julain; he's not what he seems."

She blinked away tears. "None of us are, are we?"

He looked down at her. Where were the words that would melt the icy blueness of her eyes? Where was the magic they had once shared? Hands that longed to brush away her tears stayed powerless at his sides. "I have spent the last months in virtual hell, waiting for the opportunity to come to you, to explain what happened that night. I know it looks bad, especially in light of my past behavior, but I swear on my mother's grave, no matter what lies Rachel told you, I had no idea that she was coming to my room that night. Nor would I have welcomed her had you not been there."

"Kit, I'm not blind. I've seen you with her. I know you would have preferred to have been married to her."

"Good God, whatever I may have once felt for her is long since dead and buried. I didn't risk my life to see Rachel. In fact, if I was to see her, I think I could kill her with my bare hands."

"Oh, Kit"— he grabbed her as she tried to turn away—"why should I believe you?"

He spoke quietly, but with conviction. "Believe

356

what you must, but I tell you now, I have never lied to you, not since that silly farce in England." Finally, desperation drove him to say the words that had been locked inside for so long. "Ah, Katy, don't you see? I love you. I always have. From that first moment when you stormed into your grandfather's study, I knew you were exactly what I wanted. If you only knew how many times I cursed myself for forcing you that night. I've tried so hard, ever since, to be patient, so I wouldn't frighten you again. After that night at Oaks, I began to hope we might have a future together. What would be the sense in jeopardizing all that for one night with another woman? Especially Rachel. Katy, it's you I want, and no one else will ever be able to fill my need of you."

Katy could only stare at him. An already unbelievable evening was beginning to seem more like a dream. Had he actually said he loved her? Kit saw the disbelief in her eyes and read her reaction wrong. He shrugged and in a gesture of futility, let her go. When he spoke, his voice shook, betraying his disappointment. "I said what I came to say, I guess. I hope it didn't spoil your evening. Just remember that I meant what I said. If you need me, for whatever reason, I'll be there."

His quiet words hung between them. Katy knew this was the time to tell him what he so obviously wanted to hear, but the words wouldn't come. It seemed that she wouldn't be able to breathe until she spoke, but there was so much to say. Where would she begin? Reading the confusion in his eyes, she opened her mouth to make an attempt. She wanted to beg him to stay until she could say it all, but before she could utter a word, the sound of voices drifted in their direction. One of them was Julian's.

"Katy, I've got to go."

"No, not yet." Desperately, she clung to his arm. "I haven't said anything yet. You can't go."

"I've got no choice. Julian can't find me here."

"I know, but you can't leave, not like this."

"Tell me, Katy. What is it you want to say?"

"I need more time." She held him with her eyes. "Can't you come to me again?"

He hesitated a moment. "I'll come to your room tonight. Late."

"But how? Oh, Kit, don't take any chances."

He smiled, making everything right again. "For you, love, I'd brave the entire British army. I'll be careful. But Julian is coming and I must go." He kissed her lightly. "Till tonight, love."

"Till tonight," she repeated as he vaulted over the wall and disappeared into the trees beyond. From behind, Julian's grating voice jolted her back into reality.

"Katherine, dear, where have you been? Captain Lawrence is frantic."

"I felt the need for fresh air, suddenly."

"Is anything wrong? Your voice sounds peculiar."

"Of course not. It's such a lovely night, isn't it, Julian?"

"Lovely night? What's gotten into you?"

He was right, she lectured herself. Nothing must seem out of the ordinary; no one must suspect that tonight she would lie in her lover's arms, finally able to whisper all the words that bubbled inside her. Nobody would guess how alive she was, how incredibly, insanely happy she felt. She must ignore this urge to run in the moonlight. For one last time she would hide behind the carefully constructed facade everyone would recognize. Taking Julian's arm, she forced her excitement to bubble and boil below the surface.

Concentrating on her role, Katy missed the silent

358

figure lurking in the shadows. Passing through the doors, she walked within inches of a furious Rachel. Green eyes seething with vengeance, she watched Katy stroll by. So I mean nothing to him, she thought. He would kill me with his bare hands? When I'm done, he's going to wish he had killed me. I'll teach him not to make idle threats. And then, I'll deal with Miss Goody-goody. Oh no, pretty-little-Katy, you won't have them both. When I'm finished, neither of them will want you.

Chapter 24

Two days later, Katy was on the road to Oaks. Kit had failed to keep their tryst, though she had waited, far into the night. After carefully inspecting the door to his passdgeway the following morning, she had to acknowledge that he had never made the attempt. Still, she knew he would come the next night, if he could. Yet she spent another sleepless night without him until she decided to send him a message. She would go to Oaks and find this cypress tree.

Julian remarked on her apparent ill health and taking advantage of the excuse he provided, she encouraged him to believe that maybe, just maybe, an heir was on the way. Reluctant to be escorting a pregnant woman about town, he urged her to retire to the family estates. His relief was shamefully obvious when she reassured him that she could make the trip on her own.

Oaks welcomed her. It did her good to see the fresh coat of paint and the well-trimmed hedges. With the fields coming alive, there was an air of hopefulness about the place. Waving cheerfully to the fieldhands, she thought how nice it felt to be home. All that was lacking was Kit, but now that she knew he loved her, the waiting was not so bad. He would come to her when he could.

That reminded her of her mission. As soon as she had eaten, she rushed upstairs to compose a letter. It proved more difficult than she had imagined. Putting the words on paper was no easier than saying them to his face. It was one thing to feel them but quite another to express them. Her candle had burned to the end before she was content with her efforts.

Rereading the note once, she sealed it. It could hardly contain everything she had wanted to say, but it kindled a new hope. As she rose from her desk, she glanced out the window. It must be late, she thought. Suddenly, she was quite hungry. One would think she was with child, with this strange craving for food in the middle of the night. If only she was.

Shaking herself, she tiptoed down the stairs and started for the kitchen. Just as she put her hand on the heavy, wooden door, she heard voices from within. Cautiously, she slid the door open a crack, to see Rosie stuffing supplies into a sack. Behind the slave, in the shadows, was another person but it was too dark to determine who.

There was nothing to fear from Rosie so Katy burst in on them. "What's going on in here?"

The big black woman's hands flew to her chest. "Lordy me, missy; you done scared the daylights outta me." Rosie tried to hide the sack behind her back while her visitor remained in the shadows, beyond Katy's line of vision.

"Rosie, is there anything wrong?"

"No, no, child. You go on to bed. Rosie will take care of it."

"Don't lie to me. There's something wrong; you're shaking like a leaf."

The slave looked far more guilty than afraid. Curious, Katy stepped farther into the room and the faceless intruder moved farther into the shadows. In a protective gesture, Rosie positioned herself between Katy and the visitor. Thoroughly intrigued by now, Katy moved closer. "What is it? Surely you can't think I would object to your giving food to a needy passerby? Or is it more than that?"

"Please, missy, you go on up to bed and let old Rosie take care of this. You just forget you seen anything tonight."

Reacting quickly, Katy caught sight of a thatch of red hair before the boy could hide himself. There was only one person with hair that color. "Josh Randall, what are you doing here?"

He stepped out of the shadows, strangely defiant. "I had some business with Rosie; there's no need for you to concern yourself with it."

Why was he so hostile? "Business with Rosie? In the middle of the night? I don't understand."

"You don't have to; it doesn't concern you."

Hurt, she stepped backward. "Very well, if you feel that way, I'll leave. Only first, can you give me any news of Kit? Where he is?"

"Ain't no way I'll be telling you that."

Rosie was shifting her weight, looking nervously at her mistress. Katy, mystified, looked at both of them. "Is something wrong? Josh, tell me, what's happened?"

"As if you didn't know. He's dying, thanks to you. I hope you're satisfied with your revenge; I hope it was worth it. Don't look at me like that. You let me down,

Katy. I really liked you; I thought you were a lady. But that was a vicious trick you played on the captain."

"What are you talking about? What trick?"

"I may be nothing but a stupid boy to you, but I'm not that stupid. Nobody else knew he was coming to see you. That soldier shot him in the back, right by the house, and then hunted him down like an animal. Was that what you wanted? You never gave him a chance."

All color drained from her face. "He's been shot? You have to take me to him."

"No, Katy. Even if I was stupid enough to let you take another shot at him, which I ain't, I've got my orders. You're not allowed anywhere near the ship. Rosie'll go with me. If anyone can save his life, it's her."

Lightheaded, Katy sank into a chair. "I've got to go. I can't begin to explain why it's so important, but I've got to see Kit."

"Missy, you stay here, like the boy says. I'll take care of your man for you."

Katy looked up at her. "You can't possibly think I had anything to do with this, can you? You know how much I love him. Don't you see? I've got to tell him. He has to know." She was dangerously close to hysteria.

The old woman looked at her with sympathy. "These men have powerful evidence against you. Don't matter what I think; they ain't gonna let me near that boy."

"Give me the chance to convince them. Josh, you can tie me; bring me aboard as a prisoner. I thought you Americans believed that a man was innocent until proven guilty. Don't I deserve the chance to defend myself?" Her lip began to tremble. "Don't make me beg. Please let me go to him."

"Sam won't let you."

"Then take me to Sam. Let me talk to him."

"Katy..."

"Josh, we were friends once, weren't we?" She could see he was wavering. "You've got to believe me. I swear to you that I know nothing about this shooting. Can't you see that we're wasting time arguing? If we're going to save his life, we have to get Rosie to him."

"I've got my orders."

"Look at me and tell me that I've changed any since those days on the *Irish Lass*. You trusted me then; please, trust me now."

"All right." He was still doubtful. "I'll take you to Sam. Nothing more. But I swear, if you do anything to harm the captain, I'll see to it myself that you never get off the ship."

"That's fair enough. Don't worry, you won't regret this. But let's start out. There's no time to waste."

Katy blessed the full moon for making their way easier. As it was, it was slow going. Rosie, who hadn't been on a horse in years, couldn't keep the pace. Katy had to double back, many times, barely hiding her impatience. Once they entered the swamps, she had to fall in line behind the both of them. Making their way carefully, it seemed an eternity before Josh gave a low whistle to warn the others of their arrival. Ducking under some Spanish moss, Katy was amazed to see the *Irish Lass* before her. They wasted no time in boarding her and Katy went straight to Sam.

If Josh was hostile, then Sam was doubly so. "What in tarnation are you doing here? I gave that boy orders..."

"Don't blame Josh. I forced him into it. Sam, you've got to believe me. I had nothing to do with this."

He turned his back on her. "Get Mrs. Warwick off the ship."

"Very well, Sam Culligan, we'll play this your way. I am still part owner of this ship and as your captain is no longer able to give orders, you will take orders from me. I asked you a question and I expect an answer. How is he?"

He whirled around. "How is he? Did you come to gloat? He's in there bleeding to death. Are you proud of yourself? Couldn't you have done it yourself instead of sending one of your gutless admirers to do the job? I thought you had more guts than that."

"One of my admirers?"

"Only one band of soldiers wear the green uniform."

"But that's the dragoons. Sam, I have nothing to do with Tarleton."

"Don't lie to me. You been seen with him often."

"That's true, but you can't believe I'd send that butcher after Kit? I only spoke with him to learn more about the Swamp Fox since he'd been ordered to chase him. How else could I learn what was going on? I don't even like the man; I don't like any of it. That's why I left Charleston. This is only circumstantial evidence."

"Only you and Kit, and later I, knew he was coming that night. Why was that soldier lying in wait for him? How could he know Kit would be coming, if not for you?"

"I don't know. Honestly, Sam, I have no idea."

"Go home, Katy. There's not one of us here that will take orders from you now, so you might as well go peaceably before I have the men drag you off the ship."

Breathing deeply, she kept her composure. "You're so ready to believe the worst of me, aren't you? Very well then, are you quite prepared to let me go now that I know your location? If it's revenge I'm after, what's to stop me from going to my friends and telling them where to find you?"

"Isn't it enough that you've damned near killed him?"

"It's useless to protest my innocence. I'll make a pact with you, Sam. Just let me go into him. Let me see him. Then you can lock me up or do whatever you want with me."

"Are you crazy? Or do you think I am?"

She ignored that. "Unless you are prepared to tie me up, I'm going to see him. The only way you can stop me is by force." She looked him straight in the eye. "He needs me, Sam, and I'm not going to let him down, no matter what I have to do."

For the first time, she could see doubt. "Why did you do it?"

"I didn't."

"But the soldier . . ."

"It wasn't me. I can't explain it any better than you can. I've lain awake for two nights, waiting for him to come to me, and then I had to lie to Julian so I could come to Oaks because it was the only way I knew to reach him. I've got to tell him something."

"Ah, I want to believe you, but I can't take a chance, I can't have him hurt any worse."

"Then come in with me. Have someone watch me. Tie my hands behind my back. I don't care. Just give me the chance to tell him I love him." She bit her lip.

366

"I've never told him. All this time and I've never been able to say the words. If it's too late . . ."

She was wringing her hands and in spite of himself, Sam placed a hand on her shoulder. He spoke quietly. "All right, lassie. Go on in. See what you can do."

She straightened her shoulders. "Thanks for the vote of confidence, Sam. I won't let you down. If sheer willpower alone can save him, then I won't let him die."

The scene in Kit's cabin, however, brought her close to despair. Kit lay on the blood-soaked sheets, moaning softly. Katy watched the life pour out of a hole in his back. A small cry of protest rose to her lips. Thinking she was squeamish, Sam moved to take her from the room. She brushed him off, rolled up her sleeves and with an air of determination, offered her services to Rosie.

It was a long night. The two women fought together to save his life. Though Katy was inexperienced, Rosie had generations of knowledge and it was enough for both of them. They managed to stop the flow of blood. Following Rosie's instructions, Katy bathed the wound and they applied herbs and wrapped it tightly. But he had lost a lot of blood and he began to grow feverish. Katy was given the job of keeping him quiet. When warm clothes did nothing to soothe him, she tried her lullabies. They had always worked for Midnight, and if nothing else, they served to calm herself. Her voice rang out in the still night air, causing more than one sailor to shiver. She was pleading with fate, with God himself, not to take her man away. All the while, she bathed his head and face with cool water. Her efforts eventually took effect and she noticed with relief that he was sleeping quietly. Still, she kept up until Rosie motioned her away. "You sure you ain't a witch, child? Never heard a white woman sing like that. You could charm old Lucifer hisself with that voice. It's powerful medicine; look how he's sleeping now."

"Oh, Rosie, do you suppose he'll be all right?"

"It's all in the hands of the Lord, now. You and me, we've done all we can."

Katy covered her face with her hands. "Then you mean there isn't much of a chance?"

Rosie put a hand on her head. "Now, child, don't be putting words into my mouth. That man of yours, he don't give up easily. I imagine it'll take more than a hole in his back to slow that boy down. All he needs is his sleep. Just you wait and see. Come morning, he'll be hollering like the devil for his breakfast."

"Do you really think so?"

"He ain't gonna die. You trust Rosie, I won't let him give up. Why don't you get some rest now?"

Katy stood. She was exhausted. Stretching her arms, she found they ached and her neck was stiff as well. "I suppose you're right. Only promise that you'll send for me if his condition changes. I'd like to know when he regains consciousness. I have to talk to him."

What a relief that Rosie understood. Stiffly, Katy made her way up to the deck. How odd it felt to be back on the *Irish Lass*. This time she was a stranger, not trusted and not wanted. Memories crowded in on her, making her want to cry. He's got to live, she argued with fate, I won't say good-bye again to someone I love.

She met Sam up on deck. "He's got a fighting chance, Sam, and you know that if it's a fair fight, he'll win."

"I'm sorry about last night. About doubting you."

"You no longer do? Why?"

"I saw you with him. It was like with your horse. You didn't want him to die any more than we did. I should have known that."

"I guess I understand. I probably would have done the same in your position."

He looked at her, long and hard, before turning away. "Lass, I've got something to say to you, something you're not going to like."

"Go on."

"It's about your husband. I've tried not to interfere in the past, tried to let you work out your own problems. But I've got to speak out now. He loves you, lassie."

She smiled. "I know. He told me so. I'm afraid it was hard to believe at the time."

"You can believe it. He's been mooning around like a sick calf for ages. I can't be sure how you feel but you said last night that you wanted to tell him you loved him."

"I never got the chance. He's still unconscious."

Sam shifted, uneasily. "I sure hope you love him enough because this is going to be hard on you. I'm asking you not to tell him."

Cocking her head to one side, she stared in puzzlement. "Not tell him? But why?"

"He's better off not knowing. He's got enough trouble living this double life, without the worry of you. It was a damned fool thing he did, going into Charleston, but he wouldn't be talked out of it. Said he had to see you. Can't you see? If you weren't responsible for this shooting, then someone else was. Someone knows Kit is here. It proves he's got enemies that know his vulnerable spot—you. If you told him you loved him, he'd take every chance he could to come see you, to make sure you're safe. And with every chance he took, the closer he'd come to getting himself killed. Do you want that, Katy? Do you want this to happen again?"

"Of course not. But what you're asking is unfair."

"Nothing about this war is fair. I know I'm asking too much. I can see it in your face. But the only way he'll stay away from you is if he thinks you don't want to see him. It's the only way."

"What if he dies? What if something happens and I can't be there to tell him the truth? I can't stand the idea of him believing I tried to have him killed. It's too hard, Sam, what you're asking."

He shrugged his shoulders. "It was just a thought. Don't listen to me; I'm just a foolish old man. Getting too cautious in my old age."

Katy looked at him fondly. "Go on with you, Sam Culligan. Old age, indeed. The worst of it is that I know you're right. At least, my head knows you're right; just give my heart time to get used to the idea. I'll leave. I won't return unless he takes a turn for the worse and then nothing on this earth will keep me away. And I want your promise that if there's a chance that he won't ever be coming back to me, you'll tell him about this conversation."

"You've got my solemn word on that."

She hugged him. "We're agreed then."

"You're a good girl, Katy. Forgive me for treating you the way I did."

"That's forgotten, please. I'd better leave or it will be hard to explain my absence when Lilah comes with my breakfast tray."

"Take care of yourself, lass."

370

As she turned to go, she remembered something. "By the way, I was going to tell Kit, but I never got the chance. I've been talking to Captain Lawrence. I don't know what you're doing now, but if you're still privateering, the *Olympus,* among others, is after you, with orders to shoot first and ask questions later."

"You were told not to be spying."

He was so stern. "What gratitude! Don't worry— I've left town and I've no intention of going back. I'll be waiting at Oaks for Kit to finish with this interminable war. Take care of him. See that he doesn't take chances. See that he eats and sleeps well."

"Aye, that I will. And I'll bring him home to you."

"Good-bye, Sam."

There were tears in her eyes as she left the ship, making it difficult to find her way home. But Dawn was an intelligent animal and knew the way. Oaks was still asleep when she dragged her tired feet up the stairs and to her room. Inside, she found the note she had written earlier, still on her desk. In a fit of frustration, she tore it into a thousand pieces. Throwing them all into the fireplace, she started a flame and watched them burn. She moved closer, trying to draw warmth from the blaze, but nothing could stop her shivering.

Rosie found her some time later, still in a daze. "Child, why aren't you in bed? You want to catch your death?"

Katy snapped out of her trance. "How is he?"

"I told you that boy is strong. He'll be just fine, which is more than I can say for you if you don't get out of them wet clothes. I've got one patient on the mend, I don't need another one to take his place."

Obediently, Katy undressed. Without bothering to put anything else on, she climbed under the blankets. Their sudden warmth soothed her. Kit would live. That was all that mattered. Nothing was settled between them, but as long as he survived, there was hope. Someday he would return to her as Sam had promised. He would understand the sacrifice she had made and it would all be worth it. In the meantime, however, she would have to keep the plantation going, despite Julian's bungling, to give him something to come home to. As she drifted into the long delayed sleep, she was planning what she would do first.

Chapter 25

It was a long war, and a bitter one. In the beginning, the patriots could manage only a token resistance, with the hit-and-run tactics of Marion and Sumpter. Though it did little more than annoy Cornwallis' well-trained troops, its tenaciousness gained recognition in the North. In December, General Washington assigned Nathaniel Greene to lead the Southern Continental Army, on the assumption that if the South was willing to fight, the government would do their best to help them.

Even with the added support, the patriots would still be highly outnumbered, but unlike his predecessor, Gates, Greene saw the wisdom of using the knowledge and experience of the natives. Seeking the support of Marion and Sumpter, his plan was to slowly deplete the British strength, reducing the odds, until they could fight a fair fight. Then, and only then, would he engage in combat.

To someone unaware of his strategy, as Katy was, it seemed a hopeless struggle. Though she cheered Tarleton's sound defeat at the hands of Morgan at the strange-sounding place called Cowpens, it was a long, hard winter with little good news. Greene was forever in retreat with Cornwallis close at his heels, all the way into North Carolina. With their superior knowledge of the countryside, the Americans only barely eluded their pursuers, so fast did the British march. What Katy failed to realize, however, was that in his desperation to capture Greene, Cornwallis had burnt most of his supplies. Unable to replace them on the long march, he lost more men than necessary. In the end, Greene reached the Dan River, his objective, not more than a few hours before him, and the American army escaped over the line into Virginia without having engaged in battle.

To Katy, it seemed a monumental waste of time and effort. Nothing was settled and winter was over. At this rate, the war could drag on for years. News from the North was just as discouraging. Whatever kind of genius this Washington might be, it seemed he surrounded himself with ineptitude. Clinton remained firmly entrenched in New York, with no hope of him ever being driven out. Katy celebrated her one-year anniversary alone, wondering how many others would come and go before she saw her husband again.

Kit wondered the same thing. Participating in the raids with Francis had made it easy to forget his private life, but since his injury, he had more than enough time to brood. Though he couldn't, wouldn't, believe that Katy was responsible, the doubts nagged at him. He wanted to go to her, but Sam was adamant. His disappearance had been reported to Julian and he was caught in the lie. There would be no more visits to Charleston, especially until his wound had healed.

Back in Charleston, Julian was also wondering and waiting. When he had first learned of his brother's disappearance, he had mourned the loss of his cotton. He had kept the news to himself, knowing full well that he would lose his hostess. But when she sprang the news of a child on him, an idea began to form. In all likelihood, Kit was dead; pirateers had no mercy for British sympathizers. If he was to woo the widow, unobtrusively of course, she would willingly marry him to have a father for her child. Smiling, he thought of the riches of the Farley estates. Why, he could recoup all his losses, far less dangerously than his usual methods and still have money for his pleasures.

In late November, he made a special trip to Oaks to inform Katy of Kit's unfortunate accident. Surprised by his evident concern, Katy wondered if perhaps Kit had been wrong about his brother. It seemed there was nothing he wouldn't do for her. If she chose to stay at Oaks, he hated to leave her alone with her grief, but she was free to decide for herself.

From then on, he conducted his romance through letters. Rachel had already been sent to stay with friends, as Katy was no longer there to chaperone, so there was no worry of her interference. It was essential that he go about this cautiously. It wouldn't do to frighten Katherine, just as she was beginning to trust him.

Katy had plans of her own, none of which included matrimony. With Julian being so sweet, there was a chance he would grant her request. She had only one wish; she wanted to be in control of Oaks. Someone had to stop the overseer from taking advantage of his position. More than once, she had caught him beating the slaves and she suspected him of pilfering supplies. Besides, with the business records and control of the operation of the plantation, she knew she could make it see a profit. Esther was a willing accomplice and with her help, Katy learned all she could.

In January she wrote to Julian telling him she had lost the baby. If she felt guilt about the lie, she refused to let it bother her. Now, she told Julian, she had a double grief to overcome. She must have something to do, something to take her mind off her troubles. She had an idea. Perhaps they could discuss it on his next visit?

Julian rushed to her with words of consolation. The loss of the child was a setback, but Katherine was still a link to the Farley estates, and he gave in readily to her desires. Of course she would supervise the planting; he had already given up hoping the place would make a profit, anyway. But she must promise not to overtax herself. Yes, he would speak to Wharton about it in the morning. Pleasantly surprised by her evident knowledge of the plantation's affairs, he was more than relieved to leave it in her capable hands while he spent a far more enjoyable spring in Charleston, without the usual worry of how he was going to pay for it.

Before doing anything else, he would need to free himself of Rachel Worthington. She might have been a valuable asset in the past, but her usefulness had reached its end. Kit was gone; it was impossible to taunt a dead man. And he could hardly propose to his widow with a fiancée waiting in Charleston. Rachel would have to go.

But she was too shrewd and not about to let him quietly withdraw. With sly cunning, she probed until she had the entire story. "I knew this was coming. Julian, you're a fool. However anxious you may be to believe what you're telling me, I can assure you I

376

won't be as easily hoodwinked. Do you honestly expect me, of all people, to believe that your concern is for your brother's widow, and not for her grandfather's money? I think you had better make certain that she is a widow before you start spending the money."

"All that matters is that Katherine believes she's a widow."

"Ah yes. Poor, sweet, innocent Katherine. Pity you can't see when you're being made a fool of, darling."

He squeezed her tender wrist until she cried out. "I think you'd better explain that remark."

She glared at him. "Let me go or I won't tell you anything."

With one last squeeze, he flung her wrist away. "Very well, then. What do you know."

Rubbing her wrist, she smirked. "I can't pretend to know what she's planning, but I tell you, I've seen Kit here in Charleston as late as October. And he was talking with your precious Katherine."

"You're lying!"

"Count the months. Really, Julian, you're far too trusting. She could hardly have been five months pregnant when she wore that silly costume. Unless, of course, she saw Kit after he had left. Either way, she's lying to you. You can't see it because you're so blinded by the Farley money. Which is suspicious in itself. If he's so fond of her, why doesn't she ever hear from him? And why did he allow her to marry a penniless fool like your brother? They've been lying to you, all along, and you've never questioned them."

The skin on his face was stretched taut. "Then it's time I did question. But if I discover that it's been you who's been lying, I'll kill you. I won't be made a fool of—not by you, not by anyone."

"Save your anger for your brother, darling. And his dear wife. They're the ones playing games with you, not I. What will you do?"

"I haven't been to England for a while. Perhaps I'll visit my distinguished in-law; I'm certain Farley can enlighten me."

Rachel smiled in approval. Everything was working out splendidly. That little brat would get what she deserved. There was little doubt that Julian would find enough to incriminate them both. Once Julian disposed of them, it would be simple enough to convince him to marry her. Too much valuable time had already been wasted waiting to become mistress of Oaks, and like everyone else that year of 1781, she was tired of waiting.

Chapter 26

Left to her own devices, Katy's first step was to deal with the overseer. From now on, she informed him, there was no reason for him to enter the house. As Mr. Warwick had left her in charge, she would handle the accounts in the future. Wharton was still grumbling when he left the house and Katy knew she had a battle on her hands.

Trouble broke out early. Two days later, Katy went to the kitchen to plan the menu with Lilah when she found Wharton raising his whip to Jeremy. Furious, she barked at him. "Mr. Wharton, what do you think you are doing?"

Dropping his hands to his sides, he tried to bluster his way out of the difficulty. "This nigger is too big for his britches. Needs to be taught a lesson."

"You have no right whatsoever to be touching any of the house slaves, especially since you have been instructed to stay out of the house. In the future, if any disciplining is necessary, kindly remember that I am the one to take care of it."

"You're still new here, ma'am, and you ain't familiar with our ways. They have to be taught their place or there's no living with them."

"I think you are the one who needs to be taught his place. As long as Mr. Warwick left me in charge, no one will raise a whip to these people. If I catch you at it again, I will see to it that you never work here, or any other plantation in the area, again. Do I make myself clear? I certainly hope so. Now get out of my house and don't come back unless I send for you."

By the time he was gone, Katy was trembling. She didn't actually have the authority to threaten him. She prayed he wouldn't go to Julian with this. Seeing her agitation, Jeremy helped her to a chair and made a cup of tea.

"What happened, Jeremy? What was he doing in the kitchen?"

"Caught him in the supplies again, and I did as you told me. When I told him to get out, he got nasty. Sure was happy to see you."

"I'm glad I came when I did. Though I hope we don't have any more problems with this. That man makes me nervous."

"He wouldn't dare touch you, Miz Katy. Have all of us after him if he did."

"Thank you, Jeremy, but I doubt he'd go that far. I'd hate for him to take this to Julian, though. There's no telling how he'd react."

But Wharton had already considered asking for Julian's intervention before thinking better of it. From past experience, he knew better than to criticize Mr. Warwick's latest fancy. All he had to do was bide his time till the master grew tired of her, as he had with all the others, and then he'd make sure she paid for making a fool out of him in front of all them niggers.

Everyone seemed to be biding their time that spring. Cornwallis, tired of waiting and greedy for battle with the ever-elusive Greene, marched to Guilford Courthouse, in North Carolina, with a skeleton of his former army. Satisfied at last with the odds, Greene engaged in battle. It wasn't quite the triumph Greene had anticipated, but as Esther pointed out, the British victory was a shallow one. Having lost the greater number of men, it was their turn to run for Virginia. Like so many of his contemporaries, Cornwallis was reduced to remaining on the coast, where he could be certain of supplies and support from the Royal Fleet. Without Cornwallis to contend with, South Carolina was an open field for men like Marion, Sumpter, and the dashing Harry Lee. Victory after victory encouraged the countryside to begin their preparations for peacetime.

Katy was among them. Studying Julian's accounts, she learned a startling fact. During the months of April and May of last year, Julian had received large payments from high ranking British officers. He must have been one of those Loyalists that had betrayed Charleston by selling information to the British. How many men had gone to St. Augustine prison because of him? How many of them had thought themselves his friend? Judging by his records, he had been paid well for his efforts; far better than the original Judas. Kit had known; he had tried to warn her. How odd that both brothers had been spying, for different causes. But, she reminded herself, Julian hadn't been working for a cause, merely for his greed. Where had all the money gone? A paltry sum had gone toward the refurbishing of Oaks, but most had been spent on himself. Whatever affection she might ever have felt for him died a quick and painless death as she realized how many people had lost their homes, and some perhaps their lives, to pay for Julian's gambling debts and sordid pleasures. She would never again be able to wear his diamonds, knowing what they represented.

But it strengthened her resolve. The war would soon be over and it looked as if the Americans would win, at least in the South. Even if Julian had the courage to remain, in all likelihood the new government would never allow him to keep Oaks. Kit would be their logical choice as new owner and she must plan for that. When Julian wrote to inform her that he was going North and wouldn't return until autumn, she knew what she was going to do. The cotton seed was placed in the sheds. With the money left from her portion of her dowry, she bought a variety of new crops. With Esther's advice and Jeremy's help, she planted rice, vegetables, and tobacco; all items a growing nation would need. Later, when the economy stabilized and trade resumed, Oaks could return to growing cotton. There was much to learn and much to do, but she welcomed the challenge.

Predictably, she met with resistance from the overseer. He questioned her when she informed him of her plans. "Mr. Warwick know what you're doing?"

"Are you questioning my authority, Mr. Wharton? I gave you an order and I expect you to carry it out."

"I ain't taking orders from a girl."

"No?" She gave him her haughtiest frown. "Then I suggest you pack your things and leave."

His face registered surprise and then his eyes narrowed. "You trying to fire me?"

"Not at all. The choice is entirely yours. Either you do what I, as Mr. Warwick's representative tell you to do, or you find somewhere else to work."

He was trapped and he knew it. "All right, I'll plant your tobacco for you, but I'll be laughing myself silly when the master comes home and finds out what you've done. You won't be so high and mighty then, I reckon."

He was already laughing, leaving Katy with a feeling of apprehension. Would Julian return before the American victory? Would he be angry, and if so, what would he do? Had she been overconfident in thinking she could talk him into anything? But, she reasoned, it was useless to worry about it now. What was done, was done.

Actually, she found very little time for worry in the weeks that followed. Busy from sunrise to sundown, she supervised the planting, ran the household, and balanced the books. Working in the Carolina sunshine, she soon grew tanned and healthy. The freckles that had once bothered her so now covered her nose. But who had time to bother with a sunbonnet? Who would ever seen them anyway?

Spring settled into summer. Once the crop was planted, Katy had some spare time for visiting. One day, as she was on her way to Esther's, she caught Wharton with his back to her, raising his whip to Sampson. She had surprise on her side and without thinking, she somehow managed to grab the whip by its end, taking it from his hands before he could strike. He wheeled around. As she had so often seen him do, she raised it menacingly in the air. "What were you planning to do with this, Mr. Wharton?"

He was surly. "The lazy bastard won't follow orders."

"Would you like me to use this on you? You weren't

following orders, either. You were told not to use this on the slaves, as I remember. Now get off this land before I do use it on you."

He snorted derisively. "Nobody can fire me but Mr. Warwick."

"Don't be so sure of yourself. You may not be afraid of me, but I wouldn't hesitate to give this whip to Sampson. I have a feeling that he could convince you that you were no longer needed here."

Wharton saw the big black grin. "All right, you win. This time. But I'll see you pay for this. Take it from me; you haven't heard the last of Silas Wharton."

He stomped off, leaving Katy with a bad taste in her mouth. What had she done now? She had let her temper get the better of her again. Oh, she was glad enough to be rid of him, if his going meant the end of her troubles with him. Somehow, though, she rather doubted it.

The summer passed and the crops continued to do well. So much depended on a successful season that Katy found herself in a panic if it rained for more than a day, or if it didn't rain at all and the ground was dry. Jeremy would laugh at her, saying that she'd never last out the season if she didn't quit her worrying.

Somehow, she did last. As harvest time grew nearer, she could hardly contain her excitement. Arrangements had been made for the rice and tobacco; all that was left was to get them from the fields and to the buyers. Soon she would have the proof she needed to show that she had made the right decision, but more importantly, for the first time in years, Oaks would show a profit. What a wonderful homecoming it would make for Kit.

The note from Julian brought her back down to

earth. Recognizing the seal, she opened his letter slowly. If only it could have come two weeks later, after the crops were delivered. He didn't state his business. In a curt manner, he said that he had received some startling news and it was imperative that she join him in Charleston, immediately.

No matter how curious she might be about this news, she resented his tone. Besides, she had a plantation to think of and it was harvest time. Sending off excuses, she assured him that she would come as soon as conveniently possible.

Worry returned and this time she couldn't free herself of its nagging persistence. All of her hard work, all the slaves' hard work, could well be for nothing if Julian took control out of her hands. Unless the profits were put back into the plantation, it would be no better off than when she started. Oh there was trouble ahead; she could literally feel it.

Still, she had no idea how bad the trouble was until Wharton barged into her office, two days later, accompanied by two rather large men. They stood on either side of him, like sturdy book-ends, flexing their impressive sets of muscles.

Katy tried to remain unruffled by their threatening display of strength. Haughtily, she glanced up from her books. "Please state your business, Mr. Wharton. As you can see, I am quite busy."

"Isn't that funny? That's just what we came to see you about. You see, I've been talking with Mr. Warwick about you and he seems to think I can do a better job here than a silly little girl like you."

It was difficult to say which was worse; the deliberate rudeness, or the smirk. "Do you expect me to take your word for that?"

He gave her a toothless grin. "I anticipated that. So did Mr. Warwick. That's what the boys are for—to convince you. They're gonna take you to Mr. Warwick to do some talking. Ain't you, boys?"

He looked to them for agreement. It was obvious that their physical strength far outweighed their mental prowess as they gave a hearty imitation of Wharton's grin.

"And if I refuse to go?"

"You could do that. But these boys sure had their hearts set on taking you to Charleston and you would't want to hurt their feelings, now would you? They can get awful mean."

"They wouldn't dare touch me. Julian wouldn't allow it."

"Tsk, tsk. You aren't listening. Who do you think sent them? They have orders to bring you and they tend to stick to one idea at a time. Don't you, boys?" Again they grinned, in unison, and Katy suppressed a shiver. "No, I wouldn't argue, if I was you. Go along, peaceful like. Less trouble that way."

Katy wanted to slap his weasley face. "It doesn't appear that I have a choice."

"No ma'am, I reckon it don't."

"You will permit me to pack a few things first?"

"You know, I sure hate you to be thinking that old Silas here is a hard man. But it crosses my mind that you might say something to that nigger woman of yours and I can't afford trouble with them now, not when I'm taking charge here again. No, you just hurry along with the boys and I'll send whatever you need later, soon as Mr. Warwick sends word. Oh, and just a word of caution. Best not say anything to them big bucks of yours, either. First nigger to make a move to

386

help you gets a bullet in his head for his trouble."

Helplessly, Katy was ushered into the waiting carriage, stuffed back against the cushions and denied her last look at Oaks. It seemed Wharton's men took their work seriously; they drove like maniacs and it took all her concentration just to stay on the seat. By the time she reached Charleston, she felt nothing but relief.

Julian was waiting for her in the dining room. In the middle of a bite, he motioned for her to take a seat. "Ah, Katherine. I'm flattered that you rushed all this way to join me. You must be positively famished after your journey. Won't you join me? Cook has prepared the most delicious sole . . ."

"Who do you think you are, dragging me from my work, bringing me here and threatening me?"

He raised an eyebrow. "Come now, my dear. Surely you exaggerate. Calm yourself. There's no reason to get yourself into a state. Do sit down."

She refused the seat. "Stop it, Julian. I don't know what game you are playing, but I won't have it. I'm leaving."

He played with his fingernails. "Oh no, I think not. You and I have to talk, my dear."

There was a brittleness, a sharp cracking sound to his voice. The streak of cruelty, usually well-hidden, was now in evidence. Something akin to fear clutched at her as she remembered Kit's warning not to underestimate his brother. Still, she kept a false bravado. "You'll be sorry for this, Julian."

It seemed she had said something funny. "Katherine, you are delightful. I wonder if Chris realizes how lucky he was to find you. You're probably thinking I brought you here to chastise you for the way you handled things at Oaks. On the contrary, I am quite pleased. I'm told you made a profit. I think you did a splendid job of it."

"Then if you don't mind, I'd like to get back to it."

"You're not paying attention. I have no intention of permitting you to leave. As I told you, we have to talk, you and I."

"I have nothing to discuss with you."

"Whatever happened to my sweet, devoted sister-in-law? Is your mask slipping?"

"I don't know what you're talking about."

"Don't you? I'll give you a hint. Suppose I tell you where I've been the last few months. Does the name Whitney Hall spark your memory?"

She wanted to reach out for the support of the chair but his eyes were riveted on her, watching for her reaction. "Why, that's my grandfather's home."

"Yes," he chuckled. "A delightful man, Lord Whitney. Though not at all what I expected from your description. Why, do you know, I think he had me confused with my brother."

Was it necessary to watch her that closely? "I'm afraid he's getting old. His mind wanders."

"Nonsense. He's in excellent shape. But naturally I was curious so I did a bit of investigating. His lawyers were only too happy to refresh my mind about the size of the dowry. Now where do you suppose my brother could have spent all that money?"

"I haven't the slightest idea."

"Haven't you? You know, they tell the most amusing story in Bristol, about a ship that was in such a hurry to leave before the arrival of His Majesty's troops, that they left behind some cargo? By the way, I took the liberty of bringing your trunks home with me." His cold blue eyes laughed in triumph.

Defeated, Katy took advantage of the nearest chair. Those damned trunks. If she wasn't so tired, she could have laughed at the irony of it. "You've made your point. Now what do you want?"

"Splendid. No scenes. No tears. I admire your ability to face the inevitable. It seems you have a collection of admirable traits. You're also a talented actress; you had me fooled for a time. I must say, though, that it suits my purpose to have you so accomplished."

"What exactly are your purposes?"

"Gracious, you're so impatient. You will know soon enough. In the meantime, I really do think you should eat something. Here, try some of this sole."

"I'm not hungry."

He shrugged and returned to his place. "Suit yourself. I will eat."

Katy recognized the game he played and resented the enjoyment he derived from it. He had brought her here for a purpose and she wanted to know what it was. Her only hope was by feigning indifference. "I'm far too tired for this. I'm going to my room. We can continue this in the morning."

"Don't you dare turn your back on me."

His tone made her flinch but she didn't hesitate for a second. She opened the door. "Good night, Julian."

He was on her in a second. "You won't go anywhere until I say you may."

She whined. "You're hurting me."

"I'll hurt you a great deal worse unless you do as you're told. You had better take me seriously, Katherine."

To control the rising panic, she stared him down. "Can I at least sit?"

He threw her from him and she collapsed in the nearest chair. "I would prefer to do this in a civilized manner. I do hate for things to get nasty, but believe me, if necessary, I will use force."

"Why don't you just tell me what it is you want me to do?"

"Try to understand, my dear. These are dangerous times. You see, I've rather committed myself; the British expect certain things from me."

"Are you referring to the money they gave you for spying?"

"You've been prying into matters that don't concern you. It's just as well, I suppose. It shows you just how serious this all is."

"What is?"

"You're forgetting my startling news that I've waited three days to tell you. I've discovered that my brother is a traitor. If I am to do my duty, I will have to turn him over to the authorities."

"Your own brother?"

"Half-brother. Ours is not the first family to be torn in half, so to speak, by this dreadful war."

"But they'll hang him."

"The thought did occur to me. Pity, but it can't be helped."

"You'll have to find him first."

He laughed, a dry, mirthless sound that sent chills down her spine. "That, my dear, is the least of my problems. Chris was more than anxious to rush here to your aid."

"He doesn't care what happens to me."

"Really? He's waiting upstairs for you now."

"Kit is here?"

"But of course. That's what I've been trying to tell

you. Perhaps you're beginning to realize how thorough I am. I thought it only fair to give you the opportunity to say good-bye to him."

"I don't believe you. If he's here, take me to him."

"Not quite yet. There are certain things we must discuss."

"Such as?"

He towered over her, threateningly. "Such as what you will say to him. You're not stupid. You know I brought you here for a reason. I could just as easily have presented him to the authorities without your presence, but I wanted to give you the chance to save him."

She regarded him suspiciously. "Save him? How noble of you."

"Yes, it is, isn't it? But as much as I would love to be generous, I am not in the position to give away something for nothing."

"Then you want to strike a bargain. What is it?"

"Katherine, you're a marvel. Not too many women would take this so calmly, or reasonably. Quite simple, our bargain will be that you tell my brother what I want you to say and I will let him go."

"And that's all there is to it?"

"No, not quite. I've received some dreadful news from Virginia. Cornwallis has been soundly defeated and, frankly, without his protection, I'm in a rather tenuous position here. It's imperative that I leave the country and you, my dear, will have to help me."

"Over my dead body."

"Do try not to overdramatize; it doesn't enhance your role. To be accurate, it will be Chris's dead body. Unless, of course, you go to England with me, pretending that I'm your husband."

"England? You're mad! Where would we go?"

"I rather fancied Whitney Hall."

She stared at him in amazement. "You know that my grandfather can't stand the sight of me. What makes you think he'll take us in?"

"Farley needs an heir; we will provide him with one. Besides, the old man can't live forever."

"This is insane, Julian."

He gripped her shoulder, tighter and tighter, until she almost cried out with the pain. "Nonetheless, it is the way it must be. I have no money of my own, so either you come with me, or Chris dies."

"You said I was to tell him certain things. I won't agree to anything unless I know what they are."

"Very wise of you. You know, I think I'll enjoy being married to you. I want you to convince my dear brother that you are leaving with me willingly, to make certain that he won't follow us. Otherwise, how could I take the chance of letting him go?"

This new Julian was hard and cold and she didn't for a second doubt that he would give his brother to the British. But could she face a future with him? Life with Julian and Farley would be a nightmare, but what was her alternative? He had her, and one glance at his smirking face told her he knew it.

"If you make me do this, Julian, I'll hate you for the rest of my life."

"Ah, Katherine, you never quit. What spirit! It grieves me to have to put you through this, but try to see it from my point of view. The two of you have been making a fool of me, using my name and influence for your traitorous purposes. Did you think I would never realize what you were doing? And that if I did, I would do nothing about it, that I would let you go

392

unpunished?"

She couldn't help it; she winced at the glare from those stony eyes. But Julian was enjoying himself far too much to notice. "His punishment will be the knowledge of your unfaithfulness. Contrary to what you said before, he cares a great deal about you. Or at least he did. Your punishment, my dear, will be watching his face as you tell him you are leaving him."

"What makes you think he will believe me?"

"I've seen you, remember? You will be convincing, unless you wish to see him hang."

"You're a monster."

"Is that any way to speak to your husband? Let's not waste time calling each other names. We have a job to do and the sooner we're done with it, the sooner Chris can go free."

Grabbing her wrists, he yanked her from the chair. As she stumbled after him, she thought wildly. How was she going to do this? Why England, of all places, and why Whitney Hall? There had to be a way out of this. But falling up the stairs after her ruthless captor, she was at a loss to discover what it was.

Julian flung her into her room and ordered her to get into the gown on the bed. She would want to look her best when she saw her husband. As a final touch, he draped the hideous diamonds on her neck and Katy struggled with nausea. Their weight did nothing to alleviate the gloom that engulfed her. With a heavy heart, she followed Julian down the hallway.

Kit was lying on the floor, bound and gagged, and she was horrified to see how thin and worn he looked. As the sudden light hit his eyes, he squinted up at them. His eyes narrowed in recognition and Katy felt a cold band of steel twist around her heart, pulling tighter and tighter. He looked like a caged, wild animal and she vowed that once and for all, she would set him free. Her love for him was as strong as ever, but it had caused both of them nothing but pain. He was better off without it, than like this. Drawing a deep, ragged breath, she moved to stand by Julian. If ever she had been the actress he claimed, this was the time to prove it. Assuming an indifference she didn't feel, she stared at her husband.

Julian seemed quite pleased with himself. "Where are your manners, Chris? Your wife has come to say good-bye. Stand up."

Kit dragged his chains with him to a standing position. "Excuse me, my dear, but Julian said nothing about company. I had no chance to dress." He gestured at his rags.

Did he have to be so happy to see her? It made her job all the more difficult. It took all her willpower not to rush to him, to tear at the chains that bound him. Instead, she turned to Julian, forcing her voice not to crack. "Did you have to tie him up, for God's sake?"

"Really, Katherine, this is no time to be squeamish. I could hardly take the chance that he'd bruise your lovely throat." Lifting the diamonds, his cold fingers massaged her neck, making something turn in her stomach. Watching, Kit felt the blood rush to his head. Ineffectively, he struggled with the chains.

"You see. He's an animal. He needs to be restrained."

Katy looked away. If she had to watch, it would break her. Poor, proud Kit. Whatever Julian's perversions, she had no taste for this. "Let's go, Julian."

"But you haven't said what you came to say. I've gone to a great deal of trouble for you; don't lose your courage now."

"What is it you have to say, Katy?" Kit's voice was soft, but it cut through her like a blade of steel.

When she didn't answer, Julian cut in. "Poor little brother. Your wife has come to bid you adieu."

"Is this true, Katy?"

She could only nod. If she spoke, he would know the truth. As if sensing this, Kit turned to his brother. "Then at least give us some privacy, Julian. Surely we can be left alone to say our good-byes?"

In a panic, she blurted out. "No, I don't want to be alone with him. I can say whatever I have to say with you in the room."

Julian shrugged in a gesture of helplessness. Knowing she would get little aid from him, Katy marched to the table and poured herself a whiskey. With a quick swallow, she downed it all, praying that it would provide the courage she needed. Whirling around, she found Kit's eyes on her, waiting, questioning. Nervously, she fingered the diamonds, searching for the right words."

"Chris is waiting, my dear."

Swallowing deeply, she reached for her voice. "It's just like Julian says. I'm going away with him." She should have reached deeper, for her voice was small and unnatural."

"Why?"

Think angry, she schooled herself. Think angry and don't look in his eyes. "Why? Because I'm tired of waiting for you, that's why. Tired of waiting for this infernal war to be over so I can go back to England. Did you think I could be happy here, with no money and no friends? I want more from life than you can ever give me. Julian understands me, far better than

395

you ever did. I think we will deal rather well together."
She forced herself to gaze fondly at him.

"Don't trust him, Katy."

"Trust? Are you still talking about trust? You, of all
people? I trusted you once, and look where it got me. I
warned you that if you let me down, there'd be hell to
pay. I swore I'd have my revenge and by God, I'm
going to enjoy this."

He flinched. "I thought you had forgiven me that."

She spat on the floor. "There's your forgiveness. I'll
never forgive you. Every minute since, I've plotted
and planned, waiting for the precise moment to bring
you to your knees. I've played the dutiful and loving
wife until I thought I would scream. But it was worth
it. I fooled even you, didn't I? But then, you were such
a good teacher. Julian and I have admired the way you
played your role. But it's over now, Kit, all the acting
and deceiving, for both of us. I'm going out that door
with Julian, back to England where I belong, and I
hope with all my heart I never have to see you again."

"I don't believe it, Katy. Look at me, goddammit.
Face me and tell me this is really you talking."

The cold band twisted tighter as she raised her eyes
to meet his. They were soft and yearning, pleading
with her. They had lost none of their ability to attract
her and she was being drawn to him like a magnet.
Until she died, she would be haunted by those eyes
and the pain she saw in them. "You're a fool, Kit
Warwick, especially when it comes to women. If you
refuse to believe my words, perhaps this will convince
you." She reached back to undo the clasp of the ruby
pendant she had worn beneath her gown since he had
given it to her. "Take this. Give it to some cheap little
tart who will appreciate it. I don't need it. Julian will

give me lots better, won't you, Julian?''

"Katy. . ."

Near tears, she ignored his plea. "This is useless, Julian. I'm tired of this game. Let's go."

Julian chuckled. "Katherine, Chris. Please. I hate to see you part on angry words. Come now, let's kiss and make up so you can part friends. It's so much more civilized, don't you think? No? I did try, brother dear, but you know women."

Kit's voice was bitter. "No, Julian. I thought I knew Katy but I guess I never did."

There was defeat in his words, and finality. To Katy, it was small comfort knowing she had done her job well. Kit was free to go, in more ways than one, and it hurt to know that his memory of her would be tinged with betrayal. It wasn't fair. If she had been so noble, why did she feel so sick about it? It was as if a part of her had been amputated, a vital part that would make the rest of her life unbearable. With a sob caught in her throat, she ran out of the room. Julian could stay to torment him, if he must, but she wanted no part of it.

Smiling vindictively, Julian finished the conversation for her. "Know Katy? Why of course you never did. If you had, perhaps you wouldn't have lost her. To me."

Closing the door behind him, he left Kit to brood in the darkness with his words echoing in the silence. Kit slumped back down to the floor. What did it matter what happened to him anymore? Without Katy, what the hell did it matter?

397

Chapter 27

Katy was weeping quietly in the hallway when Julian sauntered up to her. "You were magnificent, my dear. Absolutely magnificent. If only you could have seen his face when you left the room . . ."

"Stop it. Do you have to be so cruel?"

"On the contrary. It wasn't I who was cruel. 'I played the dutiful and loving wife until I thought I would scream.' That was cruel, but, oh, so splendid. I can't remember a time when I've enjoyed myself more."

Katy turned her tear-stained face to him. "I don't understand you. You have everything and he has nothing. Why must you do this?"

"Everything? Oh no, not quite everything. He has you, does he not? Or at least, he did have you. Now you are mine."

"Never!"

"Never? That's too strong a word, I think."

"I'll never forgive you for this."

"But how difficult it will make things. Try to understand. I am accustomed to taking what I want. Only two people have ever been able to thwart me. One of them was Kit and for that, he will pay.''

"Who was the other?''

His look was terrible. "His mother. I can't fathom
why my father was so infatuated with her. She could
do no wrong in his eyes. Her and her brat. They ruined
everything. I hated her, as I hate him. And I made her
pay for her stupid interfering.''

Katy was afraid to hear any more. "Your sordid
past doesn't interest me.''

He smiled maliciously. "But, darling, there should
be no secrets between us. I want you to know. I'm
proud of it. I killed her.''

"Oh God!''

"Save your oaths; she deserved it. I warned her. I
told her I wouldn't be forced into going to England for
the brat's birthday. Do you know what she did? She
scolded me. As if I were a child, her child, God forbid. I
grabbed my father's hunting knife and we fought. In
the end, I stabbed her in the stomach. Oh, I had no
real intention of killing her. She wouldn't have died if
she wasn't so determined to go to England. How
could I know that the stupid bitch would pretend
nothing was wrong? All for that damned brat of hers.
It was always 'little Kit this' and 'little Kit that'; it
made me sick. You needn't look so shocked. I did what
had to be done. If I hadn't taken action, she and her
useless son would have contrived to take everything
away. Oaks was mine. It's all mine.''

"This can't be true. I don't believe you.''

"Suit yourself. I am not bragging. I merely want
you to know what you're up against. I mean to leave
this country, with your help, and I will do whatever is
necessary to reach that goal.''

"Even murder?''

"Why not?"

"You're insane!"

All at once his features darkened and grew ugly. Katy took a step backward, afraid of what he might do. Then, as if reassured by her fright, a quick smile transformed him into the earlier Julian. "Whatever I am thinking of, chatting this way with you when there's so much to be done. Katherine, you must begin packing while I make the last-minute arrangements. Hurry along to your room, while I tend to my dear little brother."

The sudden change all but took her breath away. "You must be crazy. I'm not going anywhere with you."

"Come, come, let's not bicker. I hate to get nasty but I did warn you that I won't tolerate anyone getting in my way. When I say it's time to pack, you are going to have to learn I mean what I say." With a snap of his fingers, the two unsavory characters that had escorted her to town materialized behind him. "Gentlemen, would you please see that Mrs. Warwick finds her bedroom?"

Though he spoke pleasantly enough, there was granite in his tone and Katy could feel the hard walls of his prison closing in on her. Frustration and despair made her want to scream but what little was left of Farley pride kept her silent. With a haughtiness to rival her grandfather's, she allowed herself to be led to her room.

Somewhat unceremoniously, she was deposited among her trunks. Seeing them she was filled with a fresh supply of self-pity. Just as she was convinced that life couldn't deal her another blow, Rachel strolled into the room. In her right hand was a glittering pistol that was waved in Katy's direction. "You really should get busy. Unless, of course, you'd rather wear those dreadful things in your trunks. I wouldn't be caught dead in them, myself."

"You looked through my trunks?"

"My, my, aren't we sensitive. Naturally I looked through them; who do you think chose what you have on now? Not that I found anything worth my effort."

"I should have known that you were behind all this."

"Yes, you should have. I did try to warn you. If you had listened to me, none of this need ever have happened. You could have lived the life of a queen in England and I would have had Kit. Poor Kit. I wonder how he will enjoy his trial."

"Trial? But Julian promised . . ."

"Poor innocent. I also warned you about your naivet'e. How could he possibly release Kit now? It's so funny. Kit detests you by now, you know. How nice of you to take credit for all we've done to him. He'll go to his grave blaming you."

Katy shivered. How could she have been so stupid? "So Julian will turn him over to the authorities anyway?"

"I'm afraid so. Just think. That touching scene was totally unnecessary. The outcome would have been the same, either way."

"Except that now, I no longer have to cooperate with you. I'm not going to England."

Rachel laughed. "Your naiveté is showing again. Trust me when I say that you'll come with us—with or without your cooperation."

Her secret smile convinced Katy that whatever their plans for the future were, they didn't include her.

A convenient accident on the ship? A fire in her room as she lay sleeping? Any number of things could happen to her. After all, they didn't need any more than a body to claim her inheritance. And if Julian was willing to sacrifice his own brother for his greed, what chance did she have? Her only hope lay in making Rachel talk. Perhaps she'd let slip a clue, something that would prove useful later on. "I can understand why Julian would want me to come along, but why you? Aren't you tired of being Miss Worthington? What do you get out of this? He's using you. Don't you realize that? Now if you were to help Kit . . ."

"Give me credit for some intelligence. I heard him that night, at the Smithfield ball, telling you how he hated me."

"You heard?"

"Yes. And you thought you were so clever, didn't you?"

"But I don't understand. Why didn't you tell Julian, then?"

"At the time, I thought I could deal with it myself."

"You had him shot, didn't you?"

"Who else? Of course, by now he's blaming you for that, too. Neither one of them trusts you now. And you thought you had them wrapped around your little finger."

Any other night, Rachel's news might have shocked her, but tonight, anything seemed possible. Her situation was desperate; somehow she had to get away from these ruthless people. "Be careful not to make the same mistake, Rachel. There's danger in being overconfident."

"You're learning fast. But have no fear; I always manage to succeed. We're wasting time. You're supposed to be packing. Get busy." She waved the pistol in the direction of the trunks.

As she went through the motions of packing, an idea began to formulate in Katy's mind. If she could distract Rachel, she could easily get her pistol. With the weapon, she could free Kit before the soldiers came to take him away. As she had hoped, Rachel's eyes were glued to the gems. Tossing it carelessly on the bed, she watched as her quarry took the bait. How similar they were: both so beautiful, and so cold.

Pouncing on the pistol, she had it before Rachel was aware of what happened. "Not one word, Rachel, if you value your life. I am more than willing to give you the diamonds, but if you make a sound, you'll be wearing them in your casket. Now just move back into that chair and we'll see what we can do about keeping you in it."

"You little bitch. You haven't got a prayer. You'll never get past Julian and you know it."

"Not alone, perhaps, but I do know where to find Kit, and I like the idea of having his help. Now move. Get in that chair."

Still clutching the diamonds, Rachel did as she was told. Too late, Katy saw the barely perceptible flicker in those strange, green eyes. She heard the steps only seconds before something exploded in her brain and the world went black.

"How did this happen?"

"She tricked me, Julian."

"Obviously. I asked you to watch her carefully. Incompetence! I'm surrounded by imbeciles. She won't require your dubious supervision any longer. Come with me. The soldiers will be arriving any moment and everything must appear to be normal."

"What are you going to do with her."

"Leave her where she is. Even if she regains consciousness, which I doubt, she isn't going anywhere with the door locked and a drop of twenty feet from the windows. I'll leave my friends parted outside the door, as an added precaution."

"And what about me?"

"You will go to your room and stay there until I send for you. Ah, that must be my visitors." He rubbed his hands together. "I must say, this has proven to be such fun."

"You really are depraved."

"Yes, I know. That's what makes us so well suited, my dear. Now come along. I can't keep my company waiting." Encircling her waist, he led her out of the room, taking the candle with him. Only the firelight saved the room from total blackness, and only the click of the key in the lock disturbed the silence.

It was to this tranquil atmosphere that Katy woke. Crawling, biting, kicking, she tried to surface. There was a dim light at the end of the tunnel and she floated in its direction. As the light became brighter and warmer, the crackling logs slowly came into focus. Shaking her head, she tried to clear away the remaining fog. A sharp light flared across her eyes as the pain seared her brain. For a moment or two, she had to lie back down. Dimly, she was aware that it was essential to have her wits about her, but she couldn't seem to get her bearings. When she was finally able to open her eyes without wincing, she tried to stand. A wave of nausea tried to take her back to the swirling fog, but her senses were alert to danger and self-preservation came to her rescue. Once more she blinked, amazed at how clear her head had become.

The pistol! She must have fallen on it when she was struck from behind and luckily Julian had forgotten it. Knowing him she was sure her door would be locked. There was a way out of this; she could feel it. If only hear head didn't ache so. Perhaps the door to Kit's room was unlocked. Hurrying over, she turned the knob. It moved easily, too easily, and the door stood open. It was the door out of Kit's room that proved to be the obstacle. She dropped to the floor in anger and frustration. As if another light had exploded in her brain, it hit her. The tunnel! It had literally been staring her in the face. With renewed determination, she closed the adjoining door. Let Julian figure this one out, she thought to herself. Just as she had watched Kit do, she opened the tunnel door, rearranged the clothes in the closet behind her and slipped into the darkness beyond.

Once in the tunnel, she cursed her stupidity. Why hadn't she thought of a candle? There had been one at Kit's bedside. Debating on whether or not to go back, she decided there wasn't a second to waste. Who knew how much time had elapsed since she had been hit on the head? Julian could be in the room, searching, at this very minute. If she walked carefully, she would be fine. Besides, what she couldn't see, couldn't hurt her.

There must be stairs, she thought, and suddenly she was upon them. Inching her way down, she counted fifteen before they leveled off. Reluctant to touch the damp and chilly walls, she groped about in the darkness. It seemed an eternity, at least, but in actuality, it was a short tunnel. Soon the darkness was less intense and she was struggling through the opening.

She found herself in a clump of bushes not far from the house. Brushing off her clothes, she was about to emerge as the door opened. Seven soldiers dragged an unprotesting Kit to a waiting carriage. Close behind was Julian, shouting orders. "Don't forget to tell Captain Lawrence that he is to be considered dangerous."

"I know my duty, sir. Now, if you will excuse me." Turning his back on Julian, the young officer marched to his horse. In a huff, Julian turned on his heel and returned to the house. For a wild moment, Katy considered confronting the British but realistically, she knew she could hardly deal with seven of them.

The officer mounted his horse barely fifty feet away from where she was crouching. "Let's get this poor man to his fate, Ralston. It sickens my stomach, but I must follow orders. But the world has become a sorry place in which to live when a man's own brother turns him in."

"But he's a traitor."

"Perhaps. Still, I hated giving that man money for him. Look at him—does he look dangerous to you?"

"Looks more like he's lost his last friend."

"Let's get this sorry business over with."

"But why all the fuss? Why is he being sent to England? He doesn't look all that important to me."

"He's said to be one of Marion's men, could be a local hero. They're all nervous about that mess in Yorktown. When these people learn that Cornwallis is finished, we could have trouble. By packing this one off to England, they hope to rob the locals of a martyr."

"You don't sound too happy about it."

"It goes against the grain. A man should be tried by a jury of his peers, traitor or not." He lowered his voice. "And there's talk that he might never reach England."

"Conveniently lost at sea?"

"Still, it's hard to imagine Lawrence being party to such a scheme."

"If he has orders, he won't have much of a choice."

"I suppose not. No more than you and I. I'm grateful I don't have the job. Yet I wish I was going with them, back home. I never much cared for this war."

Echoing the sentiment, Katy held her breath as they came within inches of her hiding place. When she was certain they were gone, she emerged. Her strategy was now clear. She would go to Oaks, to Rosie. It was her only hope of reaching Sam. Further than that, she refused to think. Sam would know what to do. But she couldn't walk to Oaks. She would need a horse. Did she dare risk spiriting a horse from Julian's stable? Even as she turned in that direction, she knew she hadn't the courage to risk an encounter with her brother-in-law.

The solution was almost too easy. Trust the Smithfields to be entertaining at this hour. The poor groom, sleeping in the hay, would be explaining for a week, but all she could think of at the moment was that Kit's life was at stake. Besides, she reasoned, the British owe me a horse. Talking softly, she eased the animal out of the stable and into the moonlight. Jumping on his back, she galloped off, anxious to leave Charleston far behind.

She had forgotten the sentry. "Good evening, Major. If you will excuse me, I'm in a bit of a hurry."

"I can see that, but I can't let you pass, I'm afraid. I have my orders."

"But this is an unusual circumstance. I'm in danger."

"Danger, Mrs. Warwick?"

Danger, indeed. Think fast, Katy girl. "It's my husband. He's returned sooner than expected and you see, he's quite the jealous type. I'm so frightened that he might try to kill me. I have to get away. Please, have pity on me."

She was practically kneeling at his feet and her backward glances weren't all pretense. She could almost see Julian riding toward them. For the second time that evening, it was a convincing performance; she could see he was wavering. "Please, Major. No one need ever know. I surely won't say anything, if you won't."

The young man was remembering the vivacious Katherine Warwick, flirting outrageously at every party, and he could well believe her husband would want to kill her. But she had always been nice to him and he would hate to see her harmed. In the end, he relented. With a promise not to tell a soul, he let her go. Her smile of gratitude was just reward, he felt.

It was nearly daylight when she first spotted the chimneys of Oaks. The fields, her fields, were empty and waiting. The house stood among them, rising on its knoll, a giant spectre in the growing light. It would always stand aloof, apart from the alarming events that went on around it, offering refuge within its sturdy walls. Katy felt the urge to seek that refuge, to climb the familiar stairs and throw her tired body on her bed. Before she could do that, however, she would need to see Kit safe. Leading the horse, which she had nicknamed Black Beauty, quietly up the drive, she made her way to Rosie's cabin. She reached for the pistol, in case she should meet up with Wharton. Tonight, she wouldn't hesitate to use it on him.

Rosie was already awake. "Child, is that you? What

are you doing outside my door?"

"Oh, Rosie, I need your help."

"I can see that. Well, come on in out of that cold. It's October, you want to catch your death with no shawl on? That no-count Wharton said you were off to England, to visit your granddaddy. What are you doing here?"

"It's a long story."

"I've got plenty of time." She was watching Katy carefully.

"I don't. I've got to find Sam, or the *Irish Lass*. The British have got Kit and if we don't do something fast, they'll kill him."

"Hold on a minute. How do you know all this?"

"That was why Julian sent for me. He wants to leave the country and he needed me to go with him. I escaped, but Kit is on his way to England to stand trial. Julian gave him to the British."

"Always said that boy was unnatural. What do you want me to do?"

"God bless you, Rosie. Can you get into the house? Good. I'm going to need a new dress. And a cloak. And I have to find Sam."

"That's easy enough. They're in the swamps, waiting for their captain. They won't be happy to see you in his place."

"No, I suppose they'll blame me for it again. It can't be helped. It's our only hope."

"What are you up to, child?"

"I'm not certain, exactly. All I know is that we have to reach Kit before it's too late."

"Don't you fret. I'll get your things if you promise to eat something while I'm gone. You're gonna need your strength."

As Rosie let herself out of the cabin, Katy rummaged through the cupboards. She stuffed some bread into her mouth, not caring what she ate. Her mind was not on food but on the day ahead. Rosie found her pacing anxiously, the half-eaten loaf on the table, when she returned.

Grabbing the dress, Katy gave her intructions to tell Esther. If Katy and Sam failed, perhaps General Marion could do something. Hurrying out to Black Beauty, she flung her bundle on his back and set off for the swamps.

Just as she was convinced she was hopelessly lost, she recognized the familiar markings. She slipped under the Spanish moss, giving a low whistle, just as Josh had done. Her heart did a tumble as she sighted the *Irish Lass* waiting for her in the morning haze. Weak with relief, she jumped from the horse and ran up to the deck.

Josh's young voice rang out in the still air. "It's Katy! Sam, hurry on up here. Katy's come."

Sam, as he approached, had lightning in his eyes and thunder in his voice. "What in tarnation are you doing here?"

Katy felt the familiar sting of tears. "Oh, Sam, please, not now. It's been a long night and I don't think I can take much more. Sam, the British have got Kit."

"Damnation! I told him not to go. What's wrong with you, girl? Didn't you know better than to send for him? You knew he'd come and you knew he'd be in danger. What was so important that you needed him?"

"But I didn't. It was Julian. And Rachel. She overheard us talking and she knew about the tree." She

410

glanced at the hostile faces. They didn't believe her. But they had to. "I can see by your expressions that you don't believe me. I have no time to stand here defending myself. If Kit is to be saved, we have to act quickly. Right now, he's on his way to England and there's a good chance that he'll be disposed of before the *Olympus* ever lands. I refuse to let that happen. As half owner, I am taking command of this ship. Anyone who cares to come with me is more than welcome, but if necessary, I'll sail her myself. I won't harm her and I promise to bring her back as soon as Kit is safely on board."

They stared in astonishment. In spite of everything, Sam wanted to laugh. There she was, giving orders, taking command as if she had done this sort of thing for years. You had to give her credit for spunk; and darned if they weren't all looking at her with new respect. "I'm with you, lass. I don't know what you're planning, or even what you've done, but I can see your heart's in the right place. What do you say, men—do we shove off?"

One by one, they nodded in assent. Katy had the heady sensation of being able to accomplish anything with their help. Gone was her fatigue; her headache had vanished. With a sweeping gesture, she gave the order to set sail and smiling broadly, the crew followed her commands. Creaking and groaning as if waking from a long sleep, the *Irish Lass* slowly left her makeshift dock.

The sound of whinnying caught their attention, and Katy suddenly remembered Black Beauty. "Wait, Sam. We can't leave yet. We've got to get the horse."

"Listen, I'm as fond of animals as you, but this time, your horse will have to stay behind."

411

"But you don't understand . . ."

"Enough is enough. Let the poor animal go back to his stable."

"That's the problem; he can't. He doesn't belong at Oaks. I stole him."

His exasperation switched to disbelief and then back to exasperation. "You what?"

Feeling like a child, she tried to defend herself. "I had to, Sam. How else could I get here from Charleston?"

"Horse stealing's a hanging offense."

"Don't be silly. So is treason. Not to mention aiding in the escape of a prisoner. Or spying. What does one more crime matter, at this point? Don't you see—that's why he has to come. If he was discovered here, we would all be in trouble."

Sam seemed at a loss to know what to do so Katy gave the order to bring the horse on board. The poor animal was frightened and only she could calm him. It was a painful moment when she led him into the hold, but she knew there was no time for sentiment now. If they delayed much longer, they would lose the cover of the morning fog. She could deal with the horse, but would Sam, please, give the order to shove off again?

When she at last reached the deck, they were making their way through the eerie stillness and Katy marveled at how Sam could know where they were going. Once or twice they bogged down in the mud and sand and the men had to use long poles to free the ship. But their luck held and under the protection of the fog, they managed to slip out into the open sea.

Katy stood on the bow. It felt good to feel the roll of the waves beneath her once again, and memories of that other voyage haunted her. How much she had

412

changed since then.

"I've done as I was told, lass. Now that we're at sea, though, I think I'm entitled to some answers. I want to know what happened and I need to know where we're going."

She whirled around. "Oh, Sam; it's you. I'm sorry, I guess I was lost in my thoughts. Do you suppose Kit is all right?"

"I've no way of knowing since I still don't know what happened."

"It was awful. Julian tricked me. He made me tell Kit I was going away with him to England, and in return, he said he'd let Kit go. I thought I was doing the right thing. How could I suspect that he'd turn in his own brother? I'm afraid I was very convincing. I'm sure Kit hates me now. As much as I hate his brother."

"You mean he just let you go?"

"No, not exactly. I doubt he had any more intention of releasing me than he did Kit. I have a feeling that if I stayed around to find out, I would never have left that house alive. I wasn't about to stay. I used Kit's tunnel. I imagine my brother-in-law is somewhat confused, not to mention furious. I certianly hope so."

"I bet he is. But why would he want to kill you?"

"He's getting scared. He wants to be safely tucked away in England when the British lose. But he'll need money to live in the style he's used to and he was going to use me to get the Farley fortune. He's already been to Grandfather; that's how he learned about Kit. Once he had the money, he would hardly wish to share it with me."

"Wouldn't do him any good. The estate is all tied up with the heir, a male heir."

413

"Good. He seemed to think he could charm Grandfather and take over at Whitney Hall, especially with Kit and I dead."

"Why that unnatural, scurvy. . ."

"I know. Don't think I haven't called him every one of those names. If it's the last thing I do, I won't let him get away with it."

"Exactly how do you plan to stop him, lass?"

"The first step is to rescue Kit."

"I'm in agreement with that. I'm sure you have some crazy scheme in that head of yours."

"Yes, I do. We're going after the *Olympus.*"

"That is crazy."

"Very likely, but what else can we do? They're taking him to England, to avoid trouble here at home. If I can talk to Cecil . . ."

"Wait a minute. Maybe you got away with that plan before, but you can't expect it to work twice."

She stiffened. "Very well, Sam, I won't ask you. Just let me off and I'll handle it myself. Those soldiers said something about disposing of him at sea. No doubt he'll be shot trying to escape."

Sam whistled through his teeth. "That sounds like Julian's work, but the British must be scared to go along with it."

"They said something about Cornwallis's defeat at Yorktown."

"By God, that's great news! It could mean an end to this war with Cornwallis out of it. At least for the South."

"It won't do Kit any good, lying at the bottom of the ocean."

"You're right. We can't waste any time in getting to him."

414

"Then you'll go along with me?"

"Did you ever think otherwise? Don't give me that grin; you always knew I wouldn't let you go alone. Besides, as you always say, do I have any choice?" He shrugged, bowing to the inevitable.

Katy hugged him. "Oh, Sam, I knew I could depend on you. I know it sounds crazy, but it will work. It has to work."

Chapter 28

Captain Lawrence was sitting down to dinner when his aide informed him of a ship off the starboard bow. Damnation! These things always happened when he sat down to eat. Annoyed, he threw his napkin at his plate and followed Perkins up to the deck. Once there, it was easy to spot the vessel in question. There was something vaguely familiar about it. These damn pirates, he thought. If he wasn't in such a hurry to reach England, he'd love to give chase and blow them out of the water. To add to his vexation, it appeared this one wasn't trying to avoid confrontation with the obviously superior *Olympus*. On the contrary, it was the one giving chase. Why, of all the effrontery! Challenging the might of one of His Majesty's finest men-of-war? He'd show them, orders or not. Calling the men to their posts, he crossed over to his telescope. Just as he was about to give the order to fire away, he caught sight of a pair of waving arms. He followed the arms down to the body. Good lord, it was a woman. And not just any woman; it was Katherine Farley. No, he must stop thinking of her that way—she was a Warwick now. But what the devil was she doing out here? He smiled in secret pleasure. It would certainly be a feather in his cap to present her to Admiral Farley, safe and sound, especially after that sorry business with her husband. Yes, she would be a widow by now. Trust Katherine to brighten what would otherwise have been a tedious voyage.

Turning to Perkins, he gave the order to hold fire and weigh anchor. Typically, Perkins questioned the order. Ignoring him, Cecil gave the order himself.

He was waiting, splendid in his tailored uniform, when Katy finally arrived. Bowing low, he offered her his arm and led her to his cabin, with Sam in tow. "We seem to meet in the most unusual places, Mrs. Warwick."

Katy smiled wanly as she seated herself. "I'm afraid this isn't a very happy occasion for me, Cecil."

She was using his Christian name; things definitely looked brighter. For the time being, though, he must commiserate with her. "I know, but do try to cheer up. We won't sit back and take this."

What on earth was he talking about? Her confusion must have been apparent because he hurried to add, "Just as soon as possible, His Majesty will send fresh troops and we will re-establish ourselves in Virginia. In no time, we'll have those colonials subdued."

Oh, the war. He was right; she was supposed to be British. She simpered. "You don't know how happy that makes me, Cecil. But in the meantime, I'm in a great deal of trouble."

He was all concern. "Good heavens, Katherine, what is the matter? Please, I'd like to help."

Katy could almost feel Sam grinning behind her. "I hate to burden you, especially when you have so many other important matters on your mind. But quite honestly, I don't know where else to turn."

He moved over to pat her hand. "There, there, my dear. Don't cry. We'll see you out of your troubles. Try to tell me about it."

"Oh, Cecil, you're so strong. If only my husband had your strength." She appealed to him through wide eyes, moisture gathering on her lashes. "They say he was a spy. The soldiers came and took him away. I have no money, no home. I don't know what to do."

"It was wise of you to come to me. I will take you to the admiral myself. This has been an unpleasant experience for you, I know, but trust me and we'll soon have you smiling again."

Did he really believe her to be that shallow? "That sounds wonderful for me, but what about Kit?"

"Kit? Is that your pet, or something?"

She hated him in that moment and it was impossible to hide her annoyance. "No, of course not. Kit is my husband. Don't you see? I've got to see him."

Lawrence awoke from the daydream he had been building. "You want to see him? Whatever for? He's a traitor."

Katy's voice had a sharp edge to it. "In England, Captain, we have trials to determine guilt and innocence. He is still innocent until proven guilty by law."

"Ah, but he has been. His trial was this morning."

"What?"

"He will hang tomorrow morning."

It was as if it had been his cold voice that had passed the sentence. Katy grasped at straws. "But I was told he would be taken to England for trial."

"I have no idea where you obtained your information but yes, originally he was to accompany us back to England. The elder Mr. Warwick, however, convinced the governor that it would be in his best interest to get it over with quickly, without any fuss. So they could teach the rest of them a lesson."

"Julian! Of course. He wouldn't want the notoriety over in England. You said Kit was scheduled for execution in the morning. Is there any chance for a pardon?"

"Katherine, he was a spy. There's no clemency for treason, you should know that. You seem awfully anxious about a known criminal. Your loyalty to him is commendable, but no longer necessary."

But she was no longer listening. She had turned to face Sam whose grim face mirrored the desperation she felt. Now what? They could no longer afford to dally here. She rose to her feet. "I'm sorry, Cecil, we seem to have wasted your time. If you don't mind, I'd like to get back to my own ship. Despite his guilt, I would still like to see my husband before he dies."

"I'm afraid I can't allow that."

Eyes that were previously softened by tears were now an icy blue. "What do you mean, 'you can't allow that'?"

"Don't be upset. Surely you can see that I can't allow you to risk your life for a lost cause. Charleston is no place for you. I am confiscating your ship and I will escort you to your grandfather, where you belong. Believe me, you will thank me for this, one day."

"Don't you dare touch me. And I wouldn't advise sending for your aide, just yet." She pulled the pistol from the folds of her gown. "Yes, Cecil, I will use this, if necessary. I'm not going anywhere with you. On the contrary, you will be coming with me. Perhaps the Admiralty thinks highly enough of their young captain to exchange your life for one of their prisoners."

The two men spoke at once. "Are you crazy?"

She kept her eyes on Lawrence. Reading determination in them, and more than a little afraid of what she might do with the gun, he decided to take the path of cowardice. As much as he wanted a promotion, he wasn't a fool. Sam, on the other side of the room, watched in helpless admiration. Now where had she gotten that gun?

"Katherine, reconsider. You'll never succeed with this."

"Won't I? You'd better hope that I do, or you're a dead man."

In spite of himself, he shuddered. "You don't know my aide. Perkins is extremely conscientious. He literally smells trouble; he'll never let you off the ship."

"Us, Cecil. You're coming with me, remember? And I recall your lieutenant. I suppose we'll have to deal with him first. Call him in. You heard me, call him in." She gestured with the gun and Cecil obeyed. At the same time, she instructed Sam to wait behind the door. When Perkins marched into the room to salute his captain, Sam clubbed him over the head. "There you go, lass. Now what?"

"Cecil, do you have any whiskey? Go get it."

"What?"

"No questions, just do as you're told."

He obeyed instantly, making Katy want to giggle. Apparently, there must be something frightening about a woman with a weapon. As he presented the bottle to her, she told him to pour half it contents down the throat of his aide and the rest over his clothes. Let Perkins explain his way out of that one.

"Now, Captain Lawrence, I suggest you use all your

420

considerable wit and charm to get us off this ship alive. Remember, I have nothing to lose by putting a hole in your back and I will have the pistol pointed at you at all times. One wrong move and I will use it. You are to act as if nothing is wrong. You are merely escorting me back to Charleston, to attend to some business for me. Do you understand?''

They hurried up on deck, all with different thoughts. Lawrence was desperately trying to think of a way out of this. Sam, who couldn't believe it was happening, much less believe they would succeed, was thinking ahead to how he could protect Katy if it came down to a fight. And all Katy could think about was that they had to get to Charleston before daybreak.

With prodding, Cecil explained to his next-in-command that he was going with Mrs. Warwick but he would return by morning. Perkins was in his cabin going over some charts and he would have the orders for evening duties. If he had hoped the man would question his orders, he had forgotten how well disciplined his crew was. They left the *Olympus* without incident. Before long, to Katy's relief and Sam's amusement, they were back on the *Iris Lass* and setting sail for Charleston. Lawrence was taken below, with the horse, and secured there.

Sam was still shaking his head. "Lassie, I haven't the faintest idea what you plan to do next, but after what just happened, I can't see how it won't work."

"Oh, Sam, I was so scared." She ran to his outstretched arms.

"Scared? I think it took real courage to do what you did. And fast thinking. I was still trying to take in what he was saying and there you were, pointing a gun at him. Where on earth did you get it?"

Sheepishly, she grinned. "I wrestled Rachel for it. I knew better than to tell you I had it because I thought you might try to take it away. I thought I'd better have it, just in case. I guess it turned out well."

"Aye, that it did. You're right, though; I'd never let you carry it. But, lass, what do you intend to do now?"

"I don't know. At the time, all I could think of was that we had to get off the ship and get to Kit before they hung him. Now that we're safe, I suppose we'll have to do as I said. Offer Cecil in exchange for Kit."

"It's a crazy idea, Katy."

"It worked for General Marion when he used one of them to get Mr. Gasden and the others released from St. Augustine."

"But if it doesn't work, are you prepared to kill him?"

"Let's pray that it doesn't come to that. I don't think I could commit murder. Especially not to Cecil."

"That makes two of us. Don't worry, we'll manage somehow. We've come this far, we might as well go the distance. But we can't do anything until we reach shore so why don't you get some rest? You've been going for days. I don't want you collapsing on me."

"Thanks. I appreciate the thought, but I can't sleep. Not when I think of how close Kit is to dying. And it's all my fault. I think I'll sit here and watch the stars. It really is a beautiful night."

"You know best. I think I'll go below and visit with our prisoner. Maybe he can give more information so we don't make bloody fools of ourselves in the morning."

"Good idea. I'd go with you but I'm afraid I'd try to strangle the conceited beast. Can you believe it? He actually expected me to leave Kit to die while I flitted off with him to my grandfather. And all the Farley money, I don't doubt."

"Come now, lass. Can you blame him? You did lead him to believe that he could expect exactly that."

"I suppose you're right. I should have listened to you long ago and run off to the theatre. I seem to be a better actress than wife. Because of me, Kit is in jail and every one of you is in danger."

"Nonsense. We're all having the time of our lives. This is war, lass, and we've lived with danger for so long, I'm not sure we know how to live without it. Cheer up, Kit will be out of jail come morning. Thanks to you."

"Sam, I think I love you."

He colored. "No man could ask for more, but you should be saving those words for your husband." Kissing her on the forehead, he walked away. As she watched him go, Katy felt the heavy weight of responsibility. Despite Sam's attempts to encourage her, she knew that her crazy scheme had landed them in a dangerous situation. If she hadn't set them off on the wild goose chase, they would have stood a better chance of rescuing Kit. Instead, here they were, with a potential explosive in the person of Cecil Lawrence, and she could only hope that it didn't blow up in their faces. She sat brooding, looking out over the dark ocean, willing the wind to blow harder, wishing the distance to be shorter. It's got to work, she kept telling herself, as if the hoping could make it so.

Josh stood watching her awhile. He had something to say, but was reluctant to break in on her thoughts. He wouldn't blame her for not wanting to speak to him after the way he had acted. As he was turning to leave, she looked up and saw him. To his relief, she smiled, the same welcoming smile he remembered. Before she could change her mind, he hurried over.

"Where have you been keeping yourself, Josh? I missed you."

He beamed. "Down in the galley. With the captain gone, there's not much else for me to do. I've gotten to be a pretty good cook. Though not nearly as good as you."

She laughed. "Are you trying to pass the job off on me?"

"Ah, quit teasing. You know I meant it." He was suddenly serious. "Katy, I, uh, I, well, I just don't know how to say this but it's kinda important to me. Katy, I feel just awful about the way I spoke to you. I never should have doubted you. The captain didn't. He kept saying there must be some kind of explanation. That's why he went off so fast when he got that note."

She hugged him. "Thank you for telling me this. Though I doubt he still believes in me. I did too good a job of convincing him otherwise."

"I know, Sam told me. That's why I feel so awful. Katy, if there's anything I can do, anything at all . . ."

"Thanks, Josh, but all any of us can do is wait. And maybe pray. It's going to take a miracle to make this all come out right."

"It must have been scary on the *Olympus*. What was it like?"

"Me? Scared? Josh, I was petrified. But I remembered what you told me. I just held onto the gun and looked him in the eyes. It never would have worked with Kit, but Cecil doesn't know me as well, and he isn't at all like your captain."

"I guess not, but Katy, he sure is mad. He's not too

424

happy about sharing quarters with a horse."

Laughing, she had a change of heart. "Poor Cecil. It's not fair to take out my frustrations on him, no matter how he annoys me. He'll be thinking all us colonials are barbarians."

"Us colonials?"

"I tend to consider myself one of you. Does it bother you?"

"Aw no! It just sounded funny, hearing you say it. Funny, but kinda nice."

"It feels kinda nice to finally know where I belong. Well, come along, Josh, and let's see what we can do to make our visitor a bit more comfortable."

Still complaining, Lawrence was led to Katy's old cabin, where he was shown every courtesy, including the meal he had missed, cooked by Katy herself. By the time she had fed them all and cleaned the galley, they had spotted land. Slipping into an inlet, Sam used his vast knowledge of the swamps to bring them to a place where they could land. The horse was brought up on deck and it was finally decided that Josh would carry the note to the British.

Watching him ride off, Katy prayed that all would go well. Her stomach bubbled and burned as if it was filled with hot lava. She paced, she chewed her lips, and she waited.

"Worrying won't bring him any faster, lass."

"I can't help it. I know I should probably be sleeping, but I'm far too nervous. I keep thinking about that man Lord Rawdon had hung before he left. What was his name?"

"You mean Isaac Haynes?"

"That's him. They had far less cause to hang him than they do for Kit."

"Now wait a minute. That was an altogether different situation. He was hung for violating parole; he was used as an example."

"But Cecil said that was what they wanted Kit for, an example. Thanks to Julian. What if Josh doesn't get there in time? What if they won't let Kit go? What if they decide to sacrifice Cecil and hang him anyway?"

"And what if the sun doesn't rise in the morning? Lass, we can only wait and see. Worrying will only make your belly hurt worse."

From behind him came a cry. A rider was coming. Both Katy and Sam ran to the rail for a better look. It was Josh, all right, but he was alone. Still, just in case it was necessary, Katy gave the order to bring the prisoner topside.

She jumped on the boy before he even reached the ship. "What's happened? Where's Kit? Were you too late? Is he safe?"

"Hold on, lass. Give the boy a chance to catch his breath. He can't tell us anything when he's huffing and puffing that way."

"It's all right, Sam. He's all right. The captain is safe."

Katy felt dizzy. She whispered, "Thank God!"

Sam was more vocal. "The saints be praised. But boy, where is he?"

"There's no telling. There was an escape last night. Colonel Stuart is fit to kill, they say. Everyone is whispering about the Swamp Fox again. I didn't stay around to hear all the details; I figured you'd want to hear the good news."

"Oh, Josh, yes, of course. Thank you. But I can't help wondering about Kit. He was in bad shape when

I last saw him. You're certain that he escaped?"

Josh smiled at her. "He escaped, all right. You would have loved seeing his brother, sputtering around, all angry, and I reckon more than a little scared."

"You saw Julian?"

"Yes, and I enjoyed every minute of it. Don't worry about the captain, Katy. If he's with General Marion, like they say, he'll be safe enough."

Sam broke in. "A lot safer than us if we don't shove off soon. We'd best be getting back to Oaks; that's where he'll expect to find us."

"Of course." Katy found herself trembling. "You'd better take charge. I can't seem to control myself this morning."

Someone spoke out from behind them. "What are we going to do about him?"

All three whirled around. Standing out among the other sailors was Cecil Lawrence in his tailored uniform. He couldn't have been more obvious, nor could their predicament. Using him for ransom was one thing, but with Kit now safe, he was something of an embarrassment. Yes indeed, what were they going to do with him?

He volunteered a suggestion. "Release me, immediately."

Katy turned helplessly to Sam who was shrugging his shoulders. "I'm sorry, Cecil, but you must know I can't do that. Can you imagine explaining to your superiors how you were kidnapped off your own ship by a woman? Especially when that woman proves to be the granddaughter of Admiral Farley? What will that do to your career?"

His blustering ceased. "I'd be ruined. I am ruined."

Katy laid a hand on his arm. "I really am sorry. I know how much your career means to you. I didn't intentionally set out to ruin it. If there was any way to get you out of this, believe me, I would. You've been so kind to me in the past and I'd hate you to think me ungrateful. But you see, I love my husband very much, and you seemed to be the only way to save his life. I had no idea it would be such a mess."

To give him credit, he tried to be sympathetic. "I suppose I understand. This is, after all, a war. Though I must admit I never suspected that we were on different sides. Tell me, what do you plan to do with me now?"

"I'm afraid we'll have to turn you over to some authority as a prisoner of war."

"Wait a minute, lass. We'd have to go clear up to Virginia."

"I know, but it can't be helped."

"What about your husband? What if he comes looking for his ship? Katy, you want him roaming around with his brother on the loose?"

"You know that I don't? What else can we do?"

"I might have an idea." They had forgotten Josh, who leaned against the horse, looking very tired. "I know you want to be fair to Captain Lawrence, but I think we can do both things."

"How?"

"Someone could go after the captain. You know our prisoner can expect fair treatment from General Marion."

"No thank you. From what I've heard of your Swamp Fox, I think I'd rather take my chances as Katherine's prisoner."

"Don't be silly, Cecil. I know Francis Marion per-

428

sonally, and you have nothing to fear from him. He is a gentleman. I think it's a great idea. How about you, Sam?''

With everyone but the still protesting Cecil in agreement, Pete took off for Marion's camp while the *Irish Lass* set sail again—this time for Oaks. Once there, Katy could do nothing but wait for Pete's return. And waiting was something, despite all the practice, to which she had yet to adjust and it was certainly not something which she expected to enjoy.

Chapter 29

There was very little of the British army left in South Carolina. Charleston was their last and only stronghold. Negotiations had begun in earnest, over in England, to put an end to this costly war. Hostilities had virtually ceased. Now that the war was being carried out on the diplomatic level, no one able to estimate how long it would take to end it. Soldiers everywhere, tired of the long and bitter struggle, were laying down their arms and returning to their homes and families. Only one major force remained in South Carolina. Greene and his continentals were determinedly marching on Charleston with the conviction that it was now the colonials' turn to lay siege on the city. Though they had little chance of success without control of the harbor, they had already proven their tenacity. And as stubborn as his commander, General Marion would stay until the city was liberated. His men were free to make their own decisions, but they had been together for so long that few would leave him now.

Kit must haved decided to stay also. Otherwise, Katy reasoned, he would have returned to his ship by now. Unless he was physically unable to come. Pete had returned home from PeeDee Swamp, Marion's headquarters, after missing them by one day. Katy was all for going after the marching army, but Sam counseled her to wait. If he knew that boy, he'd be coming along any day.

Frequent visits by Esther did little to ease her mind. After Kit's rescue, she had heard nothing from the general. No news, in this case, was not good news. Another anniversary came and went and Katy became depressed. Where was her husband?

Surprisingly, Cecil eased the tedium of her wait. After the first week, he had ceased his complaining. Apparently, he had resigned himself to the fact that nothing could be done to save his career and he was making the best of things. Bored with the four walls of his cabin, he gave his word to Katy that if he was given access to the deck, he would not attempt an escape. Katy, who all too well remembered her own imprisonment in that cabin, was inclined to be sympathetic. Over Sam's disapproval, she gave permission. What Sam didn't realize was that if Cecil gave his word, he would rather die than break it.

She found she enjoyed his company. He surprised her constantly. Once he adjusted to the new life, he seemed happy with it. As he remarked to her during one of their many conversations, it was like having a holiday. In borrowed clothing and with a healthy tan, he was less the pompous dandy and more one of them. Katy found herself consulting him. Even the crew, who at first regarded him with scorn, came to recognize that his advice, given tactfully, was sound. He was a sailor, whatever his loyalties, and they all had stories to swap. It was pleasant for Katy to sit and listen to them in the evenings. Except for the conspicuous absence of her captain, it was like old times aboard the *Irish Lass*.

Lawrence, in turn, was amazed by Katy. This was a totally new Katherine, altogether different then the one from the drawing rooms of Charleston, but damned if he didn't like her better this way. But it pained him to see her so sad. Consulting with Josh, they planned a picnic, hoping the change in routine would bring a smile back to her pretty face. He was forced to wait several days to put the plan into action as it was December and rapidly growing colder. Finally, the perfect day arrived. After the chilly rain, the sun was a welcome ally and Cecil found himself as excited as a child. Instructing Josh to raid the galley for the rudiments of a good meal, he gathered blankets. If Lieutenant Perkins could see him now, he thought, shaking his head. He would be laughed off the ship. But he no longer had a ship, so what did it matter? All that mattered, strangely enough, was that his jailer laughed again.

Katy was cleaning the galley of the breakfast clutter when he found her. Slung over one arm was a basket and in the other was a bundle of blankets. There was something appealing about the sight and she responded with a smile. "Are you leaving us, Cecil?"

"Yes indeed. And so are you."

"Me? Don't tell me I'm being kidnapped now?"

"Not quite. But where I come from, when the weather turns fair after a particularly nasty spell, gentlemen are often apt to take their lady friends outdoors to enjoy the change. It is remarkable what eating in the open air can do for one's spirit. I can't promise you maples and rolling meadows, but at least there won't be ants, or worse yet, your infernal mosquitoes. What do you say? Will you join me on a picnic?"

"A picnic in December? Cecil, we'll freeze."

"Come now, where is your sense of adventure. See, I've got blankets."

"So I see." She pulled off her apron. "Perhaps you're right. Things have been dreadfully dull. I think I'd enjoy being outdoors."

"That's the spirit." He flashed her a smile. "Your young friend, Mr. Randall, has informed me of a nice spot, not too far away."

"I should have known Josh was involved in this. You two have planned everything, it would seem. Very well, give me a few minutes to change and I'll try to find something suitable for the occasion."

"That's not necessary. Wear what you have on."

"Trousers on a picnic?"

"Where we are going, they're more practical than a gown. But you may wish to bring a wrap to keep you warm."

Katy hurried off to find Josh and to borrow his jacket. She would hardly be the type of "lady friend" to go on an English picnic, but she was excited about the prospect anyway. What a wonderful idea. There was a romantic side to Cecil's nature, after all. She was looking forward to spending the day with him. This new Cecil was a vast improvement, in fact, one could say he intrigued her. Strange how things turned out. Kit, Julian, Cecil—not one of them was what she first thought them to be. There was no handsome prince on a white stallion. There was a little black and white in everyone and it was impossible to determine the ratio without knowing them well.

433

Ah, but today wasn't the day for philosophy. Today, she was going to have fun. When she met Cecil up on deck, he smiled down at her. How tall and handsome he was. If it hadn't been for Kit . . . But no, she wasn't going to think about him, either.

Cecil led her to a small clearing by the river. To their dismay, the ground was damp. Determined not to give in to a minor inconvenience, he gathered wood while Katy spread the blankets on the ground, three layers thick. Soon, Cecil had a blaze going. While she huddled next to it, he reached into the basket to spread its contents on the blanket. "I do hope your husband won't mind, but I bribed young Randall to get me a bottle of his wine. I must say, he has rather good taste, for an American."

"Even Americans can pick wine, Cecil."

"I wasn't referring to just the wine. He knows his women, too."

"Are you referring to Rachel?"

"Don't be obtuse. He married you, didn't he?"

Katy sighed. "Thank you for the compliment, but I'm afraid his taste, good or bad, had nothing whatsoever to do with his selection of me. The agreement was made long before he ever met me."

"He must have seen you somewhere. Or heard about you."

"Be honest. If you hadn't visited Whitney Hall, would you have known of my existence?"

"No, I suppose not. But I was busy with my career. I assumed that you were staying at home until your season."

"It was more like being kept at home. And there never would have been a season. Grandfather wanted to get rid of me."

434

"I find that hard to believe."

"I'm sorry. I know you think highly of him but the truth is, he actually paid Kit to marry me."

"I don't understand any of this. The admiral left me with the impression that he didn't welcome suitors."

"That was so you wouldn't get any ideas of offering for me. You're the last person he would want me to marry."

"But why? I had assumed it was because of your age. I planned to wait until after your season to approach him."

"Were you really? How odd the way things turned out. Not that it would have made a difference, I suppose. He'd never have accepted you as a suitor, anyway."

"But I have very good connections and even at that time, my prospects were outstanding."

"You weren't the problem. It was me. He was protecting you."

"Protecting me? But you're his flesh and blood."

"I tried to point that out to him, but he denied it. He thinks I'm illegitimate. It's not true and someday I will prove it to him, but that's why he couldn't stand the sight of me."

"Good lord!"

"Now do you see? Tell the truth. Would you have offered for me, knowing what my grandfather thought?"

He paused for a minute. "Truthfully, I suppose not. I had my career to consider and at the time, it was rather important to me. Still, if I had it all to do over again, I would wish for a bit of the dash of your Captain Warwick. I'd carry you off and the hell with my career."

"That's very gallant of you, but then, I've already ruined your career for you, haven't I? I feel dreadful for what I've done."

"Please don't. Who knows? I might be able to scrape out of this somehow. But in the meantime, I'm enjoying myself immensely. I've learned a great deal from you and your friends. I hate to admit it, but it seems I was wrong about everything. I was in serious danger of becoming a crashing bore. No, don't bother protesting; you know it's true. All I could think of was that damned career. I hadn't a real friend in the world. Even you avoided me."

"Oh, Cecil, that's not . . ."

"No, let me finish. Being with you has shown me the other side of this war. There's more to a man than his uniform. I spoke disparagingly of your navy. No wonder you avoided me. I called them pirates, if I'm not mistaken. Since then, I've witnessed firsthand, the loyalty, the dedication, the sacrifice, and I'd be the first to admit there's not a finer group of sailors anywhere in the world. I won't find it easy to return to my command, for more reasons than one. I'm not certain I have the heart to fight this way any longer. You see, I've begun to believe that you people deserve your freedom."

"I'm so glad you understand. I'd hate for us to be enemies again."

As he refilled her glass, he looked into her eyes. "Katherine, I realize that this is purely speculation, but please humor me. Had the admiral favored my suit, would you have considered it?"

She blushed. "On my sillier days, I used to dream or being Mrs. Cecil Lawrence."

"Damn! I should have carried you off." He leaned

closer, dangerously so. "You were a pretty girl then, but you've become a very attractive woman. If the opportunity was to present itself, I would not make the same mistake twice, even if it meant I must develop some of that dash."

Gently, she placed a finger on his lips. "Please don't."

"But he doesn't deserve you. I admire your loyalty to him, but haven't you done enough? He's left you out here, unprotected. I would never submit you to the hardships you've had to endure."

"No more, please. You don't know the whole story. I understand what you're trying to say, but it's no use. A few years ago, I would have been thrilled to hear these words, but it's too late now. I'm sorry, Cecil, but I love my husband. I always will."

He backed away. "Forgive me. I had not meant to be impertinent."

"I know that. And you weren't. How could you know? I've told you some tremendous lies. I'm not even sure what the truth is any more."

"I'm sorry, I hadn't meant to make you cry."

"I always cry. It's just that all of a sudden it seems too much to bear. Julian, Rachel, the lying, all of it."

"Would it help to talk about it?" His gentleness, which she knew she didn't deserve, nearly undid her.

"Oh, Cecil, I can't bore you with my problems."

He grinned as he handed over his handkerchief. "Whatever else you might have done to me in the past, my dear, you have never bored me."

"But it's a long story and rather complicated."

"If there's one thing I have in great quantity, it's time."

In the end, Katy told her story, from Kit's deception

to her own. Though he occasionally raised an eyebrow, he never once interrupted. When she finished, dry-eyed, he was frowning at his wine.

"Was it all lies, then? Was none of it true?"

"I was terribly single-minded about Kit, but I always enjoyed your company. I never consciously tried to avoid you. I sought you in Charleston for you, not for anything you could give me. That's why I had to stop you before. I didn't want you to say anything tht would prevent us from being friends. I would hate that." She reached over to touch his hand. "I value your friendship, more than I can say."

He put his hand over hers. "It has always been yours. I would be a liar if I didn't admit that I had always hoped for more, but I too would hate to lose what I have. I'd like to be at your side, if ever you need me."

"How can you say that after all I've done to you?"

He grinned a lopsided grin. "To be perfectly honest, I don't know. I should probably abhor the very sight of you. But I'm afraid that the excitement and adventure would go out of my life if I knew I would never see you again. Your husband is a very lucky man."

"I wish he could share your opinion. I think he's staying away because of me."

"Because of what you said to him? But surely, if he loves you, he wouldn't have believed a word of it."

"I don't know what he believes. I only know I have to see him, to explain. I have this feeling that if it isn't soon, it'll be too late."

"Why don't you go after him?"

"Me? But the fighting . . ."

"Miss Videaux said the fighting was over. It shouldn't be all that difficult to find the American

438

camp."

"Sam would never agree to it."

"Why tell him?"

"You mean, just sneak away? By myself?"

"Of course not. I'd go with you."

"You'd do that?"

"I must admit, I do like the sound of it. It could be quite an adventure, eh what?"

"But you're a British officer. What if they shoot you?"

"Do I look like a British officer in these clothes? As long as you do the talking, who will know? I trust you to see to it that your Kit said nothing, either."

"I could do better than that. While I'm finding Kit, you could wander off. You could find your way to Charleston, I'm sure."

"You'd let me go?"

"I have no desire to keep you against your will. I trust you not to say anything to get us into trouble. You could tell your superiors that you were attacked by pirates on your way back to your ship. In those clothes, they'll have to believe you. Perhaps you could even salvage something of your career. Oh, Cecil, why didn't we think of this earlier?"

He leaned closer again. "We'll have to plan this carefully."

The excitement shone on her face. "Yes, I know. We'll have to leave at night, when Sam is asleep and Salty is on watch duty. I can talk him into anything. And we'll need horses. There's Black Beauty, but we'll have to get another from Oaks."

"I thought we were trying to repair my reputation. You're involving me in horse theft."

"Dawn is mine; she was a present from Kit. And

I've already stolen the black one. Maybe you can return it for me?"

"You make me feel like a naughty schoolboy again, hatching some mischief. I think I'm going to enjoy this, you know."

"We'll need to be devious on the ship. Sam would be furious if he found out."

"Let's hope we're long gone by the time he does. When do you want to go?"

"Salty is on duty tonight. Can you be ready?"

"Tonight? You certainly don't waste time."

"I can't afford to. I'm not very good at containing my excitement. One look at my face and Sam will know. Imagine. By tomorrow, I could be seeing Kit."

"And I could be facing a court-martial."

"You're doing all this for me. You don't really want to go back."

He shook himself. "Nonsense. I just hate to call a halt to my holiday, that's all. I want to save my career just as much as you want to see your husband. What do you say to a toast to our mutual success? And let's eat, I'm famished."

He had restored the festive mood and Katy was grateful. She was going to miss him. No, he might never have Kit's dash, but still, there was something appealing about his steadfastness. She would always know where she stood with a man like him. But no matter how dependable he might be, he would never stir her emotions like Kit could, with merely a glance in her direction.

At the ship, Katy pretended a chill and like the coward she was, hid in her cabin all evening. Josh popped in with a dinner tray, but otherwise she saw no one. Pacing the cabin, she waited for the ship to settle for the night before venturing out. Crossing her fingers, she prayed she hadn't overestimated her powers of persuasion.

It proved relatively easy, however, to convince Salty that he saw nothing. It was more difficult with Cecil, but he finally agreed that Katy was the acting captain and he supposed if she gave an order, she must know what she was doing.

"You want me to pretend I ain't seen your shadow, neither?"

"Shadow? What shadow?"

Salty pointed behind her. "That one."

Katy whirled around. "Josh Randall, are you spying on me?"

"Of course not, Katy. I just wanted to go with you."

"How do you know where I'm going?"

"I don't, exactly. But I know you. I could tell you were planning something; I could see it in your eyes. Aw, let me come. I promise I won't be any trouble."

Katy pulled him into the shadows where they wouldn't be overheard. "Go back to your cabin and pretend that you never saw me."

"I think he should come, Katherine. He could protect you, should anything go wrong with either myself or your husband."

The boy's eyes grew wide. "We're going after the captain?"

"Sh! Keep your voice down. Cecil and I are going. You'll stay."

"Please, Katy, let me come. I know the way out of the swamps better than you and I know the men under the general. I'd be worth it to you, honest I would."

"Let him come."

441

She looked from one to the other and shrugged. "If you two are going to bully me, I suppose I have no choice. Go get Black Beauty, Josh, and let's get out of here."

How could she refuse when he was obviously as excited about seeing Kit as she was? She let him take the lead and they made their way to Oaks. It was an eerie night, with the moon drifting in and out of the clouds, making forms and shadows on the ground. It was a good thing Josh was with them; nothing seemed familiar to her. In her state of mind, she would have gotten lost, and those night noises were no help. Instinctively, she reached for Rachel's pistol. Its heavy presence reassured her and she felt a trifle braver.

By the time they reached the plantation, the moon had all but disappeared. The wind was picking up and Katy could feel the stirrings of winter as the dry leaves crackled and danced about their feet. What a night for a journey. Drawing her jacket tighter, she followed Josh to the stables. By common consent, she went in after her horse alone while they hid in the bushes.

Dawn was happy to see her. Whispering softly, Katy slid into her stall to prepare the horse for the ride. Something perverse in her made her grab the horse she had saved from Wharton's whip. Why should she and Josh share a horse when Julian would never notice its absence? Both horses came without a sound, somehow sensing the need for silence. As she reached the door, though, she heard a step behind her. Her breath caught and she fumbled for the pistol.

"Miz Katy, is that you?"

Her breath came out, all at once. "Sampson! Good

442

heavens, you frightened me."

"I'm mighty sorry, ma'am, but I couldn't hardly recognize you in them pants. You look like a boy—one of them that's been hanging around playing pranks, now that the British are gone. If anything happened, I could be in big trouble with the overseer. Maybe have my back torn up, like Jeremy."

"Jeremy? What happened?"

"Don't rightly know. That Wharton don't always need a reason."

"He's been using that whip again?"

"That man's soul is blacker than I am. Makes him feel more like a man to beat us."

"Us? Has he been after you, too? And the others—Rosie, Lilah?"

"We're all slaves, ain't we?"

"I had no idea it was this bad. I have some friends with me. We'll go up to the house and take care of this immediately. I presume he is staying at the house?"

"I wouldn't do that, Miz Katy. He ain't alone up there. He's got two big, powerful-looking men with him."

"Ah, Julian's hired ruffians."

"Beg your pardon?"

"I've met the gentlemen. They do pose a problem."

"And that ain't all. We all appreciate you trying to help, but you gotta remember, he's got the law on his side. There just ain't nothing you can do."

"How can I sit by and let him do this to you?"

"Please, Miz Katy, forget about us. We're used to it by now. If you was to step in, it'd only make him madder. You tried, once, and so did Master Kit, but in the end, it's always gonna be Master Julian and that demon of his that are gonna win 'cause they got the

443

law with them. Best leave things the way they are."

"But that man is contemptible."

"Don't worry, we'll get by. Been doing it all our lives. You best take your horses and get out of here before he finds you."

"Won't he punish you when he finds the horses missing?"

"He's so mad at these horses, he don't never come near the stables. By the time he finds out they're gone, you'll have brought them back."

"Are you sure?"

"As sure as I can be of anything in this life."

"I'd better go, then. I don't want to cause any more trouble."

"You never were trouble, Miz Katy. You were like sunshine to us. God bless you and good luck with whatever you is planning now."

"Thank you, Sampson. Thank you for everything. I promise that when I return, I will make it clear, once and for all, that Mr. Wharton's services are no longer needed at Oaks."

He chuckled. "I believe you just might. 'Bye, Miz Katy."

On the road to Charleston, Katy had time to consider that rash promise. The heavy weight of responsibility was again on her shoulders. There wasn't a doubt in her mind that Jeremy had been punished more for that morning in the kitchen when she had deprived Wharton of his sadistic pleasure than for any trumped-up incident that might have occurred since. Would it be best to leave things as they were? What would be best, she thought, would be to consult with her husband about this. Kit would know what to do. And how incredibly nice it would be to have somebody else making all the decisions for a change.

Chapter 30

The American camp was filled with strange men who looked as though they had taken all they would of the British and Katy prayed there wouldn't be trouble for Cecil. Glancing around at their hostile faces, she grew uneasy. So when Josh offered to go look for the captain while she and Cecil waited outside the camp, she wanted to kiss him. It really wasn't the place for her, he went on, for all that she looked like a boy. Besides, wouldn't she want to change into her dress, now that they were so close to the captain?

Cecil posted himself as guard while she ducked into some bushes with her dress. Now that we're so close, Josh had said. Her fingers were trembling too much to do up the buttons. What kind of a reception could she expect? What if he refused to see her? It had been so long. Would he be a stranger to her, no more familiar than those half-dressed men that stared at her so peculiarly? Would it be possible to remember that long ago night at Oaks, after all that had happened in between?

It was a horrible wait, and a long one. When Josh finally approached, alone, Katy's heart began to thud painfully.

"Sorry, Katy, he isn't here. He left camp this morning."

Her first reaction was relief. At least he hadn't refused to see her. "Where did he go?"

"No one seems to know for sure. Seems he's been brooding for weeks, doing nothing. This guy I talked to said it was like he was lost. That is, until this morning. I guess he got word that his brother is sailing for England tomorrow. This guy said he showed enough spark then. Just popped up, changed into some funny clothes, jumped on his horse and without a word to anybody, took off in the direction of Charleston."

"Oh, Josh, you don't suppose he went after Julian, do you?"

"Sure sounds like it."

"But that's insane. He'll never get out again."

"It doesn't sound as if your husband has any intention of getting out again, Katherine."

"What do you mean?"

"Look at it from a military point of view. Captain Warwick has deserted by leaving without permission. From what I've been told, a damned good record is in jeopardy. Would he risk a court-martial if he actually intended to return?"

"You think he plans to either kill Julian or be killed himself?"

"It certainly sounds like it. Can't say I blame him, though."

"We can't let this happen. He hasn't a chance against Julian. I've got to go to him."

"Katy, wait. I'm all for helping the captain but you'll never get past the sentry. You're wanted for kidnapping."

She looked to Cecil and he was lost in the appeal of those big, blue eyes. "Take me with you, Cecil, when you go. I'll tell them whatever you want. That I was

446

with you when the pirates attacked. I'll mention the name Farley. They'll understand that you were obligated to help me in light of my husband's defection. How could you desert me to fend for myself? They'll believe us. Oh Cecil, please?"

"Katherine, it's too dangerous. You forget your brother-in-law."

"I'll have Josh to protect me."

"And how will you get him past the sentry?"

"After your daring escape and gallant rescue of myself, we found this nice boy who offered to show us the way to Charleston. Naturally you would want to reward him, but those rogues stripped you of all your valuables. He will have to come with us until we can find someone to lend us a few pennies for him."

"Very clever. But how will you manage to get Captain Warwick out of the city, should you rescue him this time?"

"I promise not to use you for ransom, if that's worrying you. He will be Julian, of course. He wants to take one last look at his beloved Oaks before leaving the country."

"This is madness. I know I should refuse but when you look at me like that, I swear I can't remember why."

"Then you'll take me?"

"Us."

"Yes, yes, I'll take you both. But let's hurry. I'd prefer to reach Charleston before dark."

With another few hours ride ahead, Katy had more time to think. She was not nearly as confident of this new scheme as she had tried to sound. That she and Cecil could fool the British, she had little doubt. Not that the story was credible, but the threat of the approaching army would occupy their minds far more than the personal problems of one of their more reliable officers. But what chance did she actually have of saving Kit? If Julian had already turned him over to the authorities, there was nothing that even Cecil could do to save him. She could be risking all their lives for nothing.

At the sentry post, Cecil transformed himself before her eyes into the very businesslike Captain Lawrence. Accustomed to his recent casual friendliness, she watched with fascination as the guard snapped to attention. Cecil barked out his story and without waiting for permission, proceeded past the post.

"I beg your pardon, sir." The poor man looked ready to wilt. "I'm afraid the others will have to stay here."

"I don't believe I heard you right, Private."

"It's Lieutenant, sir."

"Oh really?" There was frost in his tone and his upraised brows and stony glare pointed out the tenuous position of that rank.

"It's my orders, sir. No strangers permitted in without a pass."

"And you consider Mrs. Warwick a stranger?"

"Mrs. Warwick? Excuse me, ma'am; I didn't recognize you. Of course you may pass but the boy will have to stay." He was practically stammering.

"I thought I explained that the boy must be rewarded."

Katy placed a restraining hand on Cecil's arm. "I don't wish to interfere, Captain, but the Lieutenant is only trying to do his duty. The boy can wait here." She turned to Josh. "You will be all right?"

"Sure enough, ma'am. Only please don't take too long. My ma and pa will be waiting for me."

Though he didn't like it, Cecil knew he was trapped. But he was adamant that Katherine would not go to the Warwick home without his escorting her there. They would go to headquarters, first, to avoid suspicion. As soon as that was taken care of, they'd hurry to find Kit. Much against her will, Katy followed him.

Once the introductions were made and her story given, Cecil requested permission to see Mrs. Warwick home. The poor woman had been through enough and her family would be anxious to learn of her whereabouts. Glancing meaningfully at Lawrence, his superiors told him that they quite understood his concern, but they needed details for this incredible story of his. Someone else would see Mrs. Warwick home. Horrified at the idea, Katy protested, saying it wasn't too far to walk. Nonsense, she was told; the streets were far too dangerous. It was evident that she hadn't been in town recently. With the rebel army nearing, riffraff ruled the streets, taking the law into their own hands and well-to-do Loyalists were their favorite target. Why, only last night the Smithfield home had been burned to the ground. Theirs was by no means the first. How could they take a chance with one of Charleston's most charming Tories? No, it would be an honor and a pleasure to see her safely to her family.

Struggling to keep panic out of her face, she turned to Cecil. He whispered that he'd be along directly and squeezed her hand. Not at all reassured, Katy was ushered outside to a carriage. Ever conscious of the role she must play and feeling absolutely ridiculous, she allowed herself to be placed in the seat as if she was visiting royalty. Good lord, what was she going to do if Julian answered the door? Should she run for it now?

Indecision kept her in the seat until she reached the Warwick house and then it was too late. Holding her breath, she presented a shaky hand to be helped down from the carriage. She left her destiny in the hands of fate because realistically, there was no other choice. Accompanying her escort to the door, she prayed—

just one more time, please let me get away with this.

To her amazement, Rachel answered her knock. Where were the slaves? Rachel Worthington answering a door? Something must be very, very wrong.

"Katherine? My heavens, what a wonderful surprise! Julian, darling, come see who these soldiers have brought home to us."

Katy would willingly have crawled into the nearest hole if the soldiers hadn't been supporting either arm. So this was the last of her luck. Sick with apprehension, she waited for Julian to appear, and, typically, he took his time about it. He was certainly annoyed. "So you've finally come home. Don't just stand there; come in. Tell me, where have you been all this time? No, save it for later. If you will excuse us, gentlemen, I believe my sister-in-law has a great deal of explaining to do."

Katy was speechless. It was impossible that they couldn't recognize the fact that it wasn't Julian who stood so arrogantly dismissing them. True, Kit had aged considerably in the past year, but those eyes!

"Yes, sir. Good evening to you. We recommend you lock your doors tonight. There's a mob out on the streets. Mrs. Warwick, are there messages for Captain Lawrence?"

"Just tell him that I'm safely home but I hope to see him soon. And thank you for the escort."

"It was our pleasure, ma'am."

With that, they returned to the carriage, while Katy was grabbed roughly by the arm and dragged into the house. Once the door had slammed behind them, any pretense of courtesy vanished. Pulling out a pistol, Kit motioned her into the drawing room. Katy, who had yet to recover from the surprise, stared at him blindly. Thoughts whirled through her brain, none of them very good ones, but she did as she was told. She

450

attempted to speak but she wasn't given time to form the words.

"No talking. Move!"

"But Kit . . ."

"You heard me. Get moving."

"Put away the silly gun. I'll do as you say. I'm no threat to you."

He laughed bitterly. "No threat? I made the mistake of believing that once and was given a room in the local jail for my troubles. If Rachel hadn't gotten to Marion, I'd still be rotting in that jail, or worse, swinging from the gallows. No, my dear, you're not a good risk. I'd much rather keep this pointed at where your heart is supposed to be while you march quietly into the other room."

Rachel was grinning broadly as they entered. "Isn't this wonderful? At last, we will have them both. In just a few minutes, Julian will be walking through the door . . ."

"Julian, here?"

"And you hoped never to see him again, after the way you double-crossed him."

"I what? You know very well what happened, Rachel. I was . . ."

"It's far too late, Katherine dear. You made your bed, so to speak; now you must lie on it."

"But I'm not the one who is lying. Kit, listen to me, please."

"My, my, my. So it's going to be sweet, innocent Katy again, is it? Your husband knows better than to be taken in twice. What's the matter? Has your handsome Captain Lawrence turned out to have a wife back in England? Or is this another of your devious plots to have your husband murdered. I'd give up if I were you. You've already failed twice."

"Why, you . . ."

"Shut up, both of you." Kit's voice came from the window where he was peering out into the dark. "Julian is coming. Act as if nothing is wrong. I'll be behind the door. If you so much as look in my direction, I won't hesitate to use this." He cocked the pistol.

"But, Kit, you've got to let me . . ."

"Dammit, Katy, I told you to sit down and be quiet."

Rachel smirked as Katy took her seat. Kit slid behind the door to wait for his brother's entrance.

He didn't wait long. Julian's grating voice drifted in from the hallway, whining out his displeasure. "Rachel, where the devil are you? Damnation. No servants; no one when you need them. Rachel!"

"I'm in here, Julian."

"I don't know why you insisted upon sending the servants on ahead. We're going to have to spend the night here without them, you know." The voice grew in intensity as it changed direction and approached the room. "That damned mob. People all over the streets and quite ugly, I might add. Thank God our ship is departing early tomorrow. Another day in this God-forsaken hole and I would go quite mad. This is all Katherine's fault. If she hadn't disappeared, we would have been long gone. I'd love to be on that ship now, but I simply refuse to set foot out of this house tonight. A man could be taking his life in his hands. Goodness gracious, will you look at who we have here? What a delightful surprise. Is this a bon voyage present, Rachel? Just in time to accompany us to Whitney Hall?"

"No one is going to Whitney Hall, brother dear. Raise your arms in the air, as high as you can. Come now, you can do better than that. Please, do have a seat. No, keep your hands in the air. We have some talking to do."

Julian was comical, struggling to his chair with his hands high above him. If Katy hadn't been concerned with her own affairs, she would have enjoyed his discomfort.

"Chris! And I had hoped never to see you again. You found Katherine, I see."

Rachel rushed to Kit's side. "Oh no, Julian. It seems our little Katherine has been playing each of you against each other. I think she has her eye on the handsome Captain Lawrence."

"Don't be ridiculous, Cecil is only trying to help. Kit, you've got to let me explain."

"Explain? Do you honestly expect him to believe you? Or Julian either? You've finally caught yourself, with all your lies."

Kit looked tired. "If you don't mind, my business is with my brother. I don't want to have to listen to either of you. If you can't keep still, just leave the room."

"Just what do you plan to do with me, Chris?"

"As much as I might enjoy putting a bullet through that black heart of yours, Julian, I can't be that selfish. There are a number of men, back home, that are looking forward to the prospect of a public trial. Perhaps you would like to know how it feels to face the hangman's noose."

Julian went white. "You wouldn't!"

"Give me just one excuse and I won't wait for the trial. Or I could just as easily turn you over to your Loyalist friends. All that money they gave you to outfit an army. I'm sure they'd love to know where it went. No, Julian, I imagine you're better off with my friends. With any luck at all, you might only have to spend the rest of your life behind bars."

"Just how do you propose to get me out of the city?"

"Rachel has volunteered to help me."

"Rachel? How considerate of her."

"Shut up, Katy. Rachel will come with us to lend credence to the fact that I am, in actuality, you. You, meanwhile, will be fast asleep in the back of the wagon."

"And Katherine?"

Kit flashed a cold look in her direction. "Katy can go back to her Cecil who is so anxious to help. He'll take care of her, I'm sure."

At his last word, a rock came hurling through the window. Angry voices could be heard outside. Rachel moved over to the gaping hole and peered outside. "There's a crowd gathering. Kit, we've got to hurry. If it gets much larger, they'll never let us pass."

Kit tightened his grip on the pistol. "Damn you, Julian. You've probably led them here. You must have more enemies than the entire British army. Here." He threw a bundle of clothes at him. "Put these on. And smear that dye on your face. Tonight, Mr. Warwick, you're going to learn how it feels to be a slave."

"If you think I'll degrade myself . . ."

Kit aimed the pistol. "Suit yourself."

"No, don't. I'll put the disgusting things on."

"Kit, hurry. They've got torches."

"You heard her, Julian. Hurry. We're going to walk through that crowd and you will remember there's a gun on your back."

"Kit, you're crazy. You can't possibly go into that mob. They'll kill you all."

"So concerned, Katy? Do you honestly expect me to wait around for your handsome Cecil to show up?"

"He's not my Cecil. Kit, you don't understand."

Rachel called from the windows, a hysterical note in her voice. "We'll never get through. There's too many of them now and I think they might have guns."

Kit was angry. "This is all your fault, Julian. You and your greed. You couldn't be satisfied with all you had. Even when we were children, you had to have my toys, my friends. Now look where your greed has gotten us. Most likely we'll all burn in this mausoleum of yours."

As if on cue, a torch came flying through the window. Rachel screamed and stepped back to fly into Kit's arms. Another torch followed. Katy ran over with a rug, trying to beat out the flames, but windows were breaking all over the house and the smell of smoke grew stronger.

Rachel was frantic. "What are we going to do? We can't stay in here. And if we go out, that mob will tear us apart."

"Get control of yourself. Let's go. Julian, bring those clothes with you. We're all going upstairs."

"But the smoke is twice as bad up there."

"Kit, the tunnel!"

He looked at her quickly. "Ah, I had forgotten that I trusted you once. Yes, Katy, we're going to the tunnel."

"Tunnel?" Julian's eyes narrowed speculatively. "Of course! I apologize, Katherine. It seems I underestimated you. What a pity you ran away. You and I would have made a fine team."

"Just keep moving. And don't forget I still have the gun."

Rachel was already on the second floor. "Hurry, Kit. The fire is everywhere."

Stumbling up the stairs, Katy felt the heat on their backs. Smoke was billowing out of all the rooms ahead and it was nearly impossible to breathe. Kit's door was still locked so they had to pass through Katy's room. The situation there was as bad as in the drawing room and she bumped into one of her trunks.

Those damned trunks; she hoped they'd burn.

When she finally reached the closet, her trembling fingers fumbled with the knob. It popped open and Rachel pushed past her to charge through the door. Katy was about to follow when a noise behind her caused her to look back into Kit's room. Julian and Kit were wrestling for the gun. All at once, it went flying and as Kit made a dive for it, Julian lifted a vase from a nearby table and hit him over the head. Kit toppled to the ground. Half limping, half choking, Julian staggered away, to be swallowed up in the smoke.

Katy ignored him and turned her attention to her husband. Slapping his face, she tried to bring him back to consciousness. As she kneeled down, something hit her bruised shin. Her ruby pendant! It must have fallen out of Kit's pocket when he dropped. So he had kept it, after all. Surely that was a good sign. Dropping it in her bodice, she told herself to ask him about it later.

The heat was intense. Half dragging his inert form, she called to Rachel for help. She should have saved her breath, it was scarce enough. With a desperation born out of necessity, she hauled his body to the closet. With one last shove, she had him in the passageway and the closet door shut behind them.

Sinking to the ground in exhaustion, she coughed and choked until the last of the smoke had been dredged up from her lungs. Kit groaned, then coughed, but she was too tired to go to him. It was all she could do to breathe.

"Rachel, where are you?"

It cut her like a knife. How could he have called for Rachel, who was probably miles away by now. "No, it's Katy. She went on ahead."

"And Julian?"

"He's gone. After he hit you, he went back into the

456

house. With all that smoke, he'll never make it out alive."

"He had to have those damned diamonds. Even at the last, he had to be greedy."

There was a moment or two of silence before Katy spoke. "Kit, it's beginning to get hot and there's smoke creeping in from under the door. We can't stay here. If you lean on my shoulders, I can get us down to where there's some fresh air."

"I don't need any help from you."

In the darkness, she let her extended hand drop to her side. "If only you'd let me explain."

"Good God, spare me your explanations. Let's get out of here, first. My head feels as if it is going to explode. I can't cope with any scenes at the moment."

Katy bit her lip and followed him silently. Once or twice along the way, he stumbled. Instinctively, she reached out to steady him, but he brushed her hand away. They came to the end of the tunnel with no sign of Rachel. When they stepped out into the night air, they discovered why. The angry mob had been replaced by British soldiers, one of whom was comforting Rachel.

"Oh lord—the British. This is not my night. Now what?"

"You're going to give up now, are you? For heaven's sake, you're still Julian. They'll never know the difference."

His eyes narrowed. "Unless, of course, someone informs them."

"Oh, don't worry. Give me your gun and I'll see to it that Rachel keeps quiet."

"I didn't mean Rachel."

"You can't mean me?"

"Stop playing games, Katy."

"But you can't possibly trust Rachel. She'd sell you

457

in a second if it suited her purpose. You don't know . . ."

"Trust?" There's that word again. Amazing, how often it crops up in our conversations. It's funny that you, of all people, should bring it up."

"That's why I have to explain . . ."

But he wasn't listening to her. "How you must have laughed at me, spending all that time, months, carefully, oh so carefully being patient and gentle. All so you would trust me. It never occurred to me that you couldn't be trusted. Don't look at me like that. It doesn't work anymore. And neither will your tears. You've turned them on and off so often, they no longer affect me. I've had it, Katy, with your marvelous performances, your clever little games, with you. Go to your Cecil. Let him pay the price of loving you, if he's fool enough. I've paid all I can afford. The war is over for us now. Go back to England."

"But I don't want to go to England. My home is here."

"Then I'll go. If it was possible, I'd give you that annulment now. As I can't, I'll do the next best thing. I'll make you a widow. From now on, Kit is dead and I am Julian. Much neater, actually."

He was so cold, so distant, that it frightened her. He was a stranger and she didn't know what to say to him. "Kit, please, you've got to listen to what I have to say."

"You aren't listening to me. Get it through your head, Katy. I'm not interested in what you have to say. Let's call it off, now that we're even. I've used you and you've used me. There's no reason to continue and certainly no need to explain. We both did what we had to do to survive, but in the future, I'd rather not be reminded of the life we had together. I'm sure you agree."

A sob caught in her throat. "No, Kit, please don't say that. You can't leave now. I need you." She grabbed his arm.

For a moment, his eyes registered surprise, and, while the time lay suspended between them, Katy hoped and prayed that she had reached him. Then slowly and deliberately, he peeled her fingers off his sleeve and walked away.

There was pain, so intense that it blocked her throat and the words could not get past it. What she managed was little better than a croak. "Kit, please. I love you."

He never looked back. Numbly, she watched him greet the soldiers in the same obnoxious manner of his brother. He could have been Julian, for all it mattered to her. Rachel broke away from her soldier and ran to his arms. As he patted the dark head, Katy turned away. So it had all come to this. All the hopes, all the dreams, falling down around her like the charred timbers of the Warwick mansion. What a fragile thing their love had been. There was no hope of saving it now, no more than there was of rescuing Julian's showplace. And though there should have been something worth saving in the ruins, Kit preferred to sweep it all away to rebuild elsewhere. No, she could not bear to witness Rachel's triumph.

"Katherine! Thank God. I rushed over as soon as I heard. What's wrong? Are you injured?"

Cecil had never looked better to her, spectacular in his fresh uniform and as solid as a rock. "Oh, Cecil, you came. Thank you." She couldn't help it. She ran to him and buried her head in his chest.

"What's happened? Didn't you find your husband?"

"Yes. No. Oh, Cecil, he won't even listen to me. He's over there, posing as Julian. The real Julian died in the

459

fire. I tried to explain but he wants nothing to do with me. He said he wants me to go back to England."

"But I distinctly heard him say that he plans to sail to England, himself, as scheduled. He and Miss Worthington are making plans . . ."

Katy, who thought she was beyond pain, flinched. "He's going with Rachel?"

"Katherine, I'm sorry."

"I can't believe it. I've worked so hard and long, and in the end, she's going to walk off with it all. I can't even cry about it. Isn't it amusing? Me, the big crybaby, and now when I have every reason for falling apart, there's nothing there."

"You've been through a great deal."

"It's all over, Cecil. That's what he said to me. No explanations necessary. It's all over."

"What will you do now?"

She broke away. "I don't know. For once, I don't have any crazy schemes. I never expected this. I have nowhere to go."

"Katherine, I'll be sailing soon, myself. I have to report to the Admiralty. Come with me. I'll take care of you."

His eagerness touched her but she raised a heavy hand to stop him. "No, Cecil. I know you mean well, but I don't belong there."

"You can't stay here."

"It's my home now. Josh will be waiting for me. And Sam. I'll have to explain why Kit won't be coming back. I'll stay with them until I find something to do with my life. They'll take care of me."

"Your husband is a fool. If I was in his position . . ."

"But you're not. Oh, Cecil, how nice it would be if we could decide when and whom to love. I love him. What he said to me can't change that. I can't stop loving just because he has. If I went with you, it wouldn't change things, either. I would always be thinking of him, hoping to meet him somewhere, and you know it. It wouldn't be fair to either of us."

"Then I'll go to him and tell him what he is carelessly discarding."

She clutched at his sleeve. "Please don't do that. It's no use, don't you see? You're the last person he'd listen to. He'd probably kill you. He just doesn't care about me anymore." She sighed. "The last thing I want from him is his pity. Please spare me that much."

"He should know what you've done for him."

"It's too late. Too much has been said. You don't know his pride. Please, promise you'll say nothing."

"But, Katherine . . ."

"Please give me your word."

"Very well, if it's that important to you. Are you certain that you want to go back to your friends?"

"Yes."

He held out a hand. "Then come with me. I'll see what I can do."

Down the drive, two horses stood waiting. "You've brought Dawn!"

"I thought you might need her. Can you manage?"

Nodding her head, she mounted. Cecil walked over to the group of soldiers, spoke a few words, saluted and strolled back down the drive. "Mr. Warwick asked if there was anything he could do."

"What did you tell him?"

"I assured him that I would see to your welfare."

"And what did he say to that?"

"I'm afraid he wished me luck. Katherine, are you certain you wouldn't rather stay and talk to him?"

"Can we please get out of here?"

"Very well, let's go."

He accompanied her to the sentry where he explained how poor Mrs. Warwick had just lost her home, and once again, she was permitted to pass. He took her down the road, out of sight of the guard.

"Where's young Randall?"

"Over here, sir. Did you find the captain?"

"Mrs. Warwick can explain later. At present, I want you to promise to see her safely home. She's been through too much and she's going to need you to help her. Do I have your promise?"

"Sure. You don't have to worry about Katy with me."

"Yes, I know that. Thank you, Josh. It's been a pleasure knowing you. I hate to have to say good-bye. If you ever need a job, come to me." He shook his hand. "If you don't mind, though, I'd like a few moments alone with Katherine."

Josh winked and rode off. Watching him go, Cecil sighed. "He's a remarkable lad; I'm glad you have him. I can't change your mind?"

"Oh, Cecil, not again."

"I didn't think so. I don't suppose I'll ever see you again?"

"There's no way of telling."

"Do you mean that someday when I'm sitting out in the ocean, feeling intolerably bored, I can hope to spot a ship in distress? That you will be on it, luring me into another of your crazy schemes?"

"Oh, Cecil."

"There, that's better. I had despaired of ever seeing you smile again."

"I don't know how to begin to thank you . . ."

"Nonsense. It is I who have you to thank. Think of the stories I will have for my grandchildren. I wouldn't have missed our little adventure together for all the promotions in the world. If you should ever change your mind . . ."

"I'm sorry, but you know I won't."

"So you've told me. Then I hope your captain comes to his senses before it's too late. I'd like to think that you'll be happy in your new country, smiling and laughing the way I best remember you. No, not like that. A happy smile."

"I'll be just fine. Honestly."

He looked at her, long and hard, before sitting up in the saddle. "I suppose this is good-bye, then?"

"Good-bye, Cecil. I hope that Admiralty of yours realizes they have one of the finest gentlemen ever to cross the Atlantic."

"That remains to be seen. Good luck, Katherine, with whatever you decide to do."

Kissing her hand, he turned his horse in the direction of town and rode off. As she watched him, Katy was tempted to call him back, to ward off the loneliness that was closing in on her. The adventure was over. Thinking back, she remembered the young girl she had been in England, so anxious for adventure and romance. She couldn't have known, back then, that there would come a time when she would long for the simplicity of that long-ago life. Ah, that she could travel back in time. But then, where would she go? Surely not to Whitney Hall. No, if there was any hope of righting the mess she had made of her life, it would have to be at the beginning. Still, there would be no guarantee that she would be immune to those incredible eyes of his. She knew at the core of her, no matter the circumstances, her heart would always belong to Christopher Warwick. And he didn't want it.

Josh was waiting for her. She changed back into her pants, and with no more than a shout over her shoulder, they were riding like the wind for Oaks. She had a sudden need to be home. Home. The thought of the house, standing tall and proud, welcoming her as it never failed to do, brought the long awaited tears to her eyes. As she galloped along beside Josh, she brushed those tears away. She would be fine, she had told Cecil, once the aching went away. But when would it leave her? Could she forget that stately old house or the people that lived and worked within it? Could she ever again see the sun without remembering the dream that gave it all meaning? And wouldn't the memory of that angular face, with its determination and searing blue eyes, haunt her throughout time? She fought the tears. She would forget—she had to, to survive.

Though her pride steeled her through the rest of the journey, the sight of the house, sparkling in the cold morning sun, proved her undoing. As she stared at the peaceful scene, the tears streamed down her cheeks. Josh, sensitive to her suffering, took the reins and led Dawn to the swamps. Katy bounced along behind him, oblivious to everything but her pain.

As they approached the ship, Sam came charging at them, blustering and roaring questions. Josh put a finger to his lips and nodded over at Katy. "Not now, Sam. I don't know the whole story yet, but I reckon she's had enough. Give her time and she'll tell all."

Sam squinted up at her. "Lass, what's happened?"

Suddenly conscious of her surroundings, she gulped and slid off her horse. "We didn't mean to worry you, Sam. I was so anxious about Kit that I didn't stop to think about you, I guess."

"And where's old fancy pants?"

"Fancy... oh, you mean Cecil? It's rather a long story. Do you suppose we could go inside while I tell it? I think I need a hankie and maybe a cup of coffee."

"Sure, lass." Sam held out his arms for support and she gratefully used them. It felt good to be among friends. He led her to the galley and deposited her on a bench while he fixed coffee. He placed a mug on the table in front of her. "Tell your story, lass."

She looked up in his face and was touched by the concern she saw there. "Ah, you've laced it with whiskey, haven't you? It's very good. Josh, please sit. I want you to hear this, too."

For some time, all that could be heard was her voice, droning on, breaking every now and then, but continuing unrelentingly until she had finished her story.

"Hold on, lass. None of this sounds like Kit."

"It wasn't. At least, not the Kit we know. He's changed. I would have thought he was acting, but there was no reason for it. It was just the two of us and he made it quite plain that for us, it was all over."

"You're tired. You've been through too much. Maybe you misunderstood what he was trying to say. You two could never manage to let the other know how you felt."

She gave him a weak smile. "I understood perfectly well. I wasn't imagining anything. It was in his eyes. Never, even when he was furious with me, were they that cold. He looked right through me as if I wasn't there. He doesn't care anymore. About me, about you, about anything."

"But you've got to be wrong, Katy."

"Oh, Josh, how I wish I was. All this time, even when I thought the worst about him, I never gave up hoping. I felt that if I kept my head and worked at it, eventually, he'd know we were meant for each other. Now he tells me he wants to forget the little we had. Can you imagine how that hurts? All the struggling, all the planning, all those nights praying he was safe, and for what? I'll never see him again. I had to learn the hard way that you don't necessarily get something just because you want it desperately enough. You were right, Sam. Life does have a way of messing things up."

"I said that?"

"Yes you did. Way back in England, when you were trying to warn me. And you were right about another thing. I was far too young."

"Oh, and you're such an old lady now."

"I feel ancient. There's nothing left. Nothing to work for, nothing to fight for, nothing even to hope for."

"Lass, I've never known you to give up without a fight."

"There's no fight left in me. I'm too tired."

"Now, maybe, but there's tomorrow. And the next day. We can't give up, yet."

"We?"

"Yes, we. I remember those days back in England, too. I told you that if you ever needed a shoulder to lean on, I had two of them. I've been with you from the beginning and I plan on staying till the end."

"This is the end. Kit is gone. He's Julian now. And he's left me for Rachel."

"Then we'll have to go after him, won't we, Sam?"

"Stop! Both of you. I refuse to come between you and Kit. He's going to need you more now than ever before. Someone will have to make certain that Rachel doesn't ruin him."

Sam threw his hands up in the air. "If that don't beat all. That boy dragged you away from a comfortable, if not pleasant life, put you through every kind of heartache and worry, and then takes off without a thought for your welfare and you talk about what he's gonna need? You give him all you got, risk your neck for him I don't know how many times, making sacrifice after sacrifice, and you tell me you're satisfied to sit back while that bitch runs off with him? And it doesn't make you hopping mad?"

"Sam, please. I could be mad, furious, if you want to

know the truth, but that won't change the way things are. He couldn't have cared very much if he was so ready to believe the worst of me. He could have given me the chance to explain."

"It's all my fault. I should never have made you go off without talking to him that night. Damn my interfering . . . "

"Stop it. It's nobody's fault. We all did what we thought was best, but it just wasn't good enough, I guess."

"But I made a promise to you. By God, if I have to follow him to England, I'm gonna talk some sense into that boy."

"I appreciate the thought, but it really is too late now. Kit and I might have had a chance for a life together once, but it's gone. We've lived apart too long; we're strangers to each other. It's better left the way it is. Better you use your energies in helping me find a new life."

"What about fancy pants? I could see the way he was hankering after you. What, did he run out on you too?"

"Poor Cecil. No, he offered but I told him it would never work. I have no intention of returning to England."

"But, Katy, that's your home, isn't it?"

"How can you say that, Josh? In my own way, I've fought for a piece of this country and I mean to have it. It's all I do have. I'm going to see this war through and when it's over, I want to be here when the building and growing starts. I don't know yet what I'll do, but this is my home and I belong here."

"Now you sound more like Katy."

"Thank you. But Katy is very tired now. I'm going to bed."

"If you want your old cabin back, I could have it

467

ready in a few minutes."

"Don't bother, Josh. Kit's cabin will be fine for the time being. I won't be staying long."

With a feeble wave of her hand, she silenced their protests. Planting a kiss on each forehead, she left them staring after her as she made her way to Kit's cabin. But that room held memories that taunted her. That whiskey stain on the floor, glaring at her, accusing her of impossible innocence. That young girl was gone now, lost forever in a hopelessly tangled web of her own design. So was Kit.

What she needed was to get away from here. She needed to lie in the big four-poster in her room at Oaks. And why not? It was still her home until Kit reclaimed it. As he was on his way to England by now, it was highly unlikely that he would evict her. Wharton's weasley face broke into her excitement. Damn him! All the anger that should have been directed at her husband was aimed instead at the unsuspecting overseer. Oh no, she was not about to allow that worm to defile her home. Before the hour was out, she would send him packing.

Sam and Josh, discussing plans to set sail for England, heard Dawn's whinny. Looking at each other, they heard her gallop away. They were up in seconds, and flying after her on the other horse. Katy was gesturing wildly to Lilah in the doorway as they pulled up the drive. When she saw them, she pushed Lilah aside and ran up the stairs. Taking two at a time, Sam reached Kit's doorway in time to see Katy pull out a gun and threaten the bewildered overseer. Sam put out a hand to catch Josh, who was two steps behind him.

". . . and don't think I won't use this." She waved the pistol in the air. Sam cursed himself for not taking it away from her. "I hate bullies, Mr. Wharton. You're

468

very brave against helpless slaves and women, but I doubt that even you would be foolish enough to take your chances against my gun."

He cowered in the bed. "Just don't shoot that thing."

"I won't shoot, providing you get yourself and your two bullies of my property immediately."

"It ain't your property."

"You forget yourself. It is indeed my property. If you care to follow Mr. Warwick to England, he will certify my claim. In the meantime, however, they say that possession is nine tenths of the law and as I am the one with the gun . . . "

"All right, little lady. I'll go. But I'm coming back again and when I do, you're gonna need more than that pistol to stop me."

Sam and Josh stepped into the room. "Aye and she'll have more. Mr. Christopher Warwick owns this plantation now, and me and the rest of his crew will be looking out for the lady."

"You're all traitors."

"You seem to have lost track of things. This land is under American jurisdiction now. Captain Warwick ain't a traitor; he's a hero. And a grateful government feels he's entitled to this land. So I think you'd better do as his wife says."

"There's only three of you and one is a woman. I have two men who will take care of you all."

On cue, Rosie appeared in the doorway. "You sure is talking big for a man in big trouble. Those friends you're counting on are tied to a wagon in the stable and there's a whole batch of happy slaves looking to see that they stay where they are. If I was you, I'd be down on my knees begging these people to get you outta here alive."

His surly tone dwindled into a whine. "But I've got

to pack my things."

Katy smiled. "Well now, Mr. Wharton, I would sure hate you to be thinking me a hard woman, but it occurs to me that you might want to be taking your whip and I'm afraid I can't allow that. No, you just send your new address and we'll see that you get your things."

"Why you . . ."

"Careful what you say to the lady. You heard Rosie. Could be we'd enjoy letting the slaves have a go at you."

"You couldn't do that to me."

"Don't tempt us. Just come along with us now. Rosie, Mrs. Warwick is worn out. Get her to bed, will you?"

"Sam, Josh, thanks for helping me."

"Aw, Katy, you'd do the same for us."

Sam hugged her. "Get some sleep, lass. Things will look brighter after you've rested. And give me that pistol. You've gotten yourself into enough trouble with it."

He turned his attention to Wharton who was trying to hurry into a pair of pants. Shaking his head, he grabbed an arm and pulled him out of the room. Katy shivered in disgust at the mess he had made behind him. Ripping the linens off the bed, she decided to remove all traces of his presence from the room.

"What do you think you're doing?"

"I can't stand the thought of that man sleeping in Kit's bed, Rosie. I want to scrub this room until it shines. If Kit ever returns . . ."

"All in good time, child. You gotta get some sleep, like Sam said. You're running around this house like a lunatic, first attacking men in their sleep and now going after beds. What's got into you?"

Katy ran fingers through hair that by now was half

470

pinnned up and half in her face. "I guess I'm just lashing out at everything I can think of. I feel so angry and hurt and I don't know what to do about it. There's nothing I can do."

"I want to help, child, but I don't know what you're talking about."

"Oh, Rosie, Kit is never coming back."

"But Sam said . . ."

"He was lying to get rid of Wharton."

"Seems there's a lot you have to tell me. But not now. We'll get you a hot bath and something warm to drink first."

Easily persuaded, Katy was pampered one last time. Tomorrow would be soon enough to make her own way in the world, but today she would soak in luxury. Half an hour later, propped up with pillows, she felt almost alive again and delightfully drowsy. But she had to tell Rosie what had happened before she could sleep.

The slave listened patiently but when Katy repeated that Kit was never coming home, she became angry. "My boy will come back. I know it. Didn't I raise him? He knows his responsibilities, to his wife and to all of us. I don't want to hear any more talk about you leaving, either. Your place is here until your man comes home to you."

"But he doesn't love me any more."

"So? We had this kind of talk before. You made him love you once; you can do it again. But you can't do nothing by running away."

"Rosie . . ."

"Child, do you want to leave?"

"You know that I don't. Oaks is my home."

"Then you're gonna stay. I don't want to hear no more about it. You get some sleep and in the morning, we'll talk some more."

"You mean that you'll talk and I'll obey."

Rosie actually smiled. "It sure feels good to have you back, child. You bring laughter into this old house and it needs it. You stay here, with your friends, and together we'll all see that things work out right."

"If only I could believe that."

"Wait till tomorrow to tell me what you believe. Give me that cup and I'll draw the curtains so you can sleep."

"Thanks, Rosie."

"Sweet dreams, child."

Sweet dreams. Was it possible to have sweet dreams? Could she actually permit herself to hope, one more time, that Kit would come home to her? She was utterly without hope, her common sense told her, and incurably silly. But there was that little voice, murmuring encouragement, somewhere in the back of her brain, and it seemed that as long as she drew breath, it would stay alive.

Chapter 31

Kit was aimlessly tossing darts in a makeshift meeting room on the battleship, *Champion.* Fellow refugees, mostly people he detested, sat on the benches that lined the room, each with a bottle and each with something to forget. Though Kit himself was well into his bottle, he seemed to have lost none of his accuracy with the darts.

"Well done, Mr. Warwick. So you also have a talent for darts."

Spinning around unsteadily, he took in the uniform. Good lord, it was one of Julian's friends. No, on closer inspection, it was one of Katy's friends, that Captain Lawrence. Cecil. What was he doing on the *Champion?* Maliciously, he hoped the fop had made a fool of himself and gotten stripped of his command. But maybe he didn't deserve to be called a fop. There was an air of ruggedness that he had never noticed before.

"Captain Lawrence, imagine meeting you here. Would you like to play?"

"How kind of you. I haven't tossed these since I left England. But I do enjoy the game. What do you say we make it interesting? Would you care to make a wager?"

"A wager, Captain?"

"Come now. You're known to be a sporting man."

Kit pulled out his pockets. "Sorry, old chap. I haven't a penny."

Lawrence lifted a dart and inspected it. "Did I say anything about money? No, indeed. I understand your situation and I wouldn't dream of further encumbering you. I had something different in mind."

"Name your terms?"

Lawrence looked up at him, then, and Kit had the curious sensation of being at a disadvantage. Perhaps he had better put down the brandy for a while.

"Warwick, let me be blunt. I find myself in a difficult situation. I'm trying to see to your sister-in-law's welfare and to be honest with you, she is quite distressed to find you on the ship. I can't pretend to know what goes on in the minds of females, but I did make a promise and I must do my best to keep my word. Do you understand?"

He had all of Kit's attention now. "Go on."

"I will challenge you. Winner remains on the ship."

"And the loser?"

"The loser must find other means for crossing the Atlantic."

"But there isn't another ship scheduled for weeks."

"Yes, that's quite unfortunate, but I can see no other way out of this. If I win, Katherine will be forever grateful to me, and if I lose, at least I can tell her I tried my best. One could almost say my fate was in your hands."

Kit, who couldn't imagine anything less likely, decided to meet the challenge, if for no other reason than mere curiosity. Damn, what did it matter if he went to

England today, or a month from now? "Do you know, Captain Lawrence, I don't think I've ever been able to refuse a wager and certainly not one as interesting as yours."

"Splendid. Why don't you begin."

"Wouldn't you prefer a few practice shots?"

"Ordinarily, perhaps. But I'd just as soon be done with it, if you know what I mean."

Vaguely uncomfortable with Lawrence's steady eyes on him, Kit picked up a dart and tried to get the feel of it. Ten minutes ago, it had been an extension of his arm, but suddenly, it was awkward and heavy. And did Lawrence have to keep talking while he was trying to shoot?

"Do you know, the last time I played darts was with Admiral Farley, at Whitney Hall. Are you planning on visiting the Admiral while you're over there? Oh, I'm sorry. Did I disturb your concentration? I suppose it's my turn now, isn't it?"

Lawrence was good, as Kit suspected he might be. Was there anything the man couldn't do? Fidgeting, he waited until at last it was his turn again. Lawrence picked up the thread of the conversation, just as he readied to throw.

"Funny thing about the admiral. Doesn't encourage visitors, you know. Not even relatives."

"I hadn't planned to leave London." He tried to aim again.

"I'll tell you, Warwick. It certainly is remarkable how alike you and your brother are."

Kit caught himself in time. "Oh, you know Kit, then?"

"Indirectly. Nasty business about that treason. I was supposed to take him to England on the *Olym-*

pus, you know."

"And what happened to your ship, Captain?"

"You hadn't heard? I was set upon by pirates."

"How terrible for you."

"Yes, quite. But I learned a great deal from the experience. Ah, good shot, Warwick. Tell me, was it all true, about the spying, I mean? Your brother's spying, I should say."

"I'm afraid so. But then, you would know that if you've been talking to Katherine."

Lawrence looked him in the eye. "It's amazing how many times your brother was able to capitalize on your uncanny resemblance to each other, wasn't it? Excuse me, I'm interrupting your game."

Kit tried his best, but his concentration was broken. "Your turn, Lawrence. But you knew that without looking, didn't you?"

"I beg your pardon?"

"Let's play one game at a time. When we're done with darts, there will be ample time for me to be your mouse."

Lawrence chuckled. "I suppose I'm being too obvious, but let's face it, you're far better than I at this game of intrigue."

"And you're better at the other. Did Katy tell you everything?"

"As a matter of fact, yes, she did."

"Was the game her idea? It sounds like one of her crazy plots."

"No, she knows nothing of this. Nor would she be happy with me if she did. But surely you must see that she must be spared any further pain."

"Poor Katy. Oh, excuse me, it's Katherine now, isn't it? Do you know, fool that I am, I was beginning to worry about her again. I suppose old habits are hard to break. I should have known she would find someone to take care of her. She always does."

"You do care about her, don't you?"

"I thought we were playing a game."

Lawrence sighed and took his shot. "You're a fool, Warwick. You've bungled this whole affair, right from the start. You deserve to lose her."

"And you deserve to have her. No, I don't really mean that. She'll cut you to pieces. I've seen her do it. She'll look up at you with those soft eyes of hers and all the while she'll be planning on how to stab you in the back."

"You don't know anything, Warwick. How can you judge her? She was a girl when you took her away from her home. How can you possibly know what she's had to endure? Let's get this game over with, before I say something I might regret."

But Kit's concentration had vanished. The harder he tried to win, the harder it became to send the darts where he wanted them. It seemed that all he could see was Katy's face when he had said good-bye to her. The game came down to one last shot, and in the end, his hands failed him. "It seems that you win, Lawrence."

"Don't take it so bad, Warwick. All you'll be losing is the Farley fortunes and Whitney Hall."

"Do you honestly believe that I would have anything to do with the Farley money? My last experience with it has left a bad taste in my mouth."

"Ah, but you still have your ship and unless I'm very much mistaken, you'll have that new country for which you've been fighting. You're a very fortunate man, Warwick."

"Me, fortunate? Ha! Obviously you don't know me

well."

"I know enough to tell you that if there was any way possible, I'd trade places with you in a moment."

"You're the fool, Lawrence. You have no idea what a mess you'd be getting with my life."

"Oh, but I do. You might just find that your future is brighter than you think. A lot brighter than mine, at any rate."

"What do you mean by that?"

"Pay me no heed. This war has been hard on all of us. I have enjoyed meeting you, Captain; it puts my mind to rest about a few things. I hate to terminate our conversation, but our ship is soon to set sail. A wager is a wager, after all."

"I'll have to get Rachel."

"Oh, don't disturb Miss Worthington. I'll see her safely delivered to her relatives. There's no need for her to go with you, unless of course, that's what you wish."

"Good lord, no. The last thing I need is Rachel on my neck."

"Then set your mind at ease. It will be quite an interesting voyage, don't you think?"

"By the end of the journey, they will either carry you off or present you with a medal. Between the two of them, they could eat you alive."

Lawrence laughed. "They say war is hell. By the way, Captain, Katherine mentioned that a man named Sam was looking for you. I think she said something about a place called Oaks."

"And how did she know that?"

"Ah, if only I could explain. Perhaps Sam will. At present, though, I'm afraid you will have to hurry. Here, don't forget your brandy."

"Keep it. I have a feeling you're going to need it. Take care of her, won't you?"

He smiled. "With any luck, we'll meet again and when we do, believe it or not, you'll thank me for this."

"I doubt it. But still, I wish you both luck. No, I mean it. You could say that meeting you has put my mind to rest about a few things, as well. Good-bye, Captain."

With a quick salute, he was on his way to the dock, barely making it off the ship in time. Strange, he had spent so much time hating Lawrence, and yet, he seemed a decent enough fellow. Perhaps Katy did care about him; he was her own kind, after all. One could never imagine him raping his wife. Katy would like that. Dammit, why should it still bother him that she preferred Lawrence? It was over for them. Over? It had never begun. If only she hadn't shown up. If only he could have swallowed his pride and asked her to stay. He stood on the dock, watching the *Champion* sail away. So it had finally happened. Katy was off to England with her handsome captain and there was nothing he could do to stop her. Spitting in the water, he cursed his pride. Somewhere in this God-forsaken city, there had to be a horse. Suddenly, he knew he had to be at Oaks.

Chapter 32

Like a madman, Kit took to the road, reaching the plantation by midnight. The house stood before him, not old and decrepit but rather like he had always wanted it to look. Perhaps his eyes betrayed him—the moonlight was strange and he was exhausted. Surely that was a new coat of paint. What other surprises did Julian have waiting for him? Something tugged at him to go inside. What could it matter? Whatever Sam had to say would keep another day. Tonight, he would sleep in his own bed. After the hard life of a soldier, the thought was too tempting to resist.

Inside, the house was as well kept as it had been in his mother's day. What had gotten into Julian? It wasn't like him to put money into the place; he must have been planning something. But Julian was dead. Oaks belonged to him now. Strange, he should be happier about it. Wasn't it what he had always wanted? Francis Marion had dismissed him yesterday, so the fighting was over for him. He could stay home and put in a spring crop. But something was missing. Oaks needed a woman and he needed a wife that wouldn't desert him for the first good offer to come along.

His room was warm and inviting. Lilah, at least, had not deserted him. The fire was laid, waiting to be lit. As the logs ignited, he poured a brandy and pulled a chair up to the fire. He was home, in his own home, but where was the contentment and peace he knew he should be feeling? Yes, something was missing. It was laughter, Katy's laughter. Had he ever stopped listening for it? It was as if her dancing eyes held him captive and if he got past his pride, down where the honesty was, he knew he had no desire to be free of them. Remembering how soft and yielding she had been in his arms, he could have staked his life on the fact that she had cared about him. But he had staked his life and had almost lost it. Why, then, could he only remember the sweetness of her?

Roaming aimlessly, he spotted the door to her room. He would be a fool to go in there. A fool, maybe, but no one need ever know that he had been there seeking a memory, some intangible sign that she had loved him in that room. No one need ever know that he had merely been echoing her words when he had told her he didn't want to remember. How could he forget, when for the rest of his life he would be tormented by the thought of how different their future could have been if he hadn't been forced into leaving her that night.

When he finally gathered the courage to open her door, he found himself in another world. No one had to tell him that she had designed this room for herself. She was everywhere; the very scent of her lingered in the air. If he had come seeking a memory, then he had found it. Her room was a reflection of the sweet and innocent girl she had once been. Pain stabbed at him as he realized what he had lost. He knew he should leave but his feet refused to move. His tired eyes took in every detail—the starched curtains, the fresh walls, his mother's furniture. His eyes were rooted to the nightstand. That was the ruby pendant he had given her. He felt through his pockets. How the . . .

It couldn't be. Silently, he crept forward to identify the form on the bed. He was tired, too tired to handle any more, but he couldn't deny the relief that flooded through his body. There she lay, peaceful and innocent as a child and as beautiful as ever. Was it a dream?

He must remember that she was a bitch. She had stolen the ruby, hadn't she. Taken it off him as he lay unconscious on the floor. But what was she doing here? Lawrence had said she was with him. Wasn't it what that farce of a wager had been all about? Was this a trick, another lie? God, he was weary. He couldn't think straight. All he could think of was that she was here, where he wanted her. No, he couldn't possibly mean that after all she had done to him. He wasn't tired, he was mad.

As she moved in her sleep, he knew panic. He couldn't face her, not yet. If she saw him now, she would recognize his vulnerability. He might want her back, but she mustn't ever see the power she held over him. He'd have to be an idiot to give her that ammunition twice.

Think angry, he warned himself. Remember what she did to you. She betrayed you, left you to rot in that filthy jail while she ran off with your brother. Then, when that proved poor sport, she danced off with Lawrence. Had Julian, the poor, greedy devil, really loved her? Had he, too, believed her pretty lies? Had he ever stood above her, like this, wishing for the strength to kill her, knowing all the while that if he took her life, he would be cutting off part of his own?

"Kit?" Her soft voice cut through the silence and he tried to steel himself against it. "Am I dreaming? Is that really you? But it can't be. You've gone to England."

She popped up, opening her eyes wide, wide enough to see into her soul. Kit would have expected to find satisfaction, victory, fear perhaps, but was that joy he saw in them?

Be cautious, he told himself. "I'm real enough."

She tried to rub the sleep from her eyes, seeming even more like a child to him. Straining in the semi-light, she tried to read his face, but he remained in the shadows. "I don't understand. I thought you said you were going away?"

"Someone changed my mind."

"Sam? How could he . . ."

"Sam?" His eyes narrowed. "What could Sam say to change my mind?"

Biting her lip, she hoped she hid her disappointment. It would seem he hadn't come to see her. "Who was it, then?"

"Another of your many conquests, my dear. Captain Lawrence."

"Cecil? But he promised not to tell."

Her dismay irritated him. "Your secret, whatever it may have been, is safe. Lawrence had no time to take me into his confidence. He was far too busy threatening to expose me if I didn't leave the ship. To spare you any further unpleasantries, I was told."

She had to smile at this last, precious gift from Cecil. Kit misinterpreted it. "I asked you a question, dammit. What are you doing in my house?"

Startled out of her thoughts, her smile evaporated. "I didn't think you would mind. At least until I found a place of my own. I'm sorry. I'll get my things and leave." She grabbed for her dressing gown.

Kit barred her way. "Where are you going? Nobody said anything about leaving. And stop crying."

"I'm not crying."

"Yes you are. Stop lying to me, Katy. For God's sake, can't you tell the truth anymore? Here." He handed her his handkerchief but the memories it evoked set her off again.

"I'm sorry, I know how you hate tears. If you'll just leave me alone for a minute, I'll pack my things and have the room ready for her."

"For who?"

"How stupid of me. Poor, naive Katy again. When will I learn? Of course she'll share the room with you."

"What the hell are you talking about?"

"Are you going to tell me that Rachel isn't here? You, who are so disdainful of lies?"

"Rachel again. I don't know what put that idea into your head but Rachel is on her way to England with your charming Cecil."

"For the last time, he is not 'my Cecil'. He's a friend, a very dear friend maybe, but that is all."

"Very well then. Rachel is with your very dear friend so I can see no reason for you to pack up and leave."

"You want me to stay?" She held her breath.

His eyes were cold and unreadable. "You are still my wife."

"You left me with the impression that you would rather forget the fact."

"At the time, I hadn't realized that I would now be the master here. I will need children and for that, I

484

need a wife."

She could no longer look at him. What he wanted was a broodmare, not her. "How convenient that you already have one."

"Yes, isn't it? I think you may find that it will be convenient for us both. With your dear friend gone, it would seem that you have nowhere to go. Perhaps I can't offer you the equivalent to London society, but it won't be a bad life. Soon I should have the means of providing you with the things you seem to need from life. If you want, we can rebuild the Charleston house, if Oaks is still too boring for your tastes. All I ask in return is that you don't disgrace my name in public."

He might as well have slapped her. "So it's back to the farce?"

He flinched. "So it would seem."

"Except that now, I will also be expected to entertain you in my bed. We mustn't forget the children. It's so important to carry on the glorious Warwick heritage, isn't it? And what will you tell them, Kit, when they ask why their parents hate each other?"

He held himself rigidly, but she didn't notice. Raging, she paced from one side of the room to the other, hurling words at him. "Who do you think you are? Damn you! Damn you and your stinking pride. Can you actually believe to be that shallow? That's I'd sell my body to you for a roof over my head and a few trinkets? Don't bother to answer. It's obvious that you do. Sam was right; I should be furious with you. What do you think you are, making such an offer to me? How can you have the gall to ask me not to disgrace your name when only yesterday you were running off to England with your mistress? How dare you. I hate you. Do you hear me? I hate you!"

There was nothing in his voice, no emotion, no life. "I made a vow two years ago when I took you for my wife. I have never strayed from it, nor will I ever do so. You could have done me the same courtesy."

She slapped him. The sound echoed across the room. "Damn you, Kit Warwick. You never gave me a chance. Get out of here. Get out of my sight before I say something I might regret."

"What are you doing?"

"I'm leaving." She was stuffing herself into a shirt. "I can't stay here anymore, not with you."

"And if I won't let you go?"

She pulled up the trousers and buttoned them. "Don't do this. You have your pride, at least let me have mine." She turned to go.

"Aren't you forgetting something?"

The ruby pendant dangled from his hand. A small cry escaped from her lips. As she reached out for it, he grabbed her wrist. "Not so fast, love. What makes you think I'll let you have it?"

"It's mine."

"Really? I seem to remember you giving it back to me."

She tried to break loose. "I will ask nothing else from you. Please, Kit, just this one thing?"

"What would you want with such a cheap bauble when you could have all the Warwick jewels, if you stay?"

"I don't want your bloody jewels. I only want what is mine."

"You won't get a lot of money for it."

"Why must you always think the worst of me?"

"There was a time when nobody could convince me

486

that you would turn out the way you did." With a sudden motion, he released her wrist and threw her from him.

Rubbing it, she looked up at him. "Thank you for that much. You did love me once, didn't you, Kit?"

"You know that I did."

"Then why did you stop? Why did you stop believing in me?"

Disgusted, he turned away. "Give me some credit for intelligence."

With his back to her, she felt like she was pleading with the wall. "You always bragged that you could tell when I was acting. I lived so many lies that it seems I got too good at it. It's for the best that I leave. You'd never be able to trust me again. I'm sorry things turned out the way they did." She shoved a few dresses into as sack. "When you remember me, if you ever do, try to think of me the way you did when we were here at Oaks. We were happy then, as happy as I want you to be. Good luck to you, Kit. I hope that dream of yours comes true."

When he didn't answer, she picked up the sack of clothes. "I know you don't want to hear my side of the story, but I want you to know that everything I ever did, I did for you."

Ah, the tears again. She knew it was time to leave but the door seemed miles away. How could she make her graceful exit, take her last bow, when the tears were spilling out all over the carpet? Oh lord, where was that Farley pride when she needed it most?

"Katy?"

She recognized this scene. They had played it so often that she knew what to do next. Hesitating, she hoped that this time, he would know the lines.

"I won't let you go."

The words were right but the feeling was all wrong. Sighing, she reached for the knob. "Goodbye, Kit."

"Dammit, Katy, you can't go. If you walk out that door, I won't ever see you again. This is our last chance. It doesn't matter about the past. We should be talking about the future, our future."

Her hand was glued to the door. For the life of her, she couldn't seem to budge it. She heard the footsteps and felt his warmth as he stood behind her. "I can't beg; it's just not in me. Just admitting this to you is more than I thought I could manage. My pride means nothing to me if you leave."

"I can't be your brood mare, Kit."

"I'm asking you to stay, not because I need a wife, but because I need you."

"How can you say that when you believe that I did such horrible things to you?"

He pried her fingers off the knob and turned her to face him. "Can't we forget the past? We have an opportunity to start all over again. Let's take it."

"Do you mean that?" She searched his eyes and as they melted, she knew the worst was over. "Say it, Kit. Tell me why you want to do this."

"Dammit, I know that I'm a fool, but when you look at me, Katy, I can't believe in anything but you. I love you. It's a simple as that. I love you."

She fell into his arms. "Oh, Kit, I love you so much. I had begun to despair that I would ever get the chance to tell you. Someday, I'll explain it all to you, but right now, I want to look at you, and hold you, and thank the fates for bringing you back to me. Don't ever go away again, I couldn't bear it. Oh, Kit, I love you so much."

He enfolded her in his arms, unable to take it all in, but feeling better than he had ever felt in his life. As he kissed her, the months of anger and suspicion dissolved into one night, long ago, when he had held her this way. Like that other time, nothing existed but Katy. He swept her up and carried her to the bed. Gazing into her soft, blue eyes, he knew she loved him. If he was a fool, at least he was a happy one. Whatever her motives had been, he found he trusted her now. They belonged to each other and nothing could come between them.

Nothing, but a knock at the door. "Lass, what's going on in there? Are you all right?"

She laughed. "Oh, Sam, I've never been better."

"Go away, Sam. Katy and I have some lost time to make up for."

"Kit, is that you? I tried to tell her you'd come back. Open the door. I want to talk to you."

"Kit, we've got to talk. I should explain."

"Kit, we've got to talk. I should explain."

"Not tonight, Sam Culligan. As the man said, he's all mine for the evening."

Sam chuckled. "I guess that means I don't have to be talking with him then. All right, you two. I'll see you in the morning."

Katy looked up at her husband and touched his face. "I can't seem to believe this is happening."

"I know." He covered her hand with his own. "Just an hour ago, I thought I would never see you again."

"Not tonight, love. We have a lifetime to talk. I can't take the chance that we'll start fighting again.

Tonight, I just want to love you. Please?"

Nodding, she pulled his head down close to hers. He was right; there was a lifetime for explanations. Tonight was a night for love.

Afterward

"You'll do as you're told."

"I will, will I?"

"Dammit, Katy, I won't take chances with this."

"Damn yourself. I thought you and Sam were supposed to be the finest sailors on the ocean? What's the risk?"

"You're not going."

"Then neither are you."

"I have no choice. Your grandfather's lawyers made that plain."

"That bloody money. I'm sick of it."

"You and me both. But we're going to need it. Especially now."

"I don't know why I told you about it."

"You told me because we promised never to keep anything from each other. Do you want things to be the way they were during the war?"

"You always twist my words. I'm not going to stand here screaming at you anymore. Make up your mind. Either you let me come with you or I'll find another captain that isn't so choosy about his passengers."

"Are you two fighting again? Why don't you tell me what this is all about, lass?"

"It's Kit; he's being stubborn. He won't listen to me."

"Listen to her! How do you talk sense to her when she's got her temper up?"

"You can't talk sense to a woman in her condition, boy. You just go along with whatever she says."

"I won't take chances with her life. Or the baby's."

"Always the Warwick heritage, isn't it? Sometimes I wonder what would have happened if I hadn't become pregnant. Would you have left me?"

"That's enough of that kind of talk." He put an arm around her. "You know that I don't want to leave you, ever, but I can't risk your life."

"If anything happens to the ship, I won't be in any more danger than you. And if I don't go, I'll be sick with worry. That will be far worse for the baby."

"She's right son. Besides, we need her along. We still haven't got a cook."

"Sam!"

"It's no use yelling at me. Once that little lady of yours gets something in her head, you can't get it out. You can believe her if she says she's gonna follow you anyway. And you know what trouble she always manages to get herself into when you let her out of your sight."

"Please, Kit. Take me with you?"

As he looked down into her pleading eyes, he remembered the last time she had asked that of him. If he had taken her, he could have spared them both a lot of pain. But it had all come about in the end, hadn't it? Smiling, he remembered the way it had happened.

Yes, Sam was probably right. If Katy could kidnap Lawrence, there was no telling what she would do if he left her behind. Not even Francis and Esther, who had agreed to watch after her, could control her then and dammit, didn't he want her with him? This past year or so had been the happiest of his life. Could he bear to say good-bye again? Could he take the chance that something might happen to her when he wouldn't be there to help? No, it was better to take the chance and keep her in his sight.

Katy could sense his weakening resolve. Knowing her man, she hid her elation and offered encouragement. "Between the two of you, I know I won't be in danger." She added truthfully. "Kit, I want you to be there for the birth of our child."

Sam coughed discreetly and murmured, "Hmmmmph. Guess I'd better see to getting her stuff stowed aboard. Don't want to be leaving her trunks behind this time."

Neither noticed his departure, so absorbed were they in each other. Kit pulled her closer and kissed her gently. "I think I've been outmaneuvered. Very well, Mrs. Warwick, welcome aboard. But I won't have you cooking or cleaning, do you hear? You're to take care of yourself."

"Oh, Kit, I'm only having a baby. Women are always having babies."

"But not our baby. We've fought so hard for our future. Now that the war is over, we can't be taking chances."

"Don't worry, Kit, I'll be careful. We're just beginning that dream of yours. Our baby will be a boy. No, don't you laugh at me, I know it. We have the Farley

493

money, we have Oaks, we have the *Irish Lass,* and we have our freedom. Tell me now, why would I be taking chances with that?"

"Why indeed? But just in case, I'll be watching you every minute. But we've got to stop this fighting. Why must we always quarrel?"

"We can't seem to help it. And I don't know, it certainly is nice when we kiss and make up."

"Ah yes, my favorite part. What do you say? Shall we sneak away and do a really good job of it this time?"

"Sneak away?"

"My cabin or yours?"

"Kit, really. What about the crew?"

"I tend to favor mine. After all, we've never had the chance to make love in there."

"Keep your voice down. And we did so. I told you about that night."

"So you did. That was the night you raped me."

"Will you be quiet? I didn't rape you, you asked for it."

"And you didn't ask for it that first time?"

"That was different. I . . ."

He put a finger on her lips. "Enough. Let's just go do the making up, shall we?"

He was looking at her in his little boy way and she had to laugh. "Captain Warwick, I think I could be in love with you."

He held out a hand. "Then come with me, madame, and I'll do my best to convince you."

Smiling, she took his hand and followed him to his cabin. No, it wasn't quite the daydream she had envisioned all those years ago, but still and all, as happy endings go, she couldn't have asked for better.